THE LOST DREAMER

THE LOST DREAMER

LIZZ HUERTA

FARRAR STRAUS GIROUX
NEW YORK

Farrar Straus Giroux Books for Young Readers
An imprint of Macmillan Publishing Group, LLC
120 Broadway, New York, NY 10271
fiercereads.com

Our books may be purchased in bulk for promotional, educational, or business
use. Please contact your local bookseller or the Macmillan Corporate and
Premium Sales Department at (800) 221-7945 ext. 5442 or by email at
MacmillanSpecialMarkets@macmillan.com.

Library of Congress Cataloging-in-Publication Data is available.

First edition, 2022
Book design by Mallory Grigg
Printed in the United States of America

ISBN 978-1-250-75485-1 (hardcover)
10   9   8   7   6   5   4   3   2   1

ISBN 978-0-374-39091-4 (special edition)
10   9   8   7   6   5   4   3   2   1

For my parents, Evelyn and Hector Huerta:
your love is a sacred gift

CHAPTER ONE

INDIR

The wail of a far-off conch shell woke me from my already broken sleep. I wanted to wail in response, in grief, in terror.

Dogs began barking on the outskirts of the city. Unfamiliar drum rhythms pounded in the distance, echoing off the stone walls of our temple. I rose, blood rushing through my body as I swung from my hammock. An answering conch blew thrice from our own warriors. Three cries for peace.

Delu and Zeri stirred. I knew they were in Dreaming, their bodies struggling to pull them back. I kissed them each softly, Singing a small waking Song, my voice breaking. Delu, two years older than me, opened her eyes first. Zeri, the youngest of us, began her languid waking stretch, but her eyes flew open as she realized what was happening. I reached to her, pulling her small body up from her hammock and into an embrace. Delu joined us. The conch horns were louder, the drums a steady beat, closer, closer, closer. The three of us held each other in silence. For all we'd prepared, we weren't ready.

A temple worker rushed into our chamber, a lit torch in her hand.

From within the walls of our own temple, a human wail began. All of us froze. The temple worker began trembling.

The small, familiar rituals around preparing our bodies for ceremony didn't calm me the way they usually did. As we had done countless times before, we tied on each other's sashes. I held Delu's thick braids in place as Zeri inserted the combs. Delu knelt—she was the tallest of us, born into a body that wore strength, muscle.

"Indir." Delu handed me the necklace she wanted to wear. She'd chosen carved bone jewelry to contrast her damp-earth brown skin. I held Zeri's thin braids in place as Delu pinned them up. I knelt as they did mine. We painted each other's faces with pigment mixed in rendered animal fat. The temple worker held out a reflector, and we examined ourselves in the polished and oil-lacquered wood. Our bodies were shaped differently, but we had similar faces: wide jaws, dark eyes, our lips full and wide. We looked like our mother, our aunts, like Dreamers. Our black hair rose in braids twisted into the shapes of the Twin Serpents who protected us. Zeri's mouth was, as always, relaxed. She was the serene sister. Delu's mouth constantly curved as if she were about to tell a joke or flirt. My lips were pressed together.

We gathered in a small chamber adjacent to the main gathering chamber at the center of our home, the Temple of Night. The entire city of Alcanzeh was awake, waiting. The drums grew closer. Our temple was lit for ceremony, sacred Ayan smoke hanging in the air, all of us dressed and waiting for him to come. Our mother, Safi, entered. Her two sisters followed.

"We're ready for him." Our aunt Kupi grinned. Her twin, Ixara, reflected her grin. They looked like smaller, wilder versions of our mother. All three were long-limbed with abundant hips. They had the same sharp nose, wide lips, and brown eyes that missed nothing. Kupi and Ixara were identical; the only way most could tell them apart was by Kupi's broken front tooth. She was always tonguing the sharp edge.

"Safi, if there was ever a time to be bold, it is now." Ixara snapped her fingers. Our mother inhaled, her wide nostrils flaring. She seemed to bite back her response, her lips pressed together into a thin line. Safi was the cautious one of the three. Ixara spoke her mind freely, while Kupi always tried to keep the peace between her sisters.

"He isn't the boy who was taken screaming from Alcanzeh anymore; we don't know who he is." Kupi's voice was gentle.

Safi flashed her dark eyes at her sisters, then at me.

"Sisters. My daughters," Safi spoke to all of us, but her eyes focused on mine. "We've been preparing for this. It was part of the peace agreement. Outside of anything else that happens, we are Dreamers. We keep our promises."

To my right, Delu looked as regal as our mother and aunts, her posture straight and grounded. Zeri looked as if she was a girl dressed in the robes of an elder, shifting her weight from one foot to the other the way she did when she was nervous. I was somewhere in between. Delu and I had the same roundness of hip and belly as our mother, but I was shorter so it showed differently on my body. Zeri was still growing into her body's shape and appeared younger than she was. She was born into a body of thick legs; even as a child, her thighs had rippled with beauty as she walked. We wore ceremonial tunics, embroidered with the creatures of earth, sea, and sky; dark red sashes tied beneath our breasts. All of us were crowned by our own hair, our black braids wound around our heads and pinned up in styles sacred to Dreamers.

A runner came in and whispered into Safi's ear. She inhaled sharply.

"He demands we join him at the Temple of Memory."

I looked at Safi. My mother appeared calm, but I could see the tension in her jaw, the way the vein in her throat flickered with her heartbeat. She was as frightened as the rest of us.

An Avex warrior came into the room then, her body painted with the symbols of the Twin Serpents who brought forth the waters Alcanzeh was built over. Avex protected us and the rest of the sacred city.

"We understand he refuses to meet you here. We were prepared for this and are ready," she said. "Tavovis has us standing ready at each temple; there are Avex dispersed throughout the city and watching the water canals. We have guards with Lal and Naru."

My sisters and I exchanged small smiles of pity for the warriors who thought they could guard Naru.

My mother gestured gratitude and beckoned us close as the Avex left.

"We are Dreamers," Safi said. "We are Her wisdom keepers, carriers of Her wishes. Blessed with knowing that cannot be taken, no matter what else happens. He cannot take that from us."

"The people, the beasts, the land awaken. Outside the Dream, the living is long," my aunt Kupi murmured. Her twin Ixara picked up the refrain, my mother and sisters joining in.

"What she gives cannot be taken. We are One, a weaving, a Song." My voice was barely above a whisper.

I swayed at the words, darkness flashing at the edges of my vision. My mother, my aunts, my sisters, they didn't know what could be taken. I couldn't bring myself to tell them what had been taken from me.

We emerged in a line from the Temple of Night. My mother went first, as she always did, flanked by her sisters. My sisters and I followed, Delu to my left, Zeri to my right. Avex warriors, the painted lines on their bodies shining in the torchlight, flanked us. We descended the main temple stairs. It was deep night, a time for sleeping, a time for solitude or rest with chosen beloveds. I wanted to be back in the safety of the temple, behind stone walls where curious eyes couldn't see or judge me. Every time I left the temple, I felt exposed, watched. But I was a Dreamer. I had responsibilities, even in my fragile state. I couldn't disappoint my mother; there had already been so many disappointments.

The Water Temple, which faced ours, was lit with torches. Lal, the council member for the Litéx, emerged, dressed for ceremony, her hair coiled high on her head, her wrists and ankles adorned with seashells and corals. She wore a tunic the same color as her skin, brown like ours but with a different warmth of color. She was from an island. Her round face was serene. She glanced my way and took in a deep breath: her way of reminding me to breathe. She saw my chest expand and gave me a tiny nod and inhaled again deeply. I followed her breath, but the calm wouldn't come.

Lal was the main healer at the Water Temple and knew I hated leaving the Temple of Night. She joined our procession, walking with my twin aunts. I felt safer with her present.

As we walked down the carved steps that led to the Temple of Memory, we saw the city was crowded with onlookers, people who had left their homes to witness the arrival of Alcan, after years of his absence. Everyone was curious as to what sort of man he had become. The people remembered his screams as he was dragged from the city as a boy. How he had cursed his father as the warriors carried him from the only home he had ever known.

Naru waited for us, gleaming in oil and furs, the bones and teeth decorating her body stark white against her jaguar-mottled skin. She was of the Ilkan, though she had lived among us as long as I had memory. Most in Alcanzeh seemed to be equally terrified and fascinated by her.

Our ceremonial drummers stood before their drums, still. They were listening, the approaching unfamiliar rhythms calling to them. Our ceremonial dancers shuffled, unsure of what to do while our own drums were silent. There would be, it seemed, no chance to offer our dance of welcome.

Zeri gasped and gripped my hand. I followed her gaze, my hand reaching for Delu's. My older sister brushed my hand away, her posture straight, eyes focusing on the first line of Fire Warriors approaching us.

The drummers, bodies painted red and shining, came first. They were bare-chested, and not one of them had breasts or was bound. Their drums were black, the animal skin stretched over the tops dyed the red of pooling blood. They pounded their drums with bare hands, every other step they took punctuated by the bone rattles they wore on their ankles. Some wore woven headpieces, bowls of flame balanced on top. I squeezed Zeri's hand back.

The drummers parted. A whispered gasp went through those gathered; even my mother wasn't ready.

The Fire Warriors shone. There was no other word for it. They shone with terrifying power. Their faces were painted white to resemble the skulls beneath. I swayed as they approached, everything in my body screaming at me to run, disappear. I concentrated again on my breathing. I pressed my toes into the ground as Lal had taught me, to try to ground my excess energy. Zeri squeezed my hand again, for mine had gone limp in hers.

One Fire Warrior stopped in front of where we gathered, lines of his kin fanning out behind him. He held a decorated spear in each hand; matching knives hung from his hips. Burn scars ran in two swaths on each side of his head. The stiff black hair that grew from the top of his scalp hung down to the middle of his back. A black Fire Warrior tattoo encircled his neck. He stood before us, perfectly still until the drums stopped. He was the kind of man who stood in his power without the power taking over. He was comfortable in his body. Looking at him, I felt a bite of envy. The confidence of others always made me feel small. Out of the corner of my eye, I saw Delu pull herself even taller.

My mother stepped forward. Her tunic was white, the sash wound around her waist the same red as ours but woven with the Twin Serpents that encircled her body.

"Fire Warriors." Her voice rang out over the crowd; there was no denying the power she carried. I stood up a little taller. "It has been generations since you have blessed our cities with your presence. For too long your temple has remained dark, since the sacred flames of your altars have joined ours in ceremony, in Song, in peace." She paused, letting the words she'd chosen sink in. "In peace, we welcome you back to Alcanzeh, to the sacred city of—"

"I am your king!" a voice called out from behind the Fire Warriors. I thought I saw the spear holder flinch as he stepped aside.

The man who came forward didn't carry himself like a warrior, though his body was strong. His posture was the posture of a trapped animal. Still, he moved forward, grinning. Half his face was painted the same skull-white as the Fire Warriors; the other half was bare. He carried some sort of heavy mallet in his hand, and he swung it in circles as he walked. It was Alcan.

Alcan looked expectant. He stared at my mother a long moment, waiting for her response. Safi's mouth dropped open at his announcement. She said nothing. He glanced at the Fire Warrior at his side. I suppressed a smile.

"Alcan," my mother finally said, her shoulders tensing, "welcome home to the city of your birth. We grieve with you.

Your father was a wise man, a man who followed the Dream, a man who lived his life in keeping our sacred rhythms aligned. He was a great negotiator of peace." She gestured to the carved memory stone we were gathered before.

"Dreamers." Alcan drew out the word in a way that made our name sound like a joke. "Keepers of sacred Alcanzeh, keepers of secrets. You served my father well, I understand. He trusted you. He kept you close." Alcan walked over to stand before his father's memory stone.

King Anz's carving was taller than any living person, his profile carefully chipped into the surface, symbols of his reign surrounding him. His carving was the only one painted in the Temple of Memory; each ruler before him stood watch in effigy, weathered clean of the paint the city artists tended only for living rulers. Within seasons, King Anz's effigy would be as colorless as the others.

Alcan paused briefly to reach up and touch the symbol that represented his mother, then stood back, taking in the entire stone. His eyes narrowed as he turned. He tried to match the power of my mother's voice, but he had no practice.

"The Age of Absence is ending. For nearly five hundred years, we have walked the land without guidance, without our living spirits among us. The test is nearly over; we have survived, despite the mistakes of our elders and the foolishness of those who guided them." Alcan glanced our way. I stood tall as I could, feeling the council members around me bristle, the sharp hiss of my mother's inhaled breath. "I am here to usher in a new age. It has been foretold, another Age of Fire will arrive in my lifetime." The crowd rumbled. My aunts looked at each other, mouths now pressed into twin grim lines. There had already been an Age of Fire in our legends.

Everyone gathered went completely silent. Even the dogs ceased their barking. No one breathed.

Alcan turned again to his father's effigy. The Fire Warrior at his side moved as if to stop him, but Alcan was too fast.

He lifted his mallet and smashed it across the effigy of King Anz. Once, twice, a third time, stone chips flying out and spraying all of us close by. I flinched each time, pressing myself closer to Zeri, who buried her face in my shoulder. When he was finished, his father's face was gone.

Kupi and Ixara, the only ones who seemed able to move after the shock of Alcan's desecration, stepped forward. Kupi smiled her dangerous smile, the one that had a knife hidden inside. My mother flinched as Kupi opened her mouth to speak, but didn't stop her.

"Is that a tradition from the Fire Warriors, Alcan?" Her voice was low, her words weaving something I could not yet place, but I knew my aunts and their ways. The Fire Warrior who had tried to stop Alcan closed his eyes briefly, but kept his face still.

"*King* Alcan," Alcan said, his voice as soft. Kupi wove her arm through Ixara's.

"We have our own traditions here, Alcan, ones you were born to. Your mother was a keeper of those traditions. We still need to Dream for you, no?" Kupi said, her tongue playing at her sharp tooth. She was watching Alcan's face to see how he reacted at the mention of his mother. I held my breath.

Everyone in Alcanzeh knew the stories about Alcan's screams and curses after his mother died. The child she had died birthing returned with her to the Dream.

"It is late, and you have traveled far." Safi stepped forward. My mother was always a peacekeeper. "The Fire Temple has been kept clean; your companions will be comfortable there, I am sure. The Temple of Day you were born in—"

Alcan interrupted her. "I will stay with my people in the Fire Temple," he said, staring at my mother.

I felt a shift in the crowd, tension snaking through everyone's bodies. Alcan was born to Alcanzeh, born with the sacred bite of the Twin Serpents on his chest. He was ours, even though he had been sent away. It had been a part of the peace negotiations his father made with the Fire Warriors to keep them from invading Alcanzeh and the lands under our protection. My mother stared back. She looked past him at the gathered crowd; she wanted calm above all else.

"It is late. May you and your companions rest well." She turned and walked back toward our home. We followed quickly, the crowd opening as we walked through. Naru of the Ilkan dropped back so she was the last of us. I heard her growl softly in her throat. Lal tried to Sing a calming Song in a high sweet voice, but the crowd was too agitated and her Song faltered. As we climbed the steps to the Temple of Night, I looked back and saw, for the first time in my life, the Fire Temple fully illuminated. It terrified me.

《 ☾ ● ☽ 》

My mother and aunts walked directly to the main chamber of our temple. Lal, my sisters, and I followed. A temple worker with a gift for small winds was called up, and she set the air in front of the openings in motion so that no sound would enter or leave.

Lal of the Litéx, keeper of the Water Temple, knelt in front of the Twin Serpents altar that lined one wall of the room. She Sang over the bowls of water until their surfaces vibrated. She came to each of us and made us drink. She was tall, with thick, strong legs, broad-hipped and full of power. Her people were of the sea, living in islands far to the west. The Litéx were the best healers and boat makers in close kinship with those under Alcanzeh. They guided those who lived in the seas. Lal had served in Alcanzeh since adolescence, advising the council on healing ceremonies and rituals, as well as guiding those who fished the seas on the best currents, dangerous tides. Her temple workers were healers; they daily Sang morning Songs for birth and evening Songs for those who returned to the Dream. In turn, we Dreamed for their people what storms were coming, which mountains were hungry for eruption; we warned of strange tides, dangerous currents, and she sent the messages through sea traders. She usually wore her mostly black hair in a long braid that swished to her knees when she walked.

We heard Naru before we saw her.

"I do not need guarding, you fangless, soft-bodied children of men!" she snarled, bursting into the chamber, skin mottled by the heightening of her blood. Her teeth were sharp in her mouth, musk rising from her body in sharp waves. She was as muscled as the Jaguar the Ilkan stories told they were descended from, sleek in her movements, eyes always aware and watching.

The Ilkan lived deep in the jungles somewhere far south of Alcanzeh. Naru's people had the ability to speak with the beasts of the land. When we Dreamed for the Ilkan, we spoke to the spirits of the animals they hunted or tended, bringing back strange messages we were never able to decipher, yet the messages made sense to the Ilkan. In exchange, they sent prey in the direction of hunters and provided the ceremonies held each dark moon to honor the animals killed the previous moon. Naru and any Ilkan who came to visit or train with her lived in the jungle in all seasons. They disliked stone walls and stayed close to the living earth as much as they could.

"Naru!" my mother said, waving her hands in front of her face. The rest of us coughed, eyes watering. Naru stopped and grimaced, taking a deep breath. The markings on her skin faded, her teeth lost their sharpness. Her scent softened after a moment, then disappeared.

"I don't need guarding, Safi." Naru spun to glare at the Avex she had yelled at. A young man and a young woman stood panting at the entry to the chamber. "Go, return to Tavovis, tell him I'll guard myself."

Tavovis walked into the chamber then. He dismissed the two Avex with a wave of his hand. They retreated, eyes grateful.

"You may not need guarding, Naru. I was thinking of the Fire

Warriors. Who will guard them from you?" Tavovis, leader of the Avex, smiled at her. She glowered back. Tavovis turned to my mother.

"Safi, it is worse than we thought," Tavovis said, eyes serious. "Ovis took our best runners out tonight. There are more Fire Warriors than Avex. They are outside Alcanzeh, for now."

I swallowed when I heard him say his son's name. In the before, I sometimes used to late-night whisper his name at our altar, hoping to Dream him.

My aunts started a low hiss that Naru took up. Naru's hiss was more intense; the skin on my body rippled and rose at the sound of it. Lal countered with a hum of peace. Safi pulled her lips in, proof she was truly shaken. My mother had a practiced face of strength; she showed little emotion. I hoped Tavovis would mention Ovis again, but he didn't.

"He isn't king yet; we need to Dream for him. I don't know that the Dream would allow Fire Warriors to enter and reign in our city." My mother's voice was resolute.

"I sent messages to my people, to the Litéx and the Airan when King Anz returned to the Dream. We will require witnesses," Naru said. A flash of annoyance crossed my mother's features, quick as a blink. She preferred making decisions in council, but Naru refused to let anyone sway her.

"Thank you, Naru," Ixara said.

"We cannot know what the Dream will and will not require of us, Safi," Lal said gently, looking at me. Everyone else turned to gaze at me. My face grew hot.

"I made a promise," I whispered. My aunts exchanged glances.

Naru hissed again. Tavovis smiled at me. I didn't look at my mother or sisters as I already knew what their faces would look like: Safi, resigned. My sisters, curious. And I was full of fear.

《 《 ● 》 》

The night King Anz died, I woke up thrashing, tangled in my hammock. I knew myself well enough to know sleep would not return easily.

The sacred city of Alcanzeh below was quiet, the wind blowing in westward from the sea. The late spring air was fragrant with night flowers. There were hours until morning. Torches illuminated the other stone temples, serpentine shadows dancing across the carved facades. From a platform just off our chamber, I watched a runner run down the steps of the Water Temple, leaping off the last few steps and disappearing into the city. Runners had been coming and going for days. I knelt in front of our altar, dropping a dried Ayan flower onto the flame. The flower burned, sacred smoke rose, fragrant and heady. I wondered how soon King Anz would return to the Dream. The healers had been working with him for days on end. I felt the pull of a Dream come with the sacred smoke. I gasped, trying to call upon our protections before Dream took me.

I was in a swamp of dying light. I sunk knee-deep into a substance of decay. I tried to quell the bubble of panic rising. It wasn't anywhere I had been before. I had entered too suddenly, without any safety or ceremony. I tried to speak a few words of protection, but I couldn't reach my voice. A tree rose in front of me, gnarled at the base, twisting up into a thick trunk that gave way to branches heavy with hanging leaves. The leaves moved as if each were breathing. Voices spoke out in the tone of prophecy. I felt each word thrum in my blood.

Indir, you will lose what you love most. We are sorry, but it is the only way.

I sunk deeper into the swamp. Even through the decay, I could feel living roots tendril around my feet, between my toes, pulling me gently. I didn't fight it. There was no point. I had never entered Dreaming unprotected. I was at the mercy of the Dream.

Dream for Anz, Indir. Now. The last word pounded through my entire being like a clap of thunder.

I woke up on my hands and knees, retching, my hair hanging dangerously close to the altar flame. I didn't know how long I had been gone, but the scent of Ayan smoke was still heavy in the air. I jumped up and ran out as fast as I could.

I didn't bother braiding my hair or changing out of my sleeping tunic. Had it been day, I would have never left the temple so disarrayed, but it was night, and urgency rang in my ears. I hurried down our temple stairs and ran to the Water Temple. An Avex stepped out of the shadows and blocked me as I went to climb the stairs. Her face was painted in broad white and red stripes.

"I need to Dream for the king," I said, trying to move around her. I would have usually been too nervous to speak to an Avex, or anyone I didn't know, but Dream's voice had terrified me. I had no time to be nervous.

She moved out of my way. I ran up the steps and followed the torchlights to the back of the main temple, where the healing waters that bubbled up from the earth were the hottest.

King Anz was floating in a steaming pool; herbs and medicinal plants had been added to the water, and the chamber smelled sharp, green. Sacred smoke swirled and hung in the air, trailing out into the night through star-shaped openings in the stone ceiling. Healers held his body afloat, chanting and Singing. Council members sat on stone benches at the edge of the pool. I saw my mother and aunts. I joined them. My mother was holding a skin drum, beating out a slow rhythm. My aunts were talking to Naru of the Ilkan. Nahi, Naru's acolyte at the time, had eyes swollen and rimmed red from weeping.

"I need to Dream for King Anz; it was spoken to me in Dreaming," I said quietly, but the chamber was small and my voice echoed. King Anz lifted his head. The healers supported him as he stood in the waist-deep waters. I cringed at how thin his body had become. I could see the ladders of bones on either side of his chest. The serpent bite–shaped birthmark at the center of his chest barely stood out.

"Then Dream for me." King Anz's voice was strained. I slipped into the water and went to him. Even frail and thin, his body retained the lines of his previous strength. His wounded arm was striated with spears of black and purple extending from armpit to wrist in one direction and toward his heart in the other. The healers brought him to the edge of the pool and propped him up. I sat beside him, holding his hand. He was a good king, flawed like all of us and aware of it.

"What would you like me to seek in Dreaming?" I had asked. He looked at the council members, his eyes softened and filled with tears.

"Leave us." His voice was weak, but everyone rose and left. My mother stayed, her eyes flicking back and forth between us. Anz raised his eyebrows at her, and she left, glancing back at us. We were alone.

"Indir, Truth Dreamer, tell me, does my son bear the Twin Serpents' mark?"

I blinked. Alcan had been living away from Alcanzeh for years. I held his question in my mind.

I closed my eyes, breathing in through my nose, imagining the Twin Serpents who protected us and carried our gift, awakening in my belly and heart. I exhaled through my mouth, imagining the wings of the Night Bird, who crossed from the Dream into the Waking World, unfolding from within my chest. I felt the stirrings in my blood, imagining countless tiny spiders made of light unfurling from sleep to spin webs of protection in my body. I touched my hands to my mouth and mouthed the sacred words of Dreamers; we never spoke them aloud around anyone outside of our lineage. I felt the weight of my body drop, then the rush as my mind and knowing moved from the Waking World into the Dream. I was pulled through a tunnel of vibrating light and sound.

Shapes and shadows surged around me, the hum of the eternal pulsating. I looked for the entry point sacred to Dreamers, the place we could enter, be offered visions. But I couldn't find a safe way to enter the Dream. Instead, I saw the tree again. A terror rose in me. It wasn't in a swamp this time; instead, it was formed of countless points of moving light, shifting in color and shadow. Before I could approach the tree, it flowered suddenly, blossoms of every shape and size growing until they split apart, dissolving the tree. Before I could react, forms rose before me.

I had recognized Alcan immediately, nebulous as he was. He was older, but I saw the same angry look on his face I remembered from my early childhood. He was shadowed, turning this way and that. I saw another shape beneath him. He was standing on the back of another man, wisps of smoke rising from both of them. Alcan held a burning branch. He looked through me and screamed, pressing the burning end of the branch into the center of his chest. I smelled flesh burning and tried to turn away. A new shape rose up from the miasma and floated toward me, a sphere of water. At its center pulsed the Twin Serpents' bite mark, in a bloom of dappled red. Alcan flew past me, beating at the sphere with his burning branch. The shape he had been standing on rose and stepped between Alcan and the sphere. An ache started deep in my abdomen. A new shape appeared before me. It was me. I tried to cry out. The other me stared back, her surprise mirroring mine. As I reached out to touch her, the shape of Alcan surged forward; he held a knife in his hand. I stared at the stone blade as it entered my chest. I felt myself dying and tried to scream. The Dream trembled around us, the other me opened her mouth and everything around us poured into her, splitting apart as I dissolved into darkness.

《 《 ● 》 》

I rose up sputtering from the water I'd swallowed.

"Indir?" King Anz was breathing hard. I made my way to him. His eyes were all questions. They were wide, pupils dilated. He was full of fear. No one should die in fear. I cradled his head, feeling his skin going cold despite the heat of the pool. I concentrated on my breathing, inhaling deeply, reminding myself I was safe. I hummed myself a Song of return, of safety, but it did little to soothe me.

"The Twin Serpents' mark?" He was struggling to keep his eyes open.

"I saw Alcan, but I didn't see the mark; he was standing on the shape of another man. Alcan burned the center of his own chest."

The king's eyes went wide, his fear punctuated by a groan of regret. I touched his face.

"I saw the mark of the Twin Serpents floating in a sphere of water. Alcan tried to destroy it but couldn't; the man he was standing on was between them. I saw myself. I swallowed myself, the entire Dream," I told him. I didn't tell him I had seen Alcan killing me.

Dreaming was an imperfect gift, like all gifts, but we did what we could. The Dream showed us only what She wanted us to see. King Anz closed his eyes and pulled me close so that my ear was close to his mouth.

"Tell no one, Indir, promise me. Never speak of this Dream, not even to the other Dreamers. But keep it in your memory, until it is needed." He coughed. His breath smelled of sweet rot. Inside him, his blood was already dying.

"I promise."

King Anz closed his eyes, his chest barely rising and falling. He began to slip off the steps; I heard the death rattle in his breath.

"Come back!" I cried, wrapping my arms around him just as he slipped beneath the water. Voices shouted. I was barely aware of the others that splashed into the pool around me, pushing me aside. A woman began Singing, a keening that other voices took up. Arms went around me, pulling me out of the water. My mother and aunts were beside me, their voices rising and falling in Death Song. Naru and Nahi added their voices, gasping growls that reverberated through my bones. Our king had returned to the Dream. I sat on the steps, trembling at the secret he had left me to carry alone.

CHAPTER TWO

SAYA

I landed in the Dream hard. I held my breath, hoping I wasn't in an unfriendly landscape. My body could not experience pain in the Dream, but I was so accustomed to having a body that knew pain in the Waking World, I automatically curled up to protect myself. I opened my eyes. I was in one of my favorite places, one home to generous and gentle trickster spirits. I knew the offerings I had left back on my altar had been received. Sitting up, I looked around, pretending to look for the spirits I knew were hiding, waiting to playfully attack. In many ways, these particular spirits were like small children, attention changing from one moment to the next, speaking in strange riddles I'd learned to decipher. Even if their messages didn't always make sense, the outcomes were favorable and kept my mother happy. And if my mother was happy, there were fewer tensions between us.

The landscape shifted slightly as I made my way across a flat expanse of low-growing grasses that glowed in every color imaginable. At each footstep, waves of light dispersed from my motion, same as my body as it moved through the sacred space. Above me, the sky roiled and shifted, showing a glowing blue sphere rimmed in yellow smoke. It changed into a complicated web of geometric shapes that pulsed and twisted into complicated swirls. Spirits flitted by, some small as an eyelash, others lumbering shapes that hovered to briefly observe me with unseen eyes before moving away.

A push knocked me flat onto my face. I heard laughs and knew the spirits I had been seeking had decided to show themselves. I made a game of getting up slowly, brushing the webs of unknown substance from where they clung to my skin, fine threads of whatever the Dream was made of in that particular space.

"Saya so protected coming to ask," a low voice hummed. I smiled, grateful. It was Yecacu, a spirit who loved the offerings I left. I looked toward Yecacu and waited a moment for her to shift into her familiar shape, a strange combination of some kind of Jaguar spirit and the long legs of a hoofed creature I did not recognize. Yecacu had grown her ears long and tall. Smaller spirits, shaped like frogs, clung to Yecacu's ears, chirping a Song in unison. I didn't know their names. My mother had warned me about becoming too familiar with spirits, never asking their names. Yecacu was one of a few who had offered. My hand went to the protection necklace I had worn since birth. The stones were cool; they only warmed when I was being threatened and rarely in Dreaming.

"Yecacu." I opened my hands in gratitude. "Little friends." The frog spirits chirped their greeting back.

"Nuts and grains and sweet filled leaves and a stone painted in stars," Yecacu began, listing the items I'd placed on the altar before slipping into the Dream. "Nothing living, not a drop of blood." Yecacu's eyes stared into mine, asking. I shook my head.

"I cannot offer blood," I said softly, never knowing how a spirit would react. I touched my necklace; it remained cool. Yecacu shifted for a moment into a blur of light, then re-formed.

"The nuts were enough," Yecacu sighed. The frog spirits in her ears chirped again.

"I'm living in a village of wanderers, rooted for now. What stories do you know?" It was a careful way of asking what information could be freely offered to me, for me to take back to the Waking World.

"Saya so protected doing the bidding of that woman." Yecacu stared at me. I looked away. The spirits didn't like my mother, Celay, and always made a point to tell me.

"She lost her gift when she birthed me," I said. She never failed to remind me. Yecacu stomped her feet and the frog spirits whistled sharply enough for me to cover my ears, though it didn't help. In Dreaming, every sensation took over the entire body.

"Stole," the frog spirits chirped. Yecacu flicked her ears and the frog spirits were flung off. They immediately sprouted transparent wings and flew away, chirping the entire time. We watched them go.

"Gossips," Yecacu muttered and turned her dizzying gaze back on me. "Stories then, for your offerings." She listed off small pieces of information about the villagers. An older woman with a bad cut on her foot that would poison her blood; Yecacu showed me the root that would heal her. A child had developed nightmares after being subject to his sibling's rage; the child needed a cleansing, as did the sibling. She went on and on, offering strange messages to people I lived among but barely knew.

"Thank you for these stories," I said when I thought she had finished. Yecacu pawed the ground.

"There is more, but I am not the one to tell you," she growled, turning to lick her shoulder with her bright red tongue. She hacked a few times and spit out a mouthful of hair.

"And all the stories you've offered me will bring no harm?" I prodded. I had no reason not to trust Yecacu, but it was something I always asked. I had learned the hard way.

"No harm, Saya. Though you are being harmed, you know," Yecacu said. Another reference to my mother.

"She protects me," I said. It was what I always said. It was what Celay always said.

"Where else will you go?" Yecacu asked. She knew I would say no more about my mother.

I thought. There were countless places to visit in the Dream. As a child, I had been able to access only safe places full of kind and playful spirits. I had met Yecacu there first. When my bleeding arrived three years ago, I was able to visit different worlds within Dreaming, though some terrified me. I was wary of exploring.

"The cove," I said. Yecacu raised a hoof as I slipped from her chosen landscape. The light surrounding me was a mass of pale and bright green clouds that seemed to shine and throb with power from within. The air tasted the way a lightning storm smelled, like scent from a fire that burned on no fuel but itself. I spun through, relishing the pull on all my senses until they dissolved into one, a vibration that pulsed and sang in my entire being.

I landed in the cove with a splash that sent ripples glowing out to sea and toward the shore. I floated on my back a long while, staring up at the ever-shifting space above me. It was deeper, endlessly more beautiful than the sky in the Waking World. I felt shapes in the water beneath me, quick pecks at the skin of my legs that tickled. Something with a hot mouth began to lick at my toes. I kicked out gently and whatever spirit it was swam away. I moved my arms until I was drifting further out, the water growing slightly cooler around me as it deepened. Away from the shore, ears submerged as I floated on my back, I could make out voices beneath the water, scraps of Songs and mating calls, a lament or two.

A spirit shaped like a bird drifted slowly above me on out-stretched wings. I was as long as one of her feathers. No air stirred, but she glided, looking down with bright yellow eyes. I felt her gaze on me, reading me, seeing what I had to offer. Nothing. I had no other gifts to exchange but my strange ability to enter the Dream. A gift no one in the Waking World knew about except my mother.

The bird turned a slow circle in the air, leaving a trail of dis-solving light behind her. She floated over me again. I breathed in and out, waiting for her to speak. I knew I could leave at any moment I wanted, but I was as curious about her as she seemed to be about me. There were no birds that large in the Waking World, not in any of the places my mother and I had traveled. If there were stories about birds like her in our world, I had never heard them told. The bird opened her mouth to speak.

"She is coming, Saya. Let yourself be found," the bird said. Nearby, a whale-shaped spirit breached, sending a series of small waves toward me. One splashed over my head. I sputtered and kicked my legs beneath me. When I looked up again, the bird was gone.

It was odd but not entirely out of the ordinary for Dreaming. Spirits wanted messages delivered; sometimes they offered me messages. I sensed there were more powerful beings inhabiting the Dream; I felt the displacement of them, spaces I could not enter though I was pulled toward them. My mother insisted I interact and exchange only with those satisfied by small, relatively simple offerings. The bird had asked for nothing; it was something I wouldn't mention to Celay when I returned. I was learning which silences suited us best, which secrets were my own.

《《●》》

I felt my body tense when I returned to the Waking World. I kept my eyes closed and my breathing as even as I could. I knew Celay would be watching, waiting. She had a sense as to when I would return. I felt her hand on my back, a soft stroke. As a small child, when I returned from Dreaming, I would flail and scream, shocked at the weight of my body again, the abruptness of my senses frightening me. I preferred the Dream. She always placed hands on me to calm me. I was curious as to why she continued to do so as I grew older but didn't ask, afraid she would stop. It was the only time my mother touched me with tenderness.

"You're back," Celay said. I sat up and drank the cup of water she offered. I always returned from the Dream thirsty. I swished the water around in my mouth before swallowing.

"Yecacu," I said. "And the frog spirits that live on her ears, but they were being annoying, and Yecacu sent them flying away." I knew Celay loved the stranger details from Dreaming; she loved the descriptions of the spirits.

"I didn't know they flew." Celay's voice was soft.

"They did when I saw them." I kept my tone playful. I'd noticed Celay's restlessness the past moon; her moods were unpredictable. If Celay was in a foul mood, she would accuse me of trying to make her jealous, and I would have a day of tension ahead of me. "Yecacu told me stories." I recounted most of what Yecacu had told me, but some of the stories involved things I wouldn't tell Celay. A woman living near us wanted to give birth and would require the help of a spirit. I knew Celay would take that information and use it to manipulate the young woman and her chosen. I didn't know them well, but they had always seemed friendly to me.

I gave her as many details as I could. She would get angry if she missed something, and I would be the target of her rage. I could tell she was distracted. It made me nervous.

"Eat something and prepare the basket." Celay looked at where our food supplies hung suspended from the ceiling of our home. There were bundles of dried fish and meat, bunches of roots and other dried vegetables. Enough food to last a season, but Celay lived two patterns I had grown to know too well. In one, we found a place to live, made a home, stored food, found ways to use my gift to our benefit, without revealing anything of ourselves. After settling into a rhythm— sometimes it took a moon, sometimes several seasons—Celay would grow suddenly frantic and insist we pack only what we needed. We would head toward the smaller trade routes without saying goodbye to anyone we knew. The times we were traveling, Celay was bolder in using my gift to convince those we met that she had a gift, one she refused to name.

We had been in our current home, a small haven composed of people who wandered, a place of temporary rest, for a full cycle of seasons. It was the longest we had stayed anywhere. I was trying to mentally prepare myself for our next season of wandering.

I went outside to the cooking fire behind our small home, set back from the rest of the inhabitants. The previous occupant had been an elder, once a trader until she'd grown too tired to keep moving. She had been known for finding seeds and knowing how to tend them, spreading different kinds of seeds along her trade routes. Before her death, she'd spent several seasons planting and tending different seeds from her journeys. We had come through a few moons after her death and taken up residency in the hut. I was fascinated by the plants the woman had tended and tried to keep them alive. I had mostly succeeded and was dreading the day Celay announced our departure. I wanted to stay long enough to see what I had tended bloom and give sustenance. I was surprisingly good at working with the plants, convincing them to grow in a strange landscape they had no memory for. Another elder had teased me that perhaps I did have a gift. Celay thought it had something to do with my real gift. I didn't correct her. Tending the plants was the one place in the Waking World where I felt at peace.

Celay motioned me to follow her just after midday. I sighed and lifted the heavy basket. I had found the root Yecacu had shown me in Dreaming, growing among the plants I tended. I hadn't known its use before and was grateful for the knowledge. Besides the root, the basket had Celay's tools, little tricks she used to convince others of her gift. As a child, I thought it was a game we played, telling stories to people so that they would give us things. The better the story, the more we received. Celay would then praise me after we had been given our bounty. They were offerings from people who were desperate.

We walked straight to the home of the elder with the cut on her foot. Celay shook a bracelet made of bones three times, a signal she used to let people know she carried a message for them. A few people stopped what they were doing to come see. It was part of her plan; the more who witnessed Celay using her gift, the more they trusted us and would make offerings to us. The woman limped out of her house, squinting in the light.

"The cut will not heal on its own," Celay said dramatically. "The spirits have sent you a gift to keep your blood from poisoning you." She shook the bone bracelet thrice again.

The woman's eyes widened; she chanted what sounded like

gratitude in a language I didn't know. I felt my face grow hot. I disliked large displays of emotion. I was always punished for mine. Celay seemed to enjoy emotion in others though, and turned her face kind, opening her arms wide.

"A gift, sister, though I had to search my memories long to see where to find this gift." She motioned to me. I kept my face carefully blank as I approached Celay. I reached into the basket and pulled out the root. Celay had wrapped it in woven cloth before we left our home, tying small charms around it so that the root rattled. Celay bowed her head deeply as she took the root from me and walked slowly with it in her two outstretched hands, tilting her head back and calling out loudly.

"We thank you for this gift. And I thank you for allowing me to be the one to bridge this world to what the spirits want." It wasn't untrue. She was grateful. She didn't have to do work to secure food for either of us or help in other ways. She claimed she needed large swaths of time uninterrupted in order to receive messages. If there was work that required help, I was the one who would go. Celay forbade me from talking to anyone outside of common courtesies. I pretended to be shy, though I ached for connection with others. Life with my mother was lonely.

The elder took the root and unwrapped it, careful to keep the charms. She examined the root. It was as long as her hand and half the width. Knobby tendrils protruded like hairs.

"What do I do with it?" the elder asked. I felt weak. I hadn't asked Yecacu how the root was to be used. A very important detail. I saw Celay's body tense. I looked at the root and noticed it had a familiar shape, though the color was different, like that of a root we used to clear coughs. It also looked like a root Celay had shown me, one to induce strange visions in those who consumed it.

"You will make an infusion of it, to drink," Celay replied. I gasped. The woman stared at me, then back to Celay. My mother turned to look at me, her eyes cold and full of anger. She kept her face calm, but I could tell by the clench of her jaw that she was enraged. I kept my face serene while everything in me flooded with panic. I didn't know anything about the root. I hadn't asked Yecacu, and she hadn't offered any information. A dangerous mistake. If Celay was wrong, she could kill the woman. I swallowed. I knew what it meant. Celay never stayed close when she made a dangerous mistake.

The woman limped inside and returned with a bracelet made of polished black stones, cut into rough spheres with intricate carvings. Celay took it and put it in the basket, and we continued.

It was a temporary place; it would last several cycles of seasons perhaps, if sickness, drought, or flood didn't come through. The lands we lived in were full of dangerous and unpredictable seasons. There were more established places we could live, communities that had existed for generations and had stone temples carved by unknown ancestors. However, Celay hated cities, and we had avoided them my entire life. I didn't think I would ever get close to one, not while Celay had any control over me.

We stopped at a few more homes, offering quiet advice to the family with the sons who needed cleansing. I waited outside while Celay did what she did. If she had any gift, besides her ability to deceive others, it was that she knew how to cleanse.

Everyone had a knowing of how to cleanse, but Celay had gathered knowledge across the lands we had wandered and knew several ways to rid a body of nightmares, fevers, skin reactions, and other small maladies.

《 ☾ ● ☽ 》

We were walking back to our home when someone called out. I stopped, grateful. I was not looking forward to returning home with Celay. Her anger had simmered as the day had passed. I had hoped the abundance of offerings we had been given in exchange for her messages would have calmed her. It hadn't. In my mind, I was already going over what I wanted to carry with me when we left.

The voice belonged to Ruta, the young woman Yecacu had told me needed a spirit to help conceive a child. She was near my age and lived with her mate Kinet. I knew Kinet had once been a trader and that Ruta was from a coastal people. She wove nets better than anyone.

"Celay, I need your help," Ruta panted. I noticed there were dark circles under her eyes, her face pale. Her tunic hung loosely on her frame. She had been unwell recently, which explained why her skin had paled and her usually well-braided black hair was pulled back into a messy knot that hung limply over her shoulder.

"Ruta, of course." Celay stood still, not seeming to notice how tired Ruta was. I pulled a small gourd from the basket of offerings. It had been given to us by a woman whose boil Celay had pierced. I filled it with an energizing blend of herbs I knew Celay liked to drink in the morning. My mother was already angry with me, and I felt sorry for Ruta.

"Here, please, drink this." I handed Ruta the gourd. She turned grateful eyes on me and drank deeply. Celay didn't look at me. She didn't have to. I knew exactly how she felt. Ruta handed me the empty gourd and smiled at me. Her eyes were full of something I wanted more of, gratitude, a recognition. Kindness.

"What is it you need?" Celay asked. Ruta's color was already improving after the drink; it must have been a potent brew. I knew Celay noticed too.

"Come, you'll be more comfortable in our home," I said, offering my arm out to Ruta. She looked surprised but linked her arm through mine. Anything to delay Celay's punishment.

《 ❨ ● ❩ 》

Though there was still daylight enough to see inside, Celay lit the wicks of two bowls of oil. The flames gave off a pungent smoke due to the herbs Celay had let soak in the oil. Ruta sat on a folded blanket I set up beside the altar. It was a small altar, home to no specific spirit. It held what all altars held: a bowl of water, a source of flame, earth, and something that could be used to produce sound. Ours had a carved whistle. Celay placed one bowl of flame on the altar and offered Ruta a cup of water. She accepted. I waited to see what Celay would ask of me, to leave or attend. I thought she would ask me to leave as punishment, but I was surprised when she pointed at the ground beside her. I sat.

《 《 ● 》 》

Ruta held her hands briefly over the flame on the altar and pressed them to her eyes. We stayed silent while she held whatever moment of ritual she needed. She turned to us.

"My body cannot hold a child," she said softly. A wave of despair rose in me. I knew there was nothing Celay loved more than acting as spiritual midwife for those wishing to give birth. She claimed she had served at Night Bird ceremonies before I was born. I didn't know if I believed her, though she did seem to have knowledge in that particular area.

"You know whatever I do may take time. It will require extended work for me, long periods of contemplation and solitude." Celay was preparing Ruta for service. A part of me was frustrated. I knew exactly what Ruta needed, and I could help her, but my mother would never allow it. The other part of me was grateful, because it meant we would stay where we were long enough to collect whatever Celay felt was owed to her before helping Ruta.

"We are prepared. Kinet knows how badly I want to give birth. We have much to offer in gratitude," Ruta said. Celay nodded. I could see she was pleased.

"Saya, bring me the birthing basket, the red one."

I lifted the large basket from the hook it hung from and brought it to Celay. She rummaged through until she found what she was looking for. I kept my face still, but inside I was screaming at my mother. I could see the hopeful look in Ruta's eyes. It broke my heart. The bunch of dried yellow flowers my mother handed Ruta were used to prevent birth or conception. I stared at the ground. I didn't understand Celay's motives.

Ruta took the bunch of flowers. She held her hands above the altar again for a moment and then turned to Celay with tears in her eyes.

"Thank you, Celay," she said.

"I am only the messenger; your gratitude shall go to the spirits," Celay said. She never specified any spirits, though we lived among those who had their beliefs in spirits. I knew they were real, as did everyone. We saw them interplay in our lives in small ways, but it had been generations since they had moved among us.

Ruta thanked us again and left. Celay was silent a long while, too long. I tried to prepare myself for what was coming.

"Do you know what I have sacrificed to keep you safe?" Her voice was low, each word said with precision. "My gift? I gave you my protection. You wear it. Without that, you would be dead, swallowed by the Dream. I've seen it."

The same words had been repeated to me so many times my entire life that they felt like truth. I tried to reason with myself. My mother lied to others constantly, small lies, lies that changed entire lives; why wouldn't she lie to me?

"We could have told the elder we needed her to sleep with the root one night, and we'd bring her the knowledge of how to use the root tomorrow," I said. I was tired. We had spent the entire day among people. I had barely eaten anything. After leaving the elder, Celay had told every person we met with that I was fasting while she ate what they offered. I was concerned about the elder. It was the kind of mistake that could change, or in this story, end a life.

"It was your mistake, Saya. If anything happens to that woman, it will be because of what you failed to do." Celay fell into a familiar pattern.

She ignored me while I made myself a small meal. I was waiting for her punishment. It could be anything; something in my drinking cup that would make my stomach cramp terribly but briefly, taking away my sleeping blankets, or a bowl of water splashed over my head in the night. I tried not to react to her punishments anymore, but she always found a way to make me uncomfortable, to bring me pain.

I knew no other life.

I was starting to wish I did.

CHAPTER THREE

INDIR

His scent reached me before he spoke, sharp and burnt. I pretended not to know he was behind me and concentrated on painting in the lines in the carved stone. Half a moon had passed since Alcan and his Fire Warriors had arrived in Alcanzeh. Beside me, temple workers giggled.

"What have you seen these days in Dreaming, Indir? Have you seen me yet?" Inkop asked, his voice so close I could feel his breath move the loose hairs from my braid. I tried not to shudder. Inkop was Alcan's closest adviser, the Fire Warrior I had noticed the night of their arrival.

"No."

The temple workers giggled again. I ignored them.

"Seek me in Dreaming, please." I heard the invitation in his voice and turned to face him.

"This part of the temple is for Dreamers and those who serve the Temple of Night," I said.

"I didn't know." He bowed his head but kept his black eyes on me. "Alcan told me the temples were for everyone."

I didn't doubt Alcan had given Inkop free rein to do what he pleased. Elders were muttering that Alcan was overbold. His dishonoring his father's memory stone had sent a shock through the city, but already stories were being whispered about how Alcan's actions had been justified. No doubt Alcan had planted those stories himself. He knew that rumors were a food everyone could feast on in times of uncertainty.

Inkop studied the walls.

"He isn't our king yet. There is still ceremony," I said, staring at him, trying to keep the shaking from my voice. He ignored my words.

"I came to tell you the Ilkan have arrived. Dreamers are invited to a feast in their honor tonight." He reached out and touched my face. I flinched. "Seek me in Dreaming. I promise what you see will surprise you," he said, then walked out.

I waited until he was gone, then leaned back against the wall, eyes closed, not caring that the fresh paint would get all over my tunic. My heart beat hard as a war drum.

"He likes you," one of the temple workers said.

I opened my eyes. "I'm done for the day. I will stay here alone now."

They filed out, taking the bowls of pigment and my brushes.

I looked at the carving I had been painting. The Night Bird of our legends taking seeds from the Dream and creating the Waking World we lived in. The Twin Serpents rising from the roots of the first tree, creating an opening between the Dream and where we lived, gifting our ancestors with knowing and gifts. Over the ages, many of those gifts had died out, untended, though a few remained in the lands. The Dreamers carried one of the last gifts. Through all changes, ours remained. I felt my secret rise in my chest, sending my body into a state of fear. I had told no one.

I had stopped Dreaming.

I left the chamber where I'd been working and stood outside, my eyes adjusting to the brightness. All the temples in Alcanzeh were painted, but ours was the only one that was entirely white. The midday sun glared off it. The temple plateau was the highest in the city, looking out over streets arranged in grids. Ceremonial centers were surrounded by markets, and canals of water ran through the city, some designated for consumption, others for labor. The inhabitants lived on the edges of the city. Several levels of stairs rose to where we lived. I loved Alcanzeh, even if I rarely ventured into her streets. Everyone knew what Dreamers looked like. There were always those who would approach us with gifts and desperate stories, begging us to Dream for them. It was exhausting. But the Temple of Night was a sanctuary. I went down a set of stairs to the next level and entered one of the main chambers, then to another room with large windows cut high into the stone walls.

Zeri was sorting through baskets filled with food, beads, herbs, and other offerings. The baskets were on a knee-high platform that ran the length of three walls. Temple workers surrounded her as she directed them.

"This basket is full of that yellow weed the healers love; take it to the Water Temple. Moon mother, this one is filled with ashes, but of what, I don't know. Take it to the Fire Temple, leave it on the steps, but don't go inside. Indi!" Zeri looked up. She saw the look on my face and beckoned to a temple worker. "You, please figure the rest out elsewhere. I must speak with my sister privately."

The temple workers filed out, carrying the baskets. I sat on the platform next to my sister.

At fifteen, Zeri was two years younger than me, but she was already a powerful Dreamer. She Dreamed possibility and was popular with the residents of Alcanzeh. She could Dream their lovers, their children, what paths they should choose, what kinds of offerings they should make.

"The Ilkan have arrived," I said quietly.

Zeri nodded. "You know you have paint in your hair? Turn around." I let her unbraid my long hair. Zeri took a comb from a shelf and began brushing the dried paint out.

"They arrived quickly," Zeri mused. "Delu saw strong storms in the south in her Dreaming and thought they'd be delayed."

"Inkop came to tell me; he said Alcan expects us at a feast tonight in their honor." I grimaced through my words.

Zeri nodded and leaned forward to briefly touch her forehead to my cheek.

I hated the way Inkop stared at me, a question in his eyes. From the day he'd arrived with Alcan and the other Fire Warriors, his eyes had sought me out. He found reasons to visit our temple and somehow always managed to find me and ask me what I had seen Dreaming. There was something about him that made me feel unbalanced.

The tension in my back eased as my sister combed my hair, scratching my scalp gently with her fingernails. It was something we'd done for each other since childhood.

"Delu seems to like Inkop," Zeri said as she began braiding. "I believe he's the kind who goes after what he can't have. There's something about him. I can't see him clearly."

"Do you think that, or did you Dream it?" I asked, leaning back into her. I breathed in slowly. She smelled of dried herbs, woven grasses, other offerings.

"We don't have to Dream something to know it's true." Zeri embraced me, then pulled me to my feet. "What have you seen in Dreaming?"

I felt my blood rise to my face. I looked away from my sister. I didn't know how to tell her, how to tell anyone. The shame of my secret terrified me. No one, not in any of the countless stories I knew of our bloodline, had ever lost the ability to enter Dreaming.

"I don't care to speak of my Dreams," I said.

"Indi." Zeri stood in front of me, her dark eyes serious. "If you have seen Inkop in Dreaming, I won't tell anyone. Perhaps you're Dreaming possibility and not truth. We're still young; our Dreams haven't settled."

I'd Dreamed mostly truths, victors in battle, what crops would prove fruitful, the best trade routes. My gift was rare; there hadn't been a truth Dreamer in generations. King Anz had asked me to Dream for him sparingly, not wanting to abuse my gift. I had spent the moons since my last Dream lying, repeating old Dreams I'd had before. Everyone was too distracted to notice.

"My Dreams are shadowed." This was a truth. I saw nothing, even if the way I spoke it alluded to confusing Dreams.

Zeri sighed and looked past me to make sure no one was around.

"Mine too." She looked searchingly into my eyes. I held Zeri's gaze. Zeri had the eyes of all Dreamers, a brown almost black, with a fine circle of the darkest gold surrounding the iris that appeared only in direct sunlight.

Voices came. People were entering the temple. Zeri put her arm around me, leaning her head on my shoulder. Of the three of us, Zeri and I were closest.

"She will not abandon us, sister. She never has. We will survive this. We have to."

《 ❨ ● ❩ 》

The feast was held in one of the stone-enclosed gathering spaces overlooking Alcanzeh, below where the temples were but still above the city. Mats made of woven plants were placed around the space and on raised platforms. At the far end of the gathering space, the half circle of platforms was piled with cushions for the Alcan, the council, and guests. Curious residents of Alcanzeh, some who had been trying to make impressions on and gain favor from Alcan, gossiped and laughed around the edges. There were rumors Alcan would open the city to more traders. There were other rumors of how Alcanzeh would be changing.

Walking toward the platforms, I was surprised to see the Dreamers were not sitting beside where Alcan would sit. Instead, Inkop and a few other Fire Warriors were sitting in our usual place. The council sat to the left of Alcan's cushion-laden platform, their faces pinched with disapproval. Naru was not among them. I looked for her and saw she was sitting with the Ilkan to the right of Inkop.

"Indir!" Kupi called and beckoned me forward.

I made my way to where the council was seated. My mother was deep in conversation with Lal, discussing a leak in one of the Water Temple's healing baths. My aunts motioned for me to sit beside them.

"Where are my sisters?" I asked.

"Near, I'm sure," Kupi said.

"Sit." Ixara smiled at me. I adored them. Only twelve years older than me, they were more like older sisters to me than aunts. When my fears arose, it was Kupi and Ixara I turned to. They knew the words to speak, or how to stay silent and present. My mother always tried to fix me, but my aunts knew when to sit with me in whatever grief had risen, or how to coax me into release. They had been angry with King Anz when he died, for making me keep my Dream secret. They had been quiet since his death, whispering to each other and keeping to themselves, to my mother's annoyance.

"Here they come. Delu has her dog," Ixara said sharply.

Zeri arrived with Delu and Chiki, the annoying temple worker who followed Delu everywhere.

"Delu, Chiki can't sit with us," Kupi said gently.

"She's my friend. I invited her," Delu retorted. I loved my sister, I truly did. But there were times when she frustrated me beyond belief.

Zeri sat down beside me and looked pointedly at Chiki.

There was room for only one more person. Delu looked at her companion.

"Why don't you two come sit with me?" We looked up. Inkop was standing in front of us. In honor of the feast, he had rubbed his body down with oil that glistened in the setting sun. Delu's eyes lit up at his invitation. I couldn't see what she found attractive about him.

"Thank you, we will." Delu jumped up and followed him to where he led, Chiki not far behind. Safi stopped her conversation to ask Delu a question as she passed. I couldn't hear what Delu answered, but my mother rolled her eyes and turned back to Lal, saying something that made Lal chuckle and shake her head.

A conch horn wail split the air, and everyone in the courtyard quieted and sat down. I looked sideways at Zeri, who returned my look. King Anz had never arrived with fanfare. He had always entered with everyone else. But Alcan was completely different from his father. While he had been away living with the Fire Warriors in the northern deserts, he had developed a penchant for the dramatic.

He entered slowly behind the drummers. His face was wide with a broad nose, which he accented by painting a swath of red across it to his cheekbones, ending right before his ears. Obsidian blades dangled from his stretched earlobes, and a carved tusk pierced the skin above his nose.

The drummers were young men he had brought with him from the north, though they weren't all warriors. Their faces were painted white, and they pounded out ominous rhythms on skin and bone drums, rattles around their ankles. It seemed silly to me, such formality outside of ceremony. Alcan didn't look to either side as he entered; he stared straight ahead.

"Stand!" one of the drummers shouted. A murmur went through the crowd gathered for the feast. I stood, confused. My mother stood too and hissed at my aunts, who had remained seated. They rolled their eyes and stood, arms crossed over their bodies. No one had ever stood for the king, and Alcan hadn't yet entered the ceremony where we would confirm his rule. He was the servant of the people; King Anz had always knelt before his people. I heard my aunts draw their breaths in. Their faces were set into hard lines. I heard low rumbles, growls barely held in from where Ilkan stood.

Descended from the Great Jaguar herself, the Ilkan women were lightly marked like their ancestor and were, as far as we knew, the fiercest warriors in the land. They kept the peace between the people and the beasts, able to communicate with both. At times, they used their skills to protect people, but there were also times they used their skills to protect beasts. Ilkan warriors could transform themselves at will to embody aspects of the Great Jaguar. Ilkan warriors could unsheathe claws, grow sharpened teeth, leap and run with the ferocity of the Jaguar herself. They lived in the south, far south of Alcanzeh. After Anz's death, Naru had dispatched her acolyte to their land, asking her people to send a group of warriors to Alcanzeh. No one had ever seen an Ilkan man, though they had to exist.

I stared. I knew Naru well; I had known her my entire life. Over the years, a few Ilkan had visited her. I realized Naru and those who visited Alcanzeh had adapted their style of dress to match those who lived in the city, tunics belted at the waist, their hair in simple braids.

The Ilkan who had arrived were different. The women wore head coverings made of woven grasses, bone beads, and dark feathers. Strips of jaguar fur hung over their shoulders. They wore long necklaces of different claws and teeth of the animals of the land over short, sleeveless tunics that were the same mottled brown as their skin. They were barefoot, legs tight with muscle. I looked to see if Nahi had returned with them but didn't see her. We weren't close, but I had enjoyed her company the year she had lived with Naru.

The Ilkan's bodies were casual lines of indifference against the rigidity of everyone else's. One toyed with her claw necklace. For a moment, I thought I saw the flick of a tail behind her. A tall Ilkan, with a headdress hung with carved animal teeth, caught me looking and fixed me with a cool stare. I tried to look away, but the woman's eyes were entrancing, the color of amber, with a black pupil, rimmed in thick black lashes. The woman broke into a slow smile, her eyeteeth sharp and obvious against her bitten lower lip. My face flushed as I smiled back quickly before looking away. The Ilkan had power. I could feel it.

Alcan reached his platform. He stared straight ahead. I heard one of my aunts hiss softly.

"Be seated." His voice was loud but lacked strength. "I welcome you to this feast honoring the Ilkan. They are the first to arrive to serve as witnesses." He turned to the Ilkan. The women sat as still as cats in the sun, regarding him silently with their strange eyes. They even lay about like jaguars, languid, still.

Alcan's nostrils flared.

"Let us eat!" he shouted.

Servers bearing large platters appeared. Haunches of meat, fowl, and fish were carried in; some were uncooked and placed before the Ilkan. Baskets of maize flats were passed around, bowls full of spiced sauces, cooked beans, and fungi. King Alcan pulled a knife from his belt and began eating. He turned to where Inkop was sitting to engage him in conversation.

I filled my bowl with beans and a few small, roasted fish. I sprinkled salt over my food, and dropped a pinch of salt to the ground, in gratitude. Zeri and our aunts were talking in low voices about offerings that had been left at the temple. I wasn't paying attention. I was watching the Ilkan women. They ignored the raw meat that had been placed before them. I glanced at Alcan, but he hadn't noticed, deep in conversation with one of the market leaders. I could tell she had turned her charm on, Alcan leaning toward her as she wove some tale or another. Inkop was half listening to something Delu was saying, and he watched the Ilkan, noticing the untouched meat before them. He stood and spoke.

"Are you displeased with the meal?" His question, though quiet, caught the attention of everyone gathered near.

Alcan looked up. Everyone went silent.

"Eat, eat! I had this meat brought here raw especially for you!" Alcan's smile was tight, a grimace.

The woman I'd locked eyes with stood and bowed her head slightly toward Alcan. Naru gave the woman a small nudge.

"Alcan, though we are descended from Jaguar, we eat our meat cooked, the same as you do. It has always been that way." Her voice was low, just above a growl. She bowed her head again and glanced at the pile of raw meat. Flies were buzzing around it.

"My Fire Warrior was mistaken, then." King Alcan looked at Inkop with a sneer. Inkop's face was tight and blank. "Why would you give them raw meat, Inkop? Is that how we treat our honored guests?"

The silence that followed lasted only a moment. I watched Inkop inhale slowly, look at Alcan. He seemed to be making a decision.

"I thought your true nature would appreciate the gesture," Inkop said, his voice strained.

"We are not animals, Fire Warrior." The woman stared at him. Gone was the graciousness she had exhibited while speaking to Alcan.

Alcan watched their interaction with a smile that caused the hairs on my skin to rise. He muttered something to Inkop, who winced. Alcan's eyes never left Naru's face.

"I can cook it for you." Inkop held out a hand and a small flame rose from his fingertips. Those gathered in the courtyard gasped. In stories, Fire Warriors were never to use their gifts outside of ceremony or battle.

"We would never ask you to abuse your gift," Naru spoke slowly. "There is plenty of other food for us to eat." She smiled and bowed her head. Inkop stood, looking as if he wanted to say something, but returned silently to where he sat. Delu leaned over and whispered something to him while giggling. He smiled at her and nodded his head. I felt my stomach clench.

"It appears as if it has already started." Ixara spoke low, so only those surrounding her could hear her.

"What has started?" Zeri asked.

"The witnessing," Kupi responded.

Safi stood and clapped her hands. Everyone went silent. Alcan turned to face my mother, a strange smile on his face. My memory flashed to the Dream, where I had seen him stab me. I didn't like his smile. I could see I wasn't the only one. Delu looked up from where she was speaking with Inkop, eyes going back and forth between our mother and Alcan. Zeri took my hand. The Ilkan had come to attention, their skin mottling into the hues of Jaguar, their musk pungent in the air.

"Alcan, we are grateful you have returned to the city. Once the Litéx and Airan arrive, we will begin preparations for the ceremony that will confirm you as king, protector of the people of Alcanzeh. We will guide you as you need through the sacred ways of preparing yourself," she said, opening her hands in gratitude.

Alcan stared at her a long moment and glanced back at Inkop, who looked straight ahead, not looking at Alcan. I found it strange.

"No," Alcan said.

My mother's mouth dropped open. She faltered for a moment.

"No, you don't want us to assist you in your preparation?" Safi asked slowly.

"No, I will not participate in the ceremony just yet." Alcan opened his hands as Safi had moments earlier. It was a mockery.

"Alcan, there are traditions, rituals to protect those you will serve." Safi's voice was gentle, as if she were speaking with a small child. Alcan's face hardened.

"No," Alcan said.

I felt the blood drain from my face. The Ilkan moved as a mass, some leaning forward on their arms as if about to pounce.

"Alcan." Lal spoke next, rising, her hands crossed over her chest. "I attended your birth. You were born with the Twin Serpents' mark. You have responsibilities."

Inkop stood then and crossed to stand beside Alcan. Delu looked shocked. I felt bad for her, sitting among the Fire Warriors.

"Alcan," Inkop said loudly, "the Game." I had no idea what Inkop meant, but it served to distract Alcan from whatever he was going to say next. Alcan broke into a smile.

"When my father sent me to live with the Fire Warriors, it was to unite us again after ages of absence. I would like to bring a Fire Warrior tradition back to the city of my birth. A tradition that, if the stories I was told are true, used to be practiced everywhere."

I looked at my aunts. They had both crossed their arms, staring at Alcan.

I leaned into Zeri, and she leaned back so that we were pressed shoulder to shoulder.

"If you want me to participate in the Dreamers' ceremony, then you must help me bring this tradition back to Alcanzeh. One sacrificial Game to unite us," he said.

There was a hard, still silence, as if his words had robbed any of us of the ability to speak. There were old stories about sacrificial games played in Alcanzeh in the ages before ours. Two warriors, fighting to the death, as a sacrifice to the Dream. In the oldest stories we knew about ourselves, sacrificial games temporarily enhanced the gifts of those who participated in the ceremony surrounding them.

"No." Safi said the word firmly. It almost made me laugh, how everyone's heads turned to Alcan to see how he would respond. The scent of musk rose in the air, a sign the Ilkan were agitated. Out of the corner of my eyes, I caught what I thought looked like sparks from where the Fire Warriors sat; but when I looked directly, they disappeared.

"You have the ritual in your memories, no? And protections? It will be one Game, an offering to the Dream. After that, I will enter ceremony," Alcan said. Lal stepped forward.

"We will have witnesses arriving soon. We will sit in conversation with them before we make a decision," she said. Alcan seemed to consider it for a moment. Inkop said something under his breath that made Alcan nod once.

"Of course, this would not just be a Fire Warrior ritual. We would invite the Dreamers to be a part of this," Alcan said.

Zeri and I looked at each other. None of us were warriors;

there was no way we could fight anyone. Then I thought of my aunts and thought Kupi might want to try. My mother tried to soften the tension with a laugh, but it sounded forced.

"We are not warriors, Alcan," she said, gesturing behind her to where we sat.

"I know," he said, glancing at Tavovis. "Alcanzeh is not a city of warriors."

I was almost dizzy at his disrespect. I saw Ovis rise up and cross his arms behind his father. I bit in a smile. Before my gift disappeared, I had always wished to see Ovis in Dreaming.

"We ask you to Dream for us and ask who the warriors will be. It will be to honor the Dream, this sacrifice, given freely. We will force no one to fight who does not wish to," Inkop said, stepping forward. "We were once part of Alcanzeh, and perhaps this is a way to begin opening to us again."

I heard my aunts inhale sharply, looking at each other with raised eyebrows. It had been generations since the Fire Warriors had been stripped of their name and driven from Alcanzeh. To us, it was a story, a warning against abusing gifts. The way Inkop spoke made it sound as if it were a living story for them. It had been one of our Dreamer ancestors who took their name from them and returned it to the Dream so it would live in no memory.

Alcan's mouth pouted into a sneer. I shook my head. I couldn't believe those around him allowed him to behave the way they did, my mother included. My aunts were exchanging looks with the Ilkan. I saw Lal touch her throat. If she was Singing, or humming, it was too low or too high to hear.

"We will sit in conversation when the Litéx and Airan arrive," my mother said, looking only at Inkop.

Tavovis stepped forward and spoke to Inkop. I saw Alcan's eyes narrow.

"We have many travelers arriving in Alcanzeh. The word has gone out that Alcan has returned, and there are those curious to be a part of the story. We know there are Fire Warriors outside the city—will they help us keep the peace as more travelers arrive?" I wondered why Tavovis asked this. Our stories told the Fire Warriors were our enemies and had been for generations. It had only been in the last generation that peace had started to be woven between the Fire Warriors and the lands they touched.

"We can help." The Ilkan who had stared at me earlier stood. She and Inkop regarded each other. I saw Ovis step forward. I realized Tavovis had created a distraction to break the tension.

"We will be grateful for any assistance. Markets will rise up and so will flirtation dances. We must keep the canals clean, make sure the waste trenches are seen to morning and night," Ovis said. His father clasped him on the arm and they exchanged a look of admiration. My breath caught when Ovis smiled. He was beautiful, his teeth shaped differently than any I had seen. He must have felt my eyes on him because he looked past his father right at me. I dropped my eyes and leaned into Zeri, who leaned back. The rest of the meal was subdued, people keeping their conversations low. Alcan left without speaking again, and everyone who was gathered dispersed into the night.

A Game. Fear bloomed in my body. A death as offering to the Dream. I tried to push away the memory of Alcan's blade entering my chest. I hoped the death would not be mine.

CHAPTER FOUR

SAYA

Celay made me sleep outside. It wasn't as terrible a punishment as she thought; there were things my mother did not know about me. She was terrified of flying things at night and burned different blends of herbs in our fires and altar to keep away insects. She always flinched when they came near. My body always flinched when hers did. She thought I was scared of things at night with wings. I wasn't. I took my travel hammock past the tended plants and strung it between two gnarled trees just inside where the jungle growth began. I could still see the flickers from the fire my mother had burning inside our home. A few insects made their way toward me, curious for my blood. I plucked a hair from my head, rolled it between my fingers, and held it to my lips.

"Small spirits, I offer you a piece of me. I ask that you keep insects and other creatures from disturbing my body or sleep." It was a small offering, for a specific reason. It wasn't something I did often. I had learned from a friendly spirit in Dreaming soon after my bleeding came. She had told me there were small spirits everywhere, and they loved to be of service, for small offerings. I could have used any part of my body, spit, hair, tears. But I wouldn't use blood. I was too scared of what a blood offering could bring—hungry spirits flocked to it but often had intentions of their own.

The insects buzzed away from me. I pulled a loosely woven blanket over me, for the comforting weight of it, and stared up into the growth. Night birds called out to each other, and from a distance, I could hear a man Singing a Song of desire. Another voice joined his from further away until they moved toward each other and Sang together. I smiled. It was one of the rituals I loved from the part of the world we were living in. I wondered what my Song of desire would sound like; and if one Sang out in the night that called to me, would I know how to respond?

I watched a few stars pulse through the canopy. They looked like eyes, blinking open and shut as the leaves moved in the small, high winds. The sky in the Waking World had a quality that Dreaming could not match, not for all the colors and shapes and different depths. The sky above the Waking World held a power of its own, something I could not name. I watched until the eyes began to blur and I slipped into sleep.

I did go into Dreaming, but first I had a dream, like those without my gift. It was a strange place to be, in between the Dream and the Waking World; I could not control what I said or did. I followed whatever shape it took. I noticed, not for the first time, spaces where the in-between dream seemed to thin and I could glimpse the Dream sparking through, usually for a moment or two, before disappearing. I was curious and slightly annoyed. I preferred Dreaming to the regular dreams of most people. My dream was mundane. I was tending plants as I did in the Waking World. Then I was gone.

I was Dreaming.

I was in what I knew was a desert, though I had never known one in the Waking World. Even in Dreaming, the air barely carried the memory of water. There was a creek bed, dry and overgrown with skeletal remnants of plants. There was a sensation, a hunger in the land that seemed to pulse, telling me it had once been a sacred place and wanted to be again.

I knelt at the edge of the creek, touching my fingers to one of the dried-out plants. Sharp thorns stabbed upward, begging for a snag of skin. I brushed my fingertips against them, the power dormant in the plants sparked into being. I closed my eyes and cast myself into the memory of what once was: running water, vegetation clinging to the edge of the banks, roots following their thirst, the upward rush of life in bloom, flowers beckoning insects and birds. This was a part of my gift I was learning: imagining into existence, creating where I wanted to be. I felt a push in the air, a presence discovering itself once more. I tasted the water in the air. It was happening.

"Imagine more," a rasping voice spoke.

I kept my eyes closed but inclined my head to acknowledge her presence. She was an older spirit, nearly forgotten in the Waking World—I could tell by how she seemed to smolder. I imagined water rushing forth and smiled when I heard a drip, then the whispers of water rising to tumble rocks from its path as life returned. She sighed. I opened my eyes.

"Are you the spirit of this place?" I asked, my eyes soft on her as she came into focus. She was older. She must have been the spirit Yecacu told me about, the one Ruta needed. As memory rose in the land, the spirit remembered herself as well.

"I am Wotal, and you are not from the lands where once they spoke my name," she said. I was surprised she gave me her name. She must have been still a very long time and wanted her name spoken.

"There is someone in your world who wishes to give birth, little Dreamer?" I flinched when she called me Dreamer. I was not a Dreamer, though I could enter the Dream. I was not from Alcanzeh, half a world away. I was not born to the Temple of Night. I didn't know why the gift had chosen me. My mother had warned me never to ask. I took a deep breath.

"There is a woman, Ruta, who wants to give birth, be a mother. But she has been unable to keep a child in her body. We ask for your blessing." I waited. Wotal stared into the running water, then reached her hand out to me.

"Show me her face," she said. I took her hand, gasping. A river seemed to rise within me, pulsing, vast, flooding me with joy and longing. I closed my eyes and allowed the feeling to flow through me. I wanted to grieve, I wanted to dance, I wanted to press my face to the damp earth of the creek bed and taste the memories of all the water that had ever flowed by. She released my hand and too quickly, I was myself again.

"Oh, little Dreamer." Wotal's eyes were full of pity. She touched my face, and again, briefly, I was overcome with emotions not my own.

"I'm not a Dreamer. My name is Saya. Can you not help her?" A small panic rose in me.

"I can, I will. I know what it is like to be dry and without life. She will give birth by Night Bird, though no one can guarantee what happens after." Wotal's smile was sad. "It is the way of birthing. All who birth know it. I ask that one of the child's names be mine and that they always keep an altar to me. I know that soon enough I will cease to exist in this form, but I would like to stay a little longer, offer help where I can for the turmoil that is coming."

I nodded, confused and relieved. Her eyes went to my necklace.

"You always wear that, don't you?"

My hand went to the familiar stones.

"A protection my mother had placed on me at birth," I said. She was not the first spirit to comment on my protection.

"That is the truth, even if it isn't shaped the way you believe it to be." Wotal smiled. "A gift for you, if you will accept it."

I hesitated. My mother warned me to be careful when offered gifts from spirits. Wotal sighed.

"The gift is knowledge, sweet one, nothing more. I offer it unburdened in gratitude. No one has reached me here for a very long time." Her eyes were bright with love. I found myself pulled toward them.

"Only knowledge," I said, and opened my hands in acceptance.

"That protection no longer serves you."

I flinched and pressed my hand to the stones, afraid they would begin to warm.

"I've always worn it. It keeps me safe."

"Saya, protections we carry can harm us if we've outgrown them. That is true for those of us in the Dream and those in the Waking World." She reached as if to touch my necklace. I pulled away, jarred.

Suddenly, a strange jolt trembled the entire Dream. A smile played on Wotal's lips. The air beside us began splitting, making a shrieking noise. There was darkness behind the tear, a rushing sound as it widened into a hole. The elder with the cut foot tumbled through. She looked terrified. She stared at me for a moment.

"The root was meant to be ground into a poultice and placed on your foot, daughter," Wotal said gently to the woman.

"Is this the Dream?" the elder gasped, staring at her body as it began shifting to how she saw herself in her mind.

"It is." Wotal smiled at me. I shuddered. It was a smile of knowing. I had no idea what she was doing. It terrified me.

"Saya?" The elder stared at me; I stared back. She was younger than me now, dressed in a trader's tunic, hair braided down to her hips. She had the same eyes and mouth. "Is it the root your mother gave me? Is that what's letting us be here? Where is Celay?" She looked around. Her shock had softened into awe.

"Celay cannot enter the Dream or speak to my kind," Wotal said. The elder looked puzzled, then her eyes widened as if seeing me for the first time. The Dream trembled again. She opened her mouth to speak but disappeared, the Dream closing behind her. A jagged white thread remained where the Dream had closed.

"A wound in the Dream, but some wounds are worth it." Wotal watched it float away, sighing.

"Why was she here?" I asked. My voice was high. I had never seen anyone from the Waking World in the Dream. It felt wrong. Something in the landscape had dimmed after her departure.

"Now someone else knows your secret, Saya. There is no coming back from knowing. Thank you for speaking my name. Visit me again if you wish. Consider what I've shared. That protection no longer serves you." She vanished.

The landscape began to blur as I released my need to be there. I was stunned at what Wotal had done. How had the elder been able to enter the Dream? And now she knew I could enter the Dream. Celay would make us leave immediately. I felt that truth with everything in me. I held my necklace tight against my chest, knowing each stone by heart and memory. It was a part of me.

The violet twilight spilled forward, the vibrant hum of the Dream resonating against my skin. I felt another push of presence and focused my eyes. The wound left in the Dream floated past me. Smaller wounds of the same substance had joined it. There was a darkness surrounding the wound that made me feel ill. I closed my eyes and willed myself back to my body.

((●))

I woke up and immediately jumped from my hammock. It was just before dawn. Celay was still asleep. I made my way toward the elder's home as quietly as I could. Dogs barked lazily at me as I went. A few people were already awake, and they nodded at me as I moved past. I kept my head down. I saw there was a fire burning outside the elder's home; someone was tending it. As I approached, I felt a wave of cold surprise. Ruta was kneeling at the fire, using a pair of curved wooden tongs to lift a piece of boiled root from a clay pot bubbling over the flame. She looked up at me and raised her eyebrows. She nodded her head toward the entrance of the elder's house and followed me in.

The elder stared up at me with wide eyes from her mattress on the floor. I stopped as Ruta pushed past me and knelt, placing the root in a carved-out stone. She pounded it with another stone. The root broke apart easily. Ruta added a little water and a few other herbs, then scooped the poultice from the stone and began applying it to the elder's foot. The elder sighed in relief, her eyes closing as she leaned back. Her relief was immediate. I stood in place. She'd known what to do with the root. She had been in Dreaming with me. I began to feel dizzy.

"Sit." Ruta pointed at the woven floor mat beside her. I sat. My hands were shaking. I felt Ruta staring at me. Just behind her, the elder chuckled to herself, eyes still closed.

"Is she well?" I asked. I sat on my hands to still them. Ruta noticed.

"I heard her cry out in the night while I was out walking. I came to her and she woke up with a very strange story," Ruta said carefully, watching me. I did my best not to react, but my body betrayed me. My mouth filled with spit and I had to swallow several times, breathing through my nose.

"I have to go. Celay can't find me here," I said, jumping up. I was grateful I had spent the night outside; there was no way I would have been able to leave our home without Celay noticing.

"Saya, was her story true?" Ruta asked. I panicked. I looked back and forth a few times. Her hand was on her lower belly.

"Celay can't know you know," I said quickly. "I'll help you. There is a spirit I spoke with, and I can tell you more later. I need to return home. Ruta, please, this secret keeps me safe." I felt my face grow hot as soon as I said it.

Ruta stared at me for a long moment. I couldn't wait. I started to leave. Celay would blame me and make me suffer. I had lived through it before and I could do it again. Ruta spoke.

"I won't tell. I would never want to be the reason you were unsafe. Meet me later, at the basin. During the resting period," she said. The basin was far enough away that whatever we spoke of would be private.

I nodded and rushed out. I made it back to the hammock in time to hear Celay's morning groans; her hips always ached in the morning. I gathered up my hammock and blanket. As I walked into the house, I realized the elder had made me no promise.

((●))

"Poultice," I said as soon as I entered our home. Celay was disarrayed on the floor, her scrawny legs bent in front of her. She had her tunic up and was rubbing a salve into her hips. She hissed, and flung the clay jar aimlessly. It hit another clay jar and cracked, the thick salve inside the only thing holding it together. I felt sympathy for the cracked jar. I knew what it felt like. I breathed in and out slowly, trying to calm myself. I didn't know what was holding me together, if it was fear or hope or a strange combination of the two. Celay pushed herself up.

"You stay here. Let me take care of this." I felt my heart drop at Celay's words as she grabbed a basket and hurried out. I knew arguing with her would serve no purpose but to anger her. I sent up a rare prayer, to any spirit listening and willing, that the elder not tell Celay about entering the Dream.

I sat in front of the altar after she left and lit a few dried Ayan blossoms, letting their smolder and smoke envelop me. I poured a fresh cup of water for the altar and held my hands over the flame. I felt depleted, scared. I didn't want to leave. I wanted to befriend Ruta. I wanted to tend the plants I had started to know. I was tired of moving, of using my gift to trick people into providing for us. Something was shifting. The Dream was starting to respond in a different way. I closed my eyes and tried to fit the pieces together, but they slipped away. My stomach made a noise. I rose to make myself a meal.

Celay returned and seemed relieved, though there was still anger in her eyes.

"Is she well?" I remembered asking Ruta the same thing. It felt like an entire cycle of days had passed since that moment. I watched Celay carefully.

"She said she had a dream she had to make a poultice." Celay knelt in front of the altar and put her hands over it. It was rare for her. Keeping an altar seemed mostly symbolic to her, and I rarely saw her contemplate in front of it. "Strange, but in the end, the cut on her foot will not kill her." She closed her eyes and rocked back. She fisted her hands and began kneading her hips.

"Salve?" I asked. I had carefully removed the broken pieces of pottery from the salve as my breakfast cooked. I had rewarmed the salve, straining it through a woven cloth while pouring into another vessel. Celay looked at the proffered jar. She knew I was trying to keep her happy. I hoped her pain was sharp enough to distract her from her anger at the mistake. She held out her hand and took the jar. I sighed in relief. She stretched out again on her pallet and rubbed the salve into her hips, groaning the entire time.

"My hips have never been the same since I birthed you." It was a familiar complaint of hers. My birth had been difficult, she had told me over and over again for my entire life. Another way I'd damaged her and owed her my devotion. As relief began to ease the lines around her mouth, I saw an opportunity. She would be in a temporary state of calm while her pain was subsiding.

"I'm sorry about the root," I said, head bowed.

"Look me in the eyes, Saya," Celay said. I did. Her eyes were hard, scared. She gestured toward her hips. "We can't move from place to place anymore the way we used to. My hips." She grimaced. "Mistakes can't be made. Even protected, your gift is dangerous."

Her eyes dropped to the necklace I had worn since birth. Seven stones strung on a woven cord. I knew it was real. The few times in my life it had woken up, I had been terrified. When I was in danger, the stones of the necklace would warm to an almost unbearable heat against my skin. I fingered the stones where they hung below the edge of my tunic. One of the only times Celay touched me was when she was checking the necklace cord, twice a moon, for fraying, confirming that it wasn't in danger of coming off in any other way. She never told me anything about the necklace except that she had placed it on me at my birth, and that I should never remove it. If there was a fray, Celay worked on it while I wore it, careful and diligent in a way she rarely was otherwise.

"I know," I said. I wanted to keep her calm. If I was just contrite enough, it would be easier for me to leave to meet Ruta later in the day. If she stayed in a foul mood, I was ready. I had already made a pain-relieving infusion for Celay and added a strong pinch of a pain-relieving fungus with a mild taste that I knew made her sleepy. I hoped she wouldn't recognize it. It would ease her pain immensely as well, and as she always told those she counseled, rest was vital to healing.

《《●》》

Celay found the infusion later that morning and drank it without me telling her to. I'd been tending the plants, losing myself in clearing the back of dead growth, shifting crowded places, making space where other plants had sprung up. The sun was hidden intermittently by shifting clouds high in the sky. Long shadows moved across my body, and I was contemplative. I didn't know what I was going to tell Ruta. She already knew the elder's story to be true. I could ask for her silence and offer to help her without any payment. Celay could not know.

I saw her asleep on her side of the floor. Her face was peaceful in sleep, her breathing even. I knew she would sleep deeply and wake up with almost no pain. The infusion also had a small pinch of leaves that brought on a mild euphoria; I hoped their effects would last longer than her sleep. I grabbed two large waterskins from where they hung. If she woke and saw them gone, she would believe I'd gone to get water. I would return with water, lie and tell her a spirit in Dreaming had told me to bring water from a particular source. She would believe me. She was the one who taught me to tell small lies and distortions. She never suspected that I used them against her.

I covered my hair; walking deep into the jungle would be hot, and the path to the basin was overgrown. I was approaching the basin when I heard multiple voices. I was surprised. I thought Ruta was meeting me on her own.

"Saya," Ruta came out of the growth. She looked mildly annoyed. "There is a family there. We should find somewhere else." She looked tired and hot. I made a choice. I wanted to know Ruta, and I wanted her to know me. I looked around, dropped my waterskins, and spit on my fingers. I wiped the saliva against the roots of a low, wide-leafed plant. I knelt and whispered a small ask. And waited. Ruta had a strange look on her face.

"May I ask what you're doing?" she said. I thought there was a laugh in her voice.

"You'll see. I hope." I looked around for a sign from a spirit or a spirit to make itself known. Ruta looked around as well.

"Saya, you are so strange. I'm fascinated by you," Ruta said. I stared up at her, shocked. I didn't know how to respond. I was strange, no doubt, but that was a story cultivated and created by Celay to keep people from getting too close to us. I opened my mouth to speak.

A hummingbird swooped down from the canopy then, whistling the air with her sharp body. The bird hovered in front of me, then darted to my right, then back in front of me, as if she wanted me to follow. I followed. I had seen enough hummingbirds in Dreaming to know they were able to travel between worlds. The hummingbird paused midair as I looked at Ruta. She was frozen, hands at her wide-open mouth. I motioned with my head for her to follow. She did, face in awe. There was no path, and soon, I was sweating, my breath coming hard as we followed the little messenger to where she was leading us. I could have sworn her chirps were encouraging. Every time I turned back to Ruta, she was shaking her head, smiling with closed lips. The hummingbird led us to a wide expanse of hanging vines, then darted through. I pushed my hands into the vines and felt cooler air rising. In silence, Ruta and I untangled the vines as best we could, then pushed through and gasped together.

It was a small temple. The landscape around where we lived and elsewhere was filled with small temples and places of offerings from those who had lived here before. This one was new to me, and somehow unknown. There had been no path leading to it. We pushed through the vines and saw stone stairs leading down. There was light at the bottom of the stairs. I walked down carefully, Ruta following. At the bottom, we gasped again.

It was a sunken water hole, the walls reaching up toward the open sky above it. The stone walls were practically covered in hanging vines. I turned a small circle and smiled. The temple was carved into a natural rock formation. Dirt and roots clung to the walls, but I thought I could see carvings beneath. The hummingbird chirped at me again; she was hovering over the water. Ruta had her hands over her mouth, trying to take it all in.

"What is this place, little friend?" I asked the hummingbird. She darted back into the temple and hovered in front of one of the dirt-caked walls, then flew away.

"Saya," Ruta breathed out my name. "Who are you?"

CHAPTER FIVE

INDIR

"What a strange evening," Zeri said, her arm entwined through mine as we slowly made our way back to our temple. We paused at the stone edge of the high part of the city. The city below the temples was still busy, lit with torches. We could see children playing in the night market, their parents gathered in small groups, laughing and trading. Someone was playing reeds. Voices rose in Song, and I felt familiar stabs of jealousy. I wanted to be a part of the city but had always been afraid to venture into it. I had wanted to be out there as a child, playing in the streets, laughing and fighting with the others. I had never been brave enough to try. Instead, my childhood had been full of lessons on the rituals and ceremonies sacred to Dreamers.

I smiled when I saw there were flirtation dances about to begin. Circles of residents, traders, and visitors were gathering according to desire. There were circles of elders, circles of youth, circles of men, of women, of the graced who were neither and all. The dance would become a spiral; then it would shift into a serpent shape, interweaving with the serpents from the other circles, then circles again. Those whose bodies matched in the ancient rhythm of attraction would break away, continue the dance outside their circle. Sometimes they would continue to dance until they danced away into the night; sometimes they would rejoin the dancers. I imagined I'd be one of those who would dance away from the circles alone, fully enraptured by myself, if only I knew how.

"I saw Ovis looking at you," Zeri whispered. I shook my head quickly.

"No, I don't know him very well," I said.

"We're Dreamers, Indi, everyone in Alcanzeh knows us. And Ovis looked like he knew you." She bumped her shoulder against mine. I shook my head again and concentrated on the dancers. I knew my mother and aunts sometimes joined the flirtation dances, and I suspected Delu had as well. I had never felt brave enough.

"Indi, a question." I heard the tease in my sister's voice and smiled. I looked at her, ready to refuse to answer whatever she asked. It was a game between us. Sometimes it was easy, and other times, my face betrayed my answer.

"What would you do," Zeri said, then paused dramatically, "if you were in a flirtation dance and Ovis was dancing as well? Would you dance toward him or away?"

I imagined Ovis dancing, moving in time to whatever drum was calling him. I imagined his smile as he moved toward me. I tried to bite in my lips to keep from smiling. Zeri cackled. I couldn't stop my smile.

"I might dance toward him, if I were someone who danced," I said. Zeri's smile went soft. She was, in so many ways, wiser. If I'd been born with a sadness or fear in me, Zeri had been born with wisdom. I waited for whatever she was sure to say.

"Some dance and some don't, sister. My question wasn't about the dance." We started walking back to our temple. I chose not to respond.

"I wonder if the Ilkan dance," I said, thinking back to the warriors, how at ease they were in their strength. I had known Naru most of my life, but I realized she had adapted her behavior and way of being while in Alcanzeh. The Ilkan moved in their power unlike anyone I had ever seen.

"That would be a dangerous dance, and I would be joyfully in it," Zeri said.

((●))

I tried, again, to enter the Dream that night. After my sisters drifted to sleep, I anointed myself with the sacred oil we used for ceremonial Dreaming. I knelt in front of the Twin Serpents altar until my knees ached. I stayed in my breathing. I begged the Twin Serpents, wherever they were, to bring my gift back to me. I had to Dream. I didn't know who I was without it. I stared at the Twin Serpents on the altar, bodies wound around each other's as each helped the other shed its skin. It was how our world had been born. The Night Bird had plucked the serpents from where they slept in the Dream and dropped them into the emptiness that had been the Waking World, the other half of the Dream. The Twin Serpents had twisted around each other trying to return to the Dream. In their twisting, they'd begun to shed their skins.

The first shedding of skin had created the land, the mountains, valleys, rocks, earth.

"Let me back in," I whispered. "Please. I will give you anything."

But I didn't Dream.

《 ⟨ ● ⟩ 》

We were up before dawn. We weren't the only ones. Our morning meal was crowded. Naru and the Ilkan I'd noticed the night before joined us, as well as Lal. I sat beside my aunts since they were seated closest to the Ilkan and I was curious about them.

"I am Raru. I greet you in the name of all that is sacred," the Ilkan said as I sat down.

"I am Indir. I greet you in joy," I said honestly. She went back to her meal, but I kept glancing at her, fascinated by the way her skin seemed alive with movement, the mark of the Great Jaguar seeming to ripple just out of sight.

"How soon for the Airan and Litéx?" Safi asked Delu. I hadn't realized my mother had asked my sister to Dream for her. I was grateful she hadn't asked me.

"Soon. The seas are clear and free of storm, so the Litéx will arrive within a few days. The Airan may arrive sooner—I could not see them clearly, but it appeared they were traveling faster than I thought possible," Delu said, yawning. She preferred sleeping late after a night of Dreaming, but my mother had sent temple workers to wake us all early. My mother looked down, a strange look on her face.

"Do you know who is coming?" Ixara asked, sensing, as we all did, it was a question my mother wanted to ask but wouldn't.

Delu thought for a moment.

"I saw Ali clearly, and maybe someone who is his mate," Delu said. "For the Litéx, I couldn't see them clearly but know they bring four boats."

My mother seemed to tense at Delu's answer. My aunts were looking at her with tenderness. I glanced at Zeri, but she only shrugged. My mother and aunts had a strange way with each other. Raru sniffed the air.

"Someone comes," she said.

Tavovis entered. He looked tired; there were dark circles beneath his eyes. He greeted us, then sat beside Safi. She handed him an empty bowl. He filled it, then sat back, staring at it.

"I spoke with the Avex," he said in a weary voice.

"Thank you," Safi said gently, touching him on the arm. "I know it was a lot to ask."

"Safi?" Kupi and Ixara had spoken in unison, not uncommon for them.

My mother looked at them, her eyes defiant.

"We have to prepare for many possibilities," she said. "I asked Tavovis to speak with the Avex to see if any of them would be willing to fight in a sacrificial Game."

Raru growled.

"I would fight in a sacrificial game," she said. Naru rolled her eyes.

"So would many of the Avex," Tavovis sighed. "I was surprised at how many were excited about the idea."

"The forbidden is always exciting to some," Ixara said. "If they are protected."

"And even if they are not," Kupi added, tonguing her broken tooth. She had never told anyone how the tooth had broken, but she always smiled when anyone asked and told them it was a story sacred to her.

"It would have to be fought without gifts," Tavovis said. "The Avex are powerful warriors, and well trained, but they cannot fight someone who is using their gift of fire. It would be unfair."

Everyone nodded.

"Why is this a possibility? I don't understand. A sacrificial game? Have we really come to this for the sake of peace?" Lal asked softly, her eyes filled with tears. She was always close to her emotions and let them flow through her, something I admired and was terrified of. I held everything in, just like my mother, aunts, and sisters.

Everyone looked to Safi. There were no named leaders among us, but my mother was the one everyone turned to for guidance. She took in a deep breath.

"I have something to share. Before she returned to the Dream, Bentixa saw chaos in Alcanzeh. She asked me not to tell anyone until I had to."

Kupi and Ixara hissed together.

"Why are we learning this now?" Ixara asked. Lal started a hum in her throat, and the tension eased a bit. Safi glared at her sisters.

"Let me finish speaking and you'll know." My mother's voice was a snarl. I bit in a smile. My sisters and I acted the same way with each other.

"Bentixa saw chaos as a sign calling the Twin Serpents. She said there will be great loss, and a Lost Dreamer." Her voice went soft at the end.

"The Twin Serpents? Returning? To shed another skin and bring us what? To swallow what?" Lal asked. Bentixa had been my grandmother, and she had returned to the Dream when I was very young. She used to rock me to sleep, telling me stories of our lineage.

My heart was pounding. There were only two Lost Dreamers in our stories. One who went too deep into Dreaming and never returned to her body. Another who had disappeared an age ago when the Fire Warriors lost their name and were sent into exile. I almost spoke my secret then but stopped myself. Those Dreamers had kept their gifts, their losses different than mine. And if I was to die at Alcan's hand, there was nothing to be done.

"The Twin Serpents?" Delu asked. "Here or in the Dream?" The Twin Serpents had long retreated to sleep. In our stories, they only returned to the Waking World for two reasons: to shed another skin or to swallow something that no longer served the Waking World. There was a scent sharp in the air.

Naru and Raru were perfectly still, their eyes focused sharp on Safi. Their markings were out. There were so few of us with gifts left in the Waking World, and the rarest were the Ilkan. Lal hummed deeper. Kupi reached out a hand and placed it on Naru's knee.

"Tell us more, Safi," Kupi said, her eyes wide.

My mother paced back and forth, which made me nervous. Delu pulled her knees up to her chin and wrapped her arms around them. She felt it too. Safi took another deep breath. Tavovis nodded at her.

"Bentixa asked me not to speak this Dream until I had to, and we keep our promises."

She glanced at me, nodding once. I nodded back. She continued, "Bentixa saw Alcanzeh in flames. Now that the Fire Warriors are here, I don't know if that was a symbol, or if our city will truly burn. She told me the Twin Serpents will return. She told me to speak to the Airan about the skies and what is coming. And she said there will be a Lost Dreamer who will save our gifts. This cycle is ending." She finished. There was silence. My stomach clenched, and I felt as if I was going to vomit. I didn't notice how hard I was squeezing Zeri's hand until she shook it. I released.

"How soon?" Zeri asked. Our mother's face softened for a moment.

"We cannot know. It could be this season, or it could be in years," Safi said.

"Why the Game, then?" Zeri asked.

"Each age ends in chaos," Tavovis said, leaning forward from where he sat. "Our stories tell us there is nothing to do but move toward it when it comes. Alcan seems to be a part of that chaos, and we are part of order. There is somewhere we must meet. Better in a Game than played out in the streets of Alcanzeh or somewhere else." He puffed up a little. I wondered if he, like his warriors, craved a Game. Stories about it would be told for generations.

"Chaos and order are two of the faces the Twin Serpents can wear," Lal said. "If the end of this cycle is coming, there is nothing we can do but move with it and see how the story is told through us."

There was a long silence. Lal's voice had carried the ache of prophecy in it. I didn't need my gift to feel it; everyone did.

Zeri spoke again, her voice high with emotion.

"What does Alcan want?" she asked.

"Power," Safi said simply, "and he believes power means having control over others. We know it comes from taking care of each other, and this Waking World. He is disrupting the balance the Twin Serpents asked us to help keep."

"He was born with the mark, so he has to be a part of this story, chaos or symmetry." Lal sighed.

I thought back to my Dream for King Anz and felt my face grow hot, my mouth watering as if I was going to be sick. I drank from a cup of water to try and hide whatever emotion I was showing. Out of the side of my vision, I saw Naru and Raru's nostrils flare. My fear had a scent. I pretended not to notice.

Little more was said. My mother left to meet with the leaders of markets to discuss the newly arriving crowds. Delu and her temple worker friend Chiki went to the offering rooms to sort through whatever had been brought by those who lived in lower Alcanzeh. Zeri left with Tavovis, who had beckoned to her at the meal's end.

I contemplated whether to paint or help tend the younger children of daytime temple workers in their play area. It was a risk, as the young children were either joyous or irritable early in the morning.

"Indir." Ixara was still seated as well. "We're going outside the city to spend part of the day with the Ilkan where they set up. Will you join us?"

Naru and Raru flanked Kupi as they approached us. I nodded. I was curious about the Ilkan and wanted to speak more with Raru.

As we headed down the steps, I watched my mother walk toward the stairs that led to the main market. People noticed her and nodded in greeting. She always nodded back. I hadn't yet mastered the art of walking and being seen. It still made me uncomfortable. I was dressed in a plain tunic and had covered my hair, but people still noticed us. It was impossible not to. Naru's posture had changed since being among her people. She and Raru walked with what could only be called ferocity. They moved with purpose. My aunts were fast walkers and I hurried to catch up, feeling slow and graceless compared to those around me.

《 ❲ ● ❳ 》

Alcanzeh was always beautiful, but it seemed especially vibrant that morning. The temples were bright in the morning light. In the distance, the sea shone. Smoke from cooking fires left a gray haze over the city that the afternoon winds would blow to sea. I heard Singing and looked toward the Water Temple. The healers were on the stairs, facing the rising sun, Singing the morning Song for those who had been born since the last dawn. At dusk, they would stand on the same steps and Sing the evening Song for those who had returned to the Dream since the last sunset. I didn't look toward the Fire Temple; I didn't want to see it full of people.

The sacred city was humming in the morning quiet. Birds sang and called to each other. We passed lines of trench workers who carried baskets of cooking ash that were set outside every living space each night. The ash was collected and poured into the waste trenches to keep the odor from rising. They emptied into a stream that ended a half day's walk down the coast from Alcanzeh, a place no one lived or even visited, the terrain rough, sand cliffs that gave way underfoot unexpectedly. People were given long stretches of trench duty as punishment, though everyone at some point in their lives did it. There was a council of grandmothers in the city that people took their grievances to. They were the ones who decided what punishments were suitable for which crimes. Waste trench duty was the least favorable of all the jobs people could take in the city, but those who did it were well fed and given hot baths at the ends of their days, and healers worked on their bodies once a week. Still, the fine white ash clung to the skin and hair of the trench workers even after their work for the day was done.

We headed to the place where the jungle met the city. Few lived out that way; those who did were artisans who required solitude for their work. We passed a few living spaces where weavings hung outside, and vats of dye were already bubbling, smoke rising in colors.

Entering the growth of jungle, I immediately felt the air cool. I had rarely ventured in though we lived at its edge, and I was surprised to remember how dense it was. Children in Alcanzeh were warned to stay away from the jungle or to stay near the paths. There were venomous serpents, spiders, and other ways to die. Once lost, it was difficult to find one's way out without a tracker. Most experienced trackers had once been children who couldn't resist the allure of the jungle and had grown up knowing her secrets.

We arrived at the Ilkan camp. There was a small clearing. An almost smokeless fire burned. The Ilkan from the night before introduced themselves but seemed shy. I sat down on a ground covering, my aunts sitting to one side of me, Raru on the other.

"You knew Nahi?" Raru asked me, her black eyes focused on mine. There was an intensity to her gaze that both unnerved me and drew me in.

"I did," I said, remembering Naru's former acolyte. She had been present at King Anz's death. She had left Alcanzeh soon after. "She was there when King Anz returned to the Dream."

Raru nodded. "She grieved him. I could feel it on her when she returned to us to tell us Alcan would be returning. Naru wanted some of us to come as witnesses." My aunts and Naru were deep in conversation, speaking in low voices. I tried to listen, but it was difficult to not focus on Raru.

"Why didn't she return to Alcanzeh?" I asked. Nahi had been a little older than me and had loved to watch me paint in the temple, sitting quietly behind me, handing me bowls of different-ent colored clay when I asked. It had been more a quiet companionship than a friendship, but I missed her.

"Nahi had a feeling Alcanzeh would no longer be safe. You know this," Raru said. I heard a hiss from my other side. I turned to see Naru, color out, glaring at Raru.

"We trust her, don't we? She's a part of this as much as any of us, more than any of us if the twin Dreamers are correct." Raru had barely finished speaking before Naru leaped over the fire, the jaguar marks on her skin darkening. She pinned the younger woman to the ground, growling something in her ear. Raru flipped over beneath her and sunk her head in surrender. Naru stood up, dusting off her hands, skin returning to normal, though her eyes were still bright, predatory.

I felt faint. I had never seen Naru in the grip of anger before. It shook me. Raru's words pounded my heart. What was I a part of? What had my aunts Dreamed?

"You saw me in Dreaming? What did you see?" I asked Kupi. My aunt held my gaze.

"We see much in the ever-changing Dream," she said slowly. "We all have our roles. We cannot, sweet love, tell you what we see right now." She pressed both her fists to her chest. "Know that the Dream plants seeds, and we are each one of her seeds, and nothing that happens is truly as it seems."

Ixara cleared her throat, nodding. She looked at me.

"Does my mother know you saw me in Dreaming?" I asked. Kupi and Ixara exchanged a long look.

"Your mother." Kupi stopped and thought again. "Our sister

Safi is bound by her devotion to Alcanzeh, to a certain idea of peace, to the sacred city and temple. She's good at what she does. Ixara and I are devoted to the Dream, sweet one, to a longer story than the one we are living in. You've seen our differences, and you know we each have Dreams we don't share. You have yours, no?"

I nodded, a bloom of fear sparking in my center and moving outward to the rest of my body. I carried two secrets within me: my Dream for Alcan, and the loss of my gift, which was even more unspeakable.

"There will be loss, Indir," Ixara said softly. "We all must prepare ourselves."

"A Lost Dreamer?" I asked. A spark of faint hope battled the fear I had been living with. Maybe the absence of my gift marked me as the Lost Dreamer.

"The last Lost Dreamer disappeared when the Fire Warriors had their name taken, no?" Raru asked. She was sitting down again, her arms curled around her knees.

"There is an old, seldom-told story about the last Lost Dreamer," Ixara said, her voice tight with tension. "One that is rarely spoken because it is too terrifying to consider. It is one of the reasons we are more wary of the Fire Warriors than Safi."

I felt myself go cold at her words. My aunts were collectors of stories. Traders, travelers, and wanderers all came to visit them, hoping they could bring my aunts a story they had not heard.

"Will you share it with me?" I asked, holding my breath. They looked at each other.

"You know why the Fire Warriors were stripped of their name and exiled?" Kupi asked. I nodded. Raru spoke up.

"They say it is because they were too strong and that they threatened the Dreamers," Raru said. "I hid in a tree and listened to a few of them who have set up deep in the jungle, and they did not see me."

"They abused their gift. That is part of it. They were secretly practicing blood offerings, fighting each other until there was blood, then offering that blood to spirits for strength. They did it outside of ceremony; it was dangerous, stupid. They wanted to rule Alcanzeh and beyond, to disrupt the balance," Kupi said. "There was a battle where those in Alcanzeh rose up with their gifts to drive them out. The Dreamer who was Lost was the one who went into the Dream and took their name from them. It was a dangerous ceremony. She returned changed. Then she disappeared."

I shivered. There was something they were trying to say without saying it. Blood sacrifice, a Dreamer who had disappeared. I put my hands over my mouth, then wrapped them around my body.

"There is a story that says when the Fire Warriors left the city, weakened, they took her with them to try and retrieve their name by using her for blood sacrifice," Ixara said.

I reeled back as if the words had hit me in the face. I remembered the knife in my chest. I hadn't seen any blood in the Dream but knew my body would bleed in the Waking World.

"And we let them back into Alcanzeh?" I gasped. My aunts nodded, looking dispirited.

"They cannot hurt us that way anymore," Kupi said. "Ixara and I have gone deep into the Dream and have made offerings for protections. You and your sisters are safe."

"What about you?" I asked, my relief tentative. "What about my mother?"

"Safi has her own protections, and we have ours," Ixara said. I didn't want to believe any of it.

"How am I a part of this?" I asked.

"We can't tell you any more," Kupi said, a plea in her voice. Then the tone switched as she spoke in the voice of prophecy. "Trust the Dream, Indir. Trust that what is to be yours will be yours. The story we are a part of is much longer than any of us can imagine."

"How can I trust the Dream if chaos is coming? If there will be loss? What else will be taken?" I tried to hold in my fear, but it spilled out and I began shaking. I put my head on my knees and covered my ears. I was overwhelmed, and wanted to disappear. I didn't want to be a part of a longer story; I wanted a simple story. I wanted to live and Dream, stay in the temple with those I felt safe with. I didn't want chaos. A gentle hand pulled at one of my wrists.

"Indir, see me." I opened my eyes and uncovered my ears. Naru was squatting in front of me. "See the Ilkan. Once, in the before, there were many more of us. Each cycle, there are fewer. We concentrate on surviving, on being true to our gifts and what we can offer, while we can. Do you imagine this is the story we want to be living? We prefer solitude, to stay among ourselves, but we're here because we know our survival depends on the Dreamers, on the Litéx, the Airan, the Fire Warriors. Our gifts are interconnected. And there is an imbalance; we have to try and correct it, or there is a chance none of our gifts will survive. You must practice being strong."

I saw that her pupils were dilated; her teeth had grown sharper, her nails darker. My aunts held hands behind her.

"How do you know this?" I whispered.

"We may not enter the Dream, but the Ilkan have ways of knowing this world. We know how to hear the stories of the animals, the plants, the way the roots below us communicate across distances most cannot begin to imagine. There is an imbalance. Even now, in lands we do not know, hunger is growing." Naru dipped her head. "The land is changing, and so are we."

I closed my eyes and surrendered to the rushing sound of my blood in my veins, heart pounding fast as a dance of release. I had changed. I was still changing.

"What do we do?" I asked.

"What we've always done," Raru said. "We do our best to survive. Practice being strong, Indir. We will need you."

((●))

There was another meal shared that night, but I begged off, claiming my head hurt from so much time outdoors. It wasn't a lie; everything seemed to hurt, my skin, my hearing, the sound of my own voice. I didn't want to be where anyone could find me.

I climbed to the very top of the Temple of Night, to sit beneath the carved altar to the Twin Serpents. I didn't like that there were suddenly so many secrets between Dreamers, a sign of the coming chaos. I watched the city below brighten with firelight and torch as night grew darker. There were many people in the streets. The canals and waterways shimmered dark and serpentine where they intersected the city markets and living spaces.

I wondered at what Raru had spoken and been silenced for. What was I a part of? I shivered, the idea that I was the Lost Dreamer itching at the edges of every thought. Loss, my aunts had said. I turned so I was kneeling before the Twin Serpents, their bodies twisted, skin shedding below them as their mouths opened to the sky. I lay my forehead against the base of the carving.

"Please," I begged, barely a whisper, "help me become strong but not as the Lost Dreamer. I want to live. Let me live."

A strong wind came, sharp and hot as it rushed up the side of the temple and blew over me. My hair lifted from my body, my tunic pressed tight against me. Then it was gone. I ran my fingers through my hair, loosening strands that were ready to shed. I rolled the few hairs into a small ball, then placed the bundle of hair at the base of the carving, hoping it was enough offering, hoping they were listening.

CHAPTER SIX

SAYA

"Saya, who are you? What gifts do you carry?" Ruta asked. Her eyes were wide, shining more amber than brown in the slanted light.

It was a question rarely asked. Gifts were private, and rare. They had been dwindling for generations across the lands, a slow leak of power. Those with gifts were encouraged to use them to help others, but having a strong gift could also be dangerous. My gift was strong. There were those who tried to collect and enslave the gifted strong. It was one of the reasons Celay kept us wandering my entire life.

"I can enter the Dream, and speak to small spirits, with offerings. I made an offering back near the basin, and a spirit sent the hummingbird," I said. It was the truth. There wasn't any reason to mention that the spirit may have been the humming-bird, embodied. Something in me knew, somehow, I could trust Ruta. I was fascinated by her as well. I wanted to know more about her. She seemed at peace, something I craved but didn't know if I could have.

"Why are you afraid of your mother?" she asked. I wasn't expecting the question. I felt a drop in my chest, a cold space pulsing along to my heartbeat. There were so many reasons that I didn't know where to begin. Or even if I wanted to. I never spoke openly to anyone. I felt shame for wanting to tell the truth. I didn't want Ruta to know how much control Celay had over me, over my gifts. That keeping my gift a secret was a protection.

"Let me ask you something easier, Saya. I'm sorry if my last question was too much," Ruta said. I exhaled. Any other question would be easier to answer. "Does your mother carry the same gifts as you?"

I shook my head. It felt like a betrayal for some reason.

"She knows how to read a body and cleanse, but I think it is a knowing born of a lifetime of learning." Celay learned different cleansings wherever we wandered or stayed. And she knew how to read a body for want or fear.

"Knowing is a gift, but not like the one you carry. Saya, why do you let Celay claim your gift? What's the story that led to the elder eating the root? Did she really go into the Dream?" Ruta's eyes were wide. I realized what she was asking: if there was a way for those without the gift to enter the Dream. It terrified me. A part of me felt protective of the Dream; I didn't want others appearing in and out, not knowing what kind of information they would return with to the Waking World, and how it would be used. And there were only a few of the roots left, and they seemed to me to be slow growing.

"My mother protects me. She always has. I need protecting," I said. My hand went to my necklace, beneath my tunic. Ruta noticed but didn't say anything.

"From what?" Ruta asked.

"I don't know, but I know I've been in danger before. I felt it."
I didn't mention the necklace. "As for the elder, I brought back
incomplete knowing. And Celay made a mistake in telling her
to make an infusion. I don't know how she entered the Dream,
but I did see her there." I felt my blood pounding through my
body. I had never shared so openly with another person. It was
terrifying, and something else: a rush of joy in me.

"Are you a Dreamer?" she asked. I cringed. I couldn't help it.

"No. I can just enter the Dream. I've never seen a Dreamer
there before, but I know they exist. The spirits have tried to
gossip to me about them, but Celay warned me never to talk
about Dreamers," I said.

"How does Celay know so much?" Ruta asked, crossing to
the edge of the water and dipping her hand in to take a drink.
She wiped her mouth afterward. I sat beside her and plunged
my feet in the cool water. Ripples extended out.

"Celay is very private," I finally said. As much as I wanted to
connect with Ruta, it felt wrong to use Celay's story.

"If people eat the root, they can enter the Dream?" Ruta's
voice was soft, but her words felt like a shout through my body.

"No. It's too dangerous," I said, thinking of the wound in
the Dream. I would have to dig up all of the root, dispose of it
somehow. No one else could know of it.

"It wasn't dangerous for the elder," Ruta said, and sighed. "I
know I shouldn't want to enter the Dream, but I'm curious. I
don't even know if I believe in the Dream. In the story where
I was born, it was different. If it is the same place, we have
another name for it, another way of knowing."

I waited for her to say more. She didn't. I took a deep breath and betrayed Celay more than I ever had before.

"You will give birth. A spirit, Wotal, will help," I said. Ruta covered her mouth with her hands, then threw her arms around me. I tensed up at first. I wasn't used to being touched, and I especially wasn't used to being held. It felt strange, the skin, bones, her scent close against me. I lifted my arms slowly and put them around her. I felt her chest rising and falling quickly as she laughed or cried. After a moment I relaxed into the embrace. It felt different. It made me aware of how alive I was.

I resisted briefly when Ruta pulled away.

"One of your child's names must be Wotal. You know of a Night Bird ceremony?" I asked, remembering Wotal had mentioned Night Bird.

"I do, we do. Kinet and I discovered one a day's walk from here. We have attended the ceremony many times, but . . ." She waved her hands in a downward motion in front of her body. She had never given birth.

"Celay lied," I said. "The flowers she gave you prevent birthing." Ruta's face hardened.

"Kinet and I have always questioned if we could trust Celay. We've seen the way she treats you. But after our last loss, we promised each other we'd try everything," Ruta said, staring into the water. "I don't think you trust her either. Is it too much to tell you that? I was born in a place where we speak honestly. Kinet says sometimes I say too much." I saw a small crease of worry appear between her eyes. I reached out with my thumb and smoothed it out. She relaxed.

"I don't trust my mother." I bit my lips. It was the first time I'd said it aloud. I thought of the years of building distrust, her lies and deceptions to collect offerings from those who sought her help, often at our insistence.

"Some aren't born to those who are kind," Ruta said. It was a gentle way of saying what I knew to be true. "We are of an age, no? You are not dependent on her for anything. You could leave her, or find a mate, or join a group of wanderers, discover how to use your gift for yourself."

Her words stunned me into an openmouthed silence. We were of an age. I wasn't dependent on Celay. I knew how to make my way in the world. I had never considered it. I'd thought it was enough to escape into the Dream when I wanted to. At some point, it had stopped being enough. The discomfort had been waking in me a long while, but Ruta's words brought it to the surface.

"What could I use my gift for?" I asked, mostly to myself. Ruta didn't say anything, but she watched me, her mouth curved into quiet satisfaction. I thought of the possibilities. The part of the world we lived in had seasons of unpredictable storms. I could ask in Dreaming, speak to the spirits of wind and water and sky, ask them for knowing, make offerings. I had seen drowned bodies, flattened landscapes littered with tools and broken structures. The memories stayed with me, and the stories. I could use my gift to help.

"We can help you. Kinet and I have often wondered about you; quiet, private Saya, whose eyes never miss anything. Silent Saya who always looks like she wants more," Ruta said softly.

"You don't have to do this alone if you don't want to. I think your mother has convinced you that you're nothing without her. I've seen that story lived in before."

She took my hand in hers. No one ever held my hand, or touched me because they wanted to. I was both scared of the feeling and wanted never to let go of it. I closed my eyes and exhaled a tight breath. I wanted to trust her, tell her everything, all my secrets and Celay's, explain the Dream to her in vivid detail, make her laugh.

"Wotal told me something else." My voice came out barely above a whisper. Ruta raised her eyebrows but didn't say anything. She was waiting for me to be ready. I squeezed her hand gently and pulled it away. I pulled my necklace out from under the tunic. "This is a protection I've worn since birth. Wotal told me it no longer serves me." I held the necklace away from my body, my fingers woven between the cord.

"What did it protect you from?" Ruta asked, her eyes on the necklace. The stones weren't cut or carved, just polished, natural stone in different colors.

"Danger, somehow." I swallowed, and Ruta reached out to touch a couple of the stones. "A few times in my life, the stones have grown hot. I knew it meant I was in danger." I thought back to the times the necklace had heated, how Celay had insisted we hide until the necklace was cool again. Soon after, we would be traveling hard.

"What will you do?" Ruta asked.

"I don't know," I whispered. "I'm terrified the elder will tell someone about the root. Or that she'll tell someone she went to the Dream. Everyone wants to be a part of a story, that's what Celay always says. I'm scared Celay will make us leave. And she'll never let me take the necklace off."

Ruta thought for a moment, pulling her feet out of the water and setting them on the ground to dry. Birds chirped back and forth at each other from the canopied walls of hanging plants. Sunlight glowed through the water so it appeared to be a deep blue bowl. A strange bird flew down from above and clung to a thick, hanging root. Ruta lifted her toes to scoot a small pebble into the water, and I watched the ripples move outward. I compared our bodies. She was the same height as me but had smaller bones, sharp where I was soft. Her black hair shone more, but mine was thicker. Her face was wider than mine, and her mouth was her most prominent feature.

"What do you want your story to be, Saya?" Ruta asked.

I didn't know how to answer. I looked up as if checking the position of the sun and turned.

"I should get back."

Ruta followed. She sensed my discomfort, and we walked back in friendly quiet. When our paths split, she touched her cheek to mine and continued on, humming.

《《●》》

I was surprised to see Celay sitting on a woven mat when I returned. She looked contemplative and barely glanced at me as I walked in, the waterskins heavy in my hands. I poured them into vessels and hung the skins to dry. It was late afternoon. I wondered how long Celay had slept. She looked rested when I passed her, the dark circles under her eyes faded and the whites of her eyes clearer than they had been that morning.

"Kinet brought food, as offering," Celay called from where she sat. I found the covered bowl of food and served myself a portion of the cooked fish. It had been simmered with tart red flowers that grew year-round in the part of the land we were living. I hesitated, then took a mat and my bowl outside, sitting beside Celay. I concentrated on eating the slippery pieces of fish, watching her out of the corner of my eye to see what kind of mood she was in. She seemed distracted. She held dried sinew in her lap, pulling the fibers apart.

"I haven't had fish cooked this way before," I said, saying something simple to see how she would respond.

Celay nodded, staring off into the distance. I began to worry that my mother was in a mood I could not feel. I tried again.

"How do your hips feel?" I caught a piece of fish as it tried to slip through my fingers and scooped it into my mouth.

"Better," Celay said, looking at her hands. "Good enough to travel."

I stopped chewing and swallowed. I held my breath and waited.

"A trader we know came through, one of the Iguana sisters," she said, naming a trio of traders whose bodies carried a skin difference that caused them to look as if they were covered in small scales. "She told me a story, said there is someone who could use a cleansing in the caves." The caves were not too far away from where we lived, but they were full of different healers. Celay was always cautious around other healers, making sure to keep my gift from them.

"Will we go?" I asked. Celay thought for long moments, using a stick to carve swirls into the dust at her crossed feet. I finished my meal and set the bowl down, waiting quietly.

"I will go, you'll stay here. There is something in the story—" She stopped speaking. Her eyes unfocused and her lips pursed as she stared at her hands and thought hard a long while. She glanced at me, then picked up a length of sinew and began pulling strands from it, rolling them to smoothness between her fingers. I bit the tip of my tongue between my teeth to keep my face neutral. She looked afraid, which made me feel afraid. I knew my mother to be many things, but I rarely ever saw her shaken.

"Do you want me to ask in the Dream?" I asked. The more she was appeased, the more likely we would stay. I could spend more time with Ruta, begin a friendship with Kinet.

"Promise you won't ask about it in Dreaming. It feels dangerous." Her eyes went to my necklace, and she raised her eyebrows in a question. She wanted to know if the stones had heated, warning me I was in danger. I shook my head. She nodded, a small relief flashing across her features.

"I will stop to see the elder before I leave." Celay stood and dusted off her tunic.

"You're leaving now?" I asked, glancing at the sky. It would be well after dark by the time she arrived at the caves.

"I'll take torches and return tomorrow. I was told it was a story that can only be told after dark." She thought for a moment. "Is there any more of that root for the elder? I'd like to leave her some before I go."

"No," I said, too quickly, then pretended to think for a moment. "I didn't see any more, but I can look." Celay nodded and began gathering items to take with her.

The tended plants were in their usual afternoon state of being slightly wilted from the sun. I knelt and dug through the soft earth with my hands until I found two roots, each smaller than the one we had given the elder. I made my way on my knees around to where tall, spindly plants grew. Avoiding the small thorns, I dug at their roots and nestled the two other roots against them before replacing the dirt. I would retrieve them and hide them somewhere safer once Celay left. I worried the elder would tell Celay that she had entered the Dream. I decided I would visit her after I was sure Celay had left. I exhaled. My simple mistake had complicated my life.

I carried in a different plant, one used to keep wounds free of pus and rot. Celay had a small travel pack on, two torches sticking up from the back. She was distracted, trying to untangle knots in the cords of her foot coverings. I waved the plants at her, and she took them. I handed her a water gourd. I saw her eyeing the hooks where our larger travel packs were hanging, her eyes skimming the baskets of dried travel cakes.

"Do you want me to Dream for Ruta while you're gone?" I

asked quickly. I wanted to remind her there was at least one reason to stay.

"No, not yet," she said. "I'll return tomorrow." She turned and left. My mother had never left me alone before for a night. I looked at our home. It was neat, small, and felt more spacious without her there, with the knowledge she would not return. The solitude felt strange, an emptiness that was my own, and I didn't know how to fill it. How could I think of filling a life?

I dug up the roots again and grabbed a small travel pack Celay had given to me when it had grown too worn for her. I had fixed it as best I could, weaving small pockets into the lining. I hid the roots in one of the pockets.

The sun was setting. I thought of what Ruta had asked me earlier: What did I want my story to be? I thought of the stories that had always fascinated me, about those who were brave. I thought of the Iguana sisters, how the three of them moved across the land together and apart and always on the edge of some great knowing.

I sat in front of the altar, burning Ayan flowers and letting myself drift into my breathing, watching how the smoke moved at each inhale, only to swirl away at my exhale. I hummed a small Song in my throat, something Ruta had been humming when we left the temple. I wondered what Ruta would say if I stopped by her home with Kinet. Would they welcome me or want their privacy? I was unused to having to make such a decision for myself, and it jarred me how uncomfortable it was. Time with Ruta had reminded me of how I was in Dreaming: free, myself, seen. Now that Celay was out of my life, just for one night, I realized I never had a choice. She directed how I moved in the world. For one night, I knew I had to make choices for myself. A beginning.

《 ❰ ● ❱ 》

The elder was sitting alone in front of her home. She nodded at me and pointed at a mat next to her. I sat and waited for her to speak. She was barefoot and had her cut foot in her lap. The cut had already started to heal. She traced her finger along the seam of mending skin.

"I didn't say anything to Celay, about the Dream. I didn't belong there, but you did," she said at last.

"I keep my gift sacred, for my protection," I said. She raised her eyebrows at me.

"You were wearing a necklace in Dreaming. Do you wear it here as well?" she asked. I pulled it out from under my tunic. Her eyebrows raised as she stared at it. "A strong protection," she said.

"You know what it is?" I asked. She grinned. She was missing a couple of her front teeth, and her smile was charming.

"I know protections," she said. "I gave up my name for protection." I waited for her to say more. "You don't ask questions, do you, Saya. Why is that?" the elder asked. I leaned my chin into my knees.

"Celay doesn't like questions," I said. It had been true my entire life.

The elder reached out and put a hand on my knee.

"The gifts she claims, they aren't hers, are they?" she asked gently. It was too much. First Ruta being kind to me and now the elder. I shook my head as tears ran down my face. The elder handed me a length of woven cloth. I wiped at my tears.

"She protects me," I said. The words felt false. I had been questioning them more than I ever had before. The elder nodded slowly. She traced the line on her foot.

"What if that necklace protects you the way Celay does? By keeping you from living your own life, knowing your own gifts and choosing how to use them?" she asked.

"I don't have a choice," I whispered. The elder's eyes looked past me, in memory. She sighed.

"When I was your age, I lived a life where my choices were made for me. I wasn't happy. I didn't feel alive. One day, I made a small choice for myself, then another. I became someone new; my story has been hard, but it's been mine. Small choices, Saya," she said.

I swallowed.

"You won't tell anyone about the root and the Dream?" I asked. I didn't know what else to say.

"No, Saya," she said. I grasped her hands in gratitude, trying to ignore the pity in her eyes, and left.

((●))

Ruta and Kinet were happy to see me.

"Share our meal," Kinet offered. I accepted a clay bowl of fish broth and sipped, staring into the fire. A crackling blue flame appeared, and I choked on my broth. It was a color I knew from Dreaming. I had never seen it anywhere else. My skin crawled. I stared. Ruta touched me gently on the arm.

"It's a powder that burns in colors. I had the same reaction the first time I saw it," Ruta said.

"I remember your reaction being a little louder," Kinet teased. Ruta laughed once, her smile splitting her face as she leaned into her chosen. Kinet's body was longer than Ruta's, with skin that shone a dark amber. I wondered if it was an oil or natural.

"I was a little louder," Ruta admitted. "And you noticed me." Kinet nipped at Ruta's shoulder. She laughed once again. I smiled. Her joy made me joyous.

"It would have been impossible not to. I'd been seeking a laugh like yours my entire life," Kinet said. They kissed softly. I finished my broth.

"I'm surprised Celay let you out without her," Kinet said. Ruta nodded in agreement. The ease between them made me feel brave; their love for each other made me feel safe.

"She's gone for the night, to the caves. I wanted to ask a favor," I said quickly before I could change my mind. I wanted to make a small choice, for myself.

"Ruta, will you stay the night with me? I need your help with something," I said, breathing deeply.

Kinet looked at Ruta with expectation. Ruta tilted her head at me.

"Let me gather what I need for the night," she said. She went inside. My hands began trembling. I had never spent a night with anyone other than Celay. I knew what I was going to ask of Ruta, and it terrified me.

"I'm grateful you're helping us. Ruta shared some of your story with me," Kinet said.

"It's easy to share around Ruta," I said.

"My chosen knows how to love," Kinet said, "and she chose me. A trader. She said yes to leaving behind everything she knew to follow me. I want to give her everything she wants. She wants to give birth. Saya, she told me about the flower Celay gave her. I am grateful you chose honesty."

I wasn't used to receiving gratitude. I ducked my head, nodding once.

"Will you show me the temple?" Kinet asked, surprising me.

"Of course," I said without thinking. "Tomorrow morning?"

"I'll bring a meal over in the morning in case you two are awake long into the night." Kinet smiled as Ruta came out with a bundle. They kissed tenderly, and Kinet whispered something to Ruta that made her laugh low and pull away. She looked back with a tease, then linked my arm. We walked into the night.

((●))

Ruta changed into her sleep tunic and sat in front of our altar. I heated water for an infusion and set it to seep, a mixture of calming spider-thin roots. I didn't know what the night would hold. I looked at the tunic I was wearing. I often slept in my normal clothing as everything I had already looked worn, so I didn't change. I sat beside Ruta in front of the altar and lit a dried Ayan flower. The white blossom dried in the shape of a funnel, edges brown. When Ayan blossoms bloomed, they looked like open hands. When they burned, they curled into fists. The sweet smoke rose around us.

Ruta held her hands over the flame. I dipped two fingers into the cup of water and brushed my lips with them. I was nervous; Ruta noticed. She leaned back and pulled the infusion from where I had set it to cool. She poured two cups, handing one to me. I appreciated her silence and patience.

"Will you help me?" I asked.

CHAPTER SEVEN

INDIR

The next morning, the temple was quiet. Safi was in lower Alcanzeh, meeting with the grandmothers to discuss the best places for visitors to stay. I didn't know where my aunts were. I had slept in an empty chamber, something all of us did when we wanted solitude. I had missed the shared morning meal but didn't care. I went to the area of the temple for feeding of workers, visitors, anyone who hungered. I ate a fast meal in the corner and went looking for my sisters.

Zeri was playing with temple workers' children, a tile game that was played throughout all lands and carried far by traders. Sets of tiles from across lands were traded back and forth, and long games were played across distances by certain traders who specialized in the game. There were smaller versions of the game too, like the one Zeri was playing with the others. The rules confused me; I didn't enjoy playing.

"You slept alone. Did you have Dreams you want to share?" Zeri looked up from where she sat on the ground surrounded by children only a few years younger than her. They scowled up at my interruption. A temple worker I hadn't seen before sat with them. She held the spinning tiles and raised her eyebrows at me.

"Do you play?" she asked.

"She doesn't, Dua. I've tried," Zeri said. "Indir, I'm needed here. I have a message for Tavovis, will you take it?" She glanced back down at the game.

"You can't send a temple worker?" I asked.

"Not for this message," she said. "He asked me to Dream for him. I would go to him myself, but I'm training Dua for temple work. She was sent from the Water Temple by Lal. Or you can train Dua and I'll go." It didn't look to me like she was training, but if chaos was coming, I wanted my sister to enjoy her game.

Dua glared up at me, ready to spin her tiles. I was too restless to spend my day trying to focus on training a temple worker. It would have been unfair to both of us.

"I'll go," I said.

《 《 ● 》 》

The Avex training area was at the outside of Alcanzeh, set away from the city itself. It was set up on the ruins of an ancient city whose name had returned to the Dream. There were large fields where the Avex trained in wrestling, agility, and how to tend the fresh and wastewater canals. Many younger people served as Avex for a period of time—it was considered an honor to have an Avex tattoo: three lines like a claw across the three middle fingers of the spear hand. Some who didn't have a trade or a family could stay on as Avex and rise in the ranks as trainers or leaders.

I knew where the camp was but had never had any reason to visit it before. As I approached, I heard a commotion. I saw a group of young trainees gathered and yelling. I went to see what they were shouting about.

A small dog was tied to a fallen stone pillar, where a cluster of younger Avex were antagonizing it. The dog cowered, tail between his urine-wet legs. He was crying in pain. The trainees were using slings to hurl paint-dipped stones at the clearly exhausted dog. It was impossible to tell what color he had been originally because his coat was covered in red paint, which ran in smears that looked like blood. The Fire Warriors sent out sparks from their hands whenever a stone hit the dog, to cheers.

My entire body went hot with anger. I tucked the scroll into the belt of my tunic and yelled loudly.

"Stop!"

They turned, looks of guilt on the Avex's faces. They knew cruelty to animals was seen as deeply shameful in our city.

"It's only an animal," one of the Fire Warriors taunted me. "We're betting, join us."

He flung pebbles at me. He didn't want me to join; he wanted to scare me. One hit my shoulder and fell at my feet. I didn't think. I scooped the pebble and threw it back at him. It hit him in the mouth, splitting his lip. Everyone was silent. I felt my blood pounding in my veins as his fellow Fire Warriors gathered behind him. My anger coalesced into something else, and for once, I wasn't afraid. The gathered Avex stood watching, eyes wary of the Fire Warriors, looking to each other for guidance.

The dog was pressed up against the fallen pillar, its eyes wild as it tried to free itself from the rope. I went toward the dog, but when I approached, it began to growl. I knelt, holding my hand out, but the dog just pressed itself closer against the pillar, growling. A shadow fell over me. Someone handed me a piece of meat. A low voice spoke.

"Give him this." It was Ovis.

I held the meat out, crooning softly, proud of the way I had confronted those torturing the dog. I hoped Ovis had seen my anger, hoped it had been more interesting than my usual silence. The dog sniffed the air, approaching cautiously before finally taking the meat. I brushed my hands over its head and looked into its yellow eyes, doing my best not to glance at Ovis, to appear strong.

"I apologize for the Fire Warriors. They will be disciplined." A familiar voice spoke from behind. It was Inkop. The Fire Warriors who had been torturing the animal looked uncomfortable. Inkop held one by the upper arm. Ovis glared at him.

"They are not welcome here. They're a bad influence on the Avex they interact with."

"They're bored. They crave excitement, are used to living a different kind of life. I apologize again." Inkop looked past Ovis at me. I stood, and the dog pressed itself against my leg. I stared back at Inkop, hoping my face showed my disgust.

"They threw stones not only at the dog but at Indir, a Dreamer of Alcanzeh," Ovis said. I breathed out through my nostrils slowly, the way Lal had taught me, and focused on the feeling of the air leaving my body, keeping my face calm.

"I am sorry, Indir. I don't believe they knew who you are. They will be disciplined," Inkop said.

"Dreamer or not, it was wrong," I said, surprised at myself. The residual anger in my body had turned to something that rose in bravery, strength.

"You're right, I apologize," Inkop said. I was astonished. I had expected something different from him, close as he seemed to Alcan.

"Alcan said—" one of the Fire Warriors started to speak, but Inkop silenced him with a motion of his hand. He closed his eyes briefly, his mouth tightening as if he wanted to say more. But instead, he turned and walked away, the Fire Warriors following.

"Come with me if you wish," Ovis said, scooping the dog up and walking toward the jungle. I was so surprised, I didn't say anything. Ovis had long legs and walked fast. He left the clearing, entering the jungle. I paused only a moment before following him.

Ovis came to a small stream with a pool formed at the edge of it. He waded in to his knees and crouched, the dog still in his arms. The dog flinched when he felt the water, then relaxed and dipped his head down and began drinking. Ovis held the dog in one arm and used the other arm to scoop water over his coat. I felt a small drop in my stomach at how tenderly he moved his hands over the dog's shaking body. He motioned with his head for me to join him. I didn't hesitate. I lifted my tunic, tucked the hem into my belt, and waded in. I stood beside

Ovis, running my hands through the dog's coat to release even more paint. Trembling, the dog stopped drinking, and a low growl began to vibrate in his throat.

Ovis put his hands over mine before I could pull them away and held them firmly on the dog's body. He raised his eyebrows to me and began Singing.

I knew the Song. I knew the Song in my entire body. It was a lullaby about trusting the Dream, a story Song. My mother and aunts used to Sing it to me when I was a small child. The dog relaxed. I ran my hands through his coat until the water around him ran clear. I hummed along, not able to hide the smile on my face. I felt warm despite the cool water. Ovis walked out of the water, placing the dog on the ground. I followed, smiling as the dog shook the water off, spraying us both.

"Stay away from bored warriors, little friend," Ovis said. The dog wagged its tail and trotted off into the jungle. Ovis looked at me.

"I don't trust Inkop," Ovis said.

"Because he's so close to Alcan?" I asked.

"Our spies say he and Alcan were raised like brothers, that Alcan keeps Inkop around because the Fire Warriors respect him. I don't trust him because of the way he looks at you and the other Dreamers. He wants something; I can feel it," Ovis said. I pulled my head covering forward to hide the heat that rose to my cheeks.

"He confuses me," I said, thinking about his apology earlier. "I don't know that he wants to do everything Alcan asks of him."

"But he does it. That's what matters," Ovis said. I didn't know if I agreed with him but didn't want to talk about Inkop. He shifted the conversation. "What were you doing in our training grounds, Indi?"

"I have a message for your father," I said, surprised he knew my small name. We had met on a few occasions, but I had always felt overshadowed by Delu, who knew how to speak to others in ways I had never mastered. But away from the eyes of others, I felt comfortable with him.

"I'll take you to him." He led me through the Avex camp. We passed the clearing where the young trainees had been torturing the dog, now empty. We went past another clearing where young Avex were hurling stones out of leather slings at a post while a short woman called out corrections to their form. In another clearing, they were practicing wrestling. I was fascinated at how the bodies of the wrestlers moved back and forth with restrained power. I wondered if Ovis wrestled. He led me into a small stone building with a thatched roof. Tavovis sat in the center, surrounded by other important Avex. He stood when he saw us approach.

"Ovis!" he said, shaking his head and smiling. "I heard a Dreamer outdid the Avex when she threw stones at Fire Warriors. Have you brought her here for training for the Game?" He wiggled his eyebrows and looked at me with admiration in his eyes. "I hear you hit him right in the mouth, Indir! What are you doing in our training grounds, besides defending poor creatures from Fire Warriors?"

I stood a little taller at his praise. My mothers and aunts always treated me carefully, knowing how I normally preferred to stay clear of attention. It felt rare and good to be admired.

"I didn't expect to see Fire Warriors here. They were hurting a dog, and there were Avex laughing."

The older man's mouth went into a line; he and Ovis exchanged a grim look. Tavovis sighed.

"Zeri asked me to bring you this." I handed the scroll to Tavovis, knowing how important the message had to be that my sister would use a scroll, even a small one. He unrolled it, reading the symbols quickly. His posture dropped. He stood for a moment with his head down. When he looked up, I saw his eyes shone with tears.

"In Dreaming, she saw that traders have been killed a few days north of here," he said quietly. Ovis stepped forward and put his hand on his father's shoulder.

"Maybe it was only a possibility; she Dreams in possibility." Ovis's voice was somber.

"Nothing is surprising. Nothing. Fire Warriors are in our city, traders being killed." The older Avex pressed his lips together, turning to sit back down.

"I can go. I can take a few runners, see for ourselves," Ovis said. His father shook his head.

"No, I want you here. I want you near me." Tavovis clasped his hands and nodded at me. "Thank you for bringing me the message and for stopping those trainees from killing that animal." He turned to a woman sitting next to him. "Find which Avex were torturing the dog, put them on stone-moving duty the next few days, and trench duty the next moon. Put the word out that any Avex caught with Fire Warriors will be disciplined."

"Is there anything you'd like to send back to my sister? A return message?" I shifted from one foot to the other.

"No, not today. Ovis will walk you back to your temple." He dismissed us with a nod and walked away.

"You don't have to walk me back; I know how to get there," I said, not looking at Ovis.

"My father is leader of the Avex. When he tells me to do something, I do it." He sighed. "He asked your sister to Dream about my brother. Our father has had a feeling that Tixu would be returning soon; he says he can feel his spirit being called back to Alcanzeh. And there is a fear to the feeling."

I felt a rush of empathy for him. I couldn't imagine anything happening to one of my sisters. They were my only friends, even if we didn't always get along. Losing one of them would destroy me.

"You were right though, it was only a possibility," I offered, looking up at him. It was something I had been trying to tell myself after my last Dream.

"I know. I would know if something happened to my brother, I would feel it. You would too, no? If something happened to one of your sisters?" He had stopped and was looking at me, his eyes imploring.

"Of course." I felt my face heat up again. We were walking slowly, footsteps away from where the training grounds butted up against the jungle. We were going the long way back to the temple, instead of walking straight through Alcanzeh. I was glad.

"I've been thinking about the Game," Ovis said. I stopped.

"Why?" I asked. I hated the idea of him fighting anyone, especially a Fire Warrior. I shuddered. "It doesn't bother you? The thought of dying or causing someone else's death?"

"Not if it is for the greater good of Alcanzeh, so we can move forward," he said. "And whoever fights will live forever in stories."

"Is being part of a lasting story that important to you? Wouldn't you rather live? Alcanzeh has been doing fine without playing the Game for generations," I said. My anger sprouted again, letting my words loosen.

"I enjoy using my skills. It is what I've been training for. Do you enjoy Dreaming?" he asked suddenly. I paused before answering, careful.

"I'm always happy to help our people," I said. It was an easy answer.

"I feel the same way about being an Avex warrior," he said simply. I didn't want to speak with him in conflict, I decided, and changed the subject.

"You have a voice that carries Song well." I remembered the rush of thrills running through me when he Sang to the dog. He smiled, picked up a stone, and tossed it into the jungle.

"My mother was a Sacred Singer of the Litéx. She served at the Water Temple. When he was a young man, my father was injured in a small battle. When they brought him back to Alcanzeh, the Avex took him to the Water Temple, sure he would die. At sunset, my mother came to Sing his Song of Return. When he heard her voice, he decided he had to live."

"Does she live with the Litéx?" I asked. I knew nothing of his mother.

"She returned to the Dream when my brother and I were very young."

We walked quietly. I took the cover off my head and shook my hair out, lifting it away from my neck to cool down. I was happy the braid had fallen out. I could smell the Ayan blossom— scented water I had brushed through it, and I wanted him to notice me more but had little practice in ways of flirtation. I wanted to say something but couldn't think of anything that would improve the comfortable silence between us.

"If you could be anything else besides a Dreamer, what would you be?" he asked, pausing beneath a strand of curling vines. Behind him, the jungle breathed its warm breath of insects' Song out toward us. I thought about the question. No one had ever asked me, and I had never considered it. I thought of the carvings in the temples, how much I enjoyed painting them, making them beautiful.

"An artist, or artisan. I'd be a temple painter, or serve as a weaver of stories, if they accepted me." I imagined weaving stories into long cloths that could be traded land to land. The weavers of Alcanzeh kept their artistry secret. Weavers came from far-off lands to learn. Few were accepted and of those who were, all were sworn to secrecy.

He nodded, his eyes on mine. "Indir."

I felt my name in my entire body when he spoke it. It both

terrified and thrilled me. He beckoned me to follow him into the jungle. I took a breath and followed. He walked until he was standing beneath a tree of curled vines that hung down just over our heads. I didn't know the name of the tree but knew that in a few weeks, it would explode into curtains of bright orange flowers that would hang to the ground. The vines were beginning to unfurl, but they were mostly curled tight and dark green.

Ovis grabbed one of the curled vines and held it close to his mouth. He began Singing, a low murmuring Song. I couldn't make out the words, but the melody Sang in my veins, making me want to breathe in and dance. I closed my eyes and let the Song fill me.

Behind my eyelids, I saw stars, lights streaking, exploding. Ovis stopped Singing, but I kept my eyes closed, alert to every sound in the jungle, the sun dappling through the growth to play on my skin. I heard Ovis step toward me. Something dropped over my shoulders. When I opened my eyes, I gasped. The vine had unfurled into bright blossoms that trailed down to my knees. He had draped it over my shoulders. He was a Sacred Singer.

"Does your father know?" It was all I could think of asking.

"He knows I carry the gift. And he knows I am an Avex. It was clear from a young age that my brother didn't want to be an Avex. I didn't want to disappoint my father. I trained to make him proud." His smile seemed to hold grief. "I spent some time along the Litéx, when I was young. They trained me to sense pain, to see where it gathers in the body. I don't want you to think me disrespectful, but I see something in you I recognize, a want for something you can't have. I know how that feels." He touched my cheek. I felt my face warm and dropped my eyes to the ground. His feet were bare and closer to mine than I'd expected.

"You shouldn't hide your gift for Singing," I said. "I imagine a warrior who can heal would be in great demand."

Ovis laughed, low in his throat.

"There are better trained healers with more potent gifts than mine, Indir." When he spoke my name, I looked up into his eyes. "And I do not hide my gift, I just choose who to share it with."

"I am grateful you shared it with me," I said. I didn't know how else to respond.

"I trust those who are kind to animals," he said, his smile spreading across his face, "and those who throw rocks at those who aren't." I couldn't not return his smile.

We left the vine and walked back to the temple in silence. I felt safe. I wished we could spend the entire day together, but another Avex called out to him, and when he turned to greet her, I hurried up the stairs without saying goodbye.

《 《 ● 》 》

Zeri was still playing the tile game when I returned, now with a new group of players. She saw me entering and placed her tiles down faceup.

"I surrender the offerings," she said. The others leaned to look at her tiles and groaned.

"Zeri, your tiles would have added so much to the story," a young man whined. Zeri ignored him, scooped up her tiles, and walked to another chamber, beckoning me with her chin.

"How did Tavovis receive the message?" Zeri asked.

"I sensed his grief, but he had hope too. It is only a possibility his son died, no?" I felt odd asking, but my empathy went out to the older man, and Ovis.

Zeri looked over her shoulder at me.

"I see many things in Dreaming, sister. It is possible he lives, but no traders have arrived from the north in too long. In the Dream, I see changes, routes that were once full of traders, now empty. That isn't usual."

I felt my heart sink for Ovis.

"Dua said Ovis walked you back." Zeri's voice had a smile in it. I thought of the temple worker, wondering how she had seen us and told Zeri before I had arrived.

"Tavovis had him walk me back."

"I have a feeling you'll Dream him, sister," she said.

My face burned hot. There was no possibility of Dreaming him. I shook my head.

"Impossible," I whispered.

"Is it?" Zeri asked. She stepped closer to me, gently putting her hands on my upper arms. "I think I know your secret, sister, or part of it. I saw something about you in Dreaming, one of those little flashes, almost like a memory."

I took a step backward, away from her. My throat went dry. I looked to see if the room had a drinking gourd. It did. I poured water in a clay cup and drank deeply.

"Indir. I have reason to believe you will not live here anymore," Zeri said, voice low.

I froze. The clay in my hand dropped to the floor but didn't shatter. I started shaking. I bent over, putting my hands on my knees to steady myself for a moment. I stood slowly, head bowed. I took a few deep breaths, then looked up. Zeri had a strange look on her face.

"What?" I whispered. My voice had left, and it was all I could gather.

"How long have you known?" Zeri asked, stepping in to embrace me. I embraced her back. She was shaking too. I realized Zeri still didn't know I had stopped Dreaming. I pulled away.

"Wait. What do you mean, I won't live here anymore?" I felt my blood running cold, fingers of fear moving up and down my spine. They were going to discover I had lost my gift.

"You didn't know? You haven't seen it? I thought that was why you've been acting so strange. Indi, what is going on with you? Come with me." Zeri wiped her hands clean and led us out of the room.

We went outside and up a flight of stairs and sat on a small platform that was on the temple. The temple was covered in such small places, for the Dreamers and visitors to contemplate, meditate. We sat. Zeri didn't speak; she held my hand and hummed a small tune. She knew me, knew I would speak when I was ready. I breathed until most of the panic in me eased into resignation. They would find out eventually.

"Zeri, you have to promise me not to tell anyone," I said.

Zeri nodded, face serious.

"I've stopped Dreaming." I made a choice not to tell her about Alcan plunging his knife into my chest. The other secret was almost as terrible.

My sister was silent. Her face didn't change. She looked me in the eyes.

"Zeri?" I trembled.

"Oh, sister." Zeri moved over closer and put her arms around me. I stiffened, then relaxed into her and let myself be held. I was still trembling, but Zeri rubbed circles onto my back. After a few minutes, my breathing evened.

"When did you stop?" Zeri whispered. I leaned into her.

"When King Anz died. That was my last Dream."

"And you won't tell us what you Dreamed for him?" my sister asked.

I shook my head. I had made a promise. The sphere of water made no sense to me, but it wasn't mine to tell.

"Who have you told about your loss?" My sister's voice was calm, but I saw an urgency in her eyes.

"No one. I'm too scared of what they'll say. What if I made this happen? What if I Dreamed something I wasn't supposed to? The night I Dreamed for Anz, it happened so fast, maybe I wasn't protected enough."

Zeri rocked back and forth, her eyes on the sky. She closed them briefly.

"I'll Dream for you. I'll ask and find out," she said.

"Zeri. You said you saw me leaving the temple? Alcanzeh?

Will I not be allowed to live here if my gift doesn't return?" I felt panic rise in my blood, twitching along my spine, into my hands. I clenched them. Zeri put her hands gently on mine until I released them.

"Not just the temple. I saw you leaving Alcanzeh," she said. I had a moment of relief; at least she saw me living. Then the truth of it awakened.

"What? Where will I go? I don't want to leave Alcanzeh. This is my home." I stood, panic overtaking my body. I paced back and forth, my hands clenched in my hair. Zeri had seen me in the grip of panic before. She stood to stop my pacing and placed her hands over her chest, inhaling and exhaling deeply. I did the same, out of instinct, though everything in me wanted to run, cry, hide.

"It isn't as if you won't be able to return, sister. This is your home." Zeri's voice was gentle.

I looked out over Alcanzeh. I had lived here my entire life and spent most of it inside the temple. I had rarely thought of what was outside. Did I lack imagination, or was I so set in my path as a Dreamer that I was unable to see anything else?

"Alone?" I turned to Zeri. My sister smiled.

"I only saw you, but you were smiling, speaking to someone. You looked different, stronger, happy."

I couldn't imagine myself happy outside Alcanzeh, away from those I loved.

"I'm scared I'll be forced to leave, when they find out I can't Dream. I'm broken, Zeri," I whispered.

I saw Zeri struggle. She had always been the compassionate

sister, the one who tried to reach me even when I refused to be reached.

"Stop, Indir. Maybe you're the Lost Dreamer. Perhaps it'll take your leaving for your Dreaming to return. We have to be patient with what we cannot know. I saw your face, Indir, I saw a joy I had never seen before."

I swallowed down my response and nodded.

"Trust the Dream," I said, more to placate myself than anything else.

"Trust the Dream," she repeated.

Dua, the new temple worker, ran up to us, out of breath. I stared at her. She seemed terrified and excited at the same time.

"Your mother calls; you must hurry," she gasped. "Alcan has desecrated Alcanzeh!"

CHAPTER EIGHT

SAYA

"I understand if you are uncomfortable with what I ask—" I said.

Ruta held up her hand, palm up.

"Ask then, Saya. I know discomfort and don't fear it. If it isn't something I can offer you, I'll tell you," she said. I blew on the liquid in my cup and took a sip. It was a flavor that reminded me of damp earth, with a green taste that remained in the mouth long after swallowing.

"I want to Dream without my protection, and I'd like you to be here, in case anything strange should occur," I said quickly, swallowing my infusion in one swallow. It was still hot. I breathed fast with my tongue between my teeth to cool my mouth. Ruta's face stayed serene. She poured me a cup of water.

"What do you mean by strange?" Ruta asked, her eyes going to my necklace.

"I don't know," I admitted. "Celay has never let me remove it, not once. She says it protects me, but I think she might be lying."

"What would I do if something strange were to occur?" Ruta's calm didn't break.

"Place the protection back on my body?" I said, my voice making it more a question than an answer.

Ruta nodded, her eyes moving back to the altar.

"What does your body do, here, while the rest of you is in

Dreaming?" she asked, running another Ayan blossom through the flame so that it smoked again.

"I don't know, I'm gone. Celay says it looks like I am sleeping, but I don't move. You'll know when I'm returning; I'll move again," I said, hopeful. She hadn't said yes, but she hadn't said no either.

"Turn then, let me untie it for you," Ruta said. My entire body vibrated with joy; I could feel my blood dancing in my veins to the pounding of my heart. I turned and lifted my hair. I could feel Ruta's breaths on the back of my neck. She leaned in close to try and untangle the knot, muttering a phrase in a language I didn't understand as her fingers pinched and plucked at the knot until one end dropped free. She pulled the end, and it slithered off my body. For the first time in my memory, I was without my protection. I blew an exhale through pursed lips. It felt strange, and it felt normal. I ran my fingertips over the skin where the seven stones usually pressed against. The spot was sensitive, the sensations of skin on skin more noticeable than other places I touched.

Ruta held the necklace out in her hand.

"Do you want me to hold it? To place it on the altar? Hide it away?" she asked, and again, I was grateful for her. She thought of questions I wouldn't have. I thought for a moment.

"Not the altar; I don't know how the protection works. Keep it close, next to where I'll Dream," I said.

"Are you afraid?" Ruta asked softly. I didn't answer. We moved to where we would sleep. She unrolled a sleeping mat, placing it beside mine. I carried a small oil-filled shell and lit a twisted wick in its center, then placed it near enough to where we'd sleep that we would stay softly in light as long as the wick burned.

Ruta placed the necklace beside the shell and sat cross-legged on her mat. I sat on mine beside her.

"Thank you," I said. I stretched slightly, twisting back and forth, then stretched out on my mat, pulling a light blanket over me. Ruta reached out to hold my hand.

"Thank you for trusting me with this, Saya," she said softly. I wove my fingers between hers.

"Thank you for saying yes," I said.

And then I was gone.

《 《 ● 》 》

The Dream was different, brighter, the colors even sharper than I had known they could be. And there were voices calling, shouting; some were laughing, others screamed. A small panic rose in me, but I pushed it down; it was the Dream. I had always been safe there. I reached up to touch my necklace, a lifelong habit, but I felt nothing. I saw a face hovering in front of me for a moment, teeth ripping through the fabric of the Dream, splitting it. I couldn't make out the details but didn't want to. It felt malevolent. I closed my eyes and wished myself somewhere safe.

Around me, the Dream pulsated in answer, and I felt myself being pulled. I landed on ground made of cut and fit stone. Some sort of large temple. I looked around, gasping in wonder. Carved tiles covered the stone walls around me. An altar was set up in the corner, a flame burning in a small bowl set before twisted shapes I couldn't identify. They seemed to be dancing. I heard footsteps running toward me. I pressed myself to a wall, wishing again to be somewhere safe, but I remained. Shadows moved at an entryway I hadn't noticed.

Two women came in and stood stunned before me. Their hair was arranged in a strange braided style I had never seen. Neither of them spoke, though one moved toward me, her arms outstretched. They looked alike. I realized they were sisters. I shrank back, begging the Dream to release me. I felt it respond, reluctantly. As I was pulled away, I heard them calling out. Their voices followed me, but their words didn't.

《《●》》

I woke up gasping. Ruta grabbed the necklace and put it on my neck. My entire body shook. When the stones had fallen into their familiar weight on my skin, I leaned into Ruta. She put her arms around me, crooning something under her breath as she rocked me back and forth.

"Breathe," she whispered against the side of my head. I concentrated on my breath until my body started to relax and the shaking ceased.

Alcanzeh was half a world away from where I lived, far to the north. The temple city was rumored to be beautiful, though fading. I knew few stories of the city except that it was home to Dreamers, a lineage of women who went into the Dream. I had never encountered them before, though I knew they existed.

I wondered if they knew I existed and realized probably not, given their reactions.

"I may have seen the Dreamers of Alcanzeh," I said, my voice dry. Ruta crooned, rubbing her hand in circles over my back. My body released more tension. "I went to a temple, one larger than any I have ever seen. I think it was Alcanzeh. There was an altar, with a light burning. Then two women came. They wore their hair in strange braids. They tried to come toward me, but I willed myself away."

Ruta waited, but I didn't have anything else to say.

"How do you feel now?" she asked.

"Strange," I said, pulling slightly away, touching my necklace. "Why would I need protection from the Dreamers?"

Ruta pulled back and sat for a long moment, her eyes unfocused over my right shoulder.

"You don't know if it's a protection. And you don't know if they were really Dreamers. I don't know the story you're living, Saya, but more will come. It always does. Is there any way I can help you feel less strange?" she asked. I laughed. I was alone in my home with a friend, my first night away from Celay. I had entered the Dream without my protection, possibly seen Dreamers.

"I don't think there is any way to get away from strange anymore," I sighed, stretching my legs out in front of me. Ruta went to the altar and brought me a smoldering Ayan flower.

"Breathe this in, at least. I noticed how you always moved toward the scent earlier." She held the burning blossom in front of my face. The smoke was a pale blue in the dancing light from the oil flame. I inhaled, closing my eyes. Ayan flowers grew across all known lands, at least according to stories. Something about their scent and smoke opened me to peace in small ways. I thought of the surprise on the women's faces. Their tunics had been strange, decorated in ways I'd never seen before. They hadn't seemed malicious, just surprised. They'd moved toward me as if they knew me, though that was impossible. In my shock, I had run. I should have stayed.

"Will you try again?" she asked. I shook my head.

"Not tonight, but soon." I felt unbalanced. "I asked to be taken somewhere safe. I was surprised. I didn't leave out of fear." I thought of the face I saw pressed against the Dream, the cruelty coming from it. I didn't tell Ruta. It had passed quickly.

Ruta nodded. She stretched out on her mat. I did the same. We faced each other, the oil light shadowing our faces.

"Will you speak to them if you see them again?" she asked.

I wanted to, if I was able to return to them. I didn't know when I'd be able to Dream without my necklace again.

"If I can," I yawned. Ruta pulled her knees up so they were touching mine. She was more comfortable in her body than me. Touch was rarely safe for me, but I trusted Ruta.

We spoke of small things until we drifted off to sleep. I didn't Dream again.

((●))

Kinet's whistle woke us in the morning. Ruta rolled over lazily and sighed. At some point, we had shifted to our backs, but our feet touched.

"My chosen," Ruta sighed sweetly as Kinet entered, kneeling to kiss her on the mouth. I sat up, rubbing my eyes. I had slept well, despite the shock of what I had seen in Dreaming. I stayed quiet as Kinet and Ruta exchanged morning pleasantries and embraces. I stepped outside to relieve myself and heard Ruta's laugh. I ached for a laugh like that in my life, either from my own body or from someone I cared for. I brought out bowls for the meal Kinet had made.

"Do you want to share more of your story with Kinet?" Ruta asked gently. They were sitting close, eating from the same bowl. It was a small act of intimacy that made me wistful. I nodded and explained the cut stone, the women with strange hair and tunics. Kinet listened, nodding, then spoke.

"My father will be passing through soon. He knows more about Dreamers than I do. If you choose to share your story with him, he may be able to answer questions you have."

"I would be grateful to speak with Batuk," I said. I was surprised at how easy it was to speak of what had always been secret. I expected to feel guilty sharing what I'd seen with anyone besides Celay, but it felt freeing.

We finished our meal quickly and headed toward the temple. The morning was cloudy, but there was no scent of rain in the air. The birds seemed excited, gossiping back and forth, flitting from tree to vine above and below us. A pair of hummingbirds chased each other, either vying for territory or mating.

"I wonder if there's a predator nearby," Kinet said, noticing the birds.

"Maybe your hummingbird messenger is telling stories," Ruta teased me.

"Look at Saya," I said in a high-pitched voice, pretending to be the hummingbird, "learning how to live in the Waking World."

Ruta laughed and linked an arm through mine.

"I'm grateful you're in the Waking World. You make it much more interesting," she said. I blushed. Kinet looked at me sideways, grinning.

"Thank you for inviting us to share in your story," Kinet said.

"I'm curious to see how it ends," I sighed. Kinet stopped briefly to turn to me, winking.

"Stories don't end, Saya, they just change shape."

《 《 ● 》 》

The temple seemed closer to the path since we knew where it was. Kinet stomped down much of the growth, following the trail we had left before. When we arrived, I pushed aside the vines and let Kinet enter first, Ruta and I following. Kinet barely glanced at the water and instead pulled a knife out, cutting away the growth from the stone walls, using the knife tip to gouge out dirt.

"There are carvings here; I can just make out the shape in a few places."

Ruta and I watched for a minute, then went to drink from the cool water. It reflected a deep blue under the clouded sky. Birds flitted in and out, calling out stories to each other that

I wished I could understand. Below the water's surface, I saw movement, as if a river moved deep beneath the stillness. It was possible. There were vast webs of underground rivers and streams; it was why travelers called where we lived the Belly.

"These are symbols," Kinet said. Ruta and I went to look. Kinet had cleared two carvings. They were old, chipped in places, all color washed away from the carved stone. One carving seemed familiar to me, though I couldn't recall having seen it before. Kinet stood in front of the other one.

"This is a symbol for forgetting or loss. I recognize it from my travels," Kinet said, tracing the swirl with a fingertip. "If there is a symbol of forgetting, the symbol for memory must be under some of this growth."

"I know this symbol." I stood before two lines intersecting. "I've seen it before."

"The Twin Serpents," Kinet said, glancing at me. "Though I don't know what shape their story takes here. It changes from land to land. They're sacred to the Dreamers of Alcanzeh."

I traced my fingers along the lines of their converging bodies. I knew the symbol a deeper way. In the story almost everyone shared, The Night Bird and Twin Serpents created the Waking World. I saw traces of them interwoven throughout every part of the Dream, invisible segmented twists that always seemed to float just out of sight. I looked closer and saw a different set of markings just below the symbol of the Twin Serpents. I couldn't make out the details of the shape, but it was roughly circular. As I concentrated on it, the side of my vision picked up the Twin Serpent symbol, and a memory rose strong.

"The women in the Dream had hair that looked like this symbol," I said.

"They were probably Dreamers, then," Ruta said. "Will you Dream without your necklace again? Tonight?"

I thought of Celay. There was no way to remove the necklace without her noticing—it seemed sometimes she looked at the necklace more than she looked at me.

"If I want to do it, I'll have to do it now," I said. "Celay will notice. We never sleep apart." I stared at the symbol. My body felt the pull of the Dream, inviting me to enter. It was a feeling that rarely came, but when it did, I could not ignore it.

I went close to the water's edge where a lip of stone jutted out. Ruta helped me untie the necklace, then handed it to me. I poured a small amount of water into my hand and poured it over the stone as offering. I was becoming sleepier and sleepier, a strange sensation as if I was sinking. The birds seemed to call out louder. I sank to my knees and held my necklace out over the lip of stone and dropped it. It fell, splayed. I started to sink backward. I heard Ruta's voice as if from far away, but I couldn't make out the words. I felt her arms support me as I fell into her lap. She cupped my face with her hands and spoke to me, but it was as if I was underwater. I heard Kinet shout, then a strange sensation came, a pulse in the air. I turned my head to see a large bird, bigger than any I had ever seen before, glide down on outstretched wings, beak open, heading toward me. My protection was gone, and the bird was going to kill me, I thought. I didn't care.

Ruta may have screamed, but it sounded deeper, a wail that

wrenched through my entire body. A sensation of grief arrived with an intensity that seized through me. I lost my breath. The air pulsed again as the bird dropped down.

I knew what it was going to do, and there was nothing to do to stop it. I watched, stunned and trying to catch my breath as the bird hooked my necklace in its lower beak, then rose in a pulse of air and wings. A shadow flew over me. Kinet leaped at the bird, knife in hand. I heard a splash and was able to take a breath again. I gasped as the air filled my lungs at the same moment the water from Kinet's leap at the bird splashed over me. Then I was gone.

《《 ● 》》

Dreaming came on hard, harder than I had known before. I was in a different place, new to me. I hovered above a small jungle clearing, where a man knelt in front of a stone altar barely bigger than him. The man was young, strong, but as I looked closer, I could see he was tired. There was something in him that called me, I felt him in all of me, pulsing like my own heartbeat. I found myself moving closer to him, then realized I was hovering in the air, which was not uncommon for Dreaming, but when I tried to move myself to the ground, I couldn't. I was without body. The resistance to what I wanted distracted me a moment, but then the man began Singing. He held a small hummingbird in his hand. I gasped, without sound, when I realized what he was going to do.

Sacrifice wasn't uncommon, but it wasn't a practice I was

comfortable with. The spirits always asked for blood, and I always refused. There were too many stories of how it could go wrong, what power could awaken in a spirit and let it cross to the Waking World. Despite this, I hovered closer, as if his Song was a current I was caught in. I wasn't afraid. I was fascinated.

The stone altar was surrounded by plants unfamiliar to me. They seemed to undulate and twist in colors that didn't exist in the Waking World. I observed, enraptured. The man whispered to the trembling hummingbird, bowed his head, and snapped the bird's neck. He stopped Singing and held the still bird in his hands, raising them over his head. He spoke in a low voice.

"Whatever mistakes we have made, or offenses we have caused, forgive us. All we have done has been out of love. Thank you for the safety we have known." He cleared his throat. "I ask you for another protection, as many as you can offer, when you are able to, when she needs it."

I was again distracted. A spark of light seemed to glow from the hummingbird's body. It pulsed, as small as the bird's eye, then rose out, flying upward toward me. I had known spirits to take different shapes, and this one was tiny and bright. I marveled at the spark, pulsing white, gold, then a deep blue. My body took shape again, though I was still without full control of it. I didn't care. The light flew to me, hovering in front of my eyes before moving forward and touching the center of my forehead. I felt a rush of love fill me, a joyous sense of being touched, held, seen. I closed my eyes, letting the sensation overtake me until I felt I was made of light, no boundaries between me and the Dream. It pulsed brightly, then softened. I opened my eyes.

The man had his forehead to the altar stone. I moved toward him, though I had no idea what I looked like, what shape I had taken without my protection. Whatever I was in that moment, a part of me reached out to touch him. As I did, the hummingbird sparked back to life in his hands, wings fluttering, healed. The man lifted his head quickly, eyes wide. He couldn't see me. His face was different from the faces I had known my entire life. I wished I had a voice to greet him, but it didn't matter; being close to him felt safe. I reached out with my mind, with all my intention, to let him feel the love that was filling me. He gasped, his hands going to his chest. The hummingbird flew away.

"Saya?" he asked, dark eyes staring upward as he released the bird and watched it fly away. "My child?"

((●))

I woke up as hard as I had entered Dreaming. The weight and substance of my physical body startled me. I jolted, then felt Ruta jerk behind me. She was still nestled against me. I sat up and stared at her. My mouth was open, blood pounding in my ears.

"I saw my father," I gasped. Ruta sat up, eyes wide.

"Do you know him?" she asked.

"I was born by Night Bird. I've thought that my whole life." My hand went up to touch my necklace before I remembered I no longer had it. I stood, pacing back and forth.

"Saya." Ruta's voice was tender. Her eyes shone with empathy.

"My necklace." My hands went to my chest, and I searched for the grief I was sure would come, but I felt nothing except the absence of the protection's familiar weight.

"Kinet went to see if the bird was nearby or if it dropped the necklace. We can return home. You're shaken."

"I wasn't born by Night Bird," I said. "I had a father." I pulled at my hair, my hands desperate for something to do. "Celay lied to me about my father! I saw him. He loved me, Ruta. I felt it. He was making an offering for my protection."

"You have to ask her. She can't hide this from you," she said, standing and dusting off her tunic.

"Why would she hide my father from me? Did she trick him? She said she almost died when I was born; that's why she has bad hips. When did she leave?"

"You have to ask her," Ruta repeated. "I can come with you. Kinet too."

I nodded, tapping on my chest where the necklace usually hung. Ruta put an arm around me and led me back.

《 《 ● 》 》

Celay wasn't home. Ruta heated the food Kinet had brought over earlier and made me an herbal infusion. Kinet stayed searching the area around the temple, looking for my protection. I was unable to respond to most anything Ruta said. After a while, she just sat beside me. She didn't touch me, didn't speak. It was what I needed. I kept thinking back to the man in the Dream, how I knew, I knew in my bones and blood, that he was my father. He wasn't a masked acolyte, he wasn't someone making a sacred offering. He was a man who knew my name. And loved me. I held my head in my hands and rocked back and forth. Ruta asked if she could soothe me, and I let her rub my back. I don't know how much time passed, but too soon, Celay entered.

I stared up at her, and she flinched. Her eyes went to my neck and widened.

"Your necklace, Saya, you need to put it back on." Her voice was low, edged with a threat.

"Who is my father?" I asked, standing. Ruta stood beside me. Celay glanced at Ruta, then back to me.

"You were born by Night Bird. Saya, where is your protection?" Celay said in a carefully measured voice.

"No," I said. "I was not born of Night Bird. Who is my father?"

Celay flinched. I felt a surge of power. Something had frightened her.

"Saya, you need your necklace," Celay said. Ruta stepped in front of me.

"Saya's necklace was stolen today." Ruta's voice was cheerful, as if she was teasing. Celay put her hands to her mouth, and for a moment, I thought she was going to vomit. She stared at me.

"Who? Who stole the necklace? Did someone come through while I was away? Why didn't anyone tell—" She was frantic; it unnerved me and made me even more resolute.

"A bird stole my necklace, Celay. Who is my father?" I asked again.

"A bird?" Celay put her arms out as if they were wings. If I hadn't been so angry, I would have laughed.

"A bird. And then I went into Dreaming, and Dreaming seemed very different to me. I went somewhere I had never gone before. I saw a man. He was making an offering. He said my name and I felt his love for me, Celay." I took a deep breath. "Who is he? Where is he? How long has it been since—?" My voice broke. Ruta put her arms around me, glaring at Celay.

"I can't tell you, and you can't ask in Dreaming. Saya, what have you done?" Celay's face contorted, her mouth twisting in a way that terrified me. "What have you done?" she wailed.

"What have you done, Celay?" Ruta stepped in front of me again, placing herself between Celay and me. "What lies have you told your daughter? What lies have you told everyone? We thought you had a gift. It was Saya's the entire time, and you've been claiming it. This is your child, Celay, and you use her for your own benefit. Was the necklace really a protection, or was that another one of your lies?"

CHAPTER NINE

INDIR

Zeri and I rushed past her. We could hear our mother yelling. We found her with our aunts.

"Safi, he is trying to scare us. We know this," Kupi said gently, though I could see she and Ixara both were worried. They glanced at us and held out their hands. My sisters and I joined them.

"We should have seen this coming. Did the Dream not tell you? Have you neglected your gifts? You barely spend time in the temple. You hide your Dreams from me. All you two do is whisper and exchange concerned looks, but when I ask you why, you refuse to say anything. Where do you keep disappearing to? I'm tired of it!" Safi was yelling. Zeri and I stood perfectly still. Delu creeped closer, her mouth open.

"What did he do?" I asked. I held hands with Delu on one side and Kupi on the other.

Ixara shook her head, a look of resignation on her face.

"Alcan invited a Pili as witness," she said.

I went cold, the shock flooding my body.

"They're real?" Zeri asked. "If so, why haven't I seen this in Dreaming? I thought they were a story."

"This one is real." Safi held her hands over her mouth. "There are old traders in the market who confirmed, and then they left the city at once. There are others who are fascinated—of course they are. Alcan has brought confusion to Alcanzeh; he has stories moving through the city about how dangerous we are. The Fire Warriors are charming. They're burning waste, helping the potters with their ovens, clearing dried brush from around the canals, all while asking why these acts of service aren't provided by Dreamers. Nothing of what he says makes any sense, but people enjoy chaos when it doesn't affect them. We're becoming a story before their eyes, and they love it." Safi stopped pacing back and forth. "Bentixa was right. I thought her mind had softened with age. But she was right."

Kupi and Ixara stepped forward.

"Safi, what do you mean? What did our mother say?" Ixara stood directly in front of Safi. My mother wouldn't look at her.

"We'll go greet him." Safi ignored my aunt's question.

"Safi." Kupi's voice was low and dangerous.

"After. I'll tell you after. Let's go see this Pili. We are Dreamers. We have to be strong."

There was commotion at the temple where we were to meet. We heard it even before we arrived. The Avex warriors accompanying us pushed the crowd aside. Some of those gathered were curious, many were upset. I held back while my aunts walked ahead to see what was going on.

A man was yelling at the base of the temple stairs. He was an elder, his tunic worn but clean. He had the tattoo on his face that distinguished him as a trader, though it had likely been many years since he had been on the trade routes. An Avex was trying to calm him. The old man was trying to enter the Fire Temple.

"A Pili! How could you let him into our city? This is a holy place! Pili are false! Do you know what they do? Truly know?" The man was enraged to the point of shaking. He tried to get past the Avex holding him back again but was blocked. The Avex wasn't rough with him but held firm.

"Grandfather, calm yourself." It was Ovis. I stepped closer. My aunts walked past the elder. Ixara reached out, touching the older man lightly on his shoulder, saying something I couldn't hear. The man stared as the Fire Warriors guarding the temple parted to let them up the stairs. Delu followed quickly behind, but Zeri and I stayed back, holding hands tightly, watching.

"You cannot," the old man said, tears running down his cheeks. "You cannot let them into our city. You don't know."

"I know," another voice said. It was Tavovis. He approached the old man. "I know, Kuven." He took Kuven's arm, leading him away. Ovis glanced toward us and turned away, his expression unreadable. I looked down, a drop in my stomach. I pulled Zeri up the temple steps as fast as I could.

My mother, aunts, Lal, and Naru were gathered in the main chamber, standing in a line with their backs to Zeri and me. We joined them. I tried not to shrink back when I saw the Pili.

Alcan and Inkop were standing on a platform with a strange man. He was dusty from the road, but strong. His muscles were clearly defined beneath skin the same brown as ours, but the skin looked as if it was loose, worn. He wore unfamiliar animal skins. His thin legs were scarred with circles and lines, his thin hair hanging from his skull. Even from where I was standing, I could see his face was different from any face I'd ever seen. His cheekbones were high and prominent, almost like the faces of the skull carvings. His nose was long and sharp with nostrils that tapered to a point. He turned to stare at us. I recoiled. His eyes were pale, almost clear, the pupils were dark, tiny points in his face. The man grinned; his teeth were stained a deep orange.

"The Piliti does that to their eyes and teeth," Tavovis whispered. He was standing behind us. "The more the Pili force their way into the Dream, the less color they have in their eyes."

"We are honored, of course, that you accepted our invitation," Alcan was saying loudly.

"Honor," Lal hissed below her breath. She saw me and stepped back so I could stand beside my mother.

"These are the Dreamers, and a Litéx and Ilkan." King Alcan gestured toward where we were standing.

In the fear stories told of them, the Pili were small in numbers but dangerous. They had powers that no one understood, but every land they visited suffered. Drought, strange weather patterns, and poor hunting were rumored to follow the Pili moving through a land. It was unthinkable that Alcan had invited one into Alcanzeh.

The Pili stepped forward. I cringed again when I looked at his face. Though his body said he was younger in years, he had the face of an old man, deeply lined with bags beneath his pale eyes. I heard Lal suck in her breath.

"I am overjoyed to be in your beautiful city. I am eager to add our knowledge to yours as we greet the new cycle together," he said. His voice was deep and slow, his words thick, almost as if he had just woken up. He stood before us, his smile insincere as his gaze traced over each council member and Dreamer. When his eyes reached me, a spark of interest flashed across his features, but it was gone immediately.

My mother cleared her throat. I could see she was attempting to keep calm, but the hairs on her body had all risen.

"This is a sacred city of Dreamers. We were not informed or asked if you could join us. How long do you plan on staying in Alcanzeh?" Our mother offered no formal greeting, nor did she ask his name or offer hers.

The Pili stared at her with his strange eyes. I wanted to close my eyes and return to the Dream forever; it was too much. I swayed and felt a hand press against my back. Lal, close to me, comforting. I straightened my posture and stood firmly, the way Naru did. I felt the fear dissipate a little.

"As long as your king wishes," the Pili said.

"He is not our king yet," Ixara said. "We have not Dreamed him yet. We are waiting for witnesses."

"I have seen him in the Dream," the Pili said. I felt sick.

"You cannot enter the Dream," Safi said, her voice strong.

"He can." Alcan stepped forward. Inkop was right behind him, his posture stiff. He stared at the ground, the furrow between his brows deep. I wondered what he thought of the Pili.

"I brought Piliti with me, and would like him to join you in Dreaming." His eyes moved across all of us. I stood as tall as I could, hoping I looked like a strong Dreamer of Alcanzeh.

"You are not welcome here," Safi said, her voice firm. The Pili opened his hands. Alcan smiled, watching the exchange.

"Alcanzeh is very full these days, have you noticed?" Alcan said. "So many Fire Warriors, all loyal to me. If I say he is welcome here, he is welcome here."

"You are not king yet," Kupi said.

"My father was king, and I was born with the mark. It is enough," Alcan said. "My Fire Warriors have Alcanzeh surrounded. I do what I want."

Chaos. I tried to remind myself to trust the Dream, but I felt the Dream had failed me, exiled me, abandoned me, abandoned all of us. The grief was acidic in my body, but I swallowed it down the best I could. I wanted to be as strong as my aunts, as Naru and Raru. I wanted to be strong in a different way than my mother was strong.

"I believe," the Pili said, his breath fouling the air we breathed, "you will be surprised at what I have been able to see in the Dream."

"We won't hear it," Safi said. "We're leaving." She turned, and the rest of us followed. I glanced back. Inkop was staring at me, as if in warning. I hurried to follow the others.

"See you in Dreaming," the Pili called after us.

((●))

The Temple of Night was quiet. Workers sensed our upheaval and stayed out of the way. Lal was Singing over an infusion she had prepared. Zeri was crying in the corner. Delu looked bewildered. My aunts and mother were staring at each other.

"Do you still think moving toward peace with Alcan was the right decision?" Kupi asked, eager to exchange strong words with my mother.

"Do you think I had a choice?" my mother said back, her voice low with venom. She paced back and forth, stopping to take deep breaths before moving again. Kupi opened her mouth to speak, but Ixara quieted her with a look.

"The Airan and Litéx will be here soon. We have the Ilkan, the Avex, the people in the city," Ixara said, trying to bring my mother to a place of calm.

"He has more warriors than we do," Safi said, shaking her head. "And we let him into the city. We had an arrangement; the people will see he defies his word."

"The Fire Warriors are charming on their best behavior. Already stories move through the city about how they belong here, have always belonged here. There are many excited about the prospect of a sacrificial Game," Tavovis said. "The Fire Warriors have convinced them. What is new is always exciting, even when and especially when it's dangerous. The inhabitants of Alcanzeh have always known peace; they can imagine nothing else."

"Are the people so foolish they don't realize the Fire Warriors don't have a name? That it was taken from them?" Safi wailed. I felt bile rise in me and tried to swallow hard. Lal clucked gently and rubbed a hand over my back, her low hum reaching and calming me, barely.

"Chaos comes," Delu said.

"We know, Delu," I said, frustrated. "We all feel it." I gagged, my body attempting to reject the fear that flooded me.

"Indir," Lal said gently. "I think you should go to the Water Temple and soak in the healing waters. I can feel your distress."

My mother turned.

"Are you unwell?" she asked. Her eyes seemed wild, as if nothing was making sense to her. I nodded. "Go, heal what you can, while you can. Chaos comes."

The healers of the Water Temple were gathered on the steps to Sing the sunset Song of those who had returned to the Dream. I went around to another entrance, one used by temple workers to bring in food and other supplies. A few Water Temple workers were whispering to themselves; they seemed nervous. They looked at me but didn't say anything. The air of the Water Temple was warm, heated by the steaming waters that ran beneath. I peered into a few of the main healing waters, but there were others there. I moved toward the smaller pools, with hotter water. A healer came out and asked if I needed her to assist me. I said no and kept going. I went to one of the smallest pools, where there was a cutout star-shaped hole in the wall, faint light streaming in. Oil lights were set at intervals around the pool.

I slipped off my tunic and entered the healing waters, sighing as the heat wrapped around my body. The water was almost too hot. I could smell Ayan smoke from somewhere in the temple. The evening Song echoed through as the sun set. I breathed deeply, stepping down another step, then lunged forward with a gasp. The water was hot, shocking me enough that the feeling of illness left my body, or at least, I wasn't aware of it any longer. I dipped my head back and let the heat soak my skull. I closed my eyes and floated with the sounds beyond, now muffled.

I didn't want chaos. I didn't want any of the story I found myself a part of. I felt unsafe, as if a layer of my skin had been removed and I was new and raw. Again, I tried to enter the Dream. I begged with everything I had. Nothing. I moved to the edge of the pool, leaning my forehead against the lip. I had to practice being brave, trusting the Dream and what had been chosen for me, even if it was loss. *Trust the Dream. Trust that what is to be yours, will be yours,* I repeated the words to myself.

"A gift," a voice said. I looked up, and any healing that had come from the waters disappeared.

The Pili stood at the entrance of the chamber. He was wearing only a tunic around his waist. His hair was wet, as if he had been soaking. His ribs showed; I swore I could make out his beating heart beneath. I didn't move, trying to summon the power my aunts moved with. He moved forward, leaving a bowl on the floor.

"A little Piliti, if you want more interesting Dreams, Dreamer. You can have a taste," he said, as if mocking me. I was full of terror but kept my face as blank as I could, attempting to pierce him with the practiced gaze of disdain my mother and aunts had perfected. He bowed his head and left. I stared at the bowl, curiosity taking over my body.

The Piliti was a root, gnarled and dried. It was as long as my hand. I stared at it. Was it truly a gift? I reached out for it, wondering what he meant when he told me I could have a taste.

Of his type of Dreaming? I wanted my gift back. Was the root a way back? I would do anything for its return. Had my wish been heard and answered? I picked the bowl up. The root was the girth of one of my small fingers.

I wanted it, badly. I wanted to return to the Dream. In all the stories I knew about sacred plants from healers and other stories, the plant chose the person who was to know it. I wondered how much of a taste I would need to enter the Dream again, just once more, to ask why my gift had been taken.

I had to trust the Dream, I reasoned with myself, and hadn't a gift appeared? I was dizzy from the heat of the water around me, the steam rising in clouds in the darkening room. I picked the Piliti up. It looked ordinary. I smelled it; it smelled of nothing but earth. I walked back up the stone steps and sat on a bench that was set up against one wall, wrapping myself in one of the cloths piled in the room.

Chaos was coming, that much was clear. I was already a part of it. I ached for the Dream, for the familiar shifting air, everything made of Song and light and shadow. I put the root into my mouth and scraped my teeth against it gently. The skin of the root broke easily under my teeth, and my tongue went numb where the root touched. I spit it out and rinsed my mouth with water. But the numbness remained.

((●))

I waited. Watched the steam twist and move. The oil lamps danced, their shadows warping into dancing forms on the rough stone of the walls. My eyes began following the pattern of the stones, noticing how each was spaced and aligned. I was seeking symmetry, repetition. I heard laughter from someone in another chamber. I put my tunic back on, covered my hair, and walked slowly through the temple. I left the same way I had arrived, away from the busy main stairs.

Night had fallen while I had been in the healing waters. Torches were lit around the temple. I had never noticed how the torchlight changed the color of the temples at night, the rich saturation of the pigments radiating, the color intensified by fire. I didn't want to return to the Temple of Night. I felt drawn to look at other temples, see what they looked like by torchlight. The lights were calling me, as they did in Dreaming. I followed the lights, the brightest lights, all the lights. Shining.

There were so many lights, piled on top of each other, spiraling, telling secrets only they knew. I followed the brightest to where they led me. Up. Up. I moved the way I did in the Dream, slowly, feeling the air against me, pleased at how the heat from the waters still rose from my skin, reaching for the light.

"Dreamer?" a voice asked. A face I knew. A strange face, strange scars, a beautiful mouth.

"Inkop," I said his name slowly, enjoying the way it moved across my tongue. "Do you see the lights? There are so many lights."

"I don't believe you are in your senses," he said, putting a hand gently on my shoulder, a strong hand, a hand that made fire, made light.

"Show me your fire," I said. Inkop's eyes widened, he leaned forward to sniff.

"What did you eat? Your breath is sour," he asked in a low voice, pulling me away from a room I didn't remember entering. There were more lights deeper in the temple. I wanted to follow them.

"Show me your fire," I said again. Inkop looked behind him at the other Fire Warriors, but I barely noticed them. He held out a hand, and embers seemed to glow from beneath his wrist, pulsing along to this heartbeat. I grabbed his wrist, pulling it closer to my face. Inkop pulled his hand back, cursing in a language I didn't know but felt I understood. I followed his gaze. Someone with bright teeth was moving toward us. The Pili.

"Your king is expecting you," he said. I was fascinated by his teeth. They hadn't looked like that before. He noticed and ran his tongue over them. His tongue was blood red. I recoiled.

"She is unsteady; I will accompany her," Inkop said. The Pili turned and moved deeper into the temple. Inkop held his arm out, wrist up. The embers were back again. I grabbed his arm, staring at him as he led us through the temple. He stopped us when he saw a Fire Warrior he knew, bending and whispering something urgent to him. There was a cutout in the wall that showed a volcano, the earth's blood spilling out, freshly outlined in gold. Inkop pulled me away, his hand firm on my arm. I could sense his heart in his palms, beating quickly. I felt a calm as if just waking or entering the Dream. I wanted to dance, but my body was heavy. I stumbled. Inkop put an arm around me.

He whispered something, but I couldn't make out what he said. His voice came from afar.

Inkop led me to an area open to the night sky, where flames burned in clay pots, surrounding a platform. Alcan lounged on a pallet made of furs and blankets, the Pili beside him. My head kept dropping forward. Inkop said something. I could feel the anger rising off his body in waves; it felt like flames. He moved me to a pallet on the platform, far opposite the others, stacking cushions behind me. Alcan and the Pili laughed.

"Inkop," Alcan said. "Leave us." Fear shot through my body.

"Indir has asked me to stay with her," Inkop lied smoothly, sitting so he was between the others and me. "We don't want to anger the Dreamers any more than we have." His voice took on a tone I hadn't heard before. I believed him, even though I knew I hadn't asked him to stay. Alcan grunted something.

A trio of musicians came into the courtyard as if they had been waiting. My head cleared a little as I stared at them. One began playing a reed flute, notes that were unfamiliar to me. I found myself entranced by the music as it flowed and dipped. A rattle joined in. There was a chant of low voices chasing back and forth, connecting, then moving apart to chase and connect again.

My body felt heavy. I leaned back into the pallet. There were soft animal skins stacked behind me, covered in woven blankets. I let my body sink into the warmth. Another voice spoke; it sounded like Alcan's, but from a distance, laughing. Another voice, harsh and low, came closer to me and was soon beside me, saying my name. A cup of something was brought to my dry lips. I turned my head from Inkop; I could smell him. I tried to resist, but he held my head firmly and put the cup between my teeth. It was water, cold. I hadn't realized how thirsty I was. I drank the entire cup; then Inkop gave me another. I felt the cold water enter me, move through my body. I opened my eyes, not realizing they had closed.

Inkop was in front of me, cross-legged. His back was to Alcan and the Pili. His tunic was an ashen color I had never seen worn before. I reached out to touch it. It was rough woven but soft.

"Like ashes," I said, my voice coming out strained, dry. I stared at his nose: long, starting in a slope between his eyes, angling down. I saw the oil on his face, the sweat. "You look like a bird," I said. The Pili laughed, the sound startling me. I leaned to the side, almost losing my balance.

Alcan was leaning forward, his smile so wide his eyes creased.

"I'm sure you know many interesting stories, Dreamer. Fascinating Dreams. You went into the Dream for my father, didn't you?"

"Alcan, she isn't in her senses." Inkop's voice was a war drum, reverberating in my head and chest. I sat back, the quickness of the movement making my skull feel heavy. My eyes couldn't focus. The Pili laughed. I leaned back against the furs.

"No," I echoed. My head rolled to the side, the flames of the fires burned against my eyes. I closed them for a moment. Inside, I was shouting for help, begging my body to move, to wake up. It wasn't the Dream. Lights churned and split, coming together and weaving themselves into slender shapes behind my eyelids. It reminded me of getting pulled into Dreaming, but it was different, too vivid. I couldn't focus. A weight fell on top of me. I gasped, eyes opening. I tried to move, but my body was as heavy as temple stone.

"A blanket, you're shivering." Inkop's voice sounded like hurricane winds, the rush that built up to a howl. The weight settled on me. "Try to focus on me. I'll keep you—" His words faded as I closed my eyes, exhaling widely through my mouth. I breathed the scent of the animal the blanket was made from. Sunshine, fresh growth. Fear. The knife that cut its throat. I cried out with the animal's pain.

"What did you see?" Alcan's voice made me open my eyes again.

I spoke. I don't know what I said. My voice seemed to belong to someone else. Inkop kept trying to quiet me, but my words kept coming. Whatever I said, Alcan reacted in anger, then a quiet curiosity. He stared at me, but I couldn't focus my eyes on him. He stood, hissing something to the Pili, whose laugh was sharp in my ears as they left, the musicians following. Inkop rose from beside me, calling out something to one of the Fire Warriors.

My head pounded. I was sweating and shaking at the same time. I slipped out from under the blanket that had been wrapped around my shoulders. The air felt cool; I lifted my arms, trying to dry the sweat on my body. I ran my hands over myself, trembling. Nothing hurt. My legs were asleep, so I stretched them out in front of me, wincing as the blood flowed back. I heard loud voices behind me. The Fire Warrior had returned with something. Inkop went to him.

I thought I saw sparks flying off him as he walked back to me. I rubbed my eyes. When I opened them, he was in front of me, offering a cup of steaming liquid. His eyes were wide, his face pale.

"You were not harmed; I swear by the blood of my mother and sister, by the Twin Serpents. May they end my life if I lie. Drink this. You'll feel better." He put the cup into my hands and moved to put his hands on my head to help me drink.

"No, I have it." I pulled away from him, staring at his face. I trusted him, but I didn't know why. It wasn't his oath. When I had been under the effects of the Piliti, I had felt his kindness, his fear for me radiating off him.

A bird, I had called him, before I went into the darkness. I looked at the cup in my hands: the steam coming off the liquid smelled sweet, like nectar, with a spice of herbs underneath. I looked back at Inkop.

"I don't want this." I tried to hand the cup back, but Inkop put his hands up and wouldn't take it.

"It is only an infusion, I swear by fire. You had a bad reaction to the Piliti." He closed his eyes. "I am deeply sorry that happened to you, Indir. His inviting the Pili was a surprise, though I am no longer surprised by anything he does. I stay close to try to stop him. He has harmed me too."

I remembered the musicians playing their strange Song, the lights that had risen and pulled me into them. I looked down at the fur gathered around my hips. The animal. Its memory of grass, then its cry of death. The shaking started again. I pushed myself backward, away from Inkop.

"You'll fall off the platform," he said, voice intent. I was at the edge. I swung my legs off, falling to the stones. I fell, catching myself on my hands, jarring the bones in my arms. My body burned with the impact. My palms were scraped raw.

Inkop turned and strode out of the courtyard. I sat on the edge of the platform. My whole body shook. I picked up the cup Inkop left. I sipped, spilling some down the front of my tunic. Whatever was in the infusion softened my tension. Inkop returned.

"Go to the Water Temple on your walk home. They can tend to your hands better than I. Tell them what happened, Indir, all of it. I'll do what I can from here." Inkop had a salve. I took it and gently rubbed it on my scraped palms. Inkop stood silently, not too close, and handed me two lengths of woven cloth. I wrapped them around my palms.

"What happened? What did they do?" I took a step toward him.

Inkop shook his head, his mouth creasing.

"They did nothing to your body or safety, I swear to you. I didn't leave your side. And you did nothing but answer, if what you said can be called answers, to questions that Alcan asked you."

"What did I say?" I whispered.

"Something about a ball of water, a missing Dreamer, and Alcan," Inkop said, but his eyes flashed away from mine, just for a moment. His gaze turned hard. "Indir, do not return to this temple."

"I'll never return to this temple, not if I'm surrounded by all the Avex." I turned and paused. "Thank you for the salve." I walked out as fast as I could. I had to get home.

《 《 ● 》 》

The temple steps were empty. I was grateful. I paused at the top and stared out over Alcanzeh. My head pounded, but not with pain. I walked down the steps slowly. I had to tell my mother and aunts what happened. They would be outraged. I would have to tell them I ate the root, and why. There would be questions, so many questions. I felt like answering none.

I chose to walk; moving felt better than staying still. I walked aimlessly, down the stairs and into the residential part of Alcanzeh, where people lived, where they held markets. My heart pounded.

I wandered among the streets, through the night market. I passed people laughing, fighting. I passed bodies pressed against each other. I passed elders scolding and gossiping. None knew me. I was just another citizen of Alcanzeh. I circled back around to another set of stairs that led up to the temples. I climbed slowly, head down. Someone was running down the stairs. They stopped just in front of me. I moved to the side to let the runner pass.

"Indir?" a voice asked. I looked up. Ovis. He carried an unlit torch in his hand.

"Ovis." I moved to pass him. He touched me on the arm as I passed. I flinched.

"Are you hurt?" He reached out toward one of my wrapped hands. I drew them closer to my body.

"Scrapes. I fell. I'm going to the Water Temple; the healers will tend to my hands."

"Ah, you haven't heard? The Litéx arrive tonight. Most of the healers have gone down to the sea to meet them. I was going to go myself. They were my mother's people. I feel I should be there." He gestured with the torch. "Let me look at your hands." I pulled them away.

"I apologize; I should have asked you if I could look at your hands." He looked embarrassed. "We can still go to the Water Temple; there are a few healers there, tending the very sick," Ovis offered, smiling.

"You can look at my hands. Let's go to the temple," I said.

He had said "we." I didn't feel like being alone.

CHAPTER TEN

SAYA

Celay didn't speak. No one had ever come to my defense before, and I wanted to scream, cry. I kept as still as I could instead and focused on Celay. She began pacing.

"I left your father as soon as you were born," she said. I stepped forward again so I was closer.

"What about your hips? Didn't I ruin your hips at my birth? How did you get away? Why would you leave him? Who was he?" The questions and rage poured out of me. Ruta stepped back and put her arm through mine, comforting me.

Celay ignored the questions and hurried to where she stored her herbs and plants. She was muttering to herself, tears running down her cheeks. I stood in silence, watching her, waiting for what she would do next. Her thin frame trembled. Celay used her hands to crush dried plants into powder, sniffling the entire time. I didn't know what to say or do. I had never seen my mother so shaken. A part of me wanted to comfort her, tell her it would be okay, but the larger part of me was tired of her lies, her manipulations. Ruta beside me made me feel strong.

"Pour this into water and drink it; you can't go into Dreaming tonight." Celay held a bowl of herbs out to me. I stared at it. Ruta glanced at me and smiled at Celay. She stepped forward, her head bowed. Whatever craved power in Celay softened at Ruta's demeanor. She held the bowl out. Ruta snatched it away, took it to the front entrance, and flung the contents outside. Celay stared. Ruta turned and smiled at her.

"Saya will stay at our home tonight and as long as she wishes," Ruta said. Celay was still staring out the entrance of the house where Ruta had tossed the infusion. "If you try to come for her or create problems for her, I will tell everyone living here and every trader who passes through that you lie. I will tell them you gave me tea to prevent conception when I sought your counsel on how to conceive. I still have the tea as proof, Celay."

Celay sobbed, going to her knees. I noticed for the first time how small she was. I took a step toward her, but Ruta put her hand on my arm. She shook her head. I looked back at Celay, who was rocking back and forth. I remembered the spark that had touched me in Dreaming, the love that had coursed through me, unlike anything I had ever known.

"He loved me, Celay, I felt it. You never have. You didn't even try." I ignored Celay's wails as Ruta led me away.

《 ❰ ● ❱ 》

I moved between grief and rage that evening while Ruta and Kinet sat quietly, allowing me to feel everything I needed to feel. I kept remembering my father's Song, how it seemed to bring me to life, awaken in me something I wanted but couldn't name. I spent most of the evening on my knees, forehead on the floor as I wept for the years of loneliness I had lived. For my necklace. My ignorance. Knowing I had once been loved made me feel even lonelier.

I cried until I was thirsty and dry-eyed. Ruta and Kinet sat on either side of me, rubbing my back and head. One of them scratched their nails through my scalp, soothing me. When my tears stopped, I stayed still, eyes closed. Their hands moved in comforting strokes up and down my spine.

"Can I make you an infusion?" Ruta asked. I nodded. She rose to prepare it while Kinet stayed by my side in comforting silence. I was used to hiding my emotions, but it felt safe to cry in front of them.

"Would you like either or both of us to sleep beside you?" Kinet offered.

"I'll sleep alone," I said. They'd be close by if I needed something.

I drank the infusion slowly before stretching out on the pallet of woven mats. They retreated to their sleeping area behind a grass screen. I tried to stay awake. I had no idea what awaited me in Dreaming.

《 ❰ ● ❱ 》

I landed in my cove, at the water's edge. The colors shimmered more than before; there were Songs in everything if I paid close enough attention. Spirits kept flitting in and out of my vision, disappearing as soon as I noticed them. There was a different quality to the water, currents of light moving within the depths. The sky churned as if stirred. I stared up, mesmerized. The Dream seemed more alive to me than it ever had been before. When I stepped into the water, I felt a rush of love enter my body and pulse. After a moment, the sensation quieted but remained, a low thrum of joy Singing through all of me. I swam out, delighting at glowing schools of fish and smaller creatures that rose to put their mouths to my skin, as if welcoming me home. I laughed. The waters around me laughed in return. The fish turned so they were all facing away from the shore.

A large shape was moving through the water, a deep blue glow with a bright center coming toward me. Even from our distance, I felt the whale-shaped spirit Singing my name. It rose in me, a Song I had never heard before. I opened my voice to Sing welcoming refrains, mouth wide in joy.

Before she reached me, the whale spirit began to shift. Her light grew smaller and more intense until it brightened into a mass that flashed once. She had transformed into a woman. She swam toward me, laughing. I couldn't stop myself. I laughed, swimming toward her. She pulled me into her arms, and I let myself be held as we Sang the same Song, our voices rising until it ended. She pushed me toward the shore. I couldn't stop turning to look at her. She kept laughing until we were out of the water. We collapsed on the beach.

"Saya," she said. Her eyes were dark brown, her face wide, cheeks full. I stared at her face, her body. Our legs were shaped the same.

"Who are you?" I asked.

"We carry the same Song, my child. Call me Tiya. I have been watching you your entire life." Tiya crossed her legs. "You have lived the life you were given as well as you could, even without knowing all of your gifts."

"My gifts? That Song, the one we Sang? How did I know it?" I asked.

"You have more gifts inside you than you can imagine. You aren't just a Dreamer, Saya." She leaned forward and began running her fingers through my hair, untangling it.

"Am I a Dreamer? I can enter the Dream, but calling myself a Dreamer doesn't feel natural." I didn't know why I spoke so freely to her. It had to be the Song, the one we seemed to carry between us.

Tiya threw her head back and laughed.

"You're a Dreamer. You're more." She smiled, her mouth closed and curved.

"I knew you were coming," I said, feeling comfortable. "A spirit told me during another visit a few days ago."

She paused and looked contemplative for a moment. "The message you received, about someone coming for you. It wasn't about me. An offering was completed, and it begins." Tiya gestured up toward the churning sky. "Look, see who else comes."

The center of churning mass seemed to fold in on itself before opening. A light appeared. It was a star. I looked closer and saw it was moving, slowly but clearly. I squinted and saw tails of light streaming behind it. A comet. But it was more than a comet; it seemed intelligent, as if it knew it was being watched.

"What is that? What's beginning?" I asked.

"A promise made," Tiya said. "One from long ago. Nothing to fear."

It was confusing, but I had interacted with spirits my entire life and knew their words often didn't match what they wanted to say. They spoke in riddles that only made sense to themselves. Knowing Celay wouldn't be around to make me tell her what I had seen in Dreaming made me feel lighter.

"What promise?" I asked. The woman pressed her lips together.

"One made of gifts. Now I'll awaken another of yours, if you allow me."

"Yes," I said. I was dizzy, staring at the comet. I felt alive in a way I hadn't since childhood.

Tiya moved so she was before me, face-to-face. She placed her forehead to mine and stared into my eyes. In hers I saw islands, rocky shores stirring a deep blue sea into white froth. Waves hitting the shore and sending rainbows of light up in bright sunshine.

"Open your mouth," she said.

It wasn't a kiss, not in an intimate sense. She pressed her open mouth to mine and blew her breath into me, once, twice, a third time before pulling away.

I stared at her.

"I don't feel different," I said. "What's the gift?"

Tiya laughed a long, loud laugh. It was beautiful, from deep inside her. I opened my mouth, and my laugh matched hers. Our shared laughter felt like Song.

"My Saya. This gift will show itself when it needs to." I tried to speak, but she put a finger to my lips.

She pressed her forehead to mine again, then slipped back into the water, swimming out. Another flash of light, and she was again whale-shaped. She breached, her Song ringing out in the Dream around me as her body splashed down into the water. She swam away, following one of the currents of light until she disappeared.

I jolted awake. Ruta was kneeling beside me.

"I'm so sorry to wake you, but something has happened," she said, her voice trembling.

"Is it Celay?" I sat up, shaking my head. I hadn't been ready to leave the Dream. Celay had never woken me from Dreaming. I was used to waking up and having at least a few moments of space to land back in my body.

"Come." She held her hand out and lifted me. Dogs were barking; it was still night. I heard voices murmuring, children crying. I followed Ruta outside and gasped.

The comet I had seen in Dreaming was in the sky, low on the horizon, its long tail trailing. Ruta put her arm around me. Kinet walked away from a group of people and approached us, voice low.

"Celay came out, looked at the sky, then retreated into her home. No one can get her out, and the people are seeking guidance."

"They seek guidance from a liar," Ruta whisper-hissed.

"It's a promise," I said. They both looked at me. "I saw this comet in Dreaming. A spirit told me it is a promise made long ago."

"You have to tell the people; they're scared," Kinet said. I thought of the spirit who had awakened some secret gift in me. She said my gift would arrive when needed. I didn't want to tell people I was a Dreamer. I shuddered. I had never called myself a Dreamer before, not even in my own imagination. I wasn't ready to speak it aloud. But I could try to bring them comfort.

"I'll speak to them," I said. Ruta raised her eyebrows at Kinet. Kinet nodded and called out to the gathered.

"Saya, Celay's daughter, will speak."

My face warmed. People gathered around me. I swallowed and wished I hadn't said anything. I wondered when my gift was going to show up.

"The comet is a promise made from long ago," I said, voice trembling. I didn't like the way everyone was looking at me. "It is nothing to fear."

"How do you know? Did your mother tell you?" a voice called out from the gathered crowd.

"No, my mother didn't tell me anything," I said, surprised at the heat of annoyance that rose in me when someone questioned my gift. "I spoke with a spirit."

"What did the spirit tell you? How did you speak with a spirit?" another voice asked. There was a tension in the air, a fear. The dogs felt it and barked nonstop.

"She said it was a promise and nothing to fear," I said, looking to Ruta for support.

"How can we trust you?" another voice asked, sounding frantic. Ruta turned to the crowd.

"Kaltin, I recognize your voice. Didn't Celay guide you when you lost your chosen?" Ruta asked. I bit back a smile. I had entered Dreaming to see why Kaltin's chosen had disappeared. She had grown tired of living with rock fragments from his skill as a knife and toolmaker. When I returned, Celay lied to Kaltin that he was in initiation and losing his chosen was a part of it. We received several good knives for the information, and Kaltin's grief turned into curiosity.

"Celay guided me, but we know nothing about Saya. She never speaks," Kaltin said. Others seem to agree. Kinet spoke up.

"Kaltin, what was your mother's skill? Your father's gift? Your sister's?" Kinet asked.

"We work stone, make tools," Kaltin muttered.

"The same gift from the same family, then," Kinet said slowly. "Do you think this is unique? I trust Saya and my chosen does too. We choose to believe her."

There was more grumbling, then exclamations came from deeper in the crowd. It parted. Celay walked forward. Her eyes were swollen, as if she had been crying all night. She looked terrified. She approached me, but Kinet stood between us, eyes sharp on Celay.

"Saya has a gift," Celay said, her voice low. "Listen to her." She stared at me, at the place on my chest where the necklace had always rested. I touched my throat and stared back at her. A part of me wanted to comfort her; another part of me wished to punish her.

"We're safe?" Ruta asked softly once we were back in their home.

"It is nothing to fear," I said.

"That isn't the same as being safe," Kinet sighed.

I stayed awake long after Ruta and Kinet were pulled into sleep, wondering what gift had been awakened within me.

《《●》》

I woke exhausted from the change filling my life. I felt exposed, unsteady without my necklace. I breathed deeply until the fear moved out of my body. I kept thinking of Tiya. I knew her, and she knew me. I smiled, imagining her watching me my entire life. I didn't know how, but I knew I would see her again. I went outside, where Ruta was kneeling next to the cooking fire, stirring something in a pot. She smiled, eyes tired. I knelt beside her and put my hands on her shoulders.

"Thank you, Ruta, for standing with me. For trusting me." I spoke from the same place where I Dreamed. I felt my gratitude rising in me. I hummed a fragment of the Song I had known in Dreaming. Ruta closed her eyes. My hands started to itch, and I left as if I was moving the Song from my body into Ruta's. I heard her gasp softly. I stared at her face: The dark circles under her eyes were disappearing. I pulled my hands away. Ruta blinked a few times.

"What was that?" she said, shaking her head. "Saya, you're the most surprising person I have ever known. What did you do? I barely slept last night, and now I feel rested. Saya?"

"I don't know what I did," I said. It was true.

"How do you feel? It wasn't easy to see Celay appear like a wounded animal to praise you. Will you see her?" Ruta asked.

I thought for a long moment. I wanted information, but I

didn't trust Celay. Her behavior the evening before, when she had spoken for me, had been unlike her. The loss of my necklace had changed her as well.

I thought of the hummingbird who had shown me the temple, and the one my father sacrificed while asking for my protection. I didn't want to see Celay. She would have kept me small and ignorant if she had the choice. I needed time away from her.

"I don't want to see her," I said. Ruta nodded. "I want to return to the temple."

《 《 ● 》 》

A few people stopped to ask me questions, but I gave them the same answer I had the night before. One asked me how I spoke to spirits, but Ruta chased him away. I laughed. When Kinet returned from working the shared garden, we headed to the temple.

"Celay's home looks empty," I said as we passed it. Everything was closed up. Celay hated being enclosed without flowing air.

"Interesting how you call it Celay's home and not yours," Kinet said, smiling. I shook my head and smiled back.

"I don't know how I'll go back there," I said. "I don't trust her."

"You can stay with us. We'll help you build your own home if it's what you want. You can help others, make it your trade," Kinet said.

"I don't know if that's what I want," I said.

"What do you want?" Ruta asked.

"I don't know yet," I said. We stayed silent as we made our way through the growth that led to the temple.

« « ● » »

We spent time in the water. It felt freeing to float and listen to the banter between my new friends. The day was hot, and splashing and playing freed me from the tension my body was used to carrying. Even as a child, I had rarely been allowed to act like one. Most of my play had taken place in the Dream. I shrieked and screamed along with Ruta and Kinet as we chased each other, taking turns to see who could jump further into the pool. Kinet impressed us by swimming down deep to where the current ran, disappearing. I gasped, but Ruta laughed.

"I trust Kinet's instincts, Saya. Look."

Kinet was swimming back toward us and spitting water after surfacing.

"This is part of a river—I saw light at the other end, which means this leads to another cave or temple. Should I swim through and see?" Kinet panted.

I looked at Ruta, who nodded. I nodded back. Kinet took a deep breath and dived under again while Ruta and I made our way to the edge of the pool. Ruta opened a basket she had brought with her, and we ate small cakes made of dried meat and tree fruit. I drank deeply from the cool water, feeling calmer than I had in a long while. I smiled to myself thinking of the Song from the night before. I wondered if it was a part of the gift the spirit had awakened.

"What are you smiling about?" Ruta asked.

"Everything," I said honestly. "A few days ago, I would never have imagined I would spend a night away from Celay. Or that I'd lose my protection. And everything else. I feel lighter somehow, even with the confusion."

"Or maybe not being near your mother or under her control has let you start to discover who you are," Ruta said.

"Were you raised by wisdom speakers, Ruta?" I teased. "Everything you tell me is exactly what I need to hear."

Ruta laughed. "I was raised by many wise speakers, not too many days from here, near the coast."

"Why did you leave?" I asked.

"I met Kinet, and where Kinet goes, I will follow. I can't explain it; there is something between us that calls to each other, always." She looked down at the water, where her chosen was surfacing.

"It leads to a small pond, no temple there, just vines hanging down from the high walls," Kinet said, grabbing a seed cake and devouring it. We lay in the sun a while, drying and letting our meal move through us. I was content. I never wanted the day to end.

Kinet rose and began picking at the carving again. Ruta and I stared at the unearthed symbols. They were old.

"I don't know all of these symbols."

Kinet used a stick to scrape at the dirt and debris encrusting a carving that was higher up on the wall. Dirt tumbled down, and a few spiders scurried away. Kinet stared at the carving, then turned to look at me, eyes serious.

"What is it?" Ruta's voice was low.

Kinet didn't have to interpret the carving; it was obvious. A comet, long tail curving out from its center. I felt my blood grow cold. It had to be a coincidence.

"That's strange," I choked out. Ruta's mouth was open, but then she laughed her beautiful laugh.

"Saya, your face, I wish you could see it." She wiped at her eyes. "I don't mean to laugh, but I truly wonder who you are. Is your story always this interesting?" She went to the carving. "What does it mean?" Ruta asked, shaking her head. "Is there anyone we live among who would know older symbols?"

"My mother knows some, but I don't want her to know this place." I shuddered at the thought. The temple felt personal, sacred, safe. The changes spinning toward me both thrilled and scared me. I was beginning to feel a new way of moving. It felt natural.

"The spider vines will be blooming soon," Kinet said. "This is the season my father will come. He travels sea to sea, north and south. Batuk knows symbols from different peoples. If anyone can read these, it'll be him."

"I hope he doesn't arrive during the next dark moon," Ruta said softly. "We'll be in Night Bird, and he might not wait for us to return from the ceremony. I want him to see this."

"I can ask about him in Dreaming," I offered. "Ask a spirit to see if he is coming and how soon."

Ruta's eyes lit up.

"It won't misuse your gift?" she asked. I put my arm around her shoulders, leaning into her. I was awkward, not knowing how to be affectionate. But I wanted to try.

"I'm offering, Ruta. You shared your home with me, your companionship. I've never used my gift for someone I care about. I've barely Dreamed for myself." I exhaled shakily. I wasn't used to offering.

"Thank you," Kinet said. Ruta leaned back into me, adjusting my arm around her shoulders. We dressed. Before we left, Kinet helped me form a cup from a leaf. I left it at the worn altar, in gratitude for being led to the temple.

《 《 ● 》 》

Celay wasn't home when we passed by. A few of her gossip friends were outside, talking loudly. They shouted at me that Celay was again gone for the night and asked what I had done to upset my mother. Ruta linked her arm through mine and spoke of mundane things, loudly. I shuddered as we passed. There had been something in their gazes that made me uncomfortable.

It was quieter than usual. People gathered, trading ideas and rumors about what the comet could mean. There was a sour feeling in my stomach; I could feel their fear. Kinet left us to trade for fish Ruta wanted for our evening meal. She showed me different dried plants and herbs Batuk brought from his travels, and how she used them. I was fascinated. Celay barely cooked, and when she did, the food was often overcooked and flavorless. Ruta spoke at length on the importance of salt, for preservation and for flavor. We spent the late afternoon grinding several different chiles into pastes, some to be eaten fresh, some to ferment.

Kinet arrived with fish before sunset, and we stuffed them with the paste we'd made. We roasted the fish, wrapped in leaves, over the stirred coals of the cooking fire. As we ate, the evening sky darkened, and the comet emerged near the horizon. Someone had built an offering fire, and the pungent scent of it drifted our way.

"Whatever brings comfort," I sighed. "Or that is what Celay always said."

"They believe the comet is an omen," Ruta sighed.

"I don't believe they're wrong," Kinet spoke in a tone that made me pause. I stared at the comet. For a moment, I thought I heard it Singing, a croon of sleep, rest.

Ruta was humming what sounded like a Song of desire. Kinet hummed back. They smiled and intertwined fingers. Kinet began whistling the Song. Whatever that meant to them, Ruta laughed, then moved to sit between Kinet's legs. Kinet embraced Ruta, whispering into her ear. I watched the tenderness between them with longing. I wanted to know my own. I felt embarrassed. I had no practice in flirting, and I barely spoke to anyone.

"I'm going to see if Celay has returned. If she hasn't, I'll sleep there," I said.

"Do you want us to walk with you?" Kinet asked, starting to rise.

"No, stay. If she's there, I'll return," I said. Ruta squealed out a laugh as I walked away.

Someone was Singing a Song in a language I didn't understand. Voices murmured as people walked back and forth between homes, everyone talking about the comet. When I arrived at our home, it was still empty. I found a coal in the bone ember keeper and made a fire. It was the first time I would sleep alone. I couldn't wait. I sat in front of the altar a long while, burning Ayan blossoms. I placed a selection of offerings out, a sweet root, fresh water, flowers that bloomed only at night. I hummed low to myself, attempting a Song of desire.

CHAPTER ELEVEN

INDIR

Ovis knew the Water Temple well. He led me through it, past the healing pools and up a set of stairs. He left me outside a chamber and went in alone. I heard the murmur of voices and a birthing Song, the woman's voice breaking as she Sang along with the one who attended her. Ovis returned moments later with a bowl full of scented water. He walked me up another flight of steps and then to a small alcove lit by oil fires. I looked at the small space in wonder. I had never seen it before. It was carved with creatures that seemed to move in the flickering light, great and small fish, other animals I didn't recognize.

"Put your hands in the bowl." Ovis held it out. I sat on a stone bench and started unwrapping my hands. The material stuck to the raw scrapes. I gritted my teeth, pulling the material off as slowly as I could. Ovis put the bowl down, took my hands in his, and pulled the material off quickly. I yelped in pain.

"I'm sorry. Sometimes, we are so afraid of the pain that we go into it slowly, not realizing we are prolonging our suffering." Ovis picked the bowl back up and I put my hands in it. The water was tepid.

"Do I have your permission to Sing over your hands?" Ovis asked.

"You know how?" I asked. Ovis smiled.

"The healers have taught me what they can of their gift. I haven't trained as much as I would like, but I know enough. May I Sing?"

I nodded. Ovis leaned over the bowl, took a deep breath, and began humming. The humming was low, deep in his throat; it rose and fell before he opened his mouth and Sang. He Sang intonations instead of words, a comforting melody. I felt my palms begin to itch and tried to move them, but Ovis put a hand on my wrist to stop me. I looked at him as he Sang. His eyes closed, his head fell back, the movement of the Song making the muscles at his neck and his throat rise and fall. My body went still, all thoughts melding into the cadence of his voice. His Song resonated in the entirety of me, relaxing me more deeply than I knew possible. I hadn't realized how tightly I held my shoulders, how I clenched my jaw, until the Song coaxed my body into release.

Ovis finished the Song and moved the bowl away. I looked at my palms. The skin had grown back over the scrapes, leaving shiny white patches of new growth. I flexed my fingers. The skin on my hands was a little tight, as if I'd spent too much time in water, but the pain was gone.

"Thank you," I said. I tasted salt. I put my hands to my face, feeling tears. I wiped at them with the blood-stained bandages I didn't need anymore.

"Would you like to walk to the sea with me? Come greet the Litéx?" Ovis poured the water from the bowl into a turtle shell–shaped basin, then set one of the oil lanterns into the water, where it sputtered and burned out.

I touched my fingers to the new growth of skin. My first instinct was to go home, return to the temple, give into my exhaustion and sleep. But going home meant I would have to tell my family what had happened. I wanted more time before I had to face them.

"Yes."

((●))

We didn't end up using the torch Ovis carried. The light from the swelling moon was enough. We walked in silence as we left the edges of Alcanzeh. It wasn't cold, but I wished I'd carried a covering with me. After we left the Water Temple, some fear and tension crept back into my body, enough that I wished there was something I could wrap myself in. Ovis walked beside me, his shoulder occasionally brushing mine. As we approached the path that led down to the sea, Ovis stepped off the main path to one I hadn't noticed.

"Are you feeling brave? I want to show you something, and it requires some bravery," Ovis said, a smile playing in his eyes. I couldn't stop myself from smiling back.

"I am," I said, wondering if the Piliti was still affecting me.

Ovis veered into the thick swath of jungle. I followed, elbows out to keep the plants from knocking me over. Ovis pushed through ahead of me.

"Here." He parted the growth and beckoned. I gasped.

We were on a small cliff at the edge of the sea. Beyond us, moonlight shone on the water. The tide was out, widening the beach. The sand shimmered white below us. I looked down at my feet to see we were standing on cut stone. I noticed more were tumbled around us, some broken.

"What is this?" I asked, reaching out to touch a block. It was rough, weatherworn.

"An old building or temple, from another age, I'm sure. There are remnants of past ages all over," he said, sitting on a stone.

I sat opposite him, considering him in the moonlight. He was slender but muscled. His long hair was braided into a single tight braid, the end wrapped in red leather. I had heard Avex carried knives in their braids.

"Do you have a knife in your hair?" I asked. Ovis laughed, pulled the leather wrap off the braid, and unwound his hair. It hung more than halfway down his chest.

"I carry no weapons, Indir."

I turned my head to look out over the water. Something caught my eye. I stood.

"Is the sea glowing?" I stepped up on the stone block I'd been sitting on. Out to sea, there was a patch of green, glowing water that looked as if it was moving on its own.

"Ah, time to be brave!" Ovis stood and walked to the edge of the cliff.

"I'm brave, but don't think I am jumping-off-a-cliff brave." The beach below was far enough that I shuddered, thinking how no Song could undo the damage from a cliffside fall.

"The ancestors who lived here before, who carved and cut these stones, made canals to carry water or waste out of their city." He squatted at the edge of the cliff and beckoned me over. I knelt beside him.

A stone canal was embedded in the cliff face, snaking down to the beach. It was worn smooth by generations of water coursing down it.

"How do you know about this?" I touched the stone canal. It was wide enough to sit in.

"All children of Alcanzeh know about the cliff canals. One of the mysteries all children get to explore, even though our elders try to warn us away. Years ago, a child died sliding down one of the canals."

"Then it isn't safe?"

"It was a sad set of circumstances that led to the child's death. He was here alone, and it was raining. He hit his head." Ovis shook his head.

"He returned to the Dream."

"He drowned in water a hand deep at the bottom." Ovis opened his hands in surrender. "But we are not alone, and it isn't raining. And the Litéx approach." He gestured to the glowing patch of water, which had come closer. I nodded. I wanted to slide down the cliffside, do what every other child from Alcanzeh had done before. I wanted to be brave, not for Ovis but for myself. I moved to sit on the lip of the stone canal. Ovis moved in front of me.

"Let me go first, Indi. If there is debris on the canal, I'll hit it instead of you. I'll wait for you at the bottom." He sat on the canal edge, grinned, and pushed himself off. He slid slowly at first, but then he was off, whooping and laughing in the darkness. I grinned.

I heard Ovis grunt as he arrived at the beach. I wrapped my braid around itself so it wouldn't get caught on anything and pushed off.

The stone was cool and smooth, sloping sharply down. There was a fine dusting of sand beneath me, moving with me. I couldn't stop smiling, feeling the air rush against my face. I squinted and let out my own small whoop, riding up on the side at the turn, then leveling out. I was laughing and speeding along when the canal abruptly ended, sending me flying out onto the beach. Arms grabbed at me just before I slammed into the sand, swinging me around to slow my momentum.

We didn't fall, but I staggered against Ovis. He stepped a few paces back, holding tight to me as we both regained our balance before he released me. I was still laughing from the exhilaration of flying down the cliffside. I looked up at him. His smile shone in the moonlight, taking over his entire face. He looked like a completely different man, joyful. His careful Avex posture loosened. He cleared his throat. The end of my laugh came out as a sigh. I put my hands to my cooled cheeks. I was dizzy with everything that had happened to me. I wanted desperately to hold on to the joy I was tasting. It was the strangest day I had ever known.

"Was there anything like that in your temple when you were growing up?" he asked, kneeling to open a pouch at his waist. He took out a pair of stones and a blackened slab of tile. He crumbled a bit of dry tinder on the tile before striking the stones to spark, urging a small flame. The torch sputtered, spit, and took light. The burning resin on the end had a sharp green scent.

"Nothing like that. Not even going into Dreaming feels like that." I inhaled deeply. The smoke, the salt in the air felt comforting. I felt strangely at peace. I wondered if it was an after-effect of the Piliti, but pushed away the thought.

"You'll have to tell me more about going into Dreaming one day. I'm curious, and there are so many stories about the Dreamers." He led us down the beach, walking close to the water's edge. Further down the beach, there was a fire burning, a welcome beacon for the Litéx. People were gathered around it, facing the sea.

"Stories? What kind of stories?" This was another reason I stayed close to the temple. Dreamers were whispered about as we passed. It made me deeply uncomfortable to think there were stories about me in the world, stories that grew without truth.

"Oh, you know, Alcanzeh rumors. This is a city made of stories; surely you know that. And any of us who happen to stand out, by birth or circumstance, are subject to the stories. I hear stories about myself, how I drove my brother away from Alcanzeh in shame after I beat him at wrestling and then wept for days."

"Did you do those things?" I hoped that if I kept him talking about himself, I wouldn't have to answer his question about Dreaming.

"I cried when he left. Tixu is my brother. I had never lived away from him. He was my closest friend. He wanted to leave, see lands he had heard tales of from the storytellers. He left years ago. I hope he returns. My father senses his moving closer, but I do not." Ovis moved his mouth a few times before continuing. "But I didn't drive him away. We would die for each other, gladly, if it meant the other would live."

"Do the stories bother you?" I would have been bothered.

"No, though they used to. I'm sure Dreamers also have to learn to live with such thorns. I don't believe you go into Dreaming to give yourselves to spirits to stay young and beautiful."

"What?" I stopped and put my hand on his arm. He turned to me, a small smile on his lips.

"You never heard that one? As old as Alcanzeh herself. I know it isn't true." He paused and tilted his head to the side. "Or is it?"

I was perfectly still for a minute before I realized he was teasing me. I made a face and kept walking. He caught up, putting his hand on my shoulder to stop me. His face was serious once more, his eyes steady on mine. I couldn't look away.

"Indir. There are more dangerous rumors." His voice was low.

"That in the Dream we can see who can and cannot be trusted?" I wondered if he was still teasing.

"I hope you see that in Dreaming, but I meant the whispered story about you."

"I don't know that one." I stared at the sand, feeling slightly dizzy. It hit me all at once. The day had been overlong, full of too much. I wanted to lie down on the sand and sleep.

"It is whispered you went into Dreaming for King Anz just as he died," he said. My shoulders slumped slightly.

"I did."

"And you'll tell no one what he asked you to seek in Dreaming."
His eyes were serious.

"He asked me not to," I said.

"There are other rumors," Ovis began. I walked away from him, heading toward the fire further down the beach.

"I don't care for stories that aren't true," I said when he caught up to me.

"What if the story being whispered is that Alcan isn't truly to be king?" Ovis asked. I stopped, remembering what King Anz had asked: if his child bore the mark. I hadn't seen Alcan's mark in Dreaming; he had burned his chest. I had seen the mark, in a sphere of water and light, but then he had stabbed me, making the other parts of the Dream seem less important.

"What are you saying?" I asked, my heart starting out its familiar pounding.

"Only this: Be cautious with Alcan. If I've heard the rumors, then he has too."

((●))

The rest of our short walk to the fire was in silence. I led, walking quickly despite my exhaustion. There was nowhere, it seemed, I could go, or anyone I could be with for distraction. I wanted to return to the days before King Anz died, when all I had to do was Dream when called to, describe my Dreams, interpret them, and spend the rest of my days painting and helping run the temple.

"Indir!" My aunts were, not surprisingly, at the fire, waiting for the Litéx. I joined them. Kupi put her arm around my shoulder and drew me in.

"You looked tired, sweet love," Ixara said, running her hand over my face. I turned my face toward her touch.

"The day has been moons long," I sighed, letting my body lean against Kupi's. It felt good to be held by familiar arms. Ixara stepped in close and put her cheek against mine. I loved the comfort of their soft bodies, how when they pressed against me, I felt enclosed by warmth, heat, safety.

A Song came on the breeze. Voices gathered with it, chanting in rhythm, another voice Singing a melody high above it. Everyone moved to the water's edge. Small waves broke over their feet and knees. I let go of my aunts, stepping into the water to watch the Litéx arrive.

The glow in the water was moving closer, running deep beneath the surface, as if the boats above it were giving off lights of their own. I could make out figures in the boats, tall, thick women in sleeveless tunics. Singing. A shape leaped out of the water, and I gasped along with the others on the shore. The vessels were surrounded by a family of porpoises, their gray bodies skimming the surface of the water, diving down, then jumping out, as if racing the boats. I moved deeper into the water until it was at my hips, just past where the small waves crashed. I saw other shapes, oblong dark shadows, swimming directly beneath the boats. Sea turtles, I realized; the symbol for the Litéx looked like a sea turtle. As the boats approached the shore, the green lights illuminating the vessels began to come apart, splitting into countless tiny points of glowing green that sank beneath the waves and were carried away with the currents. The beauty of the moment, punctuated by Song and the sweetness of momentarily forgetting the rest of my day, brought tears to my eyes.

A voice rang out behind me, joining in the Litéx's Song. Ovis was in the water, moving toward his mother's people, Singing. He approached the boats and others joined him; most of those on the beach had moved into the water by the time the Litéx approached. The Litéx leaped out of their boats, splashing heavily into the water, laughing. A woman hugged Ovis tightly, and I was surprised to see she was as tall as him, perhaps even taller. Others uncoiled long ropes and hauled the boats out of the water. I stepped back before I could get in the way and moved toward the shore.

My aunts stood on the beach with Lal, the Litéx council member. Tears ran down Lal's lined face as she Sang the final lines of her people's arrival Song. She had braided her graying black hair in the way of her sisters, a large, twisted coil pinned at the top of her head. She held her arms out for each Litéx, touching foreheads and lips. There were twelve Litéx; three had come on each large boat. The woman Ovis had been embracing was the last to come to Lal. She stood and stared at Lal in silence. Everyone went silent, watching. Lal began Singing the arrival Song again, arms held out, and the two women each took a turn touching her forehead and lips. Behind them, Ovis wiped his eyes.

I waited quietly while the Litéx greeted others they knew on the beach, laughing and shouting with joy. The Litéx women had skin that seemed to glow like oiled amber. Some of them had shells and white beads woven into the braids coiled into tall knots. Their feet were wide and bare, and each had a circle of threaded shells and sea stones around their ankles. They wore simple tunics cut wider than the ones in Alcanzeh, each with a length of red and black patterned material. Some wore it as a belt, others wrapped it around their shoulders. My aunts joined me.

"Shall we walk back? They have traveled a long way, and there will be time enough to spend together these coming days." Ixara didn't have to convince me. I yawned as I looked at the sky. It was late. We took the long winding path up the cliffs, and I followed behind my aunts, who walked beside each other, shoulders bumping as we wound our way back to Alcanzeh. We moved without speaking, one of my aunts humming something under her breath.

There were voices talking and laughing in the temple when we arrived. I needed to find my mother, to tell her what had happened. I dreaded it. My aunts followed the laughing voices into a brightly lit chamber. My mother sat with a woman I had never seen before, and Ali of the Airan. He was a kind man who visited our city every few years and stayed in our temple with us. He was charming, funny, and he made my mother laugh, which was rare. He and the other Airan with him were small and slender, their black hair pulled back tightly and pinned at the base of their skulls. Their tunics had hoods that hung from the back and pockets in front. They both had the large eyes of the Airan, sharply sloped noses, and short teeth. They were drinking a fermented drink, their faces loose with joy. Ali rose to greet us, embracing me and introducing his sister, Katalpa. At her greeting, Katalpa grinned wide.

"I like the shape of your face," she said to me. It was a strange compliment. I didn't know how to respond.

"Indir looks exhausted, sister, let her be," Ali said, putting an arm around me. We were the same height, but his bones were smaller. "Indir, I brought you and your sisters tunics from our weavers. I think you will appreciate the new weavings." Ali always brought us gifts when he visited.

"I love mine," my mother said, running her fingertips along a woven sash she had hung around her neck. Her smile looked younger. She was relaxed and happy for the first time in a long while. I could tell my story in the morning.

"I need rest," I said, and it came out sharper than I meant it to. Ixara raised her eyebrows at me, a question in her eyes. "There is something I have to say to you in the morning," I said quickly. "I will sleep now."

I moved out of the room without looking at anyone.

《 《 ● 》 》

Dua, the new temple worker, woke me in the morning after a deep sleep. My entire body hurt. I tried to close my eyes against the light, but Dua rocked my hammock gently.

"Your mother and aunts are speaking of you. I thought you

might want to go down and tell your own story," she said in a serious voice.

I uncovered my eyes. No one ever spoke to Dreamers with such honesty. I was surprised. And exhausted. I groaned, swinging my feet to the floor. Dua handed me a clean tunic and pointed at the basin.

"I brought you fresh water; it's warm," she said. I sunk my hands in the basin. The water was hot. I dipped a cloth into it and washed, the heat reviving me.

"Did you get this from the healing temple?" I asked Dua as she swept the sand from underneath my hammock.

"No," she said. "You should go now." She left.

I re-braided my hair slowly, trying to figure out what I was going to tell my mother and aunts. I didn't know where my sisters were. I hoped they were near so I wouldn't have to face my elders alone.

I knelt briefly at the altar.

"I trust the Dream," I breathed, my hands over the flame, trying to believe my words.

《 《 ● 》 》

I walked into the chamber. My mother leaped up from where she had been sitting. She crossed to me quickly, her hands open.

"Indir," she said, breathless. "We heard something." Her eyes were red, as if she had been crying. Kupi and Ixara stood.

"Safi, let her sit. Get her something to drink, eat," Ixara said softly. Kupi went to the corner, pouring me a cup from the jar and bringing it to me as I sat. My mother handed me a breakfast cake of soaked nuts and seeds. I chewed slowly. They didn't speak. I wondered which part of the story they had heard. I was terrified at how they were going to react.

"Indir?" My mother said. She looked exhausted.

"I lost my ability to Dream," I said.

CHAPTER TWELVE

SAYA

When I arrived in Dreaming, I arrived to a dance. Drumbeats filled the air, a heavy rhythm that resonated in every aspect of the Dream. It pounded in me as if I were a part of it. Around me, spirits in a dizzying array of shapes writhed their bodies. I marveled at spirits shaped like large birds with long, wide feathers that changed colors on beat to the drums. Jaguar-spotted spirits shaped like women leaped back and forth over my head while colorful hairless dogs danced a serpentine dance, darting between my legs. I gasped when I saw a spider-shaped spirit shoot a golden thread out from her body into the sky. Several spirits began climbing the thread, spinning around and around, howling. I had never seen anything like it before.

I couldn't stop myself from joining. I lifted my arms above my head and spun around, feeling sparks against me whenever I brushed up against a spirit. Flowers bloomed around my feet as I danced, opening their wide faces to the night and releasing a heady scent that made me want more. Above us, the comet shone in the sky, higher than it appeared in the Waking World. I wanted more, though of what I couldn't name. The drum-beats intensified and so did our movements. Soon we moved as one, rising and falling, rising and falling. The scents grew stronger. I smelled earth, rain, smoke, ocean salt. The air tasted sweet in my mouth. I opened for more.

"Dreamers never dance with us, or even notice us," a voice whispered in my ear. I spun around to see a mass of dancing lights. I blinked and moved back a few steps, the lights following. "We're happy to have you here; we've been waiting for you."

I dipped my head in gratitude.

"I've been waiting for something. Is this it?" I asked.

"This is part of it, but you should probably move somewhere else in the Dream. This place is one of temptation, and you have no training," the lights said.

"Training?" I stopped dancing, head spinning while others whirled around us. "Are Dreamers trained in Alcanzeh?"

"Yes, which is why they can't go the places you can. They trained it out of themselves." The lights blinked on and off.

I watched the way they shone. They seemed to glow softly on the edges of memory, and somehow, brightly on possibility. I was drawn to them in a way that felt enticing and dangerous. I couldn't look away. I didn't want to.

"Go now, Dreamer, go where you are called." The lights moved until they surrounded my head, my throat, my heart, spinning around and around until I couldn't even remember my own name. And then they were gone, and I was alone.

《 (●) 》

I landed near a body of still water, dizzy. The comet Sang in the sky. I called out a greeting, and a few bird-shaped spirits rose out of the water and floated toward me. I remembered why I was there.

"Batuk the trader, will he arrive soon?" I asked. The three spirits towered over me.

"Tomorrow is soon enough," they crooned in unison. I nodded while inwardly I felt frustration rise. Even without my protection, spirits were still confusing. I didn't know if they meant tomorrow in the Waking World or something longer.

"Will he help me? Or can you tell me what the symbols in the temple mean?" I asked. It was a tricky question, but I wanted to know. I hoped the offerings I'd left were enough for these spirits.

"Batuk has his part in the story." The birds stepped backward into the water and disappeared. I still felt dizzy from the speaking lights. *Go where you are called.*

I closed my eyes and listened. The Dream carried its own music, a vibrating thrum. I listened harder, wondering how to find what or who was calling me. I felt myself being pulled backward and falling. White wounds appeared in the Dream around me. They gathered together to make a web surrounded by a roiling shadow. I recoiled away, wishing I still had my necklace.

When I landed in the web, it disappeared. I was in a jungle, with hills and valleys. I lived on flatlands in the Belly, but there were hills and valleys days away. Again, I was hovering in the air. There was a stone temple rising from the growth, tall with steep steps leading to an enclosed platform. I flew closer to see what was calling me. Flies were buzzing around the platform. I looked close and saw a bowl of dark liquid on an intricately arranged altar. It was surrounded by carvings of different animals: a bird, a jaguar, a turtle, serpents. Ashes encircled other offerings: a long braid of black hair, seeds, water. A small bowl filled with burning oil cast its light. I hovered closer; there was a scent rising from the bowl, another memory I couldn't place. Peering down, I saw my own face reflected in the liquid. It was blood. I opened my mouth to gasp, and my reflection did the same. The mouth in the reflection swallowed the entire bowl, the entire night. Everything went dark.

I landed back in my body. It was deep night, silent but for insects and wind. I pulled my blanket tighter around me, breathing deeply until I was calm again.

《《●》》

I woke before dawn. I lay on my side, grateful not to have to speak of my Dream to Celay. The edge between my terror and joy was so sharp, all I could do was laugh to myself. Dreaming without my protection somehow made the Waking World more tolerable. I rolled onto my stomach and rested my head on folded arms. The pre-dawn light made everything seem blue. I let my mind wander until sleep pulled me in again.

I woke to a joyous greeting Song. It was just after dawn. I went outside and saw Ruta, Kinet, and Batuk. The spirits had been right. I stood for a moment, with a yawn that dropped into a smile. I had seen Batuk twice in my life, once in the place where we lived, and years earlier right before my bleeding started, when Celay and I had lived just near a coastal people. He looked up and saw me.

"Saya," Batuk said, crossing to me, palms open and before him in peace and greeting. I opened my palms to match his. He embraced me. I returned the embrace, the action starting to feel natural. "My children tell me there is a story you're living I should know."

Batuk listened while we ate a meal Kinet prepared and served. Ruta sat by my side, her hand on my back. It wasn't an easy story to tell. I felt shame for having helped Celay betray people she had been asked to help. Batuk's eyes widened, then narrowed on me in focus when I told him about how my protection necklace had been taken. When I told him about seeing my father, Batuk whistled low and long, shaking his head.

"And last night, three bird-shaped spirits told me you were arriving. Will you come to the temple and see if you can read the symbols?" I asked.

"I'll come," Batuk said. "None of your story surprises me. The stories from other lands are disturbing. A cycle is ending," Batuk said. "We are protected more here in the Belly, but beyond, there is hunger, a growing imbalance. The stories say even Alcanzeh suffers."

"I was told you have a part in this," I said, feeling strange. I wasn't used to sharing my Dreaming with anyone but Celay. I felt a surprising shudder of longing. I wondered where she was.

Batuk's eyes lit up, the wrinkles around his mouth creasing as he grinned.

"I'm honored. I've never met a Dreamer before, even when I lived in Alcanzeh when I was very young. They kept to themselves, and there was so much trading to do. I never visited the Temple of Night. A regret," Batuk said. "How soon can we leave to see these symbols? I want to help, in any way I can."

《 《 ● 》 》

A few people stopped us, asking Batuk when he would begin trading. He brushed them aside, arms around Kinet and Ruta. The morning air was heavy, smelling of rain. I saw clouds high above, and near the horizon, darker clouds. I tested the wind with a wet finger. The rain might not make it to us, but if it did, it wouldn't be until after midday.

I was silent most of our walk, letting Batuk tell of his journeys. He made Ruta laugh in a way I hadn't heard her laugh before, and I wanted to make Ruta laugh like that, but I didn't know how to be funny. Celay had never been funny, unless it was something unkind and cruel. Ruta's laugh was one from a place of kindness and play. I wanted more of both in my life.

Batuk whistled high to low when we entered the temple, walking slowly down the stairs. I watched him walk around in a circle, tracing his fingers over the carvings. He traced his finger over the comet image Kinet had uncovered, then took a small knife from a pouch at his waist. We had been so taken with the carving of the comet, none of us had cleared the carvings around it. Batuk used his knife to scrape away at the roots and dirt, blowing it away and wiping his fingers. He asked Kinet for water, which he then splashed over the cut stone, revealing a carving we hadn't noticed before. Two serpents, intertwined but with a line connecting their mouths. Batuk stepped back and stared. There was something about his posture that made me nervous.

"I've walked the trade routes almost my entire life, and I have seen many symbols of the Twin Serpents. I've never seen this one outside Alcanzeh." He glanced at me, and I shivered. "Saya, you say you saw the comet in Dreaming? And you visited Dreamers?"

I nodded. I didn't feel I could speak. The air around us seemed charged with tension. I could only focus on Batuk. Ruta and Kinet faded in my vision.

"This is the symbol for Dreamers, Saya, below the symbol for loss, or forgetting. And the comet—" Batuk waved his hands over it. "This story may be about you."

"How?" I asked. We leaned against the wall, Batuk facing me. His face was kind, sun worn with lines and creases. He spoke gently.

"You're used to your mother interpreting your Dreams for you. Listen, watch, trust yourself. You'll know," he said.

"I don't understand why everything is changing now." I pressed my cheek against the wall, the stone cool against my cheek.

"You no longer wear the necklace," Kinet said.

Batuk furrowed his brow.

"You say a bird took it?" he asked.

"I had never seen a bird like that before, Batuk. Kinet tried to stop it, but it seemed to know what it wanted," Ruta said.

"Have you asked in Dreaming?" Batuk used his knife to keep clearing around the Twin Serpent carving.

I thought for a moment. I remembered the spirits not answering when I asked. I shook my head.

"I don't think they'll tell me," I said, touching my neck. I couldn't stop feeling for the necklace.

"Then there is nothing to do but continue," Batuk said.

"Continue what? I haven't been doing anything." I tried to keep the impatience out of my voice.

Batuk grinned.

"Patience, little Dreamer, what is to come, will come."

((●))

Another day passed, and there was no sign of Celay. My Dreams were quiet. A part of me was worried, another part of me relieved Celay hadn't returned. I didn't want to see her, even though I somehow still missed her. She had been the one constant in my life, but my days were fuller now than they had been before. I tended plants and practiced cooking with Ruta. Batuk spent his days trading and his evenings storytelling.

Many gathered to hear his tales of far-off lands, the strange animals he had seen. He told of seeing an Ilkan, a jaguar woman.

"She walked in power and on the trade route, which was strange. There are few Ilkan left in this world, and they keep to themselves. She was dressed for travel. I met her in a market higher in the Belly. I understand the stories now, of how the Ilkan once roamed all over many lands and kept the peace. She was impossible to ignore, though some of it was out of fear. The strangest thing was that she seemed to be smelling everyone she crossed paths with. I don't know what scent she was seeking, but I hope, whoever it is, she is not seeking revenge."

I was fascinated. I had seen jaguar spirits in Dreaming, but they had always been elusive, staying at the edges of my vision and disappearing when I placed my attention upon them. Batuk told story after story. Some were frightening—droughts and hunger edging into lands they hadn't touched in generations. I sat beside Ruta and leaned into her, now more comfortable with her affection. She was joyous; the dark moon was coming, and Ruta and Kinet were soon leaving for their Night Bird ceremony. Kinet laughed at Batuk's jokes louder than anyone.

"Will you join us for Night Bird?" Ruta asked. I pulled away to smile at her in wonder. I had never been invited to a sacred ceremony before. "We leave the morning after next. Batuk will join us. The ceremony will be just Kinet and me, but this healer invites families to bring offerings as part of the ritual. If you say yes, know that the day before the dark moon must be one of joy, in preparation." Ruta smiled at the look on my face, my mouth open in surprise.

"I would love to join you. Thank you for inviting me." I embraced her, and she called me family. I missed Celay, but we'd never felt like family. Ruta and Kinet were offering me more.

((●))

I slept deeply without Dreaming that night and spent the next day preparing a pack, trading infusion blends for travel cakes. I asked, but no one had seen Celay. Every time I remembered my father's face, anger would flood me. I was content she wasn't around, but I wondered where she was, if she'd ever return. I filled a traveling pack with a sleeping blanket, water-skins, travel cakes, coverings for my feet, and medicinal herbs as gifts for the healer.

We left early the next morning, heading deep into the jungle on a path I had never walked. It had been seasons since I had traveled; I had never enjoyed it. Celay always seemed nervous, moving us fast. Batuk kept a steady pace but nothing intolerable. His pack was laden and hovered over his head. No wonder his legs were so strong. Kinet had the same legs but carried a smaller pack, as did Ruta. We laughed and talked, then lapsed into long comfortable silences. We passed a few others on the path, but I was shy with strangers, though Batuk was charming and procured us fresh fish for our evening meal. We set up in a clearing, eating our fish and contemplating the comet moving low in the sky. I slept deeply.

That night, for the first time in my life, the Dream felt unsafe. The comet hung in the space, its low Song vibrating in a tone that resonated up and down my spine. I didn't like the sensation and tried to will myself somewhere safe. I landed in the cove.

I thought of Wotal and was going to call out to her when a scream ripped through the space. The comet dimmed some. I twisted where I floated, calling out for safety. Instead, the scream elongated until it sounded like a shrill whistle. I grasped at my chest, wishing I still carried my protection.

I thought I heard a drum, but it sounded unlike any drum I had heard before, either in the Dream or Waking World. It almost hurt to listen to. Shadows seemed to move around me though I couldn't make out their shape or texture; instead of the ecstasy I felt when I had landed in the spirit dance, there was pain, agony. It brushed against me, and I recoiled and screamed inside my own head. It hurt me in a way I didn't know I could hurt, as if it was pulling my blood, my memory out of myself and destroying it.

Then a face, biting violently through the layers of Dream. Not a Dreamer, not a spirit. A man. His face was gaunt, stained white, and his eyes terrified me. They were almost all white, with tiny red pupils in the center. He opened his mouth to speak, and the stench of rot spilled out, as if his blood was poisoned and festering.

"You exist," he hissed, showing a row of frighteningly straight and filed-down teeth, "you're unprotected." He licked his lips. Beneath the drum, I heard the Song of the Comet, like a heartbeat coming to drown out everything else. The Dream seemed to tremble around him, white cracks appearing. I could feel spirits trying to reach us, but they were somehow held back. The Song rose again. I began humming it deep in my throat, as low as I could. I felt the Song as it moved through me, exploding outward from my throat in a rush of light. The man recoiled. The Dream closed shut around him. I stared at the tear. It was the largest wound I'd seen. The Dream moved toward it and tried to heal it, but it remained, a white scar hovering in empty space, smaller scars joining it.

I sunk my chin deep into the water, spirits crowding around me and placing their mouths to my body.

"What was that?" I gasped, shaking.

"Danger," the spirits said. "See the wound."

I walked out of the water, staring. Tiny lines seemed to extend out from it, thin as hair. I saw they were white cracks. Nothing in the Dream seemed able to get close.

"The Dream is wounded every time they enter," a voice said. Yecacu was on the beach. I was surprised. I had never seen her outside her strange meadow. The frog spirits on her ear chirped a greeting at me.

"Badly?" I asked. One of the frog spirits lifted its wings and rose toward the wound. It tried to get close but failed. It flew back to Yecacu in staggering motions.

"Where there is a wound in the Dream, there is weakness. We can still shape ourselves from what is broken, but it changes us. They break in more and more, uninvited, and change comes faster." Yecacu motioned at the comet. The tired frog spirit closed its eyes.

"Who are they?" I asked.

"We don't speak their name, Saya, but you will learn it. You have to. You have to keep them out," Yecacu said. "When the Dream is wounded, the Waking World is wounded as well. We weaken together, we strengthen together."

"How do I keep them out?" My heart pounded. The pain emanating from the man made me feel as if I was breaking, weakened by his presence.

"Small choices, Saya, toward what you want. I chose not to tell you how to use the root, and now you Dream for yourself and not that woman."

"Do you have a story for me?" I tried to ask in the way my mother had taught me.

"The Dream is changing, Saya, as the Waking World changes. You're a part of that change. It is your gift." She faded away.

I waded back into the water and sunk to my knees. I didn't feel ready for more change.

((●))

I woke up to Kinet and Batuk Singing a morning Song. I couldn't speak what I had seen in the Dreaming, as it was the dark moon. Ruta had to be prepared in joy only.

I joined my voice to their morning Song, hoping it wasn't too strained. I poured water for Ruta, feeding her the morning meal. Kinet wove flowers through Ruta's hair, kissing her gently on the lips while Batuk lifted Ruta's pack onto his own. It would be a day of preparing the nest for the Night Bird to bring the child they wanted. I noticed Batuk watching me as I packed up to move on, humming the morning Song. My face must have revealed my fear.

"The day is young and the walk isn't far. Saya and I will walk ahead so you may have more time to prepare the nest," Batuk said, eyebrows raised at me.

Ruta and Kinet barely seemed to notice. Kinet was massaging Ruta's feet while Ruta leaned back, biting her lip in a smile that sparked an ache in me. I wondered what it would be like to join their family. I thought of watching Ruta grow with child, Kinet taking care of her, me helping.

"Saya?" Batuk was walking ahead. I caught up, and we walked until we were out of hearing distance. The narrow traveling path was shaded by trees and vines that met overhead. I could hear running water nearby. To calm myself, I concentrated on what I could sense. I heard the birds and insects, the grunts Batuk let out while adjusting the packs. I smelled the damp morning earth, the fungal scent of spider vines blooming. I watched patterns of light dance on the ground ahead of me, trying to match my feet to where the light was moving. It reminded me of the Dream. I shuddered.

"Is there a story you want to tell?" Batuk asked in a calm voice. I saw he was looking up, eyes unfocused as the sunshine grew stronger.

"Something, or someone, tore into the Dream last night. I don't know how, but there was a man, his face painted white. He saw me. He said I was unprotected. It was terrifying, Batuk. He wounded the Dream. A spirit I know told me the Dream is changing, and I'm part of it, somehow. I have to keep them out." My words spilled out faster than I wanted. Batuk inhaled sharply. He stopped and put one knee down on the earth. He pulled out a pouch of something I didn't recognize and sprinkled it on the ground.

"Protect our path." Batuk pulled a hollow bone tube from his belt and shook out the damp grass that enclosed a live coal. He touched a piece of dried grass to the coal, then lit the powder on fire. It soaked up briefly, blue and green flames.

"What was that?" I asked when the flames had burned out. Batuk was scooping the coal back into the bone.

"A little protection for us." He kept walking. I followed.

"What was it? Or who? Am I unsafe without my protection?" I looked around us, imagining the shadows around me were hiding those who wished me harm.

"I think there are places in your story where you'll know fear. That's true for all of us." Even in conversation, he spoke like a storyteller. I wanted answers. Batuk shook his head.

"Not before the ceremony, Saya. For now, we stay in joy, for Ruta and Kinet. Do you know any traveling Songs?" he asked. I shook my head no.

By the time Ruta and Kinet caught up with us, Batuk and I were exchanging verses to a Song about a bird who migrated the wrong direction. It was the first traveling Song I learned.

《 《 ● 》 》

We arrived late in the afternoon to where the ceremony would be held. There were more people than I had imagined. I held back shyly as everyone made introductions. There were families of every shape and with as many reasons for attending. I watched a woman who was offering to nest for a family whose bodies didn't birth; she was adorned in so many flowers, I could barely see her face.

Everyone was excited and nervous. The healer had a reputation for success, and there was joy in the air as well as anxiety. I saw the faces of families who looked hopeful but restrained, as if this wasn't their first time. Batuk and I set up our sleeping area a little away from the temple where the ceremony would be. Ruta and Kinet went to the temple, where they would begin preparations for the night. Soon after the sun set, an acolyte of the healer gathered those of us who had come to make offerings.

The temple was a square platform, enclosed on three sides but open to the sky. A fire burned in the center. In the shadows, acolytes stood, masked and painted in patterns of seeds, for fertility. The healer was younger than I would have imagined, hair shorn to her skin with geometric patterns scarred across the back of her head. Her eyes were deep-set into her face, her mouth wide. Her face and robe were covered in painted birds. Birds of all kinds, sea birds, hummingbirds, birds that traveled through our skies once a year, birds I couldn't believe were real.

"Your offerings may be placed in this basket," she said, pointing to a large woven basket near the fire. I waited while others placed their offerings of jewelry, tools, different dried foods. I searched the darkened temple until I saw Ruta and Kinet seated against one of the walls on cushions. They both wore robes. I nodded my head toward them, and Kinet nodded back while Ruta kept her eyes on the fire, breathing deeply. Near them, an acolyte was dressed in a bright red robe, bird mask over his face. The mask was painted to appear feathered in every color, and a dark green beak extended past his chin. He stood perfectly still. Softly carved bird beaks were on the small altar beside them, sun-whitened and purified. Hollow reeds painted with symbols I didn't recognize stood in a clay vessel.

I moved forward and knelt to make my offerings. The healer stared at me for a moment, her eyebrows raised. I dropped a bundle of dried plants I'd brought. She pulled them out of the basket and smelled them, then looked at me again, smiling.

"This is an interesting gift," she said. I noticed glistening stones embedded in between her teeth. I must have made a face because she chuckled. "You have the look of one on a precipice." She stared at me another moment, then dismissed me.

When the offerings were complete, the healer gathered them and placed them one by one onto a wide altar. She lit bowls of flame and held them over the offerings, going to her knees, whistling a different bird Song for each flame. She was calling in the spirit of the Night Bird, so children of Night Bird could be born to those who had chosen. It was a ceremony practiced in all lands, on each dark moon. I had always believed I was a child of Night Bird but had never seen a ceremony. I wished I could stay for the ritual.

The healer took a bowl of flame to each acolyte, then dismissed us.

I nodded briefly again to Ruta and Kinet, and we left the temple. A trio of latecomers arrived and hurried past us into the temple, cursing.

《 《 ● 》 》

Batuk and I returned to where we had set up our sleeping area. Batuk made a fire while I sat, listening to the drumming coming from the temple. The dark night carried the scent of sacred smoke. There was murmuring from other fires; somewhere, a baby cried, a good omen. We ate a meal of travel cakes, then sat in silence in front of the fire. I wondered how the ceremony was going and hoped Wotal was sending her gift. Batuk spoke as if hearing my thoughts.

"May there be a birth and life in ten moons," he said. "Kinet has always loved children but never wanted to give birth. Ruta wanting to birth with Kinet makes me happy. I want my children to be happy. I want to return to a fat baby the next time I come this way."

"I want that for them too," I said.

"What do you want for yourself?" Batuk asked. The drumbeats and firelight, the feeling of being somewhere new lulled me into contemplation.

"I want to belong somewhere," I said. "To feel cared for, loved."

"Families take shape in surprising ways. That is a truth everywhere I have traveled." The drumbeats changed, growing slower. Batuk sighed. "I think the ceremony is well underway. Tell me again what you saw in Dreaming, Saya." He poured me a cup of something sweet. I held it in my hands and stared at the fire. I was exhausted—it had been more change than I was ready for. I touched my neck.

"There was a man. He bit into Dreaming with his teeth— they were strange. His face was stained white, and his breath, it was horrible. It smelled like death." I shivered and took a drink of the sweet liquid. A small rush of energy began blooming in me. "He said 'You exist unprotected,' and I couldn't move. There were strange shadows around me. They touched me, and I was full of grief and anger and fear. It didn't feel real."

Batuk gave me a sad smile.

"Grief and anger and fear are very real. If they exist here, of course they exist in the Dream." He turned to me with a look of concern on his face. "What do you know of Shadow Dreamers?" he asked.

"Shadow Dreamers?" I had never heard of a Shadow Dreamer. "Is that what wounded the Dream?"

Batuk threw a handful of crushed Ayan blossoms into our fire. They flared up, releasing their calming smoke.

"There are different ways of communicating with the Dream. The Dreamers of Alcanzeh are the most well-known. There used to be many more, cycles ago, but they have slowly died out, unable to birth anymore. The Dreamers of Alcanzeh are the last lineage of Dreamers still Dreaming. There are those who say they communicate with spirits, and perhaps they do. I have seen many strange things on the trade routes. There are those who say they can feel the Dream through dance, through drumming, those who go into long periods of isolation and silence for glimpses of the Dream. And there are those who use sacred plants to induce a state of Dreaming, though no one knows if they are truly in the Dream." He paused, tossing more Ayan blossoms into our fire. I thought of the root I had given the elder. She had definitely entered Dreaming, though without control. Batuk continued.

"Shadow Dreamers are those who enter the Dream using sacred plants and blood offering. It can be dangerous. Their minds in the Waking World are altered in ways that change them. They force their way in without invitation, an abomination, and receive gifts for the blood they have offered hungry spirits. I think you may have seen a Shadow Dreamer. What he said to you bothers me. Can you think of any reason a Shadow Dreamer would be seeking you?"

"The spirit I spoke with told me I have to keep them out. They wound the Dream, and when the Dream is wounded, this world is too." I shuddered. Batuk closed his eyes, the lines on his face pronounced in the firelight.

"Do you have spirits you know and trust? Who you can ask for protection when you enter?" he asked. I thought of Yecacu and a couple of other spirits.

"I do. I don't want to go into Dreaming tonight, but it's been pulling me stronger than ever before. I—" I shook my head. "The comet, the new stories rising around me, through me; I don't know what these changes are. I don't know how to move with them." Hot tears came to my eyes. I fisted them away.

"Saya." Batuk's voice was gentle. "You cannot deny your story, whatever it may look like. You have gifts so you can use them. It would be more dangerous—" He stopped, suddenly alert. He put his hand to his knife and sniffed the air.

"Saya?" A voice spoke from outside the light of our fire. I jumped up, heart pounding. Batuk stood quickly, his knife in his hand.

"Celay?"

It was my mother.

CHAPTER THIRTEEN

INDIR

There was silence. I closed my eyes, letting the tears spill from my face. Hands reached for me. Kupi and Ixara were embracing me. I rested my chin on Kupi's shoulder, crying silently, my face tight. I started shaking. Ixara crooned. When I opened my eyes, my mother was staring at me, horrified, her hand over her open mouth. Someone moved behind her. Dua.

"Shall I get a healer?" she asked in a quiet voice. My mother turned her face slightly but didn't take her eyes from me.

"Please," she said, her voice dry. Kupi made some sort of grunt. My mother moved forward and added herself to the embrace, stroking her hand over my head. I kept crying and felt the bodies holding me cry in response. There was still more to tell them. I pulled away, wiping my face and nose with the hem of my tunic.

"I tasted some Piliti and went to the Fire Temple. I think Alcan and the Pili convinced me to tell them stories. I don't remember. Inkop, his Fire Warrior, kept me safe. I know it. But I think I might have told them what I Dreamed for Anz. And about the Lost Dreamer." I sat back, and my tears stopped as I waited for them to react.

Kupi's head was in her hands. Ixara breathed in and out slowly, hands pressed to her stomach. My mother looked at me with more confusion than I had ever seen on her face. It was as if she didn't recognize me.

"Where did you get Piliti?" Safi asked, her face colorless. Kupi raised her head.

"From the Pili. He was at the healing temple. He offered it to me, and I thought it was an answer to me asking the Dream why I had lost my gift." My voice was raw.

"Indir, why didn't you tell me about losing your Dream? When?" Safi asked, putting her arms around me. I felt stiff. My mother wasn't known for her embraces; I preferred to be held by my aunts.

"Safi, she was scared, obviously. We have no stories for this," Ixara said, rubbing my back. Her hand felt safe, but I pulled away, wrapping my arms around myself.

They faced me. Kupi had an arm around my mother, who looked old, her face collapsed in grief.

"Is there anything else you can tell us about what you may have said to Alcan about his father?" she said. It was a careful question. She wasn't asking me to break my promise, but she was offering me a way to break my promise.

"I only know what Inkop told me," I said. "He is kind. I don't know why he stays with Alcan; he doesn't trust him. He helped me when I hurt my hands." My mother turned my hands over in hers, but there were only faint marks from where I had fallen and scraped them. "I saw Ovis after. We went to the healing temple to greet the Litéx."

"You didn't say anything to us," Kupi said.

"It didn't seem the right time," I said.

"Indir, whenever you feel you have been harmed, you tell someone so they can help you feel safe again. Have we ever made you feel unsafe?" Ixara asked. I glanced at my mother, then looked down. I heard her inhale sharply. She cleared her throat, but I could hear the tears in her voice when she spoke.

"What did Inkop tell you?" Safi asked. I decided we were in chaos; nothing mattered.

"He spoke of a sphere of water; Alcan was beating it. And I may have said something about a missing Dreamer. He didn't say Lost Dreamer, but I wasn't in my right mind. I don't know what I said." It felt terrible to tell them, but there was release in it too. My mother opened her mouth to speak, but Kupi spoke first.

"When did you stop Dreaming? How did it happen?" she asked.

"My Dream for Anz was my last Dream. And Zeri told me about a Dream she had about me. I don't know if she wishes to speak it to anyone else." I wiped at the tears that had returned and were dripping down my tunic.

"How did you keep this from anyone, Indir?" my mother asked.

"Safi, you ask the wrong questions. None of that matters now," Kupi said. My mother twisted her face but stayed silent. "We all have Dreams and more we keep private, you know that."

My mother's eyes flared with anger. I knew she and her sisters were about to argue. It relieved me; it would keep the attention off me.

"We have to tell her," Ixara said. "This is proof."

Kupi frowned but nodded.

"Tell me what?" my mother's voice raised as she asked.

"We believe Alcan may not want us to Dream for him because there is a story," Ixara said.

"There may be another child coming," Kupi said softly. My head shot up. I stared at my aunt, my heart pounding a war drum. King Anz had asked me if his child bore the mark. I had seen it in a sphere of water, not on Alcan. "There is a possibility that someone else will be shown to us in the Dream, another child of Anz."

I was stunned. I remembered the Dream: Alcan hitting a sphere of water, over and over again, screaming before he stabbed me. I wanted to tell them that part of the Dream, but it already felt like too much. My shiver turned into full-on shaking. I had told Alcan about the sphere, confirmed the story.

"That's what Alcan wanted to know," I whispered. My mother stood. She was shaking too, staring at her sisters.

"You kept this from me?" Safi hissed, pointing a finger at Kupi and Ixara. They jumped up, and I shrank back. I had witnessed arguments between them before.

"You welcomed Alcan into this city. Safi, you are so concerned with keeping the peace in this story we're living, you aren't thinking of the larger story. You Dream small, sister," Ixara said. My mouth locked up. It was an unspeakably cruel thing to say.

"I Dream small?" My mother's voice rose. "I Dream for us, for this sacred city, for everyone who lives here. I'm doing what I can to keep everyone safe."

"By welcoming the Fire Warriors and Alcan? Having us

greet the Pili? Are you trying to bring the cycle to an end all by yourself? What do you ask to see in Dreaming?" Kupi hissed.

"I see Alcan's poison has reached even the Dreamers," a voice said.

A tall Litéx woman stood in the entrance to the chamber. I recognized her as one of the women who had arrived the night before. Katalpa of the Airan stood with her. The woman gave my mother and aunts a look of disdain, then crossed, kneeling in front of me. I still had my arms wrapped around my body. She looked into my eyes and smiled.

"I am Eley of the Litéx. I greet you in the name of all that is sacred," she said.

"I am Indir," I said, trying to keep the shaking from my voice.

"Indir, I would like to speak with you about what happened last night." She noticed me flinch. "May I Sing you a Song of release first? It will help ease the discomfort, for both you and your mother."

I nodded, and she Sang a small Song, her palms open in front of her. I closed my eyes. As the Song moved through my body, my breathing came easier. I relaxed enough to feel the discomfort and tightness in my hips. When her Song ended, I opened my eyes to see my mother leaning on her sisters, tears streaming down her face. The look on her face made me ache, uncomfortable to see my mother so deep in emotion.

"Can you tell me, in your own words, what happened last night?" Eley rubbed my mother's back.

I explained as best I could. Eley frowned and shook her head.

"The cycle really is ending," Eley murmured, washing her hands in a basin of water. She approached me. "Do I have your permission to put my hands on your body?"

I looked at the tall woman. Her eyes were wide set and large, a pale brown. Her face reminded me of the moon somehow. I nodded.

"If anything feels uncomfortable or somehow wrong, tell me. This is your body, and you must listen to it." Eley ran her hands lightly over my arms, stopping at my wrists and pausing. Then she asked me to turn, and she ran her hands up my hips, then my back, pressing lightly. I winced.

"Do you feel well enough to come with me? I believe some time in healing water will help."

I glanced at my mother. I could tell Safi didn't want me to go. There was still much to discuss.

"I will come." I got up. Safi opened her mouth to speak, then thought better of it.

"Return soon," Safi said. She looked past us at my sisters. "Zeri, come here."

Zeri ducked her head and went to Safi, glancing a question at me. I was too exhausted and sad to react.

"I believe a quiet day, a day of healing, will be best for Indir." Eley's voice was firm. She put a warm hand on the middle of my back, rubbing small circles.

Safi's stare was one I hadn't seen before. There was sorrow in it, confusion. She nodded and left the room.

《 (●) 》

The tide was high. We walked down the beach, past the fishers dragging in woven nets full of their catch. A woman from the Water Temple oversaw them. She nodded to Eley and me while directing the fishers what to return to the sea as offering. Eley chatted the entire walk, telling me about life on the islands the Litéx called home. She described the coral reefs surrounding the islands, the fish and creatures that lived within.

We walked further up the beach than I'd been before until we reached a cove of sorts, a leg of land that stuck out into the water. A small river streamed out of the jungle, emptying into the cove. Over the cycles, it had formed a clear pool. Eley opened the basket and shook out a light, thin length of woven cloth. She sat on it and gestured for me to sit beside her. I did. She pulled drinking gourds and dried, green bundles out of the basket.

"This is a power place, where the river meets the sea. A sacred place. What healing we do here, whatever is created, will last. This is a place of release, Indir, of rebirth. Water is where we come from: The first sea we know is within our mothers." Eley's voice carried the timbre of Dreaming. "When the Twin Serpents shed their first skin, they did so weeping in joy, and so the seas and rivers and waters of this world were formed."

The story was sacred and comforting. I nodded.

"Have you eaten sea vines before?" Eley held out a green bundle, and I saw that it was wrapped like a savory meal cake, but with green leaves instead of husk.

"There are sea vines?" I took the bundle and began to unwrap it, but Eley stopped me and motioned for me to bite into it.

"Ah, there are entire jungles beneath the sea, as well as deserts where nothing grows, and mountain ranges, valleys. There
are volcanoes too, spitting up liquid fire that hardens into small
islands. You never go to the sea in your Dreaming?" she asked.
I swallowed a mouthful of sea vine and shook my head.

"The Water Temple in Alcanzeh is a holy place, where sacred
waters flow." Eley smiled. "Alcanzeh was built where she was
because of the springs, did you know that?"

I nodded. The sea vine contained some kind of savory paste
that filled me. Eley continued.

"When a child is living within her mother, she lives in sacred
waters. She drinks from them, breathes them. The Litéx do
not birth on land; we birth our children in the sea. All water is
sacred and can become more so in ritual." Eley stood, removing her tunic. She was naked except for her ankle decorations
and markings. Her body was dark from the sun, her stomach
bearing the sacred marks of motherhood, breasts hanging low.
She was beautiful. She held her hand out to me.

I stood, letting Eley unbraid my hair and remove my tunic.
She led me into the water. It was sun-warmed and felt like
entering one of the healing baths in the Water Temple. The
water deepened, until only our heads were out. Eley motioned
for me to lie back into the water and float.

I let myself float, hips, toes, and breasts all poking out of the
water. Eley began Singing, a high melody that at first startled
me. I relaxed as Eley guided her hands beneath my shoulders
and began moving me. I closed my eyes. The sensation of floating, of the sun on my naked body, reminded me of the feeling I

used to get right before going into Dreaming, the slipping away of the world. My chest ached with longing. I missed the safety of having a purpose. Eley lifted cupped hands, pouring water onto my forehead. It felt colder than it should have. Eley blew on my face. All my thoughts slipped away.

I don't know how long it lasted. I let Eley Sing and move me around the pool as long as the healer deemed necessary. Lights pulsed and danced behind my eyelids, reminiscent of Dreaming. I followed them until I was no longer aware of the water, of Eley, of anything.

Eley eventually guided me to the shore and lay my body on the slope of sand so I was halfway still in the water. I kept my eyes closed, relishing the sensations in my body, the small waves breaking over my hips, the ease of not thinking. A shadow moved across my face and stayed there. I didn't move, feeling Eley settle into the sand beside me. After a while, I moved my hands to my chest in the symbol of gratitude and held a hand out to Eley, eyes still closed.

"Ovis is growing in his skills." Eley held my hand palm up, tracing a finger along the skin. I opened my eyes, pulling my hand back.

"He told you about my hands?" I sat up.

"He did. He said you fell and he healed them. He has the gift. His Singing is one of many gifts my nephew has." She sighed, leaning back on her elbows. I did the same.

"Your sister was his mother?" I thought for a moment.

"Yes. I miss saying her name, but the Litéx do not speak the names of the dead unless we are in ceremony." Eley smiled sadly. "Our youngest sister, her gift was unusually strong. We begged her to stay with us, to serve the Litéx, but she insisted she was called to Alcanzeh. Somehow, she knew this was where she was meant to be." Eley sighed deeply.

"Meant to be?" I asked, twisting my hair and coiling it into itself.

"She saved Tavovis when no one else could. Tavovis has been, according to most, the best leader of the Avex in an age. He would not have lived to become leader if it hadn't been for our sister." She let sand run through her fingers. "I won't lie. I would have preferred to keep my sister, but we cannot always choose how our lives go. Her sons have visited the Litéx; Ovis spent an entire cycle of seasons with us when he was a boy. His brother Tixu found the islands a little small, though he did love stealing our boats to explore." She smiled at the memory.

"Have they heard anything about him?" I remembered taking the message to Tavovis.

Eley eyed me.

"How much time do you Dreamers spend Dreaming about what happens outside the lands you know?" she asked.

I was surprised by the question. We rarely even tried to; there was no reason.

"We usually don't." I thought of my aunts and their recent secretive ways and amended my answer. "I haven't, though I think my sisters have seen other lands and probably my aunts. The rituals we use to Dream keep us safe, but they mean we only explore a small part of the Dream." I looked at Eley. Her hair moved in the breeze coming off the sea.

Eley stood up, brushing the sand from her body. I rose and slipped on my tunic.

"There are people beyond these lands who do not believe in the Dream," Eley said as we began our walk back toward Alcanzeh.

"But we're from the Dream, don't they know that?" I felt foolish. I didn't know how much I didn't know.

Eley walked silently, staring out over the water.

"We know the Dream because it is our truth, it is our story. But there are other stories out in the world, and some of them aren't as kind as ours. We are blessed to have been born in a place that honors the Dream."

I frowned. My world was changing too fast, too soon. Eley reached out and touched my forehead with her thumb, rubbing small circles until I released the furrow.

《 《 ● 》 》

I slept hard and deep when we returned to the temple. Eley promised me privacy and quiet as long as I required it. I already felt lighter, but I wanted nothing more than rest. It was early evening by the time I woke up. A small fire burned in the room. There was a covered bowl on the bench and a clay jar with medicine inside. I stretched, expecting pain and discomfort, but I felt loose. I ate the contents of the bowl—some sort of bean—and drank from the jar. It was sweet; it tasted like flowers with a slightly bitter aftertaste. I yawned, breathing in deep, becoming alert.

A head poked in the room. It was Dua, the temple worker.

"Are you still hungry? Thirsty? Do you want me to leave? I've been standing outside so that no one bothers you," she said.

"Who would bother me?" I asked. I went to the basin of water and began washing my face and hands. The water was cool and felt good on my sleep-warmed skin.

"No one, while I'm here," Dua said. She walked into the room and stood beside me. She was odd, but there was something about her I was drawn to. She was small, almost childlike, but there was a brightness to her gaze. Her eyes missed nothing. She spoke in a way that made me curious.

"You came to our temple from the Water Temple?" I asked, changing into a different tunic. I unbraided my hair and looked for a comb. Dua handed me one.

"Yes, but before that, I was with travelers. I was born far to the north, in a desert higher and further away than where the Fire Warriors come from. The stories I was told said we were once one with the Fire Warriors, but there are almost none of us left."

"Why did you come to Alcanzeh?" I asked. She sat on the bench beside me, watching me comb my hair. Her hair was short, close to her scalp.

"I was born to a changing land. The waters were drying up and food was hard to find. Many died, even before I was born. My mother and uncle decided we had to move to a land that could sustain us. My sister and I were young, and my uncle's chosen came with us. He had warrior training and kept us safe, for a while."

"Safe from what?"

"Those who were hungry, desperate. There were five of us, and together, we seemed strong enough. We did have food; my uncle's chosen knew how to call insects from the earth, but he hid his gift from others. There were those who collected those of us with gifts, for their own needs."

"What happened?" Her story made me feel slightly different about mine.

"We were found. My uncle broke his foot one day, and we had to stay in one place. His chosen refused to leave him, and my mother knew we wouldn't survive without his gift, so we stayed. We were caught. I don't know what happened to my uncle and his chosen. My mother, sister, and I were taken by traders. We were brought south. My mother and sister were traded away from me."

I was appalled, my hands over my chest, but she seemed content, even with the pain of her story.

"You don't know what happened to your mother and sister?" I asked. Dua shook her head. She picked up the comb from where I had dropped it and ran her fingers along its edge.

"The world is very different outside Alcanzeh. It has been changing a long time. It hasn't reached here yet, but the change will come. Even with all your protections, I know Dreamers can sense it. Everyone can," she said. I realized she was older than she looked.

"Why did you choose to work here?" I asked.

She opened her mouth to say something, but stopped herself. She thought for a moment, then spoke.

"I'm curious about Dreamers. I've heard stories about you for all my seasons traveling. I wanted to see you and Alcanzeh for myself. If the cycle is ending, I thought Alcanzeh would be an interesting place to be a part of that story. And you have lots of water." She looked at the jar of water in the corner. "Hunger is hard, but thirst is terrible."

I gazed at the Twin Serpent altar. The flame was low but steady. Dua knew loss, and she was still living, following what she wanted. She had known hunger, thirst, pain I couldn't begin to imagine. I stood.

"I should speak with my mother and aunts," I said. Dua stood too.

"Are you sure? There is tension down there; there's tension everywhere in Alcanzeh, but here, tonight, in this temple, it is—" She made an expansive gesture with her hands.

"Chaos," I said.

"Chaos," she replied, then looked down and smiled at something inward. "My mother always said that chaos is a womb. What will be birthed?"

((●))

Dua walked down to the main gathering chamber with me. There were more Avex in the temple than I had seen before. I didn't see Ovis. I wondered if the story of my time at the Fire Temple had reached him.

An Avex guarded the chamber. Tendrils of hair moved around her head as she stood near the entrance to the chamber. The air moved behind her. She saw me and blew a whistle she had around her neck. Her hair stopped moving. I walked into the chamber.

It was full. There were people gathered around in a circle, on cushions. My mother sat with Tavovis. Kupi and Ixara sat opposite her with Lal and Eley. My sisters sat with the Ilkan, Ali and Katalpa sat beside each other. It was all the witnesses called to Alcanzeh.

"Indir." My mother was relieved to see me. She nodded at Katalpa. A small wind rose up from the edges of the room, blowing in a wide circle around us.

"This keeps what we say private." Katalpa smiled at me. Everyone turned to greet me. I felt strange, knowing I'd probably been a part of what they had been discussing. My sisters made room between them, each taking one of my hands. Delu leaned her chin on my shoulder.

"I'm well," I whispered.

"I don't want you to leave," Delu whispered back. I froze. Zeri had told them of her Dream. I felt dizzy. I had to tell them the rest of my last Dream.

"What are we discussing?" I asked. Everyone's faces changed.

"We're going to give him the Game," Safi said, looking serious. "Alcan said he would let us Dream for him if he has the Game. When we speak the Dream to the people, we will tell them of the coming chaos." She looked around the room for approval. Tavovis nodded, but no one else did. Katalpa spoke to me.

"The sky speakers of the Airan say the stars move in a strange dance of disappearance. Change is coming. The sky does not lie, and neither does the Dream. The Ilkan have already spoken on this." Eley hummed, then spoke. "The seas are full of strange currents these days. Creatures from our oldest stories are rising from their sleep. The seas are pulling back on themselves, more ebb than flow. The coming seasons will be hard."

"How long will the chaos last?" I asked.

"No one alive has seen the end of a cycle, or a beginning. The stories say it can be sudden, or the chaos can last seasons, years. It could be two moons or twenty years, we can't know," Lal said.

I was part of the chaos. That was becoming clearer to me. I had to tell them what else I had seen in my last Dream. I wanted to be brave.

"There is something I haven't told you, because I promised Anz not to speak of the Dream. But I can't keep that promise," I said, my voice cracking. "I can't anymore; will you allow me to tell you?"

I put my hand over the stinging feeling in the middle of my chest. Eley began humming, and Lal joined her. My mother pressed her lips together. I knew she would want me to act as Dreamer, keep my promise to King Anz. My aunts opened their hands.

"Tell us," Kupi and Ixara spoke as one. I inhaled deeply, relieved.

"At the end of my Dream for Anz, Alcan stabbed me. I felt myself dying." My breath shook as I spoke, but I spoke. It was terrifying and felt right.

My mother's face went wide in horror, her hands covering her mouth. Ali rose and knelt before me, his hands on my shoulders.

"Look at me, Indir," he said. I looked into his eyes. They were dark, shining with either rage or love, I couldn't tell. Everyone faded away. "You are not going to die, not by Alcan's hand or anyone else's. It could have been a symbol, no?"

He looked at my aunts. Kupi nodded, her face certain. Ixara was in front of my mother, urging her to drink something.

"He will not harm you." Raru showed her fangs. Eley and Lal held hands, humming as they gazed at me. I was surrounded by people who loved me, would protect me. I wanted to cry but instead sat up straighter.

"It was a symbol," my mother said. She didn't rise; she was completely still, her eyes on mine. "It was a symbol for losing your gift. And Zeri saw you leaving Alcanzeh. You will live." Her words sounded forced.

"You will leave." Ali turned to face the rest of the council. Even though he was small, he moved with strength and spoke with knowing. "She has to leave Alcanzeh," he repeated.

"In case it wasn't a symbol," Delu whispered close to my ear. I felt Zeri reach around me and pinch her.

"We are going to Dream tomorrow," Safi said. "For Alcan, to see who the warriors are to be. I'll ask where she should go." She wasn't speaking to me, but to everyone gathered.

"Any of us will welcome you where we live," Katalpa said, her hands over her chest.

"When told of Zeri's Dream, Ovis said he would be willing

to travel as guard, if it would make you feel safer," Eley said, smiling.

I don't know what kind of face I made, but my skin grew hot.

"That is very kind of him," I said. Zeri pressed closer to me. I couldn't see it, but I could feel her smile. "Am I still a Dreamer?" I asked. "Am I the Lost Dreamer?"

Safi opened her mouth and let out a long exhale.

"I don't believe you are the Lost Dreamer," my mother said softly. "But I will ask in the Dream. You can't be lost if we know you're leaving."

I swallowed. She hadn't answered my first question.

"You are a Dreamer. Nothing changes that," Kupi said, worrying the gap in her teeth with her tongue. "We spin into chaos, and we either survive it or we don't. You will survive this, Indir, I know it. It was a symbol." Ixara nodded in agreement.

"I don't want to leave," I said, though the thought of Ovis offering to guard me was one I wanted more time with.

"We have to respect the cycles, little Dreamer, all of us," Naru said. I remembered what she said about the Ilkan barely surviving the other cycles.

"No one can know she's leaving," Tavovis said. He had been silent the entire time. I'd forgotten his presence. "We don't know what she told Alcan when he had the Piliti given to her. He may not have understood it as a symbol."

My peace vanished. Alcan could have understood the Dream as a sign.

"Indir, I promise to you on all that is sacred, we will get you out of Alcanzeh. Ovis will accompany you," he said. He turned to my mother and started talking about the fastest ways away from the city. Others leaned in. It was too much for me. My sisters noticed.

"How kind of Ovis," Zeri whispered. I tried not to smile. "You can choose him now; you don't have to Dream him. Have you considered that?"

I hadn't. A small gift in the face of my loss. I shook my head.

"He won't choose me," I whispered back. Delu rolled her eyes.

"He offered to accompany you, Indir," she said.

"He's Avex, it's what they do. He probably thought I'd be more comfortable traveling with a guard I know," I said.

"Yes, he wants to make you comfortable," Zeri whispered.

"Very comfortable, keeping you safe," Delu added. I tried not to smile. It was one spot of light in the darkness.

"At least you know your role in the coming chaos, or part of it," Delu said. "We have to live the story here in Alcanzeh." I heard the longing in her voice. I knew my sister saw other lands as part of her gift. In the Dream, she was able to fly over strange landscapes different from the ones we knew. Sometimes, I didn't believe the things she told us, but she wasn't a liar.

"You get to Dream," I said. It felt good to be able to speak it. Almost no one treated me differently for it. I glanced at my mother. Her head was bent close with Ali, his hand on her upper arm. Katalpa watched them, glanced at me and looked away quickly.

"They travel on giant birds," Delu whispered to me. I turned to see if she was joking. "That's why I saw them traveling so fast, but I couldn't see the birds. They keep them secret from Alcan and everyone else. Katalpa took me into the jungle today to meet them. Each leg is as tall as us. You can imagine the rest."

I tried to imagine a bird that large but couldn't; it seemed out of a story. But everything seemed to be out of a story.

Zeri cleared her throat.

"Delu and I are to Dream the warriors, one each," she said. "Delu will ask to Dream the Fire Warrior, and I will Dream the warrior from Alcanzeh."

"Safi wanted to Dream the warriors, but Kupi and Ixara insisted it be us. They told Safi she was too trained. It was an argument heard through the entire temple while you were at your healing," Delu said.

"What will I do tomorrow night while you're in Dreaming? I shouldn't be a part of the ceremony if I can't Dream." It ached in me that everyone would be in ritual but me.

"You'll be with us, sister," Delu said. "You will sleep and Dream between us like you always do."

CHAPTER FOURTEEN

SAYA

My mother stepped into the light of the fire. Her head was shorn, her eyes red rimmed with exhaustion. Someone was with her. A man stepped into the light. Older and wiry, he carried a fear on him I could almost smell. He carried a pack, and protections dangled from his tunic: small bundles of bone, braided grasses, beads. I took a step back.

"I know this man. He is Chanut, a trader." Batuk's voice was calm, but I sensed a question. "Though when our paths crossed a few seasons ago, he didn't look this old. What happened to you, Chanut?"

Chanut mumbled something while I stared at Celay. Her lips were dry and cracked. I handed her my waterskin and watched her drink deeply. She wiped her hand on her mouth and squatted down.

"Are you hungry?" I asked, my voice low. I felt my blood rushing through my body. The drumming from the temple rose in tempo, as if in response. A wind blew in from the north, blowing the fire into higher flames. Celay nodded. Chanut squatted beside her. I handed them both travel cakes while Batuk watched us. After they finished eating, they sat back. Celay elbowed Chanut out of silence.

"I have heard your name before, Saya. Someone seeks you," Chanut said, staring into the fire. I sat up straighter, pulling my blanket around my shoulders. I didn't know if my shivering started with his words or the wind.

"Chanut, you fool," Batuk spit. "You're terrifying her. Never start a story in the middle."

Chanut blinked. I blinked.

"A wailing woman, on the dark moon. She screams your name. She searches for you. She is close."

I sat back, dizzy. The smoke from the fire blew in my face. I coughed. Someone in the temple began Singing a high, slow Song that carried through the darkness. The Song of Night Bird. I shook my head back and forth. I felt strange. I didn't know if I was feeling the ceremony or something else. Batuk hissed and stomped one foot three times.

"Saya. Chanut has eaten more sacred plants than anyone I have ever met and not in ceremony," Batuk said, voice firm and low. Chanut looked startled.

"Batuk, I swear to you—"

"You swore to an entire family there was a toad as large as a temple living in the underground rivers beneath them." Batuk stared at Chanut, who flinched. "And you took an entire tree as your lover once, then told everyone you met about it, until your next story, which I do not believe you want me to repeat."

My mouth was open, as was Celay's. She touched her hands to her bare scalp.

"Did you sacrifice your hair for this information, Celay?" Batuk asked, eyes narrowed at Chanut. I was speechless. I didn't know whether to laugh or scream. The Song from the temple grew louder as the drumming rose to a peak.

"I did," Celay said, and slumped forward. I wanted to comfort her, but I was wary. Had this been another part of her manipulations? I didn't know.

The drums stopped, and voices cried out in unison from the temple, a cry to the spirit of the Night Bird, a call to nest.

Everyone at every fire went quiet. The silence stretched on. Bird and insect Song filled the night, and the wind seemed sharper as it blew through the wild growth around us. Then, silence dropped over everything completely. I gasped. Not a bird, not an insect, even the winds stilled. The ceremony in the temple was complete. I hoped the offerings had been accepted, that Ruta would birth.

"It's silent," Celay said in a whisper, her eyes wide. At another fire, someone shouted and pointed skyward.

A large shape was circling high above, its silhouette outlined against the stars.

"The Night Bird!" someone gasped from another fire. Voices exclaimed in awe, but I knew they were wrong. I recognized the shape of the bird, the pulse of air that moved when it flapped its wings.

"That's the bird that took my necklace," I whispered. Chanut smothered a yelp and ran into the growth. Celay started chanting something. I had never heard her chant before. The fear in me rose as bile in my throat. I fisted my hands and pressed them to the earth. I couldn't see the comet; the growth was too thick, but I imagined I could hear its Song, faintly, just outside my fear.

There was a scream from the jungle and then sounds of thrashing. Batuk rose with his knife in his hand. The scream broke the silence, and the night was once again filled with the sounds of life. It seemed louder than before, a frenzied Song of insects and other creatures of night.

I stood, my arms wrapped around me. Celay moved so she was between me and the jungle. She held her hands out on either side, as if she could block me from whatever had screamed. There was a thrashing coming toward us. Chanut ran out of the jungle, stumbling, his hands bleeding from a fall he must have taken. His face was pale.

"A beast," he gasped, hiding behind Batuk. Batuk sniffed the air and gave Chanut a look of disdain. Chanut lifted his head over Batuk's shoulder and peered toward the dark. I barely heard the murmurs from the other fires. Chanut was staring at something. There was a scent in the air, sharp and pungent but not unpleasant. Yellow eyes appeared in the dark. I whimpered. Celay stepped back so that I was pressed against her. I could feel her shaking.

The yellow eyes seemed to glow, as if they carried their own light. The scent became stronger.

A woman stepped into the firelight. She was taller than me, but I was too entranced by her eyes to see anything else. Her eyes were focused on me, and she sniffed the air.

"Ilkan! See? A beast!" Chanut cried. Batuk hissed at him and lowered his knife.

"We greet you in all that is sacred." Batuk put his knife back into his belt and opened his hands in greeting. The Ilkan didn't look at him. Celay made a strange noise.

"Saya." The Ilkan's voice was a low growl. I peeked around Celay, who had her arms back, trying to enclose me in her body. The Ilkan's eyes were intense but not unkind. I noticed the markings on her skin, how they seemed like shadows or scars, the same as a jaguar. I looked over the rest of her. She was dressed in a short tunic, her legs strong, muscled. Her fingernails were a dark brown, shining, like the claws of a jaguar. Her hair was black, pulled back and tight at the back of her head. She was beautiful in a mesmerizing way. I couldn't believe she was real.

"I know you, Saya. You're not safe here," she growled again.

"Stay away from her," Celay gasped, stepping back and forcing me to move.

"She isn't yours, Celay," the Ilkan growled. Batuk was looking back and forth between them.

"What do you mean she isn't safe?" Batuk asked. His knife was in his hand again. Out of the sides of my eyes, I could see other people moving toward our fire. The Ilkan sniffed the air again.

"Saya, you are not safe here. Come with me," the Ilkan said, stepping forward. "Ilkan cannot lie."

"They can't," Batuk said. He looked past Celay at me. "If she says you aren't safe, you aren't."

The circling bird cried out. I flinched.

"Who are you?" I asked, my voice dry in my throat. The Ilkan opened her hands.

"I am called Nahi," she said.

"Saya," Celay said. "You cannot go with her; you don't know her. Haven't I always kept you safe? Haven't I?"

"I know who she is, Celay. Does *she* know who she is?" Nahi said, the marks on her skin darkening.

Celay put her hands over her face and crouched down, rocking back and forth.

"Celay, you are a fool," Batuk spit. He stepped around her and grabbed my arms. "I trust the Ilkan over Celay. Listen to yourself, Saya, listen to your knowing. What do you want to do? If something comes for you, I'll do my best to keep you safe, but the Ilkan have better instincts than we do. Decide, quickly."

He released my arms, and I made a choice. I grabbed my travel pack. Chanut joined Celay on the ground, rocking back and forth to her same rhythm. I would have laughed at the sight, had there been time. My body was alert, ready for movement.

"I trust you," I said to Nahi. I didn't know I was going to speak it. It came unbidden, but I knew it was true. I turned to Batuk. "Tell Ruta and Kinet I will return."

"Travel safe, Dreamer." Batuk embraced me briefly, nodding at Nahi, who was already at the edge of the jungle. I looked down at Celay. She was watching me with expectation, as if there was something she wanted to hear from me. I had nothing to say.

"I'll follow you," I said to the Ilkan. She reached for my hand and pulled me after her.

❨ ☾ ● ☽ ❩

The night was dark, but her eyes were sharp. Her hand was hot in mine, pulling me close. Sometimes, she paused to tell me where there was something I needed to be aware of. I sensed the air above moving when the circling bird moved her wings. Day and night birds called back and forth in frenzied Song. Vines and leaves scratched against me. My breathing came hard. The Ilkan noticed and paused, putting a waterskin into my hand. I drank deeply, then stopped. There was another sound, beneath the night sounds. It was more a feeling, like another heartbeat moving through all the plants, the very earth beneath us.

Nahi stopped, dropping to the ground and placing her hand against it. I did the same. A low vibration pulsed.

"They use the ground to seek us, Dreamer," Nahi said. "I have seen these trackers before. They have gifts that allow them to communicate with the roots beneath us. There's a chance that they will pass if we don't move. It may not work." She stood, her eyes narrowing. "I'm not really in the mood to kill; I have an aching tooth, but I'll fight if I have to."

I stayed crouched on the ground, trying to take in everything said. I was being tracked by people who communicated with roots, and she was ready to fight or kill. I let my eyes become unfocused, attempting to clear my mind. As I did, the Song of the Comet reached me once more. I felt it in my hands, which began itching. I grabbed a vine with one hand to pull myself up. As I hummed the Song of the Comet to soothe myself, a heat seemed to pull at my hand. I followed it until I was touching Nahi's jaw. She flinched away at first, then let me touch her. Her skin was as soft as the leaves we used to clean babies. It was hot, and my fingers seemed to want to move on their own. I traced them along her jaw until they reached the place right below her ear. The skin seemed to pulse, and my fingers pressed into it. Nahi didn't flinch, but her eyes narrowed. I let the Song move from my throat into my mouth. My fingertips began to tingle as something flowed from me into Nahi, in the shape of the Song. It lasted a few breaths, then receded. I pulled my hand away. Nahi opened and closed her mouth, grinning.

"You're a Singer too?" Her smile was wide, her teeth sharp. "Look at the vine in your hand, Saya."

I hadn't let it go. It had grown longer, thicker, curling on the ground.

"Ask it for more, see if it can lift you," Nahi hissed, keeping perfectly still as the vibration came harder.

I wove my arm through the vine. I pressed my forehead to it. I could feel it growing, countless invisible rivers of current moving within, forming walls, tunnels, tendrils.

"Carry me," I whispered to the Song of the Comet. For a moment, nothing happened. I deepened my voice so I felt it not only in my throat, but in my breasts, belly, shoulders. I closed my eyes as it pressed around me. It wasn't the Song; it was the vine. It had grown, wrapping itself around my body, forming a seat that cradled me, lifting me up into the trees. I kept Singing. It felt natural, joyous. Beneath my fear, the Song was stronger. It not only moved in me, it was me.

I gasped as I broke through the canopy, the vine coiling on itself below me, holding tight. The stars were a net of light across the bowl of darkness, the comet humming on the edge. I heard breathing. Looking down, I saw Nahi's face staring up at me with a grin so wide, I could see the sharpness of all her teeth.

I couldn't feel the vibration anymore but knew when the trackers were close by the way she went perfectly still. The markings on her face darkened so her eyes were rimmed in black lines, her nostrils were wider, her ears moving slightly into points. Her shoulders were roped with muscle in the shape of a jaguar. I didn't want to move. I wanted to stare at her. Her eyes were moving from one side to the other as she tracked whoever was moving through the jungle beneath us. I strained, listening for their footfalls. I held my breath. Voices spoke in a language I didn't understand. I wasn't as frightened as I thought; I was in awe at the shape my story was taking. I was being cradled by a vine, protected by an Ilkan, while unknown trackers sought me out. I leaned my head back and closed my eyes. I wanted to laugh. Not being protected was more interesting than I could have imagined.

"Stay here," Nahi whispered when the sounds had passed. She leaped to another tree, then another, until she disappeared. I shifted slightly. The vine seemed to sense my discomfort and moved to match what my body wanted. A new gift, as Singer. A gift from Tiya.

A man's scream ripped through the night, followed by an animal snarl. The scream ended abruptly. I waited for more, but the night was filled only with night sounds. I shivered. I had left my travel blanket.

Nahi called up.

"You can come down if you want to, unless you want to spend your night in the tree."

I pressed my face to the vine again and hummed, asking to be brought back to the ground. It moved slowly, then picked up speed. When I was on the ground again, it simply hung.

I saw Nahi's eyes but barely the rest of her.

"Those two will no longer bother us tonight, but I think one of them was able to pound a message into the earth. There may be more," Nahi said. Her voice was lower to the ground. I realized she was squatting when a small fire sparked to life in a shell she had pulled from her hip pack. I sat down on the other side of her. I tried not to flinch when I noticed traces of blood at the edges of her mouth. She noticed and darted out her lip to lick them away.

"I honor my gifts, even if they make others uncomfortable," Nahi said.

"I need to learn that," I mumbled, exhausted. "Will we return to the others?" I yawned, then turned it into a hum. I didn't know how I knew what to do. It came to me as if I had always known. The vine moved beneath me, then cradled my body again, now longer, like a hammock.

Nahi shook her head.

"It doesn't look like we'll go anywhere, not until you've had a cycle or two of sleep. Rest. I will make sure no one comes. I'll tell you what I can when you wake."

"I have so many questions." I wanted to keep speaking with Nahi, but my body needed rest.

I slept deeply and did not Dream.

《 《 ● 》 》

The stars had shifted and were starting to disappear when Nahi woke me.

"Saya," she growled. I opened my eyes. The jungle was gray-green shadow with flashes of colorful wings as the morning birds began to move.

"Story," I yawned. I was too tired to say anything else. Nahi handed me her waterskin, which she had filled while I slept. She handed me a traveling cake, and I began chewing at it.

"Change comes; it has been coming a very long time. I am part of it and you are part of it, and that is what I can tell you," she said. I choked.

"That isn't a story," I said after a drink of water.

"Saya." Her voice was serious. "There was a ritual involved, and I cannot speak your story to you. I am a part of it, and you are in a much longer story. A time of intensity begins. You know this. I was finally able to track you and others will as well. I don't think you're safe on land."

"On land," I said, staring at the ground beneath me. "Am I to live in the trees?" I laughed. I was exhausted. I didn't want to go back, but I missed the before. I rubbed at my arms to try and calm myself.

Nahi smiled, but it was sad.

"May I embrace you, Saya? I think it will help calm you," she said, rising and opening her arms. Her face was kind. I could see her better in the dawning light. She was older than me, her features beautiful. Her eyes were wide set in cheekbones shaped like that of a jaguar. I stepped from the vine and let her enfold me in her arms. Her body ran warmer than mine, her skin much softer. I could feel the strength in her arms and shoulders. She smelled like earth with a sharp undertone that made me think of tree sap. I exhaled. She began swinging slightly back and forth, rocking me with her. It felt like a mother's embrace, one I had never known. I started to cry. Nahi held me.

"I don't want to live in trees," I said, then heard myself and giggled. Nahi laughed too, a high cackle that brought me the same joy Ruta's laugh did. I hoped my friends weren't too worried about me. The embrace ended, and we sat back down. I felt lighter.

"Saya, I know little about you except that you are a Dreamer and Singer. What else do you want me to know about your story? What do you want to know of mine?" Nahi asked.

I told her my story as quickly as I could, my strange life of wandering with Celay, how we made our way in the world. I told her how my Dreaming and Waking lives had both started to change, about the loss of my necklace.

"Good bird," she murmured, then urged me to continue.

When I finished, Nahi sat back with a strange look on her face. She held her hands over her belly, closing her eyes. I wondered if she was to birth.

"A cycle is ending, truly. The comet is an old promise. It comes with change; it always has." Nahi sighed. I decided to offer her the same question she had offered me.

"What do you want me to know of your story?" I leaned back against the vine, my hands in the earth. I was feeling for vibrations, but if there were any, they were too faint to feel.

"I was born to the Ilkan. When my bleeding arrived, I went to Alcanzeh to study and serve as acolyte to the Ilkan serving there. When their king died, I left and have been living a sacred story ever since. Yours is a sacred story too. It isn't easy, Saya. There are sacrifices. I have had to leave what I love most behind. I would like to help you be safe. Will you travel with me until you are safe? Don't answer me yet. Breathe with it first."

I leaned back against the vine, breathing in and out. Nahi groomed herself, using a rolled-up leaf to clean beneath her sharp nails. I was traveling with an Ilkan. I'd had to leave those I cared about. I sighed. It seemed that every time a gift arrived to change my story, there was something else to grieve. Nahi squinted and looked up toward the sky. It reminded me.

"That bird, it was the one who took my necklace. Do you know it?" I asked.

"She comes from the Airan, far, far to the north and east. She is a messenger, among other things. She flies between here and the bird whose nest she was born to. She isn't fully grown." She laughed at my face. "This world is much bigger than the Belly, young friend. Will you travel with me?"

I would, but there was more I wanted first.

"How do you know Celay?" I asked.

"I have never met her before, but I know a part of her story." Nahi's nostrils flared, and her lips pressed into a thin line. "Do you want to return to her? Or bring her with us? It would slow us, but if you want her near, I understand."

I stared at the face she made. She didn't trust my mother either.

"I am happy to travel away from her," I exhaled. "I wanted more life, and the Dream heard me."

"Have you ever been on a boat?" she asked.

CHAPTER FIFTEEN

INDIR

I was sitting in our ritual of silent contemplation with my sisters the next day when our aunts entered.

"Come, we're going to cleanse at the Water Temple," Ixara beckoned.

"I thought I wasn't to leave the temple," I said. It had been decided the night before that I was to stay close. "Where's Safi?"

"Safi went to prepare in her own way; she'll return soon. There are Avex to walk us there and wait. You will be safe," Kupi said. "We wish to speak to you without your mother present."

My sisters and I exchanged looks.

"Those are my favorite conversations." Zeri grinned. We always loved it when our aunts shared knowing with us that our mother didn't think we were ready for.

((●))

It felt strange to enter the healing temple again. I wondered who'd found the rest of the root I'd tasted and shuddered, hoping they had offered it back to the earth with the other used plants they disposed of daily.

Our aunts led us to the main bath, where I had Dreamed for the last time. The bath was surrounded by bowls full of healing plants. An altar was already set up, a bowl of flame before it. There were bowls of salt for our cleansing.

We disrobed and began using the salt to scrub our bodies, helping each other with places we wouldn't reach on our own. The afternoon sunshine streaked in through high cutout stone windows, dancing on the surface of the steaming water. When we were scrubbed, we entered slowly, Singing a cleansing Song, a Song of release. I didn't like the way my voice sounded alone but enjoyed how it sounded raised in Song with others.

Zeri had a clear high voice. She moved to the edge of the pool, picking up the bowls of medicine and sprinkling their contents over the water. The scent rose in the steam, sharp and green. I lay back and floated, moving my arms until I was floating in a patch of sunlight. I heard the murmuring voices of those I loved and felt safe.

"My beautiful Dreamers," Kupi sighed. She had moved to me, kissing me on the cheek. I blinked up at her, smiling. I was going to miss my aunts when I left Alcanzeh. I would miss everyone, but I knew I would ache for their guidance most of all.

"We want to speak to you about Dreaming," Kupi said. We joined her at the edge of the pool. She and Ixara looked sad, somehow. "We've been part of your training, just as we were trained by our mother and aunts before they passed into the Dream. Your mother is very dedicated to her gift as a Dreamer, but you know we disagree with her about certain ways of being."

We nodded. Ixara continued.

"Our rituals and protections have served us well for generations, but there have also been fewer of us born. Kupi and

I made a choice when we were near your age, to explore the Dream a little further, without our mother or Safi's knowing."

Delu grinned at Zeri. I could see they were both excited by the idea of exploring the wider Dream. I would have been excited too, had I been able to Dream. I sunk down so the water was at my neck.

"We have spoken with spirits," Kupi said. I rose out of the water. Outside of very deep ritual, we were told never to speak with spirits. Only to ask the Dream to show us what we needed, to shape in front of us what we could bring back to Alcanzeh.

"It isn't dangerous?" Zeri asked in awe.

"It is," Ixara said simply. "But we believe it is more dangerous to be ignorant of what is coming. Your mother doesn't look beyond Alcanzeh when she asks to Dream. As if by concentrating on Alcanzeh, she can save it."

"What will happen to Alcanzeh?" Delu gasped.

"Alcanzeh will change, and eventually, something new will be built on the bones of the city we love in, live in," Kupi said. "Though that story should not come in our lifetimes."

"Delu, Zeri, you have your roles in this beyond what you Dream tonight. You will be living here when the cycle ends; we know that much. Indir, you will return to Alcanzeh, but first, you must seek the Lost Dreamer."

"How? I've never left Alcanzeh. Am I to become a wanderer?" I gasped, ducking back down into the comforting heat of the water. "How will I know her?" My mind raced with too many thoughts to hold any one in place. I wasn't the Lost Dreamer, just a Dreamer who'd lost her gift.

"That's what we can tell you. We believe . . ." Kupi put her hands out, and we linked to make a circle. "We believe the chaos will begin tonight." I swallowed and shivered despite the heat of water.

She'd spoken in the voice of prophecy.

《 《 ● 》 》

There was a strange wind blowing from the south when we left the Water Temple. It whipped our tunics against our bodies, lifting our hair into long black rivers that streaked out from our heads. Dark clouds gathered in power on the horizon, black and gray with a tinge of green. The smell of rain and more was in the air. We entered the temple to find workers rushing around, some securing the entrances with woven mats while others lit bowls of flame against the early darkness.

Our mother had returned and was setting up the Dreaming altar, preparing the sacred blankets we were to Dream on. Or, that they were going to Dream on. I hadn't spoken to my mother about what I would do that evening. I let my sisters go up to our chamber; Kupi and Ixara went to the offering rooms.

"Will I be a part of the ritual?" I asked from the entryway to the room that held the Dreaming altar. It was where we Dreamed together in ritual a few times a year. My mother didn't look up.

"You will," she said. "You're still a Dreamer." She rearranged something in front of the altar.

"Are you angry with me?" I felt myself starting to shake as I spoke. Safi had been a good mother, but we had always struggled to connect. She looked at me, a look of disbelief on her face.

"Indir, no. Why would you ask me that?" She crossed to me but stopped short of embracing me. I realized I had grown taller than her at some point. She looked up into my eyes, half-moons of shadow beneath hers.

"You haven't said anything about my loss," I said, crossing my arms over my chest. I exhaled. I had to speak it. I would be gone soon, and there would be no other chance. I didn't want any more regrets.

Safi shook her head.

"I'm sorry. I haven't said anything because I thought you were angry with me. I feel like this is my failure—I should have trained you better." She began to cry softly. A part of me wanted to embrace her, but her words stunned me.

"You think this is my fault? That if I had been better trained, if I'd known more, I would still be able to Dream?" My words came out as a hiss. I braced one hand against the wall.

"That's not what I meant, Indir, it isn't. I know this isn't your fault, but we have no story for this. I don't know what to believe or why it's happening."

"The cycle is ending. There will be chaos, everyone says so," I said.

"We're Dreamers, Indir. We are protected," she said. I saw she believed it. I closed my mouth, beginning to understand what my aunts had spoken of.

"How will I participate in the ritual?" I asked. There was no point in continuing the conversation. She seemed relieved. A stab of grief shot through my heart, and I looked at the Dreaming platforms. There were only four. She followed my gaze.

"Kupi and Ixara say they're Dreaming on the Twin Serpent altar tonight." She bit in her lips. She didn't like it.

"In this storm?" The Twin Serpent altar was covered but only had three walls. The storm would be strong; the scent of it was undeniable. I remembered what they said about the chaos beginning.

"Kupi and Ixara do what they want. They always have," my mother said. I heard the bitterness in her voice, and a seed of empathy bloomed in me. She was unhappy. She was scared.

《 《 ● 》 》

We ate a small evening meal of clear broth, followed by an infusion that would help us rest. The storm was crackling in the air, wind rattling the mats across the entrances. I heard thunder rumble in the distance. The air seemed alive, raising the hair on my body when I moved certain ways. Our meal was quiet. Safi tried to talk.

"Zeri and Delu, you know what to ask?" she asked.

"Safi," Ixara said. "They know.

"And you two, what will you Dream?" my mother asked, her voice tight.

"What we always ask: for the Dream to show us what we need to know." Kupi sighed.

"And I'm asking to see who Indir will go with when she

leaves, where she will live while this passes," Safi said. "Is there anyone you think you'd like to live near?"

I shook my head.

"I don't know. The Airan are so far away, and I know almost nothing about them, but I know Ali. I like the Ilkan, but I don't know how they live, if I could be comfortable. Maybe the Litéx?" I said. I thought of living on their islands, learning more about their healing gifts. Maybe living among them would heal my gift back to me.

"I will ask if living with them will be best for you," my mother said. I kept my eyes down so she wouldn't notice my disappointment. Even when she spoke of Dreaming, she spoke as if she had some control over what was possible.

"I am grateful," I said.

"Are you two certain you want to sleep on the Twin Serpent altar?" Safi asked my aunts as they entered. "It doesn't seem safe." She picked at the peeling paint on her drinking cup, using a fingernail to scratch at the moon cycle design.

"It is what we have chosen, sister," Ixara said. "We have our reasons."

The wind howled outside, ferocious and angry. I shuddered. It sounded like the beginning of the promised chaos.

《 《 ● 》 》

We gathered in the Dreaming chamber, wearing the embroidered tunics of ceremonial Dreaming. A pattern of the Twin Serpents ran up the center of each tunic, brown and blue patterns of lines and waves, tongues meeting, then curling upward to re-form into twisting bodies. The tunics were narrow at the top but flared out at the knee-length hem to allow for movement. Our hair was unbound, anointed with sacred oil made from Ayan flowers. Kupi and Ixara wore heavier cloaks coated with beeswax; they would be under the storm. They wore leggings and seemed to have additional clothing underneath. I didn't envy them the night ahead. I wondered how they would Dream in such a storm. I didn't mind rain and storms, as long as I wasn't out in them.

Safi pulled out her skin drum. Her drum was painted with creatures of land, sea, and air. Her long black hair was hanging almost to her knees, but her skull was wrapped tightly in material matching her tunic. Kupi, Ixara, my sisters, and I formed a circle, Safi at the edge closest to the altar.

Safi called out our sacred words, beating her drum once. It resounded through the whole chamber. We echoed the words. Safi began beating out a slow, even rhythm.

"We come to you," Safi called.

"We come to you," we echoed.

"We trust the Dream," my mother called out, eyes closed. Delu spoke next.

"I trust the Dream to show me which Fire Warrior will serve the Dream best in the sacrificial game."

"We trust the Dream," we replied.

"I trust the Dream to show me which warrior from Alcanzeh will serve the Dream best in the sacrificial game," Zeri said.

"We trust the Dream," we replied.

"I trust the Dream to show me where my daughter Indir should live, in safety, until her return," Safi said.

"We trust the Dream."

Kupi and Ixara spoke as one.

"We trust the Dream and the sacrifices we make to keep knowing Her," they said, eyes closed.

"We trust the Dream." There was a silence, and I realized they were waiting for me to join the ritual. I felt awkward participating. I couldn't Dream. It felt dishonest, somehow, to act as if I could. I did it anyway.

"I trust the Dream and my part in this story," I said. Perhaps if I spoke it aloud, I would believe it.

"We trust the Dream."

Safi began Singing, a low, wordless chant that one by one the rest of the Dreamers took up. It was part of our ritual to begin in Song. Our altar was laden with offerings: food, jewelry, sacred plants, water.

When we were finished, Safi put her drum down. She went to Kupi and Ixara.

"Don't feel you have to stay out there if the rains become too much," she said, eyebrows furrowed.

"Oh, Safi." Ixara smiled. "The Dream will keep us. We are grateful for your care." Kupi nodded.

"I'll ask a temple worker to stay at the bottom of the stairs leading to the altar. If you need anything in the night, shout down," my mother said.

"That is a wonderful idea, Safi. I love the way your mind works." Kupi kissed Safi on the center of her forehead. My aunts turned to my sisters and me. They embraced us all as well.

"Trust the Dream," Ixara whispered in my ear. Kupi held my eyes for a long moment. She seemed on the verge of tears. They held hands and left.

I lay on my pallet, my sisters on either side. Safi was across the chamber, in front of the altar, already spread out, slipping into the Dream. We had our own small ritual no one else knew about. I turned to each of my sisters and touched my fingers to their lips. They did the same for me and each other. As a child, I had always chewed my lips; Delu started touching them to stop me, and our ritual was born. My sisters held my hands until they too slipped away, their bodies going slack, eyes moving behind closed lids.

Outside, the rains began pounding. I could hear them even from deep within the temple. I shivered, though the air was hot, heavy in the chamber.

I wondered where I would go. I could go south with the Ilkan, live among them. I would have to become stronger; the Ilkan lived much closer to the natural world than I was used to. Or I could live with the Litéx, learn the underwater world they spoke of. I thought I might like to be surrounded by water, learn more about Ovis, how the gifts he carried were shaped by his mother's people.

I turned on my side, thoughts dissolving into one another. Ovis. The Pili. Chaos. A new city built over Alcanzeh, long after our story moved into the Dream. I drifted to sleep.

I'll return for you. The voice spoke as if it were in my head. I opened my eyes: No one in the chamber had spoken. Everyone was still deep in Dreaming. Delu had a line of spit coming out of her mouth. Safi groaned. But I knew I'd heard a voice. I looked at the altar. Had the Dream spoken to me? No. I knew what that felt like, what it sounded like. I waited to hear if the voice came again. It didn't. I curled on my side and fell back asleep.

Quickly. I sat up. The voice had come again; I was sure of it. I looked around. *Tighter,* the voice said again, as if in my head. I wrapped my arms tightly around myself. The sounds of the rain decreased until they stopped, and the night Song of insects and birds took up tentatively, then in full force. I stayed up for a long while, staring at the patterns of dancing light on the stones above me until sleep pulled me in.

((●))

A scream ripped through the entire temple. My eyes flew open. I sat up, gasping. Zeri and Delu were up too. Safi was already running out of the chamber. My sisters and I followed.

A temple worker was screaming, pulling at her hair. Other temple workers surrounded her, trying to calm her, but the girl was distraught, shaking. Safi slapped the girl across her face, and the girl stopped screaming and went completely still, mouth open in shock. My mother had never struck anyone. I was shaking, my entire body filled with dread. The temple worker's feet were covered in blood. There were red footprints behind her.

Safi's face went pale at the sight of the girl's feet. I pushed past my mother and the temple workers, following the dark prints.

My blood went cold when I saw where they had come from. The stairs that led to the Twin Serpent altar were soaked in blood.

I heard my mother screaming my name but I ignored her. I ran up the steps, each one more sticky than the last. Flies buzzed around the small red pools. When I got to the top, all the breath was pulled from my body. I wanted to scream but couldn't find my voice. I turned away from the sight and squatted down, my legs unable to support my weight. I saw my own feet were covered in Kupi and Ixara's blood.

《 《 ● 》 》

When I awoke, I was laid out on a pallet, wearing an unfamiliar tunic. My sisters sat near me, their eyes swollen from crying. I sat up, remembering, and began to shake. Zeri leaned into me. Delu was still beside us, her mouth hung open, her eyes blank.

"Ixara, Kupi," I said, my voice small. Delu shook her head slowly, tears spilling from her eyes. I sobbed, feeling as though my entire body would split from the pain cleaving me from head to groin. My legs were numb, scrubbed raw of blood. Voices shouted from outside the chamber.

Eley strode in, face stricken. Lal followed her. I saw blood on their tunics, as if they had been kneeling in it. The Litéx sisters spoke, but all I heard was sounds. I could understand no words. Lal left the room, calling out for someone. I lay back on my pallet and closed my eyes. Drums rang out from somewhere. Another voice, masculine, joined the cacophony.

Arms went around me, lifting me from the pallet, cradling

me as if I was a small child. Ovis. I knew his scent. I rested my head against his shoulder, tears running into his tunic. I said nothing as he carried me out of the temple, down the steps. Other voices called out, but Ovis ignored them, his strides long. My eyes were closed against the sun. I felt Ovis carrying me up another set of stairs; I felt the shade of stone. I smelled the water before he eased me into it. The warmth seeped into me. He reclined me on the stones, my head resting on the steps, body floating.

"Indi," he said. I didn't open my eyes. I hadn't asked him how he knew my small name, what my family called me.

"Why do you call me Indi?" I whispered. He didn't answer for a long moment.

"I heard one of your sisters call you that, once. It is how I've always thought of you." His answer was simple.

I put my arms over my head and pushed myself off the step, floating. My body felt odd, as if it didn't belong to me. Tears streamed out of my eyes into the water. I wept. Hands stroked my cheek, cupping my head, and Ovis moved me through the water as Eley had. My legs trembled; I couldn't stop them.

"May I Sing?" Ovis's breath was warm on my face. I nodded. He began a lament, a grieving Song for those who crossed into the Dream without notice. I opened my eyes. My aunts had been acting strangely for days. Had they known?

"Where are their bodies?" I asked aloud. I didn't expect an answer. Ovis's eyes were closed, his face wet with his own tears. I reached up to touch his face and pulled him down until his mouth was on mine.

The kiss was wet, salty, our lips slippery with tears and bath water. Ovis sank into the water, pulling me down with him until only our heads were above water. I wrapped my weight-less self around him, anchoring myself to his heat, my legs around his waist. He was weightless too, and we drifted and sank underwater, kissing, then came up, sputtering. I heard a familiar voice calling my name. Delu. I yanked myself away from Ovis and went to the stairs. Delu came in with a dry tunic.

"Indi?" Her voice was strained. I rose out of the water, my tunic clinging to my body. I felt, not better, but less agitated. Still, my heart pounded out a war drum. Either from my grief or Ovis's kiss.

"I'm here, Del." I embraced my sister. Delu looked past me at Ovis. He was still in the water, completely wet. "Ovis brought me into the bath, to get my senses back after . . ." I didn't finish.

"Come back, please. Zeri and I don't know what to do about Safi. We need you." She hurried out of the chamber. I looked back at Ovis, still standing waist-deep in the water. I sighed, made the gesture of gratitude, and followed my sister.

《《●》》

Our temple was surrounded by a crowd. Avex stood before it, keeping the people back. A man was shouting that it had been the Pili. Word had traveled fast.

Safi was sitting in the main chamber, on the stone floor. Her face looked haggard.

I went to my mother and kneeled in front of her.

"Safi?"

My mother looked at me as if she was a stranger. Her eyes were blank. She was in disbelief.

"My sisters," Safi said, her voice raw as if she had been screaming. I tried to embrace her, but she stayed stiff, not moving or seeming to notice anything. I looked up to where Zeri was in the corner, whispering with Lal. Ali strode in. Lal went to speak to him, but he ignored her, going to Safi. He pulled her up from the stone floor and embraced her. I gaped. My mother softened in his arms, her posture going slack, and she leaned into him, tears streaming down her face. Lal's eyes were round in shock as well. It felt too intimate. I turned away.

"Alcan comes," Naru said, entering the chamber.

I ached for my aunts. They would have known what to do, who to ask for, how to calm Safi. Their levity and joy were painfully absent. I swallowed the lump in my throat. Safi let go of Ali, her eyes small and bright with unshed tears.

"Let him come. I blame him for this." Safi's voice was as hard as temple stone. Naru went to her.

"Safi, sister. This isn't the time for confrontation," Naru said softly, her eyes flashing to Ali's for help. He tried to whisper something to Safi, but she pushed him away.

"Let him come. I'll tell him exactly what we think of him," Safi spit. Naru stood in front of her, body taut. She looked wilder than I had ever seen her, the scent of her sharp in the air.

"What did the temple worker say happened?" Zeri asked. Safi's posture dropped. Naru rubbed her hand along her back, and my mother began weeping anew. She spoke through her tears, words broken by her ragged breathing.

"She said it was raining most of the night. She stayed awake; the storm kept her up. Just before dawn, the storm moved on. She waited, expecting—" Safi stopped, eyebrows creasing into a furrow. "She waited, and then she heard the flies. She went up and . . ." Safi closed her eyes, tears spilling out.

《《●》》

"Two less Dreamers to concern myself with." Alcan's voice rang through the chamber. He was dressed like a Fire Warrior, vest open to reveal the scar in the center of his chest. He stood framed by the entrance, Fire Warriors flanking him on either side. Inkop was not with him.

"Two Dreamers who died Dreaming for you," Safi said, dark eyes on his. They stared at each other for several long moments.

"I don't believe your sisters are dead," Alcan said slowly, eyes fixed on Safi. My mother looked as if she wanted to lunge at him, tear every hair from his head. Beside her, Ali tensed.

"Then please, Alcan," Safi said his name as if it were a curse, in slow measure, "tell me where my sisters are. Or better yet, perhaps you can ask your Pili."

"I don't know where your sisters are; that's your secret. Dreamers are very good at keeping secrets." Alcan glanced at me, eyes mocking. I stood taller, wanting to appear stronger than I felt.

"You can't believe they can be alive. You didn't see the blood!" Safi was shouting. Ali and Naru encircled her, trying to speak calming words.

"I saw no blood. All I know is that last night, the first night you Dreamers were to Dream for me, two of you disappeared." Alcan stood his ground, the Fire Warriors with him completely stoic.

"They are gone, their bodies are gone, and all that was left was blood and hair," Safi said, deflating. "Tell me how it is possible, Alcan? Do you want to know what I believe? I believe it was your Pili friend. He found a way to kill them, to use their blood—" Her voice broke in a sob.

I clung to my sisters. I hadn't considered the idea. Kupi and Ixara sacrificed for a dark ritual so the Pili could somehow get powers for himself or Alcan.

"I don't pretend to know the rituals of the Dreamers of Alcanzeh. I do know you protect each other, that you keep secrets." Alcan was motionless. I saw the vein in his neck pounding; his heart was beating fast.

"They're gone, my sisters are gone." Safi bent forward, hands on her knees, hair falling forward. She let out a wail that made the hairs on my neck stand up. I had never heard anyone make a sound like that.

"Did you Dream that? Is it another Dream you're hiding from me?" Alcan stared at me, then at my mother. He looked around the chamber. "Of course, I still need to know who did Dream. The Game will be played in two nights. If your warrior wins, I might consider letting you Dream for me."

It was cruel. Our entire world had changed, and Alcan wanted to play a game.

"Not now," Safi murmured, still bent over, her tears falling from her face, making dark spots on the stone floor. Ali turned suddenly, a wind rising from him as he moved. Alcan's eyes went wide. He stepped backward.

"You will not desecrate our grief, Alcan. And you will answer for this." Ali's voice held a terrifying calm. He spoke with a power I hadn't known he possessed. It made me shake. Alcan paled. His Fire Warrior guards stepped beside him.

"I have nothing to answer for. You did this," Alcan hissed, but the bluster had gone out of him. Something about Ali had shaken him. I was impressed. Alcan opened his mouth to speak again but turned and walked out of the room, shouting for everyone to get out of his way.

《 《 ● 》 》

We wailed. We wept. I sank into arms and was held. I held. We couldn't rest. We couldn't keep our eyes open. We ached, alone and with each other. We were each alone. We each kept reaching out for Kupi and Ixara with our minds. We felt absence. We sunk. We were touched. We spoke words none of us would ever remember speaking. We were silent. We received. We gave. We lit fires at our altars. Our bodies were altars of grief. We didn't speak of Dreams or of kings or chaos or cycles ending. We broke.

Then it was time for our midday meal.

Ali helped us move to the gathering chamber. Naru and Raru draped gray mourning cloths over our bodies as we sat slumped. Lal and Eley served us steaming bowls of broth, offering to feed us. We sat in silence. No one spoke. The absence of my aunts was a presence. It was a hole. The world had shifted.

"Chaos," I whispered. My sisters looked at me and nodded. "They said the chaos would begin and it did."

My mother raised her head. "More secrets. Why did they choose to sleep up there? In that storm? How did the Pili get to them?" She began to weep again softly.

"Safi, Alcanzeh isn't safe. This is proof. Have you considered leaving with your daughters?" Lal asked gently. My mother's head snapped up.

"We will never leave Alcanzeh. This is the sacred city of Dreamers." Her face collapsed into grief again.

"Is it still sacred?" Delu asked. "After what happened?"

"We aren't leaving," Safi said.

"I am," I said, rubbing at my dry eyes. Safi lifted her head, tears spilling down her cheeks. Ali put an arm around her, and she leaned into him. I had no idea they were close, but she fit against his body in ease. His tears ran down his cheeks into her hair.

"You will go with the Ilkan," Safi said. "I saw you with Nahi. You must go to her. It is what the Dream showed me."

I looked at the Ilkan. Their eyes were kind, open with emotion.

"Where do the Ilkan live?" I asked. I knew they lived in the south but didn't know if they lived near either coast or somewhere in the middle.

"We live close enough to the volcano belt to see the smoke on clear days," Raru said. She looked pleased. "I will take you. You'll be safe with me."

"And Ovis." Delu smiled at me sideways. I felt my face grow warm.

Zeri sobbed once, slamming a hand down hard, flipping the bowl she'd been eating from. Broth spilled everywhere. We stared. Zeri never lost her temper. She put her head in her hands.

"I hate the chaos. I hate that it's taking everything." She raised her head, tears streaming down her face. "Not Ovis, he isn't going with you. I'm so sorry, Indir."

I sat up straight. Everything else in the room disappeared.

"You saw him?" I barely had a voice. My chest felt hollow.

Zeri exhaled.

"Son of Tavovis and the Singer; a voice in the Dream told me. I'm so sorry."

"Who will he be fighting?" I tried to imagine Ovis in the game arena, rushing toward an unseen opponent.

"Inkop." Delu was trembling.

I closed my eyes. I wished it to be anyone else.

"If Ovis wins he can still accompany me," I said, hoping he wouldn't be too injured or required to stay otherwise.

"Indir," Ali said. "We want you to leave as soon as you can, during the Game. Alcanzeh isn't safe. The Dream has spoken. Alcan is dangerous to you."

"That's too soon. We haven't had the ritual for Kupi and Ixara; I have to be here for that. I'm not ready. I can't leave yet." I turned to my sisters, who looked as horrified as I felt.

My mother stood and crossed the room, kneeling in front of me. She put her hands on my shoulders, staring into my eyes.

"Indir. I cannot lose you. It would kill me. I can't risk anything happening to you in this city. Trust the Dream, daughter. Trust me. Please. Your sisters and I will be safe here." She spoke as if she had to convince herself. I knew I had to leave; the Dream had shown it. I didn't want to, but the sooner I left, the sooner I would be able to return.

"The ritual for Kupi and Ixara?" I asked.

My mother blinked. She had been expecting a different reaction, but I was too tired to do anything but accept what was before me.

"We'll perform the ritual tonight. There aren't any bodies to pre—" She stopped herself, swallowing hard.

I nodded, unable to speak. I sat back, and my sisters wrapped their arms around me. Their bodies were warm and real against the pain of the story we were living. My skin stuck to their skin, and I wondered how long it would be until I could touch them again.

CHAPTER SIXTEEN

SAYA

We walked through the jungle, away from any path. I tested my newly arrived gift of Singing, humming to part plants, surprised when they listened to me. Nahi had her own way of communicating with the world around us, listening to insect Songs and bird calls, touching her hand to certain roots. She found us a spring when we were thirsty and followed birds to a tree heavy with fruit. She told me a little more about the Ilkan.

"There are few of us left. We live private lives. We are most comfortable with creatures of the earth. We live in alignment with the living world. We cannot Sing or heal, but we have a knowing that is a deep instinct. It shows us changes. The Ilkan live knowing we are all interconnected. And there's been a growing imbalance. The animals sense it, as do the plants, the serpents, spiders, birds. It must be the one you were told about in the Dream."

I told her more about my life with Celay as we made our way through the jungle, following no path. She stopped a few times to place her hands to the earth and then pick up speed. I had a feeling there was someone following us, but Nahi didn't want to frighten me. She thanked me several times for trusting her. I trusted Batuk, and he had trusted Nahi. I was learning myself each step we took, how I was eager to talk, share, to listen. A part of me felt grief for leaving Celay. She had looked broken. I knew how that felt.

We walked through the day, silences growing longer as afternoon softened toward evening. I was tired but kept up as best I could. Nahi moved us faster. The jungle Song intensified, as if the world around us was sensing something we could not. I began to smell salt in the air. We were nearing the coast.

The sun was setting when we broke through to a cliffside. Nahi sniffed the air. She pushed me toward a vine that hung over the edge and hissed.

"Sing your way down, now." She removed her travel pack, tossing it to the ground, and leaped back into the jungle, moving faster than I thought was possible. I heard grunts and growls from inside the canopy.

I seized the end of the vine and began Singing. I was so tired the Song had a difficult time moving from my throat into my chest. I cleared my throat a few times, then started again. The vine listened and responded. It wrapped itself around me and began growing, lowering down over the edge of the cliff. A shout came from above, and I clung to the vine. The setting sun was bright in my eyes, a shining path of light splitting the ocean from horizon to shore. The sandy cliffs were soft as I descended past violet flowers that grew like long tongues from the crevices in the red earth. They moved as if licking the air as I passed, the Song calling to them. A hummingbird hovered near my face briefly, the setting sun reflecting a crescent moon of light in her eye. She chirped and sipped at an unfurling night blossom.

I reached the sandy ground. The sun dipped halfway below

the horizon, the sky stained orange and pink, streaking the few clouds in color. I heard more shouts above me. I had come further than I'd imagined. I strained to see anything. Something flew off the cliff and tumbled down the rock face to the earth. I ran to see what it was.

I cringed when I saw the blood, soaking into the sand. It was a pack, though not the one Nahi had been wearing. I hurried away from it, deciding not to look up anymore. I heard a whistle.

There was a boat near to shore with two bodies in it. It was unlike any boats I had seen before: long and wide, decorated with markings all over that I didn't recognize. A long, thick pole was strapped down in the center, wrapped in woven material. It was a boat for traveling long distances. One of the people in the boat raised a hand and waved it at me, then pointed to the cliff.

Nahi was on the vine, leaping her way down. She landed on all fours, then rose. Her hands had changed. Her nails had grown into black claws, her hands more muscled. There was blood splattered across her chest, and her color was out. She adjusted her hip pack, then crossed to the bloody pack that had come from the cliff. She dug through it, and when she found whatever she was looking for, she called out in a strange yowl that made the skin on my body rise. Moments later, some sort of rodent leaped out of the cliff toward Nahi. She leaned down and spoke to it. The rodent rose on its back legs, sniffing, then took whatever Nahi had found in the pack and ran off, back up the cliff, disappearing over the edge.

"We were being tracked, but no one else is near now," she said, plunging her hands into the sand. When she removed them, sand stuck to the blood. She brushed the sand away; it took the blood off with it. "More friends, if you are willing to trust." She gestured behind me.

Two women splashed out of the boat, pulling it along with them to shore. The older woman carried a small light. I stared at her face. Her features were different from any I had ever seen. I had seen marked bodies before, but never with the intricacy of detail the woman wore on her face. Her skin was dyed in swirls and dots that extended down her chin and across her jawline. They reminded me of waves. Her lower lip was dyed a dark color. Her eyes were long with dark centers and thick lashes. Her skin was sun-darkened, and she had the eye lines of one who stared at horizons.

"A Singer?" the younger woman said, an eager look on her face. I looked at her, mouth open. She reminded me of myself. We were the same height, near the same age. Her hair was shorter than mine, cut close to her head. She moved with easy confidence.

"You heard me?" I asked. I liked her face. It was honest, watching me carefully. I wanted her to have a good impression of me. I thought of what Nahi said and repeated it.

"I honor my gifts, even if it makes others uncomfortable," I said, hoping I sounded as sure as Nahi did when she said it. I saw the Ilkan smile from the side of my eye. The young woman laughed.

"I'm not uncomfortable. We Sing too, though our Song is different. Where did you learn yours?" she asked. I opened my mouth to speak, but the woman with her interrupted.

"I am Ahkal, and this is my child Yixu. We greet you in the name of all that is sacred."

"I am Saya. I greet you in the name of all that is sacred," I said, opening my hands. They mirrored the gesture.

"Where did you learn your Song?" Yixu asked again.

"Yixu," Ahkal said in a tone Yixu must have understood, because she stepped back.

"Saya, will you let us help you on your journey?" Ahkal asked. I looked back up toward the cliff. The tongue flowers had retreated when the sun set. The cliff looked bloodied in the dusk, the night blossoms blooming a dark violet. I shuddered, not wanting to think about who had been seeking me out.

"Who's following me?" I asked. Nahi and Ahkal looked at each other. I groaned. Yixu nodded, as if she agreed.

"I've told her as little as I can," Nahi said, jumping into the boat, holding a hand out to me. I crossed my arms. I was exhausted and confused. I wanted more.

"I know almost nothing. I know I'm a Singer, though I just discovered that. I was told in the Dream that I'm a Dreamer too." It felt strange to say aloud. Ahkal didn't look surprised.

"A Dreamer? Are you from Alcanzeh?" Yixu asked. I shook my head. Ahkal stopped her again.

"You are being pursued by someone who wishes your story

not to exist, thinking it can change a larger story," she said, her voice serious.

"Someone wishes to kill me?" I gasped, my hand flying to my neck.

"We're here to keep you safe, Saya," Ahkal said.

"How far will we go? Will I be able to return? What about my mother?" I asked. I knew I was going to get into the boat, but I wasn't ready to yet.

"Your mother wants you safe," Nahi said. I furrowed my brow.

"How do you know? You said you didn't know Celay." My mood was getting sour, but they were patient. I wanted to indulge the feeling. I rarely had a chance to go into my frustration with anyone.

"Your mother wants you safe," Ahkal repeated, running her hand over her daughter's hair. "But if you wish to stay on land, Nahi will do what she can to protect you from those who pursue you. I will stay on the water with Yixu, to keep her safe." Ahkal put her arm around her daughter. Yixu shrugged her arm off.

"I'd get in the boat," Yixu offered. "You will get used to them not telling you anything. I can share my Song with you, and you can teach me yours." She dipped her head a little. I think she wanted to make a good impression on me too.

"I can share what I know, but it isn't very much," I sighed. Yixu held her hand out, pulling me into the boat. I sat beside her. Nahi sat near the front, her hands braced. Ahkal let out a brief cry of Song, and a wave surged forward, lifting the boat and pulling it back.

Yixu started Singing. I felt a thrill in my body. I wanted to

Sing, but I didn't know the Song. I listened as Ahkal joined in, her voice carrying the same Song but in a different tone. The effect was beautiful. It was a simple Song, a refrain repeated over and over. I took a breath and added my voice to theirs in a language that was beyond language. Joy rose in me as our voices joined, pushing away the terror that had taken over my body. Nahi turned from the front of the boat, grinning.

I faltered in the Song when I noticed a glow rising from the water. Countless tiny points of light rose, affixing themselves to the vessel on all sides, and streaming back in its wake. Fish swam around us, some pushing the boat forward. It reminded me of the Dream. We surged forward, and I saw that other fish had risen to help move the boat forward. I hung onto the sides and grinned as drops of water splashed across my face and body. We rose and skipped over the waves faster than I thought possible. I opened my mouth to Sing again, and my voice rose high, loud and clear in the coming night. I closed my eyes, feeling as if I were flying. I heard a large splash, and I opened my eyes just in time to see a large shape rise out of the water and crash down not far from us. A whale. For a moment, I thought it was the spirit from Dreaming, but that was impossible.

The boat slowed as Ahkal and Yixu let the Song fade. The shore was just a shadow now. I stopped Singing as well and just stared up, gripping the sides of the boat as it moved through the waves. Nahi wrapped a cloth around her head to keep the spray off her face. It made me notice that the air was cooler. I rubbed at my arms. Yixu pulled a blanket out of a basket from under our bench, and I wrapped it around my shoulders.

"What is your Song? What is this?" I waved my hand over the glow in the water surrounding the boat. It seemed to push us forward.

"I am of the Kemi, far, far to the north of here. It is one of our Songs. Those are our friends; they hear our Song and come to us," Ahkal said. I had never heard of the Kemi.

"Kemi are Singers?" I asked.

"Singing is one of the gifts offered to us," Ahkal said. I turned to Yixu.

"Sing," Yixu said eagerly, reaching to take my hand, smiling. I smiled back. She lit something in a clay jar, a small flame that barely sputtered, letting out a glow so we could see each other's faces. The comet was a hair-thin sliver rising in the sky.

I opened my mouth and began Singing the Song of the Comet. I closed my eyes and let the Song build in me, word-less, moving through me as we moved through the waves. The wind lifted my voice and carried it away. I heard Yixu try to join along, but after a moment, she stopped. I Sang until I felt the Song begin to release. Nahi was curled up, asleep. Yixu was squeezing my hand.

"She doesn't like boats." She pointed at Nahi with her chin. "Are you of the Litéx?"

Yixu released my hand, leaning forward, elbow resting on her knees. She had a small marking going down the center of her chin, the beginning of a design. I shook my head.

"I don't know the Litéx," I answered. I had heard of them, briefly. Healers who lived on islands far to the west.

"My father's mother was of the Litéx. I feel your Song when you Sing; I feel it in my body. Perhaps we are family," Yixu said.

"My sweet fish, I am not of the Litéx, and I feel your Song when you Sing. The Kemi and Litéx share a gift; it is shaped differently, but it is the same gift. You may be recognizing the gift, Yixu," Ahkal said softly.

"I believe you, and I believe myself too," Yixu said, frowning. Ahkal barked out a laugh.

"My father was a Singer, but I don't know anything about him. I thought I was born by Night Bird until recently," I said. Yixu nodded.

"My father died before I was born," she said. "I never knew his Song, though my mother tried to teach it to me. I want to travel to the Litéx, but my mother says one can only travel to their islands in groups. One boat alone is too dangerous."

I loved the way she spoke, openly and without fear. I wanted to share too.

"I heard my father's Song in the Dream. I saw him, but I don't know anything about him," I said shyly.

"I wonder if you could see my father in the Dream," Yixu said.

"Yixu," Ahkal said in a tone of voice I recognized as a warning. Yixu rolled her eyes.

"I speak my mind too much, my mother says. But I don't know why I shouldn't speak what I'm thinking. It makes living easier, don't you think?" she asked.

We hit a large wave, and water sprayed all over us. Ahkal and

Yixu started Singing again. Something large nudged the boat from beneath, and we changed direction slightly. Ahkal had her hand on a piece of wood that extended into the water; she adjusted it, and we moved smoothly on the waves again. Nahi pulled a blanket tighter around her body.

"I haven't spoken to many other people besides my mother. She preferred I didn't speak with others." I tried to say what was on my mind, the way Yixu did. She leaned toward me, eyes wide.

"You have a strange mother too, then?" She glanced past me at Ahkal and laughed. Ahkal was shaking her head, smiling. I laughed, looking at the comet.

"The Songs I know, I know from Dreaming. One was offered to me by a whale spirit, the other by the comet." I gestured toward the horizon.

"Which one did you Sing us?" Yixu asked, looking excited.

"The comet."

"Sing the other Song from Dreaming," Yixu said, grinning. I started Singing it. I closed my eyes, remembering the joy I'd felt when the spirit and I had moved toward each other in the Dream. The Song rose from a different place, as if it wanted to be known. I faltered when I heard a response.

I opened my eyes. Nahi was awake again, staring out over the water. A family of whales was near the boat, their large bodies visible just beneath the surface. There were at least four of them in different sizes. The glow that carried the boat clung to them, the whales shining a shadowy green in the water. They were Singing, following the Song I held. I rose, slightly unbalanced. Yixu held out a hand and steadied me. I let the blanket fall from my shoulders, the Song radiating out of my body. I raised my hands in the air, my head back. It felt natural. One of the whales disappeared, diving low. It rose in a rush, almost completely out of the water, and crashed down. Other creatures were rising to the surface.

When the Song had moved from me, I sat down hard. The gift was new, and it tired me. Yixu moved so she was pressed against my side, then leaned her head on my shoulder. It was awkward for me, unused to touch, but I put my arm around her. She sighed.

"I want to know that Song. I felt it even more than the comet Song. I don't care what my mother says; I believe we're kin."

Ahkal smiled a strange smile at the sky, shaking her head. She pulled a basket out from under the bench and handed me a dark bundle, then tossed one to Yixu, who immediately began eating. I took a bite and realized I was hungry, starving. It was some sort of salted leaf, wrapped around smoked fish. It was strange but satisfying, and by the time I finished, I wanted more. But I didn't ask. Ahkal was chewing slowly, gazing out over the water to where the comet hovered above the horizon. She turned to me and spoke.

"There is an island near here, for those who journey by boat. It has places for travelers to sleep, fresh water. It's a sacred resting place, protected from anyone who wishes to do harm to travelers. We'll stop there for the night."

"I didn't know places like that existed," I said. The food had filled me, and I felt sleepy. I leaned against Yixu a little to see how she would react. She turned, and I leaned backward into her, the back of my head against her shoulder. Singing with her had made me trust her; it was the same feeling I had with Ruta.

Yixu leaned closer and started Singing in a language I didn't understand, but I felt the ache of the words. It was a sleeping Song, one for babies and small children. Whatever gift she carried in her voice soothed me, and my posture softened.

I leaned against her more and let myself be sung to sleep.

CHAPTER SEVENTEEN

INDIR

The night was cool; strange for the season. The air smelled clean, of salt, smoke, and the damp green of the jungle. The steps to the Twin Serpent altar had been scrubbed clean. I still looked for traces of blood, but I saw none. Someone had already set up the pile of wood, herbs, Ayan blossoms, and sacred oil-soaked tinder. Ali, Naru, Raru, and Lal joined us.

We stood in a circle before the Twin Serpents. I refused to look at them. I was too angry to gaze upon their forms. Lighting the fire would start seven nights of mourning for the Dreamers. My mother and sisters would not attend the sacrificial Game. I was curious to see how many in Alcanzeh would mourn with the Dreamers and how many would attend the Game. The city would split behind me as I left.

Safi lit the fire with a torch. We held hands. The Twin Serpents flickered in the firelight.

Lal began Singing, a Death Song I had never heard before. It was about returning to the Dream, a lament for those left behind, our grief. Then, the tempo changed and the tone of the Song shifted, from grief to the joy that those returning to the Dream felt. I listened but felt none of the peace that usually filled me when I heard a Death Song. It was the first time anyone I loved had returned to the Dream. I ached for sleep, a Dreamless sleep, dark, away from my pain.

When Lal finished Singing, Naru turned to Safi, opening a pouch at her hip. She poured out several small objects and placed them atop the bundle with Kupi and Ixara's hair.

"Teeth from our sister the Jaguar. May she protect your sisters, always," Naru said, pressing her forehead to Safi's and stepping aside.

Ali turned to Safi and untied a long, blue feather from his cloak. He put it on top of the bundle, placing one hand on top of it and the other on Safi's forearm. "May the winds guide our sisters, keep their path clear." He touched her forehead with his. My mother choked out a sob, then swallowed it.

Lal unhooked a small, stoppered gourd from a rope around her neck and placed it on the bundle. Tears ran down her face.

"Let them be healed on their journey, their thirst quenched, their fears washed away." Safi let out another sob when Lal's forehead met hers.

Safi knelt. She beckoned us to join her. We did, enclosing the circle. Safi leaned in, and we put our arms around each other's shoulders. Safi's tears spilled down her face onto the pile she had placed in a basket she had woven herself. Zeri began crying next, followed by Delu. I couldn't cry, even though I wanted to. My grief was so vast my body could not recognize it and respond. My tears would not be a part of the ritual.

We knelt for what felt like moons, eyes on the folded cloth

that held offerings for Kupi and Ixara. We were silent, breathing shaking breaths. Then, one by one, we sat back. The blood rushed back into my lower legs and feet, making them tingle with small stabs of pain. I remained still.

"May the Dream welcome them with Song, may Kupi and Ixara join our ancestors and guide us. May we live in a way that honors," my mother's voice broke, "my sisters, Kupi and Ixara." Safi placed the basket of offerings over the flame. It caught quickly and began smoking as it was devoured by the sacred fire. I ached. I felt as if a part of myself was burning, dying, being turned to ash before my eyes.

《《●》》

The next morning, the temple was a quiet place. Our mother retreated to the Water Temple to grieve for her sisters, and for what was to come. My sisters and I barely left our chamber. We sat in silence mostly, taking turns sharing hammocks, swinging ourselves as a comfort. The Avex posted outside stopped anyone from entering the temple. From the platform off my chamber, I could see offerings piling up at the foot of the main staircase. There were several baskets, bowls, wreaths of flowers, and food. At midday, temple workers gathered the baskets and brought them into the temple. I had been restless all day, trying to think of what I would take with me. I needed a distraction. I went to see what the offerings were.

《《●》》

Dua was at the entrance to the chamber. She heard me approach and glanced inside.

"Dua." I wasn't surprised to see her. She had quickly become familiar.

"Aren't you preparing?" Dua whispered, looking me up and down.

"How do you know?" I whispered back.

"Delu told me," she said. I frowned. Delu should have stayed quiet. but staying quiet was outside her skills.

I looked past her, a sudden joy awakening in my blood.

"Indir," Ovis said from where he was kneeling inside the chamber. The contents of several baskets was spread before him. He was sorting the offerings into piles. Around him, temple workers unpacked baskets, giggling and handing the contents over to him. My joy turned to terror, remembering he had to fight in the Game.

"Ovis, what are you doing?" I crossed and knelt opposite him, looking at the piles in front of him, not meeting his eyes.

"Your mother asked that we examine the offerings, to make sure nothing is coming into the temple that may be dangerous," he said, running his hand through a basket of dried maize kernels.

"Shouldn't you be preparing for . . . ?" My voice trailed off. His eyes were bright and serious on mine. I tilted my head. Did he know he was to fight the Game? He saw my look and nodded once, briefly, the motion exactly like his father's.

"Indir needs to speak to Ovis alone," Dua announced to the other temple workers, surprising me. The temple workers looked at us. Ovis smiled at them. They grinned back, giggling, and left. Dua beckoned me close.

"Do you want me to help you prepare a pack?" she whispered. "I can start without you and get the most important parts ready while you speak with your friend." I embraced her quickly. Her skin was hot against mine. I nodded, and she darted away.

"You know about the sacrificial Game?" I whispered to Ovis. We knelt opposite each other, offerings spread between. He gazed at me for a long while before nodding.

"I am an Avex. It will be an honor." His words were practiced, but I saw in him a hunger. He wanted something else.

"You know I'm leaving," I said, my voice low. I didn't look at him. I plunged one hand into a basket of grains. He reached forward, slipping his hand into the basket, grasping mine. I dropped my chin to my chest and closed my eyes. It was as if the center of me was in our intertwined hands, pulsing, tender.

He pushed the basket away from us, walking on his knees to me. He lifted me, pulling my body to his. I let myself be held, chest to chest, thighs to thighs, my cheek against the skin of his chest. He inhaled and exhaled against my ear. He kissed the side of my face slowly, dragging his lips toward my mouth. He kissed me with tenderness. I reached back with more urgency, a hunger to feel his mouth and tongue on mine. I pulled away. We were both breathing hard.

"You know I can't Dream?" I asked. He answered with a nod, kissing me again. I pulled back, looking into his dark eyes. "I would have asked, made every offering to have seen you in

Dreaming," I said. I went to kiss him, but Ovis smiled, touching my lips with his fingertips.

"It is better like this. I know you're here with me because you want to be, not because you saw me in Dreaming."

"I didn't have to Dream you to know. I would have chosen you for myself." I breathed into him, my lips against his. "I choose you." My lips tightened away from his in a smile. He was smiling too. He pressed his forehead to the center of my forehead.

"I choose you." He pressed his mouth back to mine. He bit my bottom lip playfully, gazing into me so that my blood heated in my body.

"When?" I whispered. It was barely midday. There were hours until I was expected to disappear for sleep.

"Tonight?" He lifted me against him, hands beneath my hips. I giggled, pushing his hands away so my knees were on the ground again.

"You don't have to prepare for the Game?" I murmured. He shook his head.

"I'll prepare later. I want to be with you tonight."

"Tonight." I told him how to find the chamber where I would wait for him. He kissed me one last time and left.

《 《 ● 》 》

I had to distract myself until evening.

"I need your help," I told my sisters. They looked up from where they were sharing a hammock, legs intertwined. "I need to prepare. What do I take with me? What will I need? Dua is helping, but I need you."

Zeri untangled herself from Delu and swung out of the hammock. This was one of her gifts, preparing and organizing. Delu looked at me sideways, and we both smiled.

"We'll take over one of the sorting chambers, say we aren't to be disturbed. Get a guard at the door. I'll send a worker to the storerooms to select some things I know we have piled up down there. I'll make something up: we're sending traders to get us . . . something." Zeri shot up the stairs, already calling out to a temple worker. Delu and I followed her down to a storage chamber. Zeri had already sent most of the temple workers away and set oil lamps out for light.

"We don't know what the journey will be, so you have to be prepared." Zeri was breathless. She opened a large basket, pulling out a strange frame of wood with material hanging from it. "This is old, but I remember seeing it in the stores years ago when I was a child. It belonged to a trader who passed into the Dream while visiting Alcanzeh. A traveling pack. Stand."

I stood. Zeri placed it across my back, tying wide straps around my hips, across my chest and shoulders. It was large but light. Delu stared at me with a skeptical look on her face.

"I don't know if this is right," Delu said, her voice full of doubt. "Not if Indir has to move quickly at any point."

"She can leave the pack behind if she has to move fast," Zeri countered.

"With all her supplies in it? Isn't Raru moving her through the jungle? That pack doesn't look—"

"Then you do it," Zeri snapped. She tried to untie the straps, but her frustration made her pull the straps even tighter. I gasped at the pain across my chest and yanked the whole thing off. It clattered to the floor.

Zeri huffed, her face red. I touched her shoulder gently.

"None of us know how to prepare for this, sister." I tried to pull her in, but Zeri moved away. She sat on the bench, her head in her hands. Tears streamed down her cheeks.

"Indir is leaving, and I feel like I have no part in this story. I have to do something. I will curl up and retreat into the Dream if I don't have something to do."

"Zeri, you are a part of this story. We're all scared, little love." Delu tried to reason.

Zeri wiped at her face with the hem of her tunic. She hadn't changed out of her sleeping tunic.

"Zeri." She looked up when I spoke her name in the tone of authority our mother used. "Get up and change out of your sleeping tunic. Drink some water and come back to help me prepare. You're good at this kind of thing and I'm not."

Zeri sniffed but stood. She pulled me into a tight embrace. I could feel her shaking; the fear and uncertainty that coursed through her body reflected mine. When Delu joined us, Zeri pulled away and left the chamber. We stared after her.

"Delu, how will we survive this?" I asked.

"I don't know," Delu said. She opened her mouth to say something else but bit in her lips. She took my hand. I looked at our hands, fingers intertwined. We had the same hands, though hers were fuller than mine. My nails were short and square while hers were long and shiny from the oils she constantly rubbed into them to keep them strong. Our mother had the same hands. I wondered if I would ever touch hands like mine again. We sat for a while that way, not speaking.

Zeri walked back into the chamber.

"I found help," she said. Her eyes were bright. Raru entered behind her.

"Raru." I rose and pressed my cheek to hers briefly. Her face was warm.

"Dreamer, I am sorry for all you have endured these days," she said in her low voice.

"I have to trust the Dream," I said. "You'll be my guide. What do I need to bring with me for our journey?" I motioned with my hands to the various bowls. Raru looked at the pack on the floor with a sneer.

"I am an excellent guide, Indir. You will need none of this."

There was a snort from the doorway. Dua stood there, laden with baskets and packages.

"Indir has never even left this city, or washed her own tunic, prepared her own food, let alone traveled through the jungle for how long?" Dua set her gaze on Raru.

"Who are you?" Raru asked, turning her full attention to Dua as the young woman set down her packages.

"I am Dua. How long will you be guiding Indir? Through the jungle full of biting insects, sharp rocks, poisonous plants?"

"We will travel until we arrive. Are you—?"

Dua didn't let her finish.

"Where will she sleep? On the ground? Or in a tree, curled up next to you?"

I tried not to smile. Zeri didn't hide the grin on her face. Dua stood with her hands on her hips, staring at Raru.

"I hadn't considered that," Raru said, her face and arms mottling slightly as her color came out.

"What can you take with you? How much can you carry at the pace you will be traveling?" Dua asked.

"Not very much."

Dua snorted again and turned to the baskets she'd brought up. Raru's color deepened even more. She knelt beside Dua.

"You'll need this." Dua held out a small bowl filled with salve. "To protect her from insect bites. It will also soothe her feet when they tire."

"Insects?" I asked.

"Biting insects," Dua corrected.

"They don't bother me," Raru said, sniffing at the bowl. Dua rolled her eyes.

"Of course they don't, you're—" Dua waved her hand up and down at Raru.

"Of the Ilkan." Raru's eyes were bright.

"Yes. You're Ilkan, so you must be strong. How much can you carry?" Dua asked, sitting cross-legged on the floor.

"What do I have to bring with me?" I interrupted.

"Nothing, Indir, we are an abundant people," Raru said. Dua hissed softly.

"I'm going to set up a pack for you." Dua ignored Raru and

began arranging items on the floor. "I hope Raru will be carrying the burden of what you take."

Raru tilted her head in affirmation. For a moment, I could have sworn I saw the flick of a tail behind her, but it was a shadow on the wall.

《 ❲ ● ❳ 》

I could hardly breathe, waiting for the night to arrive. I ate with my sisters. They tried to engage me in conversation, but they were both distracted in their own thoughts and only going through the motions of conversation. Delu looked like she was on the verge of tears several times during the meal. I excused myself and went to our chamber, where I sat in front of the altar, dazed. I had no doubts about choosing Ovis. Even in grief, and because of it, I wanted something for myself.

My sisters wandered in eventually. I stayed in front of the altar. I heard Delu sighing, collapsing into her hammock. Zeri busied herself at the basin, splashing water for what felt like an eternity. After much sighing and moving about the room, I heard the creak of Zeri's hammock. I stood and walked to mine, getting in to wait.

My sisters eventually drifted to sleep, their breathing deep. Delu snored slightly. I would tell them, but I wanted it to myself, a secret that was, for once, beautiful. I waited a little longer, then slipped from my hammock. Holding my breath, I tiptoed out of the chamber, and I walked down the hall to the entrance of the darkened chamber, waiting a moment before entering.

It was mostly dark. Moonlight from the shrinking moon illuminated a corner of the room in a silver glow. I sat against the darkest wall, knees pulled to my chest, waiting. Every detail of the room was vivid and sharp. The moonlight on the stone floor, the small spider's web that stretched across a section of exterior platform, half formed, the spider eagerly weaving.

I suddenly sat up in the dark. Someone was in the room, but it wasn't Ovis. The scent was more primal. I looked around but saw no one. The sound of my own breathing seemed to fill the room. I leaped to my feet just as a shape emerged from the shadows. Inkop. He didn't say anything; he stood still, waiting for me to acknowledge him.

"I didn't mean to frighten you," he whispered. "I need to speak with you."

I opened and closed my mouth several times before managing to speak. Inkop was almost the last person I had expected to be there.

"How did you get past the Avex? How did you find me?" I whispered, trying to will my heart to slow.

"The Avex aren't the only well-trained warriors and trackers in this city, Indir. You need to leave Alcanzeh." Inkop sunk back into the shadows, leaning against the wall. I took a step toward him, then looked to the outdoor platform. I didn't know when Ovis was coming.

"Indir, Alcan wants to hurt you. He wants your secret to disappear; he'll do anything for it."

"Why are you telling me this? Aren't you his friend? Or do you just want to keep me frightened before he comes for me?"

I whisper-shouted at him. Inkop put his hands up, his face contorted, as if my words physically hurt him.

"Never, Indir. I'm on your side, I promise you." He rubbed his hands across his face.

"Why?" My hands were cold with fear. I crossed my arms across my chest.

"Alcan is my brother," Inkop said, stepping forward so that his face was in the pale light that had filtered into the room from the rising moon.

"What?" I barely breathed the word, staring at Inkop, trying to see if he was lying or trying to trick me.

"I ask that you don't share this story. I'm only telling you so you may trust me."

"Tell me," I whispered.

"My mother worked here in Alcanzeh. She knew King Anz right before he chose Alcan's mother. She left when she found out she was with child. She didn't tell him. Anz came to where we lived two years after I was born, when he was working toward peace. When he saw me, he knew. He lived with us while he worked on the peace negotiations. He promised me he would send my brother to live with me one day."

"And when he returned to Alcanzeh, he sent Alcan to live with you," I whispered. It seemed impossible.

"It was part of the peace agreement. A future king living among the Fire Warriors as a sign of peace. Alcan arrived angry, emotional. I hoped training with us would temper his rage, but it did the opposite. He poured everything into training with the Fire Warriors. He was always trying to prove he was better than me." Inkop's jaw was tight as he spoke. He moved it back and forth to try to loosen it.

"That doesn't make any sense. Alcan hates his father." I moved closer to Inkop, to see his eyes more clearly.

Inkop jutted his chin forward. "He hates our father because our father loved me. And his mother loved Anz. My brother always places himself in the center of the emotions of others. He will never be satisfied."

"He knew you were his brother?" I was dizzy with the aftereffects of fear. The story he told felt impossible, but as I listened deeper, with my body, it made sense. All my senses were heightened; my mind was half expecting Ovis to land in the room.

"He knew. He was born with the Serpents' mark, not me. He always reminded me of it. He would tell me my gift of fire was the only reason I was stronger than him, so I trained to use it as little as I could." Inkop's eyes were steady on mine. "A few moons before our father died, I noticed Alcan always wore his vest closed. I thought it was strange; he had always been proud of the Twin Serpents' mark on his chest, proclaiming that it marked him as the next guide and ruler of the people." Inkop's eyes became unfocused, remembering.

"His mark," I said. Inkop nodded.

"We lived together, in my mother's home. I had an older sister, Koya. One night, I heard Koya make a sound while we were sleeping. Alcan was trying to convince Koya to choose him, even after she refused. When I confronted him, he jumped up.

His vest was open. I saw where the mark had once been." Inkop's face was drawn. I reached out and took his hand.

"He wasn't punished?" I whispered. His hand was rough, thick with muscle.

"The next day, he confessed he had been wrong and apologized on his knees. He took a torch and promised that if he wasn't asked to leave, he would burn his mark and be sworn to the Fire Warriors forever, especially when he was king. He burned himself as he said it. There was no way to tell if what my sister and I saw was real. The Fire Warriors were so eager to have the power of a king that they ignored what my sister told them. I did not." Inkop's hand tensed; I squeezed back, then let go.

"Why are you telling me this?" I asked.

"I want you to know I stand with Alcanzeh, with you, even though it looks like I've sided with Alcan. I know strategy, how to get close to an enemy, how patience is essential in long battles."

"How can you help?" I rubbed my eyes.

"You tell me," Inkop said, opening his hands. I thought about it.

"I'm leaving Alcanzeh." I took in a shaking breath, hoping I was right to trust him. My heart fell to my stomach as I heard a whistle close by.

"How can I help?" he asked. I stepped forward into the light. His face showed he was relieved I was choosing to trust him. I heard Ovis before I saw him, a rush of air that blew past me and toward Inkop.

Inkop stepped away from the attack, then went into a fighter stance as Ovis spun, ready to attack again. I moved quickly to try and get between them, but they stepped lightly away from me, circling each other.

"She wants you to leave her alone," Ovis growled.

"This isn't where our fight will be." Inkop let a flash of fire out from one of his palms; it was white, bright enough so that when Ovis and I opened our eyes, the Fire Warrior was gone. Ovis was about to run off after him, but I spoke.

"Ovis," I said his name with a tone that caused him to stop and turn.

"Are you hurt?" he asked, running his hands along my arms. He was tight with energy and his warrior training.

"I am not. I agreed to speak to him, but I didn't know he would come here," I said, shaking off his hands. I had enough nervous energy of my own; I didn't need any more of his.

"I didn't know." Ovis took a deep breath to calm himself. I did the same. Ovis opened his arms, and I went to him. His body was hot from the blood rush of the near-fight. I pressed myself against him anyway, wrapping my arms around his neck. I breathed in the scent of him, my face against his shoulder. I hated the thought of leaving him behind when I left Alcanzeh. Knowing he would be fighting in the Game was worse.

"He's on our side," I whispered, my lips brushing against his skin. Ovis pushed me back, his eyes confused.

"How can you know?" Ovis looked as if he wanted to ask more.

"I know. He has shown himself to be different." I took one of Ovis's hands and began kissing the knuckles.

"What does he want?" Ovis stepped closer to me, lifting the hand I held so it was between our mouths.

"To help." I kissed him.

We stopped speaking. In that silence, everything between us was spoken. My breathing was his breathing, his sweat was my sweat. I chose him with every stretch of skin on my body, with every hair. He kissed lifetimes into me. I kissed him with every Dream I'd ever had.

It was beautiful. Awkward and natural at the same time. I let my mind go inward, cocoon away while every other sense of mine heightened in new awareness. I never knew my tongue had instinct. I never knew I could hear the Song in someone else's body and how it harmonized with my own. I never knew sacred existed in such ways outside the Dream. I never knew my body could become an altar. I never knew how to surrender, receive.

"I'll win," he promised me.

I believed him.

He left too soon. I returned to where my sisters slept, my body soft with exhaustion, joy.

CHAPTER EIGHTEEN

SAYA

Yixu tightened her arms around me as the boat hit harder waves.
I woke up. The stopping island was a mass in the dark ahead of
us. Two small fires glowed from the shore. Ahkal Sang a high,
fast Song that sounded like gratitude as the glow broke up
around us, sinking as the wave delivered us to the shore. Nahi
and Ahkal jumped out, pulling the boat ashore. I yawned. We
had landed between the fires. They were untended. I hopped
out of the boat, groaning as my legs became used to solid
ground again. I fell once, then rose and waited for my balance
to return.

"The shelters are ahead," Ahkal called out as she tied the boat
up. "You and Yixu go sleep; we'll secure the boat and tell the
keeper we're here."

Yixu walked up to me, rolling her eyes.

"They want to speak alone but think we can't figure that out,"
she whispered. "Have you ever seen a friendly fire?" I shook
my head. The fire was in a stone column half as tall as we were,
with a bowl where the fire burned.

"The keeper of the island tends these; they burn on a secret
gift the keeper shares with no one, and they only burn when
needed," she said. I looked at the flame. It was shrinking. It
burned itself down to light blue flames that glowed out from

porous rocks. We walked toward one of the stone shelters set on higher ground. There was another small flame glowing inside, as well as sleep platforms and a jar of water.

"Where's the keeper?" I asked. Yixu was stretching, bending over and moving side to side. I joined her, feeling awkward, then relieved as I realized how tense my body was.

"She only comes if called. This place isn't only for travelers, but for anyone who wishes time alone." Yixu sat with her legs in front of her, her fingers reaching toward her toes. I did the same and felt pops of relief across my lower back. "A moon ago, my mother heard a story that made her curious. I don't know what it was, but it must have been important. She brought me to one of these stopping islands and left me, for half a moon. I worked with the keeper on that island, learning a little of their ways. My mother had never left me before, and it was strange to be without her, especially when the comet appeared. I wasn't used to Singing alone, and even with friends that come to my Song, I wanted my mother. When she returned, it was with Nahi. They have a story between them they won't share. And now you are with us. What do you know?"

I was tired but explained to her the best I could what had happened since the bird had told me someone was coming.

"Was it my mother? The whale? The bird that took your necklace? Nahi?" Yixu asked. We were facing each other on our sides on platforms. The small flame flickered just enough light. A cooler breeze moved through.

"I don't know, I don't know anything. And then that face in the Dream? The trackers?" I shuddered.

"You must be part of a sacred story," Yixu yawned. "Things like this only happen in sacred stories." Her eyes widened. "That means I'm part of a sacred story!"

"I'm grateful I'm not in it alone." I yawned too.

"Will you go into Dreaming tonight?" Yixu asked. I shuddered.

"I don't know. The last time I went into the Dream, I saw that man. It was horrible. Then people started tracking me in this world, trying to end my story. I don't know if I want to go into the Dream." My words were honest.

"Go into the Dream," Yixu sighed. She motioned for me to turn around so that we were facing the same direction. She pressed up behind me, an arm slung around my waist. I put my hand on her forearm. "I'll Sing you a protection."

She began Singing. I felt her breath in my hair. I fell asleep feeling safe.

《 《 ● 》 》

I was in the water in the Dream: a sea, warm, salty. There was no shore in any direction. There were small waves, and I floated through them easily. Below me, I could sense curious spirits. I felt heat. I looked down into the water. A red glow rose, liquid inside of liquid. It became hotter, but not so hot the water was uncomfortable. It bubbled up. When it broke the surface, it hardened into black rock. It kept growing over itself. The higher parts began to sprout green grass that grew quickly, and trees arose, lushness spreading beneath an expanse of twisting webs of red light. An island was born in front of me. It had a scent outside my memories but was still familiar. Sand extended out from the shore, rising beneath my feet. I walked onto the island, and the sand radiated silver and gold ripples wherever I stepped.

Tiya came from the tall grasses, parting them with her hands, sticking her head out and laughing. Then she leaped out, running toward me on strong legs. I ran up the beach and was swung up into her arms. I heard waves crashing joyously on rocks, their own Song filling the night as we held on to each other. She glowed with joy; it radiated off her in visible waves that reminded me of dust in sideways sunlight, disappearing and seeming to re-form at each movement of her body.

"You found your gift." She smiled at me. I heard whale Song somewhere in the water behind us, countless voices gathered in gratitude.

"I'm a Singer," I said with a smile that attempted to match her joy. I felt as if I would split. I turned my head toward the whale Song, understanding something without understanding it.

"You travel with our kin," she said. "They recognize your Song."

"Yixu?" I said, thinking of my sweet and strange new friend. "Or the whales that followed the boat?"

She walked us to the edge of the water. The comet seemed closer: I could make out two tails clearer than before.

"There is more than Song connecting you," she answered, not answering. I didn't mind. I let the sky web take my attention; it pulsed with rays of brighter red light running along the strands.

"Someone came into the Dream the last time I was here, a

man. He bit his way through. I couldn't move; it was terrifying," I said, hoping Tiya would offer something in return, tell me more of my story.

"They cannot hurt you while you are here," she said. "He entered with a ritual that does nothing but spread chaos. It was dangerous, what he opens and invites."

"And then there was someone trying to harm me in the Waking World. They were tracking me," I said, trying to hold on to the joy.

"There was, and there is. You have switched one protection for another," she said, humming.

"Nahi and Ahkal? Batuk? I think Yixu would protect me; we have a knowing with each other," I said, eager to keep her talking. A spirit shaped like a sea turtle dragged her body onto the sand, flippers pulling her forward. Tiya knelt. The turtle came to her and began churning up the sand with her back flippers.

"Your best protections are your gifts." She bent forward, watching the sea turtle dig her nest with a look of love on her face. "Do you know these friends can swim between the Dream and where you live?" She reached her hand and touched the turtle's shell lightly. The markings on its back lit up, the webbing matching the dancing lights in the sky. The turtle began dropping eggs from her body, shining globes of yellow covered in a thick liquid that smelled of salt and ferment.

"My Dreaming and Singing?" I asked. I contemplated for a moment. "My Singing has already saved me. You awakened it at the right time."

Tiya laughed.

"It was already in you. I just reminded you. Think of the plants you tend, Saya."

I lifted my head at her words. It was true. My tended plants, from different lands, had flourished under my care. Many had been practically dead when I first found them. I thought of Ruta, Kinet.

"Are Ruta and Kinet safe? Is Celay?" I asked.

"She made choices and was aware of what she did. She is scared, but safe. Ruta and Kinet too."

I wondered when I would see them again.

"Will I survive my story?" I asked. I didn't know where the question came from. I was just starting to live an interesting life, discover how to connect with others in the Waking World. I didn't want it to end. I had an awakening curiosity.

"None of us survive our stories, sweet child; we just live them the best we can, while we can." I groaned. It was exactly what I would expect a spirit to say. She laughed, mouth wide open, head back. Her throat looked as if it were full of stars.

"What next?" I asked, feeling Yixu would be proud of me for being so direct.

She gestured toward the sea turtle who had finished laying her eggs and was covering the nest with glowing sand.

"You know what you need to, for now. For this world and the Waking." A wave rose and crashed over us. I shook the water from my body and wiped my eyes. Tiya and the turtle were both gone. The island began sinking around me, bubbling at the edges in sparkling froth. I sank with the island, floating again.

I heard her laugh and nothing else but Song. I swam for a while, enjoying how light my body felt. The whales Sang.

I ducked my head underwater to hear them better. I understood them without knowing what they Sang. I heard my name and swam toward it as it took over my body. I felt a lightness, as if my form was dissolving. I saw the shape of a whale and moved toward it. It greeted me in Song. Without trying, whale Song emerged from another part of my body. I tried to put my hands over my mouth, but I no longer had hands. I exhaled my held breath, which bubbled from the back of my neck. I had shifted into the shape of a whale. I tried to kick my feet but found a large tail instead. Moving my body up through the water, I emerged in my new shape. All my senses were different. The Dream air tasted strange to me, alive, shivering itself over my slick whale skin. I submerged again, letting myself sink.

A young whale, a calf really, rose toward me, pressing the front of its head beneath mine, a playful greeting. It fell sideways, deeper, an eye inviting me. I followed. As the sea grew darker, my senses sharpened with Song, another knowing. A sea turtle spirit, maybe the one from the beach, drifted in front of my vision, her shell glowing like a spiderweb formed of light. She pointed her head down and began spiraling downward. I followed, but she disappeared. I wondered if she had crossed into the Waking World. A large shape brushed against me; it wasn't malevolent, but it wasn't friendly. My mind tried to make out its shape, but it seemed like a dark cloud. I made my way to the surface, enjoying the way the water seemed to be speaking to me, whispering threads of stories. I felt my body pulling me back.

《 《 ● 》 》

"Did you enter the Dream?" Yixu half whispered against the back of my head. I stretched my back; she rolled away and sat up. Her hair was sticking out from all directions. Ahkal groaned and pulled her blanket over her head. "My mother likes to sleep late sometimes. Come with me. There will be a meal."

I followed Yixu out. The morning was gray, the sea calm. I saw other stone buildings on the small island, but they were empty. There was a fire burning further down the beach. The keeper, I thought. Yixu uncovered a basket of small crispy fish and popped an entire fish into her mouth. I did the same, the bones crunching between my teeth, the fish salty. I swallowed.

"I became a whale last night," I said to Yixu. She did a little sideways dance of joy.

"Did you breathe from your head?" she asked.

"The back of my neck, or that's what it felt like. I couldn't see underwater, but I could feel the world around me."

Yixu sighed. "I would love to be a whale; they travel so much faster and further than we can."

I told her about the island being born, Tiya and the turtle.

Nahi joined us, scratching her neck.

"Sand fleas," she grumbled. "They love my blood." Yixu went to the boat to get a salve for her. Ahkal joined us.

"Where will we go?" I asked, drinking a sweet juice the keeper had left in a clay jar for us. Sand fleas kept hopping on the lip of the jar, and Nahi licked the rim, swallowing them down. I tried not to make a face of disgust.

"Getting your blood back?" I asked. Nahi paused for a moment, then roared a laugh.

"The serious one can play too." She grinned. It felt good to make her laugh. Ahkal seemed relaxed.

"There is a bigger island up the coast. With our friends, we can be there by sunset," Ahkal said. "How does your body feel today, Saya? You're not used to being on the water."

"Or being chased through the jungle," I said. "I'm tired, but I'm ready. Let's keep me safe." I told them about what I had seen in Dreaming. A part of the story seemed to worry Ahkal, but she didn't speak on it, directing us instead to clean up and prepare the boat for journey.

Right before we left, someone approached the boat. It was the keeper. She was short with a wide, lush body and a shaved head. Her breasts swung side to side as she walked toward us, a look of concern on her face.

"A storm comes from a strange direction," she said, pointing south with her chin. I looked but didn't see anything. Ahkal leaped from the boat into the water, which came to her waist. She Sang with her hands beneath the water, then seemed to listen. She and the keeper exchanged a look.

"How fast can you travel? Or will you make it to shore? You are welcome to stay here, but I see you have movement tight in your bodies and eyes," the keeper said.

"Three of us are Singers. That should make us fast enough,"

Ahkal said, but there was a sense of uncertainty in her voice. "It'll be a rough ride, but we can stay close to shore if we have to." Nahi groaned. I remembered she didn't like the boat.

The keeper opened the pouch at her waist and pulled out four whistles.

"Take these. Their sound carries far. There will be boats in the water after the storm passes for those who wish to see and hunt for what has been churned up." She handed each of us a whistle, each strung on braided cord. The small sensation of weight, though different than my necklace, was comforting.

"We thank you," Ahkal said. I climbed into the boat while everyone else pushed it into the water. Ahkal cried out a Song, and a wave rose to carry us away.

《 《 ● 》 》

On the water, Ahkal and Yixu taught me a movement Song of the Kemi. It took a few tries, but soon, I was matching them in voice and tone. Fish rose up around us, but not in the numbers they had before.

"Are there fewer fish in this part of the sea?" I asked. Ahkal didn't say anything, turning to look behind us at the gathering clouds moving closer. A wind had come up and had a strange scent on it, smoke and something sharp that made me want to sneeze. Nahi was miserable in the choppy waves. She sat in the front of the boat, wrapped in a blanket, her hands clutched tightly to the bench she sat on, posture tense. Her eyes were closed, and there was a frozen snarl on her lips. Yixu gave her some kind of root to chew, to keep the sickness from taking over. Nahi gnawed on it, groaning.

Yixu tied a length of cloth around her head, then tied one around mine. The wind made it hard to hear each other speak, but we Sang, the same refrain over and over. The friends called up struggled to push us through the churning water. We were trying to move toward the shore, but the sea lurched against us.

Yixu tried to shout something at me, but the wind carried her voice away. I leaned closer, but the boat rocked, slapped by a wave. I grabbed onto the side. Yixu pointed at the back of her neck and then at the water. I shook my head. She moved her hand sharply upward, paused, then let it crash down into her lap. The movement reminded me of something. I realized she wanted me to Sing to the whales. They were large enough to move the boat through the waves.

I took in a wet inhale of breath as rain began pouring down. It was a cold rain, but it smelled unnatural. I dipped my head, tucking my chin into my chest, and began Singing, coughing several times to clear the wet from my throat. It was almost impossible to hear my own voice over the roar of wind and waves. I knelt in the water that was beginning to gather on the bottom of the boat and put my hands over my ears. I Sang with all the power in my body. I Sang until my throat burned, trying to expand the Song out the way I had in Dreaming when I had taken the whale shape.

The boat jerked hard. I braced myself. There was another movement, gentler. The boat was turning. I kept Singing, feeling the shift. The whales had come. I lifted my face, Singing into the rain. It poured in and out of my open mouth. I felt a power move through me that had me shaking. I was no longer cold, no longer afraid. I Sang until I felt the edges of the Dream in my Song and Sang gratitude. The rain started to soften, though the waves were still high. I looked over the side of the boat and saw a massive gray shape pressed tightly against the boat.

"There's one on the other side; keep Singing," Yixu said, her voice raw. I Sang as we moved toward the blur of shore barely visible in the rain. The clouds above us were swirling, a strange circle with an open mouth of bright blue sky at the top. Ahkal shaded her eyes and stared at it.

"I've seen a storm like this before. It isn't natural; this has been called," she said.

Nahi growled, shaking the water from her body. "We're in a moment of gathering. It grows. I can smell it. Saya, can you ask your kin to swim any faster?" I nodded but felt a drop in my body when she called them my kin. It felt true, but my body didn't recognize it yet.

The whales could not swim any faster. The sea started to grow tall, and our boat dropped, tilting on the side. I faltered in my Song as the sky darkened and the whales moved away. They disappeared below the frothing waves. I called out in Song, but Ahkal raised her hands.

"They know better than we do. There will have to be another way," she called from where she stood. She looked hard at Yixu and nodded once, crossing her arms over her chest and making a gesture with her hands. Yixu nodded back and mimicked the motion.

Ahkal stepped wide and began moving her body in an unfamiliar way, eyes closed. She rocked back and forth with the boat. Yixu motioned for me to sit next to her. I huddled up against her. Nahi moved from one side of the boat to the other, looking over the sides.

"Something comes," she growled, her teeth growing into fangs, her nails growing black and curved. Her color rose, the spots growing dark and mottled. Her eyes were bright yellow again, shining in the smothering gray. A mist rose from the sea. Ahkal started moving her hands over herself, starting at her feet, flinging her hands outward, then her knees, repeating the motion. She threw her hands over her head and let out a wail that splintered my fear. The markings on her skin seemed to tremble. Ahkal exhaled through pursed lips. A current rose, lighter in color than the rest of the water, a pale blue surrounding the boat, surging it forward. I fell back against Yixu at the motion and held on as the called current churned us forward. It seemed to pause, then changed direction, heading south. I squinted at Yixu; the rain had returned.

"The current knows better than we do," she shouted at the unasked question in my mouth. I nodded. Nahi snarled, then yowled, a high-pitched half scream that made me shake once, hard. Something long and red rose out of the water, trying to reach into the boat. Nahi swiped at it with her claws, striking it and drawing a spray of red from where she had punctured the creature's skin. Ahkal was wailing louder, doing some sort of dance to a rhythm I couldn't understand. I screamed in fear, using my feet to propel myself away from where Nahi battled the strange thing attacking the boat. Yixu pressed back, screaming in my ear.

"Sing!" she screamed. I hummed first, one hand pressed to my throat, trying to move past the terror taking over my body. The strange shape that had risen from the sea disappeared, but Nahi was hopping from side to side, seeing where it would rise again. Saliva dripped from her fangs, her lips pulled back in a snarl. The Song came, though I felt it had barely anything to do with me. It rose out of my body of its own desire. Yixu Sang a different Song behind me, both of us watching Nahi, waiting for the creature to strike again. Ahkal was in her dance still, the lines of her skin seeming to deepen until they looked like gouges carved into her flesh. The pale current of sea churned beneath us, carrying us forward. Pink froth rose. Nahi leapt toward it, dropping into a crouch.

The creature came up from the water again; it looked like an enormous spider but with fewer arms. Its eyes glowed like coals. It struggled to stay in one place as the current kept trying to push it away. Waves battled the river; the wind poured down on us as if blown breath from the sky. The rain slapped. Nahi swiped at a long arm that rose into the boat. Her nails got caught for a moment and the arm jerked her off her feet, but she leaped backward. She regained her balance, pulling her claw out, swatting at it with her other hand. The creature submerged again, then rose out in a jerk, hooking three arms into the boat. Claws the size of my forearm jutted from their ends as it sidestepped its way toward Ahkal.

Ahkal was in a trance, unaware of everything except for whatever she was creating with her Song and body. Yixu screamed her mother's name, but Ahkal didn't answer. Nahi leaped past us, throwing herself between Ahkal and the creature. She sunk her teeth into one of the joints on the creature's arm and shook her head, breaking the appendage away. She flung her head to the side, letting the body part fall into the foam. There was a spray of blood as the creature sunk once again.

I Sang. I Sang with rage, with all the frustration in my body. I wasn't ready for my story to end. I wanted to survive it, to see what was next.

The current surged, lifting the boat partially out of the water, as if to get it further away from the creature. The thing swam away, then sped again toward the boat. Nahi prepared in a crouch, as if to leap on it. I Sang with desperation, not knowing if my throat even made sound anymore. Right before the creature reached the boat, a whale shot straight up beneath it, flinging it high into the air. Without the buoyancy of the water, the thing flailed, arms spinning as it tried to control its descent back toward the water. Another whale leaped beneath, tossing it into the air again. I heard crunching; the creature was breaking, dripping in its own blood. It sank into the waves. The current gentled, the blood and blue mixing to violet, then blue again.

Nahi clung to the side of the boat, panting. Ahkal began to

sway. Yixu pushed me aside and ran to her mother, easing her down to the bottom of the boat. Tears streamed down Yixu's face. I stumbled my way toward them, touching Nahi briefly in gratitude. She stared into the water, waiting to see if the creature would surface.

Ahkal's markings were normal again and duller than before. She was perfectly still, but I could see her breathing. The rain still lashed, the waves still crashed, but there was a shift in the tension. The current below us still carried us swiftly toward the shore. I had no Song left in me. I crawled my way toward where Yixu held her mother, Singing to her ear. As I reached them, the river surged again. A long red arm struck out of the water, hooking itself around Nahi. Nahi sank her claws into it, hissing and thrashing as it pulled her overboard and into the waves. I screamed out the last of my voice, spinning to look at Yixu. She hadn't noticed. I stumbled toward them, trying to get Yixu's attention, to tell her what had happened.

I wanted to Sing but was too raw with fear and terror. I tried to see if Nahi's shape was visible beneath the water, but it was churning too much for me to see anything.

Yixu lifted her head, an arm raised to point at the long piece of wood her mother had used to steer the boat. Her face broke my heart; she cradled her mother against her chest, rocking back and forth. She closed her eyes. I grabbed the wood and felt the tension in it. I pulled it toward me until it seemed to lock into a rhythm, but I had to keep my hand on it to hold it steady. I looked over the side of the boat, trying to see Nahi, but there was nothing.

The current fell apart, but it didn't matter; we were close to shore. The rain softened to a mist, the sea soothing itself into an unnatural stillness. I hummed the Song of the Kemi they had taught me. A rocky coast came into view; there was nowhere to land. The boat was surrounded again by fish and other creatures of the sea. In the Song, I asked them to steer us near a safe place to land. They listened, bodies swaying to the Song as they moved us north along the coast until we came to a cove with a thin strip of beach. Yixu's eyes rose when the boat hit the sand. She gently put her unconscious mother down and leaped from the boat. I jumped out and helped her pull the boat ashore. We were both soaking wet. Yixu pulled out a sharp stake and twisted it into the sand, tying the boat to it.

I tried to speak, but I had no voice left. I pointed at my throat and shook my head. Yixu pointed at hers and nodded; she had screamed her voice away too. We got back into the boat. Yixu pulled a waterproof basket out and handed it to me, pointing at the shore. I left the boat and dragged myself up the beach, basket behind me. When I found a dry spot under a rocky overhang, I opened the basket and pulled out dry blankets. I set them up, then went back to the boat. Yixu had taken another long blanket and moved it beneath her mother. We each took an end and eased Ahkal to the shore, then dragged her to the sheltered overhang. Yixu dug through a pack and found the material to make a small fire. I gathered whatever I could find that looked like it would burn and returned to feed the fire.

Yixu had covered Ahkal in a pile of blankets. Her eyes widened as I returned, looking behind me. She made a snarling face and clawed her hands to mimic an Ilkan. My eyes filled with tears. I shook my head, my hands over my heart. Yixu slapped her hands over her mouth, more tears streaming down her face. She opened her arms out to me and I went into them. We held each other, sobbing silently, the only sounds our ragged breathing, cracking of the fire, and dripping rain. We wept until we were exhausted. She lay on one side of Ahkal. I lay on the other. We held hands over Ahkal's sleeping body and fell asleep.

((●))

I landed hard in a field of undulating silver grasses that moved as if underwater. The comet's Song rang through the Dream, louder than before. There was a frenzy of energy, the outlines of shapes moved and thickened the air. I felt I was breathing in spirits. I fell to my knees; the exhaustion from the Waking World had followed me into the Dream. I wanted to lie down and fall asleep but instead lay back and let the grass caress my body.

I began weeping, thinking of Nahi. I hoped her death had come quickly. Small spirits clustered on my face, invisible tongues lapping up the sacred salt of my body. I didn't have the energy to brush them away. Let them taste what they wanted. I rolled over and put my head into the crook of my arm, curling my body up, letting the sobs rise and fall through me. I screamed in grief and rage at some point. The spirits drinking my tears disappeared at the pain in my voice. My life was just beginning to become my own, and already it was filled with more pain and fear than I had thought possible. I felt different small shapes settle on my body as I cried, little heats pressing into me in comfort.

"Someone help me," I moaned. The new spirits that had settled onto my body shifted when I spoke, rearranging themselves so they covered my heart. When I sat up, most of them fluttered away. I drew my knees to my chest and waited. There were two winged frogs, one on each knee. I didn't know if they were the same who lived on Yecacu. They chirped at me. I chirped back. One lifted her wings out and fluttered to my face, licking at a loose eyelash. She held it on her tongue in front of her eyes before swallowing it.

"You should have asked first," I said. I looked up. "Someone help me, please," I repeated. "Ahkal is injured. Nahi was taken by something strange; it wasn't of our world. Did it drag her here?" I asked the Dream. There was no response.

The grass several body lengths away from me began to part into two paths, moved by invisible spirits. Or so I thought. As the parted grass moved closer, I saw two serpents winding their way toward me.

They stopped in front of me, raising their bodies so their heads were level with mine. The frogs fluttered to my shoulders.

"You called for help?" they asked in one voice.

"Are you the Twin Serpents?" I asked. They looked ordinary to me; I'd imagined the Twin Serpents would be something else. The frogs on my shoulders chirped in laughter.

"We are two serpents," they said together.

"Can you help heal Ahkal? She won't awaken; I don't know what happened. And my voice, and Yixu's voice. And if Nahi lives?"

The serpents laughed, twisting their bodies around each other. "You have never asked for yourself before, Saya." Their shared voice was a sharp whisper.

"I didn't know who I was before," I answered, mesmerized by the scales on their bodies that started to shimmer as they twisted themselves together in a braided dance. Lights and shadows blinked out from the spaces between their bodies.

"Do you know who you are now?" they asked, pausing their dance. One let out a long tongue, drawing in one of the frog spirits. She flew off my shoulder, reaching her tongue out to touch the serpent's tongue with her own, then fell to the ground and hopped away, chirping in joy.

"I'm a Dreamer, a Singer, a friend, a daughter to someone who once loved me, someone I've never met." I thought of the man, my father, from my Dream.

"You are the Lost Dreamer," they said.

"Who?" I asked.

"There are stories about you, stories that last lifetimes and beyond, forward, backward. You are the decider," they said.

I wanted to ask what I was to decide but had more important questions. I would think about it another time. It sounded like a story that would take several Dreams to untangle, if ever.

"Ahkal, can you help her? Please? Yixu can't lose her mother, not like this, while trying to protect me." I started crying again.

"You are worth being protected; we will help."

"Thank you," I bowed my head in gratitude.

"You too will soon be in your mother's arms," they whispered. The frog on my shoulder began beating her wings, floating toward the serpents, moving back and forth as if in hesitation. The joyous chirps of her companion Sang from elsewhere in the moving grass. It didn't go as well for the second frog spirit. I gasped as one of the serpents snapped out and swallowed the frog, gulping as the spirit's body moved down her throat. I reconsidered asking for their help.

"You won't harm me, or anyone I care about," I said. It was a clumsy way to ask.

"No harm," they said.

"Celay is coming?" I wondered why. There was no way I was going to return to the life we had been living. Though I did want to return to Ruta and Kinet.

"Celay and others," they said. "Show us your wrists."

I hesitated a moment, glancing at the lump that used to be the frog spirit.

"No harm," they said. I held out my wrists.

They struck at the same time, sinking fangs I hadn't seen into each of my wrists. I gasped, throwing my head back at the sensation of opening skin, something warm and cold entering my body at the same time. I started to cry out, but the sound froze in my throat. I blinked my eyes at the twisting sky of web and yearning, then looked at my wrists to see if the serpents had finished with whatever I had allowed them to do. Each serpent had their head in the wounds they had bitten open, sliding their bodies inside me quickly. My wrists closed up as soon as they disappeared. I gasped as a rush of emotions swam through me. I could feel them, formless, swimming through my limbs, my hips, each hinge of knee and elbow, growing and shrinking as they explored. I felt them twist up and down my spine before settling, one in my chest and the other in my belly.

I thought of the swallowed frog spirit and wondered if it was inside me too. I willed myself back to body, wondering what new chaos I would awaken to.

CHAPTER NINETEEN

INDIR

Safi came into our chamber before dawn, waking us. I was exhausted. Zeri groaned. Delu was awake, her eyes wide on me. She looked as if she'd barely slept.

"Alcan wishes to speak with us about the Game." Safi's voice was urgent. My sisters and I sat up. I couldn't believe her.

"Is he here? Did you let him in?" I asked in a tone that matched Kupi and Ixara's. My mother noticed, her jaw clenching.

"We need to keep him content," Safi said briskly. "He wants to ask us something; he says it's urgent. He's waiting for us on the far platform. Simple tunics. We're in mourning." It was a space that wasn't inside the temple but opened to it.

"No," I said, rising. "He doesn't get to choose. Why do you keep appeasing him?" Thinking of my aunts made me feel strong. They would have been proud of me for challenging my mother.

Safi's mouth was drawn into a thin line.

"Alcanzeh is full of Fire Warriors and traders." Her voice was hard and low. "They outnumber the Avex. Indir, until you're out of Alcanzeh, we appease Alcan."

My heart pounded. I didn't want to see Alcan, knowing he wanted to harm me. I wished for my aunts. When we were dressed, we followed Safi to the far side of the temple. Safi and

Zeri walked ahead. Delu walked as if underwater. I paused and let her catch up, weaving my arm through hers.

"Why is she making us do this? What can he want?" I asked. I rubbed her arm. I knew what it felt like to be lost.

Right before we reached the platform, Delu stopped.

"Indir, I went into the Dream last night," she said. Her lower lip was trembling. I shook my head.

"Tell me after we speak with Alcan, please," I begged her. "I need to pretend to be strong."

Delu nodded. Her face was full of grief.

Alcan was dressed in a plain tunic. It made him look younger than he was. Several Fire Warriors were with him. My mother faced him, her face blank. My sisters and I stood on either side of her.

"I want a sunset ceremony to the Dream, before the Game tonight, in front of all of Alcanzeh," he said, hands open in front of him. Zeri coughed. I looked sideways at Safi. She stared at him, eyes grazing his simple clothing. I didn't trust him. I knew she wanted to keep him happy. She nodded once.

"We're in mourning, Alcan. We told you we wouldn't attend the Game. If you want to come here for ceremony—"

He interrupted her.

"No, the ceremony will be on the Game field, in front of all of Alcanzeh." He smiled, and it terrified me. "If you can't perform the ceremony, the Pili has agreed to it."

My mother stepped backward. It was the worst thing he could have said to her. She inhaled deeply through her nose and spoke quickly.

"We are in mourning. Our heads will be covered, and we will wear veils. We won't attend the Game." The strain in her voice made Alcan's smile grow wider.

"I am grateful," Alcan said, lowering his head slightly. When he lifted his head again, he was staring at me. "And thank you, Indir—you gave my Pili friend something to seek when he enters the Dream. A sphere of water, a Lost Dreamer." He tapped his fingers over his heart, the same place he had stabbed me in the Dream. I didn't react. He left, the Fire Warriors following him.

I was shaking when we returned to our chamber. Alcan's parting words burned like a live coal in my belly. Safi accompanied us, all of us silent.

"He doesn't know what it means. He was trying to intimidate you," Safi said, pacing back and forth.

"He knows enough," I said.

"We can't think about that now," Zeri said. "How is Indir going to escape if she has to attend the ceremony?"

Our mother stopped pacing and looked at me.

"Your sisters and I will wear veils. Indir, you'll stay behind. I have a plan."

"I don't know if I'm ready," I said.

"You're ready. Raru and Dua spent the night preparing your travel pack. They're still in the chamber, resting," she said. "Spend the day with your sisters. I have to prepare for the ceremony." I wanted to vomit. My mother's formality had returned. I wanted the softer, grief-stricken side of her back. She seemed more real to me that way.

"I don't want to leave," I whispered, hoping she would comfort me.

"You will return." I waited for her to say more. She turned to leave and said, "Ali will arrive soon. He has a gift for you."

I wanted more from her.

((●))

Delu and Zeri left to eat a morning meal, whispering. I wasn't hungry. Ali arrived, looking older with grief. The lines that ran from his nostrils along either side of his mouth were deeper. He looked exhausted.

"I have a protection for you, if you want it," he said, barely above a whisper. He was holding a pouch. "These stones will offer you protection. Carry them with you."

He opened the pouch, shaking the contents into his palm. A jumble of colored stones spilled into his hand.

"Each of these has meaning; I can share the meanings with you, if you wish," he said. I nodded, and he poured them into my open hands. They warmed immediately.

"They're warm," I said. Ali frowned and nodded.

"They heat up when someone wishes the wearer harm. It is an honor to carry them. They have not been seen for many years. They appear when they're needed, and they appeared in my travel pack when I was traveling from our home. Carry these, and no one will be able to see you, not trackers, not Dreamers, not the Pili, or anyone who seeks you or wishes to do you harm."

"My mother and sisters won't see me?" I asked. It seemed impossible.

"It isn't forever, Indir, only until you return. Or until it chooses someone else," Ali said. "Or you may offer it to another, but I don't think you should. Not until the chaos has passed."

There were seven stones: one amber with a tiny sprouting seed in the middle, a stone that looked as if it was made of sand, another of porous blue rock, another red and orange, and a green bead that looked as if it carried the jungle within it. One shimmered in a riot of dark violets and greens, and the last wasn't stone but bone.

Ali started to tell me what each stone meant, but my sisters burst into the chamber, each with red eyes and swollen faces. Ali opened his arms to them, and to my surprise, they went to him, embracing.

"She has protection now," Ali said. "You won't be able to see or seek her in Dreaming."

"Can we speak with Indir alone, please?" Zeri seemed nervous, shifting from foot to foot. Her fingernails were bitten down, something she hadn't done since childhood. Delu wiped her face on the hem of her tunic.

"I am grateful, Ali," I said. I embraced him.

I turned to my sisters and exhaled, remembering the joy of the night. I wanted to share it with them.

"Ovis came, and we chose each other," I said.

I didn't know what I was expecting, but my sisters seemed upset at my sharing. Zeri put her fist to her mouth, pointing a finger at Delu, then at me.

"I went into the Dream last night, Indi," Delu said. I didn't care; I kept speaking.

"Ovis is going to win the Game, I know it. And he's going to find us. I'll ask Raru to leave a trail if he can't track us because of this." I poured the beads back into the pouch.

"Indir, listen to Delu, please." Zeri's voice awoke a terror in me I could not name.

"I Dreamed another Dreamer," Delu started. I interrupted her.

"Oh, Delu. The Lost Dreamer. Can you tell me where she is? When I find her, I can return. You remember Kupi and Ixara said that, right?" Hope bloomed through every part of me. Delu's face didn't change.

"I Dreamed of my daughter," Delu said, "with Inkop. The next season of spiders." She bit in her lips to stop her chin from shaking.

"You're going to birth a Dreamer? With Inkop? You can trust him," I added, wonder and sadness competing in me. I wouldn't be there to see it. Then, the meaning of her words flooded me. I put my arm out to steady myself.

"Inkop wins the Game. Indir. I'm so sorry." Delu embraced me. I didn't respond. I pushed her away. I could still smell Ovis on my skin. I wanted it to last as long as possible.

"I don't understand," I said. "He's coming with me. I feel it in my bones and blood." I looked back and forth between my sisters.

Zeri shook her head.

"Delu told me this morning. We decided it would be better

to tell you than for you to be expecting him and receive only disappointment," Zeri said.

"I have to speak with him. Do you know where he is? It hasn't been that long since he left," I said. "Can we send Dua? She'll find him."

"He went to the sea with Eley. There are boat travelers arriving from all over, and they went to help organize them and check the waste tunnels. Then he has to prepare for the ceremony," Delu said gently.

"I can't," I said, sinking to the bench. "I can't survive this. I don't know how to be someone who doesn't Dream, who doesn't live in this temple or even in Alcanzeh. I know nothing of the Ilkan. How will I live with them? How am I supposed to find the Lost Dreamer?"

"Follow the stories," Zeri said. It was a phrase repeated at the beginning of each tile game she played. I raised my eyebrows at her, then opened my arms.

"I don't know how to be without you. I wish you could see me in Dreaming; then I would know you were there, somewhere."

"We'll find a way to be with you, the way Kupi and Ixara said they will always be with us." Delu wrapped herself into our circle.

"You're going to have a baby." I was weak with my grief. I had no idea how I would walk the jungle at night with Raru. "And Ovis will be the sacrifice." I didn't want to imagine the Waking World without him.

"You'll find the Lost Dreamer. You'll return, think of that,"

Zeri said. "Indir, this grief, it's part of the chaos. It has to be. And still, you need to leave, stay safe. Let's go see what Raru and Dua have prepared."

《《●》》

Dua and Raru were sitting side by side against the stone wall in the chamber. They looked up at me. It was clear neither of them had slept. Dua's hair was tangled, her tunic torn at the side. Raru had a small tuft of hair at her temple that looked like it had been scorched.

"Were you two playing with fire?" Zeri teased. They both wore smiles I had never seen before. I knew that feeling well, even if it hadn't lasted.

"The end of the cycle has started, so we're all playing with fire. We have to take joy where we can." Dua grinned, leaning against Raru. Raru nuzzled her head.

"Don't blame it on the cycle, sweet flame. We do not take joy; joy takes us," Raru said, standing, and Dua followed. "The pack is ready. You should try it on."

I put on the pack of food and other necessities Dua and Raru had deemed necessary. I wore the pouch holding the protection stones under my tunic.

"Squat," Dua ordered. My sisters giggled. I looked at Raru. She lazed on her side on a stone bench, her upper body supported on one elbow. Raru nodded. I squatted, then rose up.

"Again," Dua ordered. I squatted. Again and again, until I was out of breath.

"Crawl across the floor," she said. I looked to Raru for help, but she seemed to be enjoying the scene. I went to my hands and knees and began crawling back and forth. The bag slid from my back and dragged between my legs. I paused to untangle it from my tunic while Dua clucked her tongue.

"We need to shorten the straps. And, Dreamer, you'll be wearing travel clothing. Sit up. Try this." Dua handed me the stiff cone of shaped hide that was for passing water. I stared at it in my hand.

"No, I won't," I said as my sisters burst out laughing.

"There is a waste pot in the corner; we will give you privacy. You don't want to squat in a jungle." Dua led everyone out of the chamber, pulling the screen behind her. I stared at the cone and sighed. I didn't want to squat in the jungle.

《 《 ● 》 》

We spent the rest of the morning and early afternoon in a quiet, sad tenderness. I wanted to memorize each moment with my sisters. We ate. We climbed to the Twin Serpent altar and sat, staring out over the city. The sounds of drums and songs floated up to us. Laughter, excitement, arguments. Everyone trusted that life would continue the way it had been, even with Alcan as king, because Alcanzeh had only known safety for generations. They had no idea chaos was coming. Delu sat on one side of me, Zeri on the other. They leaned into me. We didn't cry. We held each other, not knowing when we would be together again.

Too soon, a temple worker called us downstairs. Our mother was waiting for us in our chamber with three ceremonial tunics. I stared at the one meant for me. I wouldn't be wearing it.

"Why is this here?" I asked, touching the tunic. It was beautiful, one I hadn't seen before. There was a headpiece as well, with a veil.

"A young woman will arrive soon. She is the same height and shape as you. She will wear this tunic and accompany us to the ceremony," my mother said. "She's bringing travel clothing and a temple servant's tunic. You'll wear the travel clothes beneath the tunic when you leave tonight. Dua has already taken your travel pack into the jungle—Raru knows where. Tonight, you'll hear a whistle and leave with Dua carrying night baskets, as if you're going to the waste canals. Raru will meet you and take you south." It was a lot to take in, but I nodded. I had no other choice.

"I trust the Dream," I said, knowing it was what she wanted to hear. Safi softened, just as I'd hoped she would. She opened her arms.

"Daughter." Her eyes were exhausted, red from crying and sleeplessness. I stepped into her embrace, which lasted less than a breath before she pushed me back and gazed into my eyes. "You will return." She pressed her cheek to mine and left the chamber. I blinked after her.

"Was that her goodbye?" I asked. Delu and Zeri didn't say anything. I stared at the tunics.

A young woman appeared in the doorway, wearing a long dress I recognized from the Water Temple. She carried a satchel.

"Thank you for doing this. What is your name?" I said.

"Better if your sisters do not know my name, but for today, you may call me sister." She smiled. I smiled back, even though I wanted to scream. It was all happening too fast. I had to become the person I needed to be to survive. I didn't know if I was ready. The temple worker and I were the same height— she was more slender than I, but I doubted it would be noticeable underneath the ceremonial tunic. She stripped off her dress. Beneath, she was dressed in traveling clothes: a sleeved long tunic, leggings, and travel sandals. She began removing her clothing and looked at me expectantly.

My sisters watched as I put on the travel clothing. I was shaking. Delu combed out my hair and braided it tightly. Zeri wound the braid around my head, pulling pins from her own hair to hold mine in place.

I sat and watched as my sisters and the decoy Indir dressed. First, undertunics that were so long they nearly brushed the floor, edged in frayed fabric that rustled like feathers. Over that, they slipped on the ceremonial tunics. Decoy Indir spent a good amount of time tying woven sashes around my sisters before tying her own. She placed netting over her own face, then excused herself, saying she would let us say our goodbyes in private.

"Thank you," I said.

Her face was serene. She leaned over and pressed her forehead to mine. "Anything for the Dream." She left.

Delu and Zeri looked stunning, even without their head-dresses on. The red of the tunics was the richest I'd ever seen, darkening to almost black in the folds, vibrant and shimmering where the light hit.

"It's time," I said.

((●))

Downstairs, my mother and sisters stood around me in the main chamber.

We didn't speak. We held each other, rocking back and forth. We took turns holding each other in different patterns, shifting, a dance of embraces and grief.

"You will return," Safi said, her mouth pressed against my shoulder.

"You will return," my sisters said together. It reminded me of Kupi and Ixara speaking as one. I breathed through the shudder of pain in my chest.

"I will," I said.

We walked through the temple together. My mother had dismissed all the temple workers so they could attend the ceremony. Ali and the young woman dressed as me were waiting, large baskets on the floor in front of them.

"Indir." Ali held me once again. "I will think of you every day. May the Dream keep you safe." He kissed the center of my forehead and pulled back, staring into my eyes. "You carry gifts you aren't aware of yet. May they show themselves to you and help you on this journey. I know I will see you again; I swear it by all the air I have ever breathed. This is temporary, my little bird; you will return."

One last embrace. One last time in the arms of those I loved most in the world. We didn't speak. We held. We held more. We released. They left. I put my arms against the wall and exhaled slowly as the solitude pressed itself around me. A hand touched my shoulder, and I jumped.

"I made you an infusion; it will give you energy. I packed the leaves in a yellow pouch in your travel pack," Dua said.

It was too sweet for me, but I drank it. The sun was close to setting. My sisters and mother would arrive just in time for the ceremony. Dua led me to a small storeroom at the back of the temple. I sneezed at the racks of drying plants and roots. I tried to imagine Ovis, preparing for the Game, not knowing he would soon return to the Dream. I sat on the floor, pulled my knees up, and rested my head on them.

"It will always hurt, but there will be days when it hurts less," Dua said softly. I watched the dark orange rays of setting sunlight move across the floor outside the storeroom, lengthening, then disappearing. Drums sounded from the city, louder than I had ever heard them before. Cries and invocations followed; the hair on my arms rose. The voices quieted, but the drums remained.

The stones in the pouch around my neck heated suddenly. I gasped, pressing my hand to my chest. Dua watched me, then moved silently to the entryway, her nostrils flaring. The heat intensified; I breathed through it as silently as I could. Dua tilted her head, then motioned for me to move further back. I crouched behind a rack of plants. My eyes watered; the drying plants had eyelash-thin petals, and they rose around me at any movement. I pinched my mouth closed. There was a thud. The pouch of heated stones stayed hot against my chest.

"Are we kin?" a soft voice asked. I wondered if a temple worker had wandered back in, but Dua let out a low hiss.

"You're a Fire Warrior," Dua said. I couldn't tell if her voice carried awe or surprise.

"Did people really believe we would let our brothers come to Alcanzeh alone? They came to prepare the way for us," the voice said. "Are we kin?"

"What are you doing in this temple?" Dua asked. The flower petals were landing on my face. One landed on my eyelashes and I brushed it away, but the motion of my hand only made more rise.

"We just arrived. We're exploring the city. You aren't from Alcanzeh, little one." The voice was gentle, kind in a way that seemed to soothe even as her words deceived. I lifted the neck of my tunic to cover my face.

"Why are you in this temple?" Dua's voice was low.

"We're exploring the city. We want to see if we find anyone interesting. I find you interesting. Why are you here when everyone else is at the ceremony?" The woman's voice terrified me. I tried to see her through the racks, but Dua stood in the doorway, blocking my view.

"I don't like crowds, so I was sorting roots." Dua's voice was light.

I ducked deeper as a shadow moved across the doorway. The woman was in the room. I couldn't figure out why Dua wasn't stopping her. The heat of the stones grew almost unbearable, but I refused to pull the pouch away from my skin. I had no weapons, no way to protect myself if the woman wanted to do me harm.

Footsteps grew closer to where I was hiding. Flower petals rushed upward in the movement of air from her approach. Before I could think it through, I rose, grabbing bunches of the drying flowers and smacking them together hard in front of me, my tunic still over my face, eyes squeezed shut.

There was a flash of heat and light behind my closed eyelids. I tried to prepare myself for whatever pain was coming, but there was nothing but burning. I opened my eyes. Dua was crouched over the body of a tall woman. The woman was dead. Blood ran from her eyes and the corners of her mouth. There was a burn mark on the floor around her. Dua looked up at me. I stared, my hands over my mouth. Dua had a gift of fire. I backed away slowly.

"Do you trust me?" Dua asked softly. It was the same question Inkop had asked me. I pressed my hand against my chest and noticed the stones in the pouch had cooled down again. I was out of danger. I nodded.

"Are you a—" I started to ask, but Dua shook her head.

"Old stories say we were once one, but that was a long time ago. I have to burn the body, Indir," she said. She wasn't asking for permission, but I nodded. I watched as she placed her hands on the woman's chest. She bent her head, whispering something in a language I didn't understand. She leaned over and kissed the lips of the body. Her hands seemed to glow for a moment, and the woman slowly blackened, then turned to ash.

There had been no flame I could see. I helped her sweep the ashes against a wall and lean a drying rack over them.

"We should go; there may be others exploring the city," Dua said. She handed me the basket I was to carry. I followed her out the back entrance, pulled the head cover over my face, and tried to match her pace.

"Why are we going this way?" I asked when she led me down stairs leading toward the center of Alcanzeh. Dua stepped close to me.

"The city is full of people; it will be easier to stay concealed among them," she whispered. She smelled like smoke. I recoiled. The stones didn't heat, so I followed.

I saw people who had clearly traveled far to be in Alcanzeh. There were short, full-bodied women whose legs were stained or scarred red from knee to ankle. A man who looked like Ali had large black birds on each shoulder, but his cloak wasn't made of feathers; instead, it was decorated with hundreds of small shells beaded onto the dark blue fabric. There were Fire Warriors and other people from the north with neck tattoos, though none had burn marks on their bodies like Alcan's warriors.

I felt the stones beneath my tunic as we moved through the crowd. I kept my face covered. The drums of the ceremony called to me. I longed to be in ritual with those I loved most. I longed to see Ovis one last time, feel his eyes on mine.

Dua led me to a shadowy area at the edge of the city. The homes were dark but for their altar fires. The artisans and others who lived in the city must have been at the celebration.

Dua looked behind to see if anyone had followed us. She entered a stone building and put down her basket. A small altar fire burned, but it was otherwise empty. She helped me out of the white tunic, folding it and putting it in one of the baskets, then removed her own tunic and unrolled the leggings of her travel clothing. She went to the back, beckoning me to follow.

She slipped into the jungle. It was dark as soon as we entered, the drums of ceremony behind us. She held a small jar of flame in her hand; I didn't know where it had come from. We walked along a trail for a while before moving away from it. The lights and sounds of Alcanzeh faded away as the night seemed to thicken around us.

"Dreamer, careful, please." She helped me over the growth I had caught my foot in. The tops of my feet were already scratched. I was surprised at how sharply they stung—we weren't even to my pack yet. I began to panic. I didn't know if I could survive traveling. I didn't feel strong enough.

"The story constantly changes, for each of us," Dua said. "I feel your pain, Indir. I know what it's like to be away from those you love most. I won't lie: The story ahead will be difficult, but I think you'll begin to appreciate the gifts. It doesn't feel like it now, but you will."

"How long?" I asked. We had slowed. I wondered how close Raru was.

"There are gifts along the way, always. I was taken three years ago, traded south for more moons than I can count. One day, out of nowhere, a group of traders attacked the people who held us captive. One of them was always laughing, always joking. He's the one who told me stories about Alcanzeh, stories about his city. His name was Tixu." My head reeled back as if someone had slapped me.

"Tixu," I said, stunned. "Brother of Ovis."

"Son of Tavovis," Dua finished. The words rang somehow familiar. I shook my head to shake the buzz I was feeling.

"Indir." The vines parted, and Raru appeared, her color out in the faint glow of Dua's light. Behind her was a shape I knew. Ovis. I gasped.

Then everything went black.

《 《 ● 》 》

When I came to, I was on my back on the ground, my head in Ovis's lap. Raru grabbed my hands and pulled me up. We began moving through the jungle. I struggled to keep up, even with Raru supporting me.

"Ovis, how?" I asked. My fear had turned into disbelief.

"My brother came to me. He arrived in Alcanzeh yesterday, by boat. He told me we had to switch places, that he had to fight instead of me. He had a knowing; he insisted." Ovis was close behind me. When I stumbled, he steadied me, and I could smell the salty earth scent of him, a scent I thought I'd never know again.

"I can keep going," I insisted when Raru wanted to pause to let me rest.

"Come, then," Raru said. We followed her.

I stayed as close to Ovis in the jungle as I could. I had endless questions, but the only thing I could think of was how grateful I was to not be alone. He helped me over some of the rougher terrain. But even with his help, and Raru behind me, I kept falling. I wasn't used to walking on uneven ground. Raru stopped suddenly, spinning around. The stones grew hot against my chest. I pressed myself against Ovis.

There was a rush of air, and a flash of flame came at us. Raru leaped to put herself between us and the flame. She yowled in pain. The fine hairs of her skin were singed, little trails of light running up and down her arms and shoulders. Ovis threw me to the ground. There was another burst of flame, but it went sideways.

"What a coward this Avex warrior is," a voice sneered. I didn't recognize it. Raru cowered on the ground, licking at her shoulders. Dua crouched over her. The Fire Warrior lit something in his hand and came toward us. I shuddered, but he didn't seem to hear me.

Raru leaped up then and attacked the Fire Warrior who had burned her. I could smell burning hair and skin. I felt a spray of blood as Raru tore his throat out with her teeth. He fell. Her snarl held an edge of pain. She was injured.

Dua stepped forward, putting her hands to the man's chest. He blackened and turned to ash. Ovis inhaled sharply but didn't say anything. Raru licked at her wounds.

"I'm injured. Take her, Ovis," she said as Dua crouched over her.

"I don't know how to get her to where the Ilkan live," Ovis said. The scent of burning flesh made my stomach turn.

"It doesn't matter; just take her somewhere safe. You have a way, go." Dua tossed the pack to Ovis and put her arm under Raru. I waited to see if Ovis would offer to heal Raru, but he stood and pulled me up.

I knelt to briefly touch Raru, and she growled. There were pink patches of open skin all over her arms and shoulders. I hoped she would heal from her injuries.

I touched Dua quickly on the face, then let Ovis lead us toward the coast, away from Alcanzeh, into our unknown story.

CHAPTER TWENTY

SAYA

It was drizzling. I sat up. Ahkal was still unconscious. Yixu had her nose pressed to her mother's, whispering. She didn't look at me, concentrating on whatever she was saying to Ahkal. I was hungry. We had to eat, to drink. I walked to the boat and dug through the soaking mess at the bottom. Baskets were overturned, but most of them were watertight. I found my travel pack, soaking wet, and moved it to the pile I was gathering to take back. I added a basket with herbs and cooking vessels. I dragged it all in a net up the beach.

I thought I felt a strange weight in my chest and stomach and kept thinking about the serpents entering my body. I would attempt to Sing over Ahkal, but I knew I needed food and water in order to have strength to do anything. I relit the fire and took an empty skin to look for water. I found a spring running from a crevice of the stone wall and filled the skin. I set the water to heat. I discovered a watertight basket with dry tunics inside.

"We should change her," I rasped to Yixu. My voice was coming back. She nodded. It was difficult, but we managed to get the damp tunic off Ahkal's body. Yixu washed her mother with heated water while I combed the sand out of Ahkal's hair. We put a fresh tunic on Ahkal, then lay her back down. We washed and changed ourselves, then drank an infusion of waking herbs.

We nibbled on something Yixu called sea vines. They were filling, salty. I ate two, then immediately regretted the second one.

"I went into the Dream. I asked for help with Ahkal," I said softly when our meal was finished. Yixu was trying to pour liquid into her mother's mouth, but it just dribbled out.

"We should Sing," Yixu said in a small voice. I didn't know if she'd heard anything I'd said.

We Sang with dry and scratched throats. We Sang the comet Song, the whale Song, Songs of the Kemi, but still, Ahkal slept.

"The serpents I was with in the Dream said they'd help me," I said, after we had tried and failed to make up Songs. I chose not to tell Yixu how one had swallowed a spirit in front of my eyes. I didn't want her to think they were dangerous. And they were inside me. I put one hand over my belly and another over my heart, trying to sense if they were still there, somehow in the Waking World.

"Celay is coming," I told Yixu, trying to get her attention away from her mother. My heart ached for Yixu. She looked up.

"Why?" she asked.

"I don't know, but I was told in Dreaming, with others. Probably Batuk."

"What happened to Nahi?" she finally asked. I couldn't speak it; I shook my head and crossed my hands over my heart. Yixu's face was pure grief.

We took turns sleeping and Singing until night fell. I offered to stay awake with Ahkal so Yixu could sleep. I Sang her down with a sleeping Song I had heard mothers Sing their children in different places we had traveled over my life. Yixu snored.

I let myself wonder at what the Dream had shown me. I knew I was a Dreamer but had no idea how I was lost. I watched the comet. It was higher in the sky than it had ever been and seemed to be splitting in two.

Ahkal didn't stir, but she didn't seem to be in discomfort or pain. I stroked her face with a damp cloth, then did the same to Yixu.

"She only sleeps," a voice said from behind me. I startled, turning my upper body around to see who had spoken. "She only sleeps. I know this because I know her gift."

A woman my height stepped into the barest light of the fire. I could only see her lower body. She had the legs of a hardened traveler, muscled and scarred, with wide feet. There were markings on her feet and the front of her legs. Her leggings were frayed and stained, and her wrists were covered in bead bracelets in different types of seeds.

"How do you know her gift?" I whispered.

"I have traveled with Kemi before," the woman said, not moving. I felt as if the serpent around my heart was unwinding, awakening.

"Who are you?" It was a rude way for me to ask, but I was exhausted, and wary. I didn't know if I could protect us. She laughed, strained.

"I don't have a name at this moment, but that will change," she said.

"How long?" I asked.

"Until I have my name again?" she asked.

"No." I felt annoyance rise in me. "How long until Ahkal wakes up?"

The woman swallowed in a laugh. I could hear the smile in her voice.

"Tomorrow, midday at the latest. I will stand guard. I promise you, I mean no harm. I swear it by the Twin Serpents." She gestured to the splitting comet. It did resemble serpents. There was something in me that knew she spoke truth. I was exhausted and wanted nothing more than sleep. A Dreamless sleep, I told myself, hoping it would work.

"No harm." I settled down beside Yixu who hadn't stirred. "And keep a lookout; my mother is coming." As I drifted away, I felt a pang of guilt. I hadn't offered her my name. It was rude of me.

Yixu poked me awake in the morning. Her eyes were close to mine.

"There's a woman here," she mouthed at me.

"Is your voice still gone?" I whispered, worried.

"No," she said in a regular voice, then moved her eyes to indicate I look over her shoulder. The woman was on the beach away from us, sitting cross-legged in the gray morning light. She had a strange bag at her side, hardened skins shaped in a way that made no sense to me. Her head was shaved, and there were markings all over her scalp. She was strong, with a shape that looked like it knew how to fight and move fast. There was a stillness to her that I envied. I wanted to sit like that, to be that strong and present.

Yixu poked me again.

"She says she has traveled with Kemi before and that your mother will awaken today. She said she knows your mother's gift," I said. Yixu leaped up before I had finished speaking.

"I am Yixu," she called. "I greet you in the name of all that is sacred. When will my mother awaken?"

The woman turned. She was beautiful, older than me. Her eyes were her strongest feature, large with dark brown centers that seemed to take in everything. She glanced past Yixu at me and offered a small smile with raised eyebrows. I lifted my hand in greeting.

"Yixu, I greet you in the name of all that is sacred. I use no name for now. She will awaken soon." The woman rose to her feet. "Let me make you a morning meal."

The woman kept glancing at me while she cooked. I stared back, fascinated by her. She moved with a grace and power that reminded me of the Ilkan, but she was not Ilkan. She seemed familiar. I didn't speak. Yixu was speaking enough for the both of us, and Ahkal.

"What kind of Kemi boats did you travel in? My mother says there are many kinds, but I have only known ours. Was it a tusk vessel? A long seal boat? A sisterhood raft?"

"I never asked the name," the woman said, pouring some grains from a pouch into warm water. She sprinkled dried fungi on top and used a long spoon to push them further into the pot. Whatever she was making smelled good. I was hungry and sleepy. I itched too. I wondered if there were sand fleas.

"Do the fleas bother you?" The woman dug through her

strange pack and handed me a stoppered clay jar wrapped in twine. I smelled it.

"I made it. It soothes the bites and prevents them from landing on you. It carries a scent we can't detect but is unpleasant to the fleas," she said.

"Where did you learn that? Are you a healer? I've never seen your markings before; can you tell me what they mean?" Yixu was a nervous talker. She spoke quickly, moving between checking on her mother and closely watching the woman.

"I follow stories, and many of the stories have teachings I use, from plants to ways of moving in this world." The woman had a strange accent.

"How do you follow stories? Is that another way of calling yourself a storyteller? Did you follow a story to us?" Yixu stuck a finger into the pot and tasted whatever the woman had made. She stuck her tongue out at me sideways with an excited look on her face; it must have tasted good. The woman handed her a small bowl filled with food. Yixu swallowed a large mouthful and closed her eyes in pleasure.

"I don't tell stories; I follow them. Stories have lives of their own. I've learned how to follow ones that are true. It has taken half my life. And yes. I followed a story here, with help. I'm here for the Lost Dreamer." Her breathing shifted. She blew out as if she was nervous. A Song started in my blood. I didn't know it, but I knew it.

"The Lost Dreamer?" Yixu's mouth was full; she tried to swallow a bit, then turned to me and asked, "Are you lost?"

The woman laughed.

"I've been imagining this moment longer than you can know, Saya. And now that it's here, after searching for you, I don't know what to do." She held her hands out to the fire, then placed them over her chest. The Song in me rose even higher.

"You know my name?" I asked. She nodded once. "You're the one. I was told to let myself be found."

"Who told you?" She turned her body toward me. I felt dizzy with the presence of her. I was entranced by the marks on her skin; I wanted to stare at them but kept my eyes on hers. I listened to my knowing. I trusted her.

"I was told in Dreaming," I said.

"You just enter the Dream? No ritual? No protection?" Her eyes held a strange expression; I couldn't tell if it was confusion or something else.

My hand went to where my necklace had always been. It seemed an entire lifetime since I'd worn it.

"I had a protection," I said. "A necklace, but it was taken."

The woman rocked back so she was sitting in the sand. I did the same. She leaned back and gazed at the sky, her eyes lingering on the clouds hanging suspended over the horizon. She breathed in and out slowly, a smile pulling at her mouth but never quite fulfilling its promise.

"Who told you I was coming?" She turned to me.

"A giant bird, then a few other spirits," I said.

"You speak with spirits." She exhaled loudly and laughed once. "No training, no ritual, no ceremony, and you speak with spirits. Oh, Saya, there is so much to know."

"Why have you been looking for me? Are you going to train me? How do you know who I am?" I asked.

The woman smiled at me. "I used to enter the Dream, a long time ago. I saw you there, before you entered this world."

"Do you know Celay? My mother? She used to enter the Dream and told me I took her gift from her."

"I know Celay," she said, her voice tight. "You say she's coming?"

"I was told in Dreaming yesterday," I said. The woman's eyes were hard.

"Is she good to you?" Her voice dropped. I glanced at Yixu; she had served herself another portion of what the woman had cooked and was sipping at it in a cup held in both hands. She peered back and forth at us over the lip of the cup.

I inhaled deeply before I answered. I trusted her; I didn't know why or how, but the Song in me felt right.

"She kept me safe," I said. The woman's head reared back and her nostrils flared. Her hands fisted in her lap. She released them and stood. She walked away from us, down the beach. Yixu and I watched her.

"She's strange. I like her," Yixu said. "Have you tasted this?" She held the cup out to me. It was savory, rich, salty. The dried fungus had bloomed into tender slivers that offered a satisfying chew. I watched the woman. She went to the surf, letting the small waves break over her ankles, her arms wrapped around herself. She started walking down the coast, away from us. A part of me wanted to follow her. I was drawn to her pain.

I wanted to know what a Lost Dreamer was and why she'd needed to find me.

《《●》》

"Yi," a voice rasped. Ahkal was waking up. Yixu scooted to her mother's side and bent over her.

"You're back. I was so scared. I needed you and I thought you were gone and I didn't know what I was going to do. What happened? Don't tell me, rest. You need to drink—" Yixu stopped talking. Ahkal had taken Yixu's hand and pressed it to her own mouth. Yixu began crying.

"I'm here," Ahkal's voice was rough. I poured a cup of water and brought it to them. Yixu helped her mother sit up and drink. I poured another cup of the morning meal and handed it to them. Ahkal sipped it and looked at us, surprised. She tasted it, opening and closing her mouth. She looked around.

"Did you make this, Saya? Did Nahi? These aren't flavors Yixu and I carry with us," she asked, her color starting to come back.

Yixu and I both dropped our eyes. I exhaled hard. I didn't want to speak the words. I looked up at Yixu, who had the same look of dread on her face I felt on mine.

"Nahi's gone," Yixu whispered.

Ahkal sank back again, her eyes squeezed shut. Tears slipped out of the corners of her eyes. She crossed her hands over her chest, her mouth a grimace of pain. The tendons on her neck stood out as she tried to hold in a wail. It came out anyway, long and loud, a piercing cry that sliced through me. The markings on her skin darkened for a moment as her face filled with blood. She wailed once, twice, then exhaled loudly, breathing in and out with her mouth open. She kept crying. Yixu rubbed at her mother's arms, stroking gently back and forth with her fingertips, a tender touch. I rocked with the pain of her wail.

I felt a different kind of movement in my chest, the Song from earlier growing stronger. I couldn't hear it, but I could feel it.

"You grieve." The woman had returned and stood before Ahkal. She must have heard the wailing.

Ahkal sat up and stared, her hands over her mouth. She had a wild look on her face. She had gone from grief to joy so quickly, I wondered if she was still unwell from her ritual on the boat.

"It's you," Ahkal gasped. "After all these years, we were right. I can't believe you're in front of me—"

Yixu interrupted her mother.

"Don't say her name. She told us she uses no name."

"Thank you for seeing me, Yixu," the woman said. She spoke to Ahkal. "She is very much your daughter."

"You gave up your name?" Ahkal asked.

The woman ran her hands along her scalp and looked at me.

"A ritual at the Spider Temple. I have no name until someone who loves me speaks it."

Ahkal laughed.

"I love you. Would you like me to speak your name? Is the ritual complete?"

The woman looked at me with brimming eyes, her mouth wide with a nervous smile.

"It is."

"Indir," Ahkal said. Indir dropped to Ahkal. They embraced tightly, crying and laughing at the same time. Yixu and I exchanged glances. Yixu didn't seem to know who Indir was.

"Sister," Ahkal pulled away, holding Indir's face in her hands.

"You have a sister?" Yixu's voice rose.

"No, we are kin another way." Ahkal dropped her voice and stared into Indir's eyes.

"Would you like to do it alone?" she asked. Indir shook her head. Ahkal opened her arms to Yixu. Her daughter moved into them.

Indir turned to me. She looked into my eyes. I felt a stirring in my chest and belly; her gaze was full of love.

"Saya, I am the woman who birthed you. I am your mother," she said.

I knew it was true. The Song in me rose, rushing through blood, bone, skin. Something within me leaped in joy and recognition. I stared at her and saw myself begin to take form. Our hands were the same, as well as the shapes of our feet. Her nose was different than mine, but our eyes were similar. I looked at every part of her, seeing myself woven through her skin, her movements. Her eyes were scared, full of tears. Her chin trembled.

"How?" I breathed out.

"Celay took you from me." Her voice was a hiss. "She helped me birth you. I was far from home. In my birthing pains, I confessed who I was, what I knew you to be. In my pain, I said things I should have never said to her."

"You didn't look for me?" I asked, my voice louder than I intended. My mind raced, wondering what my life would have looked like if she had found me.

"I've never stopped seeking you, Saya. I put my protection on you as soon as you breathed for the first time outside my body. I couldn't track you, couldn't find any seer or healer across the land who could find you. I couldn't return home and ask my sisters for help, not without you."

"Where is home?" I asked. I felt myself drawn to her.

"How are we kin?" Yixu interrupted. I was relieved for the distraction.

"My chosen and your mother's chosen were brothers, Ovis and Tixu," Indir said. "Ahkal helped Ovis and me escape Alcanzeh."

"Cousins?" Yixu squealed. Ahkal pulled her closer and whispered in her ear. Yixu pulled her lips in.

"Alcanzeh? You're a Dreamer, then? Why haven't I ever seen you? You never tried to find me in Dreaming?" I asked, my heart beating faster than I thought possible.

"I can't Dream anymore. It stopped moons before leaving Alcanzeh. And even if I had kept my gift, the stones would have kept me from being able to see you. I have been coming toward you for your entire life, Saya. And even though I can't enter Her anymore, I trust the Dream." Indir's voice was soft. My mother's voice.

I looked at Ahkal and Yixu. I didn't know what to do, how to react.

"This is a lot of story, Saya. Would you like some time alone?"

Ahkal asked. I saw that her question pained Indir; the latter's lips tightened into a line I knew my own to take.

"No, I want to know more. How did you find me? How did you find us?" I asked.

Indir whistled, and a shadow moved over us. I saw the large bird that had taken my necklace. It was followed by an even larger bird, with legs as tall as me. It landed with a puff of air that sent sand out in all directions. The birds looked at us with large red eyes.

"Indir!" Ahkal exclaimed. The birds regarded us, then went to their knees, turning their heads to peck at their underwings. Yixu crawled to me and took my hand, leaning her head on my shoulder. I pressed into her. My cousin. Family. I had family. It felt strange.

"She's your mother? How do you feel? Look at those birds," Yixu said.

Indir was watching us. I felt her eyes on me. I turned my head and pressed my face into Yixu's tunic. I felt dizzy, like my body didn't fit into my skin anymore. Yixu began humming, rocking back and forth. It eased me.

"She Sings," Indir said softly to Ahkal.

"I Sing too," I said into Yixu's shirt. I wanted her to know me; I wanted to tell her everything, but I didn't know how to begin.

"Your father Sang, as did his mother. You carry her name. She was Saya too. A healer of the Litéx. Saya, I can't believe how much you resemble my sisters." Indir held her hands over her heart. She was sitting on her knees, close but not too close.

"You have sisters?" I asked.

"Two, Delu and Zeri. They stayed in Alcanzeh. I know nothing of them; it has been years since I left. My mother, Safi, lived there too. In the Temple of Night, where I was born." Her voice was gentle, offering me my own story in a quiet way.

"I think I saw your sisters," I said. Indir's mouth opened.

"In the Dream, did they look well? Did you see my mother?" Indir asked. I shook my head.

"It was right after I lost my protection. They were surprised to see me. I didn't know where I was. I got scared and left." I watched her face go through a series of transformations. I didn't know how to read her yet, but I wanted to learn.

"They live," she exhaled. "Thank you for telling me."

"Can I touch you?" The question came out of my body before I knew what I was saying, but it felt right. Her face opened up, eyebrows raising.

"I would like that," she said, swallowing hard.

I felt stiff at first. I knelt in front of her. I stared into her eyes, touching her cheek with my fingertips. There was a part of me struggling to reach her the way I wanted to. And I wanted to. I opened my arms. Her face tightened as she rose on her knees and embraced me. Her breath shook as she exhaled. She was strong, her arms muscled beneath my arms as we leaned into each other. Her scent was close to my own but sweeter, stronger. I inhaled deeply and felt my body relax into a knowing and comfort I didn't know I could feel. She tightened her arms around me, breathing into my hair.

"Saya," she sighed.

"I'm your daughter," I said.

"You're my daughter," she said. "The Lost Dreamer. I found you."

I pulled away.

"Tell me more," I said, holding on to her forearms. The closer I looked at her, the stranger it was. I thought of Celay's face. I had never thought anything about our differences, though I had always felt apart from her. I would have been closer, if she had allowed it. The more I stared at Indir, the closer to her I felt.

"You've seen the comet. I believe you've felt the changes. You lost your protection. There is a story about you, the Lost Dreamer. The story says you will be in Alcanzeh at the end of the cycle." She gestured to the sky. "It's here. The chaos has deepened. Do you want to go to Alcanzeh?"

"What do you mean, does she want to go? There's a story about her. Of course we're going to Alcanzeh!" Yixu had popped out of her mother's arms. "Indir, don't you want to see Alcanzeh? Don't you want to know why all these strange things are happening around you? The sea creature that took Nahi? Do you think—"

"Nahi's gone?" Indir put her hands over her mouth. I looked sideways at Yixu, who looked guilty for speaking it so casually.

"Yesterday," Ahkal said, "by a creature of chaos. There still may be a chance; she can swim, and she can fight."

Indir nodded, but there was pain around her eyes.

"Saya, I have walked stranger paths than you can imagine these years seeking you. I need to return to Alcanzeh. It was foretold in Dreaming. I need to see my sisters, see my mother if she is alive. I made promises. I want you to come with me, but I won't make the choice for you."

"What about the story?" Yixu whined. "Saya, do you want to see why you have a story?"

I was confused. I wanted to know Indir more, to learn her, let her learn me, explore the rising Song of connection between us. But I also wanted to return to Ruta and Kinet, to tend my plants and live simply.

"Is Saya's father in Alcanzeh?" Yixu asked. Indir's face turned emotionless.

"Ovis disappeared years ago while looking for Saya. I have known nothing of him since the morning he left. Not even stories." Her voice was even and controlled, but I could hear something sharp beneath her words, like a hidden knife.

"I saw him in the Dream too," I whispered. Indir's eyes widened.

"He lives?" she asked.

"I don't know. I saw him at an altar, sacrificing a humming-bird at a temple. The hummingbird came back to life," I said. Whatever hope had bloomed in Indir withered. Her posture went a little softer.

"He did that the day you were born," she said softly. "Celay took you seven days later."

I tried to imagine what Indir had suffered, what we had both suffered because of Celay. I recalled how, in Dreaming, no spirit ever said Celay was my mother; they referred to her by her name. And when they had spoken of my mother, I had always been confused.

"Saya." Indir put her hands up. "There are those who don't want you in Alcanzeh. There is a story about you. I'll do my best to keep you safe, but Alcan, the one who rules the city, wishes me harm. He doesn't know you exist."

"I exist," I said, remembering the Shadow Dreamer. "I think he knows I exist. I saw a Shadow Dreamer. He tore into the Dream, wounded it. I was told I needed to keep him out. I don't know if there are more." Indir's eyes went hard.

"The Pili," Indir said.

"I have to go, I think," I said.

Yixu squealed.

"Yixu, they haven't invited us, and I don't know we would accept," Ahkal said. Yixu froze. Ahkal stepped forward.

"Getting to Alcanzeh by boat will be faster than foot. Or will you ride the birds?"

"Xeynan; it is what they are called among the Airan," Indir said. "They'll fly home and tell the Airan that the Lost Dreamer is on her way to Alcanzeh. They'll want to send witnesses."

"When do we leave?" Yixu hopped from one foot to another. Just watching her made me tired. I realized I was deeply tired.

"I still need rest." I sat down on the blanket I had slept on the night before.

"Rest, Dreamer. Ahkal too," Indir said. Ahkal had closed her eyes again, a small smile on her lips. "Yixu and I will talk quietly somewhere nearby. I can see her curiosity, and I want to honor it. I won't tell her any of our story yet; that's for us, when you're ready," Indir said.

The way she spoke, with kindness, offering me a choice, was so new to me, it confused me. I nodded. I pulled the blanket around me and closed my eyes.

《 ☾ ● ☽ 》

I didn't want to go into the Dream but was pulled in anyway. I landed on the side of a mountain. Tall trees stretched up around me, bright blue with leaves that moved from violet to white. Their roots glowed from beneath the ground, stretching out in every direction in complicated webs. Spirits shaped like spiders scurried up and down the trunk, their green bodies trailing almost invisible threads of light. I leaned against one of the trees, and delighted spiders ran across my body. I waited. I didn't know what was coming, but I knew there would be a visitation. I could feel a presence moving toward me. I tapped at my chest and felt a stirring that was matched in my stomach. I had no idea why the serpents were inside me, but it felt right, like they had always been there.

"She found you," a voice spoke. I turned, but it was a spirit that wouldn't let itself be looked at directly. I felt the glow of the voice, a mass hovering somewhere around me, or several.

"She wants to go to Alcanzeh; I'm going with her," I said. There was a humming in the air, an agreement.

"They Dream differently there, know that," the voice said. I was confused, but that was nothing new in Dreaming.

"How?" I asked.

"Ask your mother," the voice said. I thought for a moment, seeing the spirit's reflection glow violet on the bodies of the spiders running over me in undetectable patterns.

"She can't Dream, she told me," I said. I wanted to look up, but each time I did, my ability to see faded away.

"You can bring her. She'll have to face a wound," the voice said.

"I don't know how," I said. I was tired. I wanted rest.

"You'll know how. Rest here a while, Dreamer. Call yourself a nest, form it around you, ask for protection. You will return to the Waking World when your body there has what it needs." The blue light faded away.

I leaned back against the tree and imagined a nest, large enough to curl up into. The spiders on my body leaped into action and began weaving around me. It wasn't the nest I had imagined for myself, but it was comforting, surrounding me on all sides. I was in a cocoon of glowing strands. I felt them pressing around me, tingles of light that seemed to penetrate my skin. I closed my eyes and rested.

《《●》》

It was late afternoon when I awoke. I opened my eyes to see Indir sitting near me, her arms wrapped around her bent knees. She was smiling at me. The Xeynan were gone.

"You Dream like my sister Zeri, your aunt. She threw her arms over her head too, when returning to her body. Or, she used to," Indir said. It made me uncomfortable that she knew something about me that I didn't know about myself.

Ahkal was sitting in front of the fire, watching us interact. She motioned to me. I rose and sat beside her, and she moved closer, putting her arm around me.

"It's a lot to learn at once," she whispered against the side of my head. I nodded. It felt good to be held. Indir rose and walked to where our packs and other items were spread out to dry. In the distance, I could see Yixu cleaning out the boat.

"Trust the Dream," I said, echoing something Indir had said.

"Trust yourself too," Ahkal said. I put a hand over my heart and the other over my stomach. I exhaled slowly. Trusting myself was new. Yixu noticed I was awake and waved me over.

I passed Indir as she shook out items from the boat that were covered in sand. Yixu was backlit by the setting sun. Squatting in the boat, she used a hand broom to sweep sand onto a long, wide leaf. Most of the water was out of the boat. Yixu called to me as I approached. Indir walked away to give us privacy.

"We're cousins, and you have found your mother. And we're going to Alcanzeh to follow your story. Saya, I have never been happier in my life," she said. I leaned against the edge of the boat.

"Even with sea creatures of chaos who rise from unnatural storms and steal away our friends?" I asked.

"You heard what my mother said; there's still a chance. Nahi can swim. I choose to believe she survived." Yixu looked out at the sea. "How do you feel?"

"I went into Dreaming and rested there. I feel stronger." I paused. "A spirit told me I could bring Indir into the Dream with me, that I know how. But I don't know how," I admitted. "I don't know if I want to."

"Why not? She's a Dreamer, or was, of Alcanzeh. She can probably teach you different ways of entering, or something you can't even imagine yet," Yixu insisted. I was grateful for the way she lived, open, honest, eager for more. My eagerness was deep but not as loud as hers.

"What if I do it wrong and harm her? What if she enters the Dream with me and tells me I've been doing it wrong, that the way I used the Dream was dangerous? What if I wound the Dream even more? What if I lose my ability to Dream like she did?" I asked.

Yixu sat on the bench, leaning her forearms on her knees.

"If a spirit suggested it to you, I think it will be safe. But you know the Dream better than I do."

I nodded. I had to trust myself.

《《●》》

Indir was cooking again, speaking to Ahkal in a low voice. I sat next to her and felt her go still. I inhaled her scent and found myself wanting to be closer to her.

"You didn't ask me what I saw in Dreaming today," I said. Her face was a question.

"It isn't my place to ask," she said. "Did Celay ask you to tell her?"

"She didn't ask. I had to," I said, fascinated by how Indir's face twisted, unable to keep in her emotion. "Do you want to go into the Dream with me?" I asked.

Her hand went to her throat.

"How?" Indir asked. Out of the side of my eye, I could see Ahkal's mouth had dropped open.

"A spirit told me I know how. Perhaps by Singing? One of the Songs I was gifted?" Or the one I felt in me when I was near her. I didn't want to mention that one yet.

She nodded.

"Is there a ritual or ceremony or any particular way you enter?" she asked.

"I just go," I said honestly.

"Did the spirit tell you anything else you choose to share?" Indir asked. I thought for a moment.

"You have a wound around the way in, but it can be healed?" I said, trying to remember what the spirit had told me.

"Piliti," she said, her eyes dropping, mouth tightening. She raised her eyes to mine. "You use Piliti?" There was disapproval in her voice.

"I don't know what Piliti is," I said. She seemed relieved.

"A root," she said.

"Oh, I think I know the root." I jumped up and went to my travel pack, dried stiff from the sun. It was even more tattered than before, but I found the root hidden away in one of the pockets. It had dried. I brought it to Indir. She held out her hand and stared at the root when I gave it to her. I could see her thoughts taking her somewhere uncomfortable, and I hummed a little in my throat. Ahkal nodded her approval from where she sat, arm draped around Yixu.

"I have a story with this root," Indir said softly. "One that isn't easy to think about, but if you think it's a way . . ." She raised her eyes to me. "I want to see my sisters." I nodded.

"So tonight you will Dream." Ahkal clapped her hands once. "Let us share a meal first."

《《●》》

Ahkal cooked some sort of sea vine Yixu had found on the beach, with shellfish she steamed open in the fire and a spicy sauce to pour over everything. It was delicious.

"I remember eating this meal when you helped us escape Alcanzeh," Indir sighed after eating. She had eaten most of the shellfish on her own—it had been too chewy for me.

"How did you escape Alcanzeh? How did you lose me?" I asked.

Indir sat back and began to tell our story.

CHAPTER TWENTY-ONE

INDIR

For all that Ovis and I had trained as Avex and Dreamer, we had little experience in the world outside Alcanzeh, or outside of who we had always known us to be. The night we escaped Alcanzeh was one of the most terrifying of my life. And then we met Ahkal.

We walked half the night through the jungle, sometimes only going by the scent of the sea. My stone pouch was warm, but it didn't get hot again. I was wild with terror at getting caught, with worry for Raru, with excitement for Ovis joining me. I don't know how I walked through that jungle; I was unused to traveling, but something in me kept moving forward. Then we arrived at a cliff. Below us, the ocean crashed on a beach. I saw the flickering light from a fire on a boat, but I saw no way down. I let my exhaustion collapse me. Ovis had a stronger body, and he went off to seek a path. He returned and guided me wordlessly, arm around my shoulder.

Ovis stopped and pointed with his chin. There was a stone canal, like the one we had used to get to the beach where the Litéx had arrived. This one was much steeper. When I peered over the edge, I saw the canal was cracked and broken in several places. I looked at Ovis.

"I hope that the speed will keep us from hurting ourselves

on the way down." Ovis sat, promising to catch me at the bottom. I didn't watch him go, but I heard him grunt a few times.

I dropped and sent myself off before I could change my mind. I yelped when my bottom hit hard against jagged places where the stone had cracked or broken. A broken piece of stone hit me in the hip hard, and I cried out in pain. Then I was falling. Ovis was ready for me and caught me before I hit the sand too forcefully. I stood, wincing at the pain in my hip. Ovis dropped to his knees and pressed his lips against my hip, murmuring a Song of healing. I closed my eyes and sighed as the pain dissolved at his Song.

Someone whistled a call at us. There was a woman in a large boat. She wore a length of cloth around her head.

"I am Ahkal," the woman said in a dry voice. "Tixu said you would come. It is time."

Ahkal helped me into the boat and handed me a scarf identical to hers. She helped me wrap it around my head while Ovis pushed the boat into the water and jumped in.

When we were far enough away from shore, Ahkal removed the scarf from her face but kept it wound around her head. She was unlike anyone I could have even imagined. Her eyes were dark brown, narrow and long with thick eyebrows above. Her face was covered in beautiful markings. She sat at the back of the boat, holding on to some sort of pole that extended into the water. We were moving impossibly fast. I peered over the side of the boat and gasped: a school of fish followed the boat, pushing it forward. I shook my head and looked at Ahkal, but she was looking past me. Ovis was hunched over, his jaw clenched. He swallowed.

"I am used to a different type of boat. Where did you say you were from, Ahkal?" he asked, his voice shaky.

"I am of the Kemi. Your brother trusts me, Ovis. That is all you need to know," Ahkal said.

The type of boat Ahkal carried us in moved through the water in a way that made Ovis sick. The days we traveled, he spent in the front of the boat. Ahkal gave him a root to keep his sickness away, and it made him sleep. She and I began sharing our stories, the ways we had to leave our homes. I cried to her and she cried to me, telling me her story. She was with child and would not return to her people.

She took us south along the coast. At night, we stopped on beaches and rested; the days were spent traveling, hoping we wouldn't be tracked. She took us to a river that led inland, nowhere near where the Ilkan were rumored to live. I made the choice to trust the Dream, to know I would find Nahi when I was supposed to.

Ahkal left us at a place she had heard of from other travelers. A land that had vast underground rivers, north of the Belly and more hidden away from the world. It seemed like the perfect place for us to hide. I discovered my travel pack was full of beads, jewelry, other things we could trade for. Ovis and I found a small village of wanderers and made a home, choosing each other again and again. Wild in our joy, though we both grieved our losses. Then we found out I was to give birth.

I knew I was birthing a Dreamer. I was halfway through the

nesting when the child I carried pulled me into the Dream and showed me her face. I knew then I had found the Lost Dreamer. She was inside me. I was both terrified and thrilled. I told Ovis and we . . . we were so young. We thought it meant the cycle was ending and we would return to Alcanzeh. After the Dreamer was born.

There was a woman. She was kind. She was near my age and knew plants, knew some small rituals. She was curious about me, about the necklace I wore. She lived beside us and would share her meals with us. She realized I didn't know how to cook. She was kind and taught me, though she wasn't very good at it herself. I didn't tell her who I was, but we spoke of our lives in other ways. She was from another land, and she didn't want to speak of it. Her name was Celay. She had been traveling alone for years. She knew how to help ease the swelling of my feet. She knew how to be patient with me as I learned skills I would have known had I not been born and raised in a temple. It was then I began to truly see how unprepared I was for the wider world. And I was going to be a mother. I was terrified, but Celay comforted me, telling me I would know how. It was in me.

My birthing was not easy. I was in pain for two days and two nights.

Celay stood on one side of me, Ovis on the other as we paced. It was past midday on the third day of my birthing. Those around us had grown used to my groans. Women came out of their homes when we passed, offering tips, support, sympathy. I ignored them. The pain was one of splitting, of expanding, shrinking, pressure, everything in the wrong place. It was hot.

Not just the heat of my body shifting to open itself for new life; the heat of day bore down on us, even through the foliage. The three of us were covered in sweat. Another pain nearly brought me to my knees. Ovis supported me, and I grit my teeth through it. After, I panted.

"I can't, Ovis." I leaned my forehead on his shoulder. Celay cleared her throat.

"Indir, you can," Ovis said. I glanced at him and then at Celay.

I cursed. "I will die of heat even before I am a mother."

Ovis lifted me and carried me back to our home. The pains continued. By night, I was exhausted, on the floor on my hands and knees. Between waves of pain, I panted and drank water and passed water. I'd ripped off my tunic as soon as we'd entered our home. I couldn't stand anything touching my skin. Ovis had found a toolmaker to make the stones that Ali had given me into a necklace. I pulled the necklace off and draped it over the altar in our home. I didn't want anything touching my skin. Everything about me was raw. Evening came.

"Keep imagining your child," Celay said as she tried to soothe me. It was near the middle of the night. I was delirious with pain. My jaw hurt from clenching. My throat was sore. I existed as only pain and want. I wanted the pain to end. I wanted my mother, my sisters. When I began to weep, Celay sent Ovis for more water, assuring him it was normal. He looked horrible, helpless, guilty.

"Push, Indir. Soon, you will have a child," Celay said.

"Daughter," I sobbed, close to delirium. "She Dreams. I saw

her. I want my mother. I want to go back to Alcanzeh. To the Temple of Night." I tried to push at the waves of pain. To push. A fire grew inside me, at my center. It took me, consumed me, obliterated all thought. I felt Ovis return. He spoke to me through the burning. I didn't understand a word.

"I need to be outside," I groaned.

Ovis lifted me. I whimpered as he carried me to the Ayan tree behind our home. The sky was clear. Night insects sang at the ripeness of the moon. He set me down, and I leaned against the tree as another wave of pain brought me to my knees. When it passed, Ovis lifted me to my feet. He leaned against the Ayan, feet spread wide, and pulled me between his legs, turning me so I faced away from him.

He Sang.

Ovis Sang. He wrapped his arms around my belly until all of my weight was pressed against him. He Sang. I lifted my arms over my head and held on to his neck. Another pain came, but it was different, a loosening. I cried out in relief. Ovis Sang. Through each widening ache, he Sang. I felt movement in my body. Another wave while Ovis held me up, the backs of my thighs pressed against the front of his thighs and we moved into a squat together. The pain passed, and I breathed deeply, in and out. I glanced up. The moon was nearly full. At the next wave of pain, something in my body released, and I pushed down, grunting through the pain. I felt as if I were splitting apart. I groaned until the groan became a yell. I pushed, sweating, aching.

A weight pushed between my legs from my center. I put my

hands between my legs and felt hair, bone. I gasped at the next pain and pushed once more. The pain broke open. A hot, wet mass slid into my hands, and I pulled it to my chest. Ovis's hands were over mine, checking each limb, squeezing. A cry. Wailing. I sobbed. I leaned against Ovis. We sobbed. Our small, wet daughter added her voice to ours. Ovis began a birth Song. Around us, above us, the Ayan vines bloomed. Saya.

I barely noticed Celay squatting beside me; I barely noticed the afterbirth coming out of me. There was nothing in the world but you, new, hot, sticky, naked.

I barely noticed Celay cutting the cord that bound us as one. I barely noticed the blanket around my shoulders and the nervous relief in Ovis's laugh as he gently led us into our home.

I barely noticed the Ayan tree, the flowers blooming out of season, called forth by your father's birth Song.

I barely noticed Celay, watching, contemplating.

I was sluggish with exhaustion, all my remaining energy focused on you. Eyes, fingernails, a face shaped like your father's. Black hair. You smelled of eternity, promise. Everything, every single pain and sacrifice were at once worth it. Celay tended my body as I lay on my pallet, staring at you in the moonlight streaming through the doorway.

I didn't need the Dream. I had you.

Your father touched your face and laughed like a child. We both laughed like children. When you opened your mouth and pulled my nipple into you, we gasped and watched. It hurt, but no pain ever felt as beautiful. After you drank your first fill, Celay swaddled you and placed you in my arms. I memorized every moment. You fell asleep. I began to follow you to sleep, the weight of you against the outside of my body the greatest wonder of my life. Just before sleep overtook me, I raised my head. Your father was sitting on the floor beside the bed and watching us.

"The protection necklace. We have to put it on her." I indicated toward the altar.

Ovis brought it over and put it over your head. It was as long as your body. He took a knife and cut the thin leather strip, shortening it and retying the knot. He slipped it over your head. We slept.

((●))

When you were days old, my milk began to dry. Nothing worked. Another mother living near us fed you from her milk, but I was bereft. I went to Celay. She had been attentive since your birth, bringing us food, teaching me how to hold you so you'd grow to have a strong neck. Celay assured me it was normal. I was a new mother, in a new environment. She opened her tunic. She showed me her breasts. They were round, full.

"Friend," she called me. "I have been trying different plants for milk." She squeezed her breast, and a dribble of milk dripped out. I was jealous, dry. You started crying, and Celay's nipples hardened and began releasing milk. She held her arms out, and I gave you to her. You drank until you were full. I felt empty. Celay comforted me.

"I will brew you milk medicine and bring it to you tonight," she said. I pulled you to my chest and wept. I felt as if I had failed you.

I have played that night over in my head more times than I can count. I have lived that night in nightmares. I have offered my own blood as sacrifice, begging for an answer. I have screamed for days. I have disappeared into silences that have lasted moons. I have sought answers in temples. I have sought anyone rumored to have a gift. I have sought out those who read the stars and those who cut open living creatures to read their entrails.

I remember it was a night of rain.

I remember Celay coming to visit us with bowls of food and tea. I remember her eyes were bright.

I remember feeling safe, my daughter in my arms.

I remember laughing. I remember leaning over to smell you, the earthy sweetness that rose from your skin. I remember laughing again, lifting your tiny foot to my lips, kissing it, biting it gently with my teeth. In the days since your birth, you'd only grown more perfect, your eyes staring up into mine. Everything I needed to know about life was in you. I kissed your soft feet and laughed at something your father said. I don't remember what he said. I know I leaned into him, he put his arm around me—and it was morning. You were gone.

I remember confusion. I remember reaching and finding only empty air. I remember screaming. I remember screaming until I had no voice. I remember Ovis shouting and calling your name. His mother's name, Saya.

I folded into myself, going over every moment. Ovis left, a few others went with him. There were many directions to search. He swore he would find you.

People came, as people do in times of tragedy. Other mothers held me. I was held. Their weeping joined mine. No one could understand why Celay would have taken you. I remembered the words that had spilled from me in my birthing time. She knew you were a Dreamer.

I bound my belly with the help of the women. Each wore her devastation in a different form of kindness. They helped me pack, gave me food, carved me a map of symbols, drilling each meaning into my memory. They knew. Not one of them would have waited. They gave me what I needed: hope.

I traveled the lands back and forth. I hardened in ways I didn't know a person could harden. I allowed myself one night of grief a month. When the moon was dark, I allowed myself my wailing. I wept into the night, seeking you with my broken heart. I made mistakes; I almost died. Still, I moved toward you, Saya. Always.

CHAPTER TWENTY-TWO

SAYA

No one spoke. Night insects trilled to each other. The sea crashed out a gentle percussion that sounded like loss. Indir had become a different person when she told the tale. Yixu was crushed against her mother's side, tears spilling down her face, soaking into the neck of her tunic. Ahkal held her daughter tightly, staring into the fire. I felt Indir's words, their lament, their pain. I wanted to offer her something, but I didn't know what I could give.

"You found me," I whispered. She nodded.

"I found you." She reached a hand out to me. "Take me to the Dream." I nodded.

"You'll create a small wound in the Dream that cannot be healed, but I heard Wotal say that some wounds are worth it," I said. She bit in her lips. I did the same.

"The Dream has wounded me. I will live with wounding the Dream," she said.

((●))

We debated back and forth over the best way for Indir to take in the Piliti. She spoke of having once eaten a taste in Alcanzeh. She didn't say it, but I could tell by her grimace it must have been a terrible experience. She took the root in and whispered to it, pressing it against her chest.

"I can Sing over it, maybe the Song of the Comet?" I offered. It felt right, a truth I didn't have to question.

"Would you like to hear the words we used, the rituals?" Indir asked.

"No," I said. I wasn't interested; I wanted no training. Not yet. Indir seemed surprised.

We decided to make an infusion of the root; I would Sing over it while Indir drank it. We would Dream together. I could see she was nervous; she fingered the seed bracelets around her wrists in contemplation.

When the root finished soaking, I lit an Ayan blossom. The knowledge that I had been born beneath a blooming Ayan tree added something even more sacred to the smoke. I was full of awe in a way I had only known in the Dream.

Ahkal poured the infusion into a carved cup she had brought out. It was of the Kemi, she explained, one of the last items she had of home. It seemed appropriate. Yixu sat back, watching, a look of expectation on her face.

We set up a small nest of blankets and sat facing each other, legs crossed. I held the infusion in both hands. Indir had braided my hair in a way that I did not know but remembered from the Dream. Her sisters had worn their hair the same way.

I Sang. I Sang with all the blood in my body. I Sang from my bones, and I Sang from all the parts of myself I was beginning to learn. I Sang for Ovis, who I'd never known. I Sang with joy for Indir, who birthed me. I Sang for Ahkal and Yixu and even for Celay, who had, in her own way, kept me safe. I Sang for the years of loss between us and the story ahead of us. When I finished the Song, Indir held out her hands and took the cup. She closed her eyes and sighed deeply before drinking it all down at once. She grimaced and wiped her mouth with the back of her hand.

"It will be different this time," she said to herself. I felt the pull of the Dream. I lay down on my side, and she lay in front of me, facing me. We held hands. Indir's eyes began to grow blurry; she closed her eyes and groaned. I Sang. My Song reached her, and she smiled at my voice, my breath on her face.

"Touch my mouth with your hands," my mother said. I did, and we were gone.

((●))

I entered, and Indir followed, connected by the Song. A red tunnel carried us in a blur. The comet Sang out past the wild whirring of wherever we were. Indir clung to me as if she were the child and I her mother. She had her face pressed to my shoulder, eyes closed. I wrapped my arms around her and whispered against the side of her head.

"Look," I said. The red whirring had slowed, though we still floated through it. Outside the tunnel, we saw strange landscapes of color and shape. Spirits pressed their faces to the tunnel, their mouths open as they watched us pass.

"It was never like this for me," my mother said in awe. I felt like her daughter in the Dream, as if I had always known her. I could hear the Song in her blood, quiet but persistent, how it matched mine.

"Show us Alcanzeh; take us to where the Dreamers are," I Sang. The tunnel responded. The red grew darker until it was almost black, shimmering with bright blue flashes of light moving the opposite direction we did.

We landed on a stone floor. It was dark but for a small altar that burned in the corner. Barely. It seemed abandoned. White wounds floated in the air. Indir stood, turning in a circle.

"This is one of the places we entered; it's shaped like the Temple of Night, connected to it somehow. It doesn't look the same. Something's wrong." She stared at the floating wounds, then knelt in front of the altar, holding her hands over the flame.

I looked around. The wounds in this part of the Dream hadn't joined together. There were countless small wounds, each surrounded by absence.

"Sisters," Indir whispered. There was a call from somewhere, a voice that resonated against the stone walls. Indir's head snapped up. I looked around but didn't see anyone. I felt a discomfort, a familiar tearing sensation. I ran to my mother and threw my arms around her.

"We have to leave; something is breaking in," I said. I recognized the feeling in my body. Someone had sensed us.

I saw the Dream begin to split over the altar. I placed my body between the split and my mother, raising my voice in Song. The tear stopped opening but was still there. A face tried to press through, ashen, mouth full of glowing teeth.

"Indir!" Voices called from elsewhere in the temple. "Come! Indir, come!" They screamed it over and over.

My mother pushed past me, running toward the voices. I glanced at the wound in the Dream. It was closing, but the other wounds were attracted to it. I turned and ran after Indir, feeling the shadows gathering behind me.

The Dream changed shape as soon as I was outside the temple. I almost ran into Indir, who had stopped, her hands over her mouth. Above us, the Dream was a tangle of glowing wounds. No color or light shone except through rare gaps. It looked like a net over us. I turned, but the temple behind us had disappeared. Swallowed by the Dream. There was no sound. It was an absence, pressing toward us. I opened my mouth to Sing, but felt a slither in my stomach. I looked past Indir and saw an opening.

I threw my arms around her, pushing her toward the glowing lights. They seemed to be reaching for us. The net of wounds grew thinner as we approached it. We broke through and were hovering over a city; the comet was at the horizon.

It had to be Alcanzeh, but it looked nothing like the stories told. The temples were bare stone with patches of old paint. There were broken stones piled everywhere as we moved above the city. The air was thick with smoke we couldn't smell. It was night, but few fires burned. Even the temples were dark.

"The water canals are dry." The pain in her voice ached in my own chest. The city began to waver below us before turning to smoke.

"The Dreamers," I said. The temple we had landed in

re-formed around us, the altar fire illuminating offerings that hadn't been there before. Indir was squatting on the floor, her head in her hands. I put my hand on her head to try and soothe her. I felt a pulling. I heard gasps.

Three women had appeared behind us. Indir lifted her head slowly, her hands still over her mouth. She shook, her eyes wide.

The shortest of the women rushed forward.

"Indir?" Her voice was faint. My mother stood but didn't move forward.

"Zeri?" Indir asked. Zeri nodded; her eyes flew to me.

"You found the Lost Dreamer?" Zeri asked, her voice growing softer.

My mother nodded. One of the other women rushed forward. The youngest held back; she was thin, with shadows beneath her eyes.

"Save yourself, sister. Don't return. The Dream has twisted. It's closing to us. We don't know what's true anymore. Stay away from Alcanzeh." The woman glanced back at the younger woman. She was near my age.

"Delu," Indir cried. She tried to get closer to her sister, but there was a resistance between us. "Delu, I've trusted the Dream since I left. It's all I've had. I've been following the story."

There was a tearing sound, and the three Dreamers disappeared. I didn't wait; I touched Indir and willed us back.

((●))

We woke tangled together. The fire was still burning. We hadn't been gone a long time, but we were both sweating. Ahkal knelt over us, Singing. Yixu stood behind her, a shell of burning Ayan blossoms in one hand. My mother and I were covered in sweat.

"Alcanzeh is dry." Indir kept her eyes closed. "They don't want us to return." She curled on her side. I looked at Ahkal, who held her fingers to her lips. She put a blanket over Indir and beckoned me into the night.

"That wasn't easy for her. Let her rest," Ahkal said. I paced back and forth.

"She doesn't want to go back? After all of that?" I asked.

"Those weren't her words." Ahkal's voice was gentle. She was right. I knelt, putting my hands in the sand. My breathing was fast. The Dreamers had barely looked at me. They'd looked frightened. I knew that feeling. I thought of the wider Dream they couldn't reach, everything that was possible. I stared at the comet. It was a promise, but I didn't know of what.

I walked back to the fire and lay on my blanket. Indir had turned so she was facing the night. I didn't touch her. Yixu gave me a small smile from the other side of the fire. I closed my eyes.

《 《 ● 》 》

I landed hard in the Dream. I called out to every spirit I knew. I called Yecacu, Wotal, Tiya, every unnamed spirit I was familiar with. I felt them around me, but they didn't take shape. There were other presences as well. I ignored them.

"Show me," I demanded. "Show me the story, the promise."

The Dream shifted around me quickly. I was in a temple. I was over islands. I flew past high cliffs, stairs carved into them. I was underwater. I was in a pool made of cut stone. I was in the jungle. I saw faces I didn't recognize, stretching past. Some looked like mine, while others had skin in shades I had never seen before. I saw Ruta and Kinet walking to the temple we'd found, without me. I stood waist-deep in water, surrounded by tall women. I saw Ilkan and strangers. I was crawling underground. I hovered over a familiar sea. I saw a boat with strange sails carrying Celay and Batuk. There was a whale beside their boat, and they were pulling someone off the whale's back. It was Nahi. I was in Alcanzeh again, but on the steps of a temple. The temple had fires burning inside. I followed the fires. I saw a wound, pulsing, cracking outward, growing. It clawed into the Dream. I moved closer. There was a man beside it, holding a burning torch to his chest. He stared at me. I felt the heat of his hatred, his fear. He thrust the torch toward me. I opened my mouth to scream and swallowed him, the web, the entire Dream. I heard the sound of rushing water on stone.

《 《 ● 》 》

It was morning. There was a whistle in the distance, from the sea. I sat up. Indir watched me. Her eyes were tired, her mouth set in a sad line. Yixu and Ahkal were down the beach, their eyes shielded by their hands as they stared out to sea.

"I'm following the story, to Alcanzeh," I said. "Come with me."

ACKNOWLEDGMENTS

Gratitude and Love:

Familia, living and ancestral, this story is for and because of you. My parents, Evelyn and Hector, your phenomenal love is the greatest gift I could have been born to; I am endlessly grateful for who you are, how you have always supported me and these dreams. My sisters, Deanna and Christina, for always making me laugh and keeping me real, you are diamonds. Mamía y Amor, por su apoyo y las herencias. The extended fam: Huertas, Jordan-Sadlocks, Brosz fam, Gerenas, Blankenbillers, too many of you to name. The best crew of sacred aunts around: Hilda, Silvia, Lily, Patty, Eva, Liz, Nilsa, Jeanette, Maria, Brenda, Sheryl. To my endless dozens of cousins. The niblings: Lucia, Maya, Elijah, and Manny, little sacred seeds I am blessed beyond language to know and love. May you all see my love for you and for us in these weavings.

To my beloved chosen family. Vanessa Mártir for always telling me *you got this,* your fierce love and endless cackles. Katia Ruiz for being such an enthusiastic hype-man/early reader. Charlotte Kaufman, I love you endlessly, friend, no words. Jennine Capó Crucet for listening hard, being my CPR and partner in cry-laughing. Yvonne Schmeltz, your love, friendship, and survival kits saved me more times than I can ever, ever tell you. Gelfing for sacred time travel, for bringing me to the temple. Forever love to the years of support from: Patricia

Engel, Andrea Serrano, Beau Lynott, Sonja Peteranderl, Seth Combs, Hari Alluri, Nadia Chaney, Daniel Hernandez, Jean Guerrero, Adriana Ramirez, Marissa Johnston-Valenzuela. Lea, Alli, and Nava Urguby, Xochitl Gonzalez, Chris Abani, Paul Tourkin, Adrian Martinez, V Zamora, Cher Johnson, Paul Flores, Gabriel LeBlanc, Lali Sanchez, Christine Lee, Lisa Factora-Borchers. All of you have helped birth this story. Your friendships and love have shaped me, uplifted me, made my life a more miraculous place to live and Dream.

To my team: agents David Patterson and Aemilia Phillips, your trust in me and my work is a gift that deepens daily. Erin Stein for believing in this story and seeing the possibilities in ways that both terrified and thrilled me; deepest gratitude and love. Wesley Turner for your sharp eye and brilliant suggestions, I am so grateful. Trisha de Guzman for coming in enthusiastic and ready to go, with such strong faith and belief, thank you.

This book was born and written on stolen Kumeyaay land. Eyaay ahan.